The Blossoming Bough

ETHEL MANNIN

THE BLOSSOMING BOUGH

'There grows a tree in the garden,
With blossoms that tremble and shake,
I lay my hands on its bark
And I feel that my heart must break.'
From *The Love Songs of Connacht.*
(*Translated from the Gaelic by Dr. Hyde.*)

JARROLDS *Publishers* (LONDON) *Limited*
(*Founded in* 1770)
47 PRINCES GATE, S.W.7
LONDON :: NEW YORK :: MELBOURNE

ACKNOWLEDGMENTS AND DEDICATION

Various people have helped with this book, notably my daughter, Jean Porteous, John McNair of the Independent Labour Party, and Joaquin Delso de Miguel of the F.A.I. (*Federación Anarquista Iberica*), and to them the book is gratefully and affectionately dedicated.

The quotation on the title page appears by courtesy of His Excellency the President of Ireland, Dr. Douglas Hyde.

E. M.

Contents

PART I

BALLYRANNON

I

IN the spring, when the grass is like a green fire, it is so brilliant, sheep graze on the terraces of Ballyrannon Castle gardens, trampling the daffodils and narcissi that roll in golden and white waves down to the lake's edge. Then the April showers beat in through the glassless windows, and gales sweeping up the lake from the Atlantic cause doors to bang in rooms long uninhabited. On the main façade of the castle, between crumbling towers, ancient ivy has fallen away in a solid mat and swings in the wind. There is lichen on most of the trees now, and the library is stuffed with hay.

Visitors to that part of Ireland are always interested. They want to know if it is a 'real' castle, or a sham, and who lived there, and why it is being allowed to fall into a ruin. When they learn that it was the home of Michael Harrigan, the author, they stare with fresh interest. Some of them remember something about a son. . . .

Amongst the rushes and wild irises at the edge of the lake Flynn Harrigan's boat lies a foot or more under water; the floorboards rotted long ago. He called it the *Kingfisher*, and he painted it blue in 1933, the year he went away.

Neither Flynn nor Bridie Harrigan had any memory of their mother—she who had all the daffodils planted, and rowed out to the island in the middle of the lake to plant some there with her own hands. Flynn was barely three, and Bridie only a few months old, when she ran away to Dublin, leaving her children, but taking her horse.

She had no place in the West. It was not amusing, and she was full of gaiety and vitality and wild mischief. Mike at a Dublin ball was a darling; Mike writing his books in the West, amongst the stones of Connacht, was a bore; and after a time living in a castle was not compensation enough. Indeed, when the castle was Ballyrannon it could even be an embarrassment. It was a product of the nineteenth century, ugly and pretentious. At one period it had been known as Harrigan's Folly. Its foundations might be said to be set in rye-whisky, distilled in the North. Mike's father was the last of the 'Whisky Harrigans', and when he died he had nothing to leave but the already decaying castle.

By that time Mike had already established himself as a writer and was married to 'pretty, witty Kitty' Shann. Flynn was born in 1913, a year after their marriage. Kitty Harrigan arrived back in Dublin shortly after the Easter Week rising, and Dublin under martial law was not the Dublin she had known; but she had escaped the timelessness of the West. Mike made no attempt to get her back. He was prepared to spend unlimited time and trouble schooling a horse, but not a woman.· The question of pride was also involved. Various members of the Shann family wrote commiserating, offering advice and excuses, assuring him that she was merely young and wilful and would return. He ignored all their letters and in time they ceased to write and he lost touch with them and all track of her. It was the talk of the countryside, but he was completely indifferent to the scandal. He drank a good deal, went to a good many balls, made numerous visits to Dublin, spending the greater part of his precarious income away from Ballyrannon, and let the place go to rack and ruin. His sympathies were openly Republican, and the day of Roger Casement's execution he hung crape from the castle windows and flew a white, green and gold flag at half-mast.

Of those stormy years Flynn knew little. The castle was raided by Free Staters in 1921, but Mike was away in Dublin when that happened and it was believed he was 'on the run'. He came back in time to meet the Black and Tans. That was something Flynn remembered vividly—a posse of mounted soldiers, a thundering of rifle-butts on the door, and the demand, 'Open in the King's name!' Then his father unarmed at a window, smiling, contemptuous, and his quiet counter-demand, 'Whose king?' The half-grudging admiration Flynn knew for his father all his life began in that moment.

Neither of the Harrigan children loved their father. They were never permitted to come close enough to him. He was away a good deal, in Dublin, London, Paris, sometimes for months on end. He insisted that he wrote best about Ireland when away from it, and full, he said, of a bogus nostalgia. He never wrote so feelingly of his native bog, he would say, as when he was in a Montparnasse café and drenched in Pernod. Quite early on Flynn came to recognise this cynicism in his father and to hate it. It was a long time before he was able to recognise Mike Harrigan's qualities as a writer, which emerged not in spite of himself but because of himself, from a basic integrity.

The children were brought up by the village woman Kitty Harrigan had engaged as nurse when Flynn was born. Her name was Emma Faherty, and for some reason—some Paris association—Mike nicknamed her Tante Emma. She was a widow with a scattered grown-up family. She was already fifty when she came to the Harrigans, and a hard life had aged her, so that before she was sixty she was already an old woman. She told the children stories of her childhood and girlhood down in Kerry, but they could not imagine her as anything but old.

During Kitty's brief reign there had been both indoor and outdoor servants at the castle; when she went her income went with her, and the servants left, one by one, till only old Mrs. Faherty remained. Then the slow deterioration set in. First the gardens went; they were overgrown in a summer, Kitty's flowers struggling up through jungles of weeds, until finally the weeds triumphed, except for the daffodils in the spring, and in the summer a few roses still clinging to crumbling walls and broken pergolas and refusing to revert to the briar.

Within a few years Mike shamelessly had a sale, in order to meet some of his more pressing debts. He stripped the place down to the barest essentials, and when it was all over, and, with the exception of the kitchen and the library, and a few bedrooms fitted up with servants' furniture, was as empty as a barn, declared that it was a dam' sight better like that, 'more honest'. He would sell the castle, too, by God, if he could find anyone fool enough to buy it.

The children enjoyed the sale. They had no idea there were so many people in the world as turned up for it. It was like a fair-day, only the crowd was bigger. People arrived on horseback—sometimes two on the same horse—on bicycles, on foot; in donkey-carts, pony-traps, side-cars. There were even a few motor-cars. Flynn and Bridie had also no idea the castle contained so many chairs and tables and cabinets, so many pictures and rugs, so much china and glass and silver. To tell the truth, Mike had not known it himself. Generations of Harrigans had collected a great deal, and Kitty had added to it. It was high time the place was 'turned out'. Kitty had left a good many of her clothes behind, and he listened to them being bid for without any feeling except surprise that a woman should find it necessary to own so many articles of dress. People cluttered up their lives with possessions, he thought ; books were the only legitimate accumulations ; for the rest, one should be able to live in a suit-case. One should be mobile. That was important. Mother of God, to be tied down to Ballyrannon, to be tied down to Ireland itself, for that matter ! You almost felt the ivy creeping in your soul to think of it. . . .

It amused him, passing from one hot, crowded room to another, to observe how people would buy things for the sake of buying them, things they could not possibly want, because they could not resist 'a bargain', for the sheer sake of possession, and because they could not endure to see some-one else come by them. He watched Charlie O'Brien, the horse-coper, as unscrupulous a faker of horseflesh as ever wore riding-breeches, buying up kitchenware the way you'd think he was going to be married, if you didn't know it was because you'd see him with it all spread out in the market-place on the next fair-day, asking for each item as much as he'd paid for the lot, pretty near. He watched old Mrs. Milligan give Mrs. O'Flaherty a black eye for trying to make away with a cruet that had been knocked down to her. He saw an old man who owned nothing but a ragged cloth cap bid for a leather hat-box with a red silk lining. . . . Ah well, when all the junk had changed hands he would pay some of the scoundrels in Galway and Dublin and Ballyrannon who considered that he owed them money, and then he would be off abroad again.

He hardly thought about Flynn and Bridie. He had an idea that the less you bothered about children the better. Somehow they grew up and in time became human beings to whom you could talk. His sister, Christabel O'Donal, 'the actress', as she was always referred to, made flying visits out from Dublin periodically and lectured him on his duty to the children. She was always wanting to take them back with her, have them brought up 'properly', with her own child, Katherine, but Tante Emma fought for the children like the most possessive mother, and the children clung to her and cried, and Christabel was always defeated in her good intentions.

"They're all right, Chris," Mike would insist, "They're healthy and they're happy—what else is necessary ?"

"They're unwashed and uncombed, and not a shoe to their feet. God help them !" Christabel would protest, "They might be gipsies !"

At which Mike would laugh. "And so they might, and what would be wrong with that ?"

Almost in tears, then, she would declare her brother to be 'impossible'. Mike would smile and shrug and offer no comment. It was what Kitty had always said of him. It was what people invariably said of you when you did not conform to orthodox ideas. He had a general reputation for being impossible. He knew very well what they chattered at literary Dublin tea-parties and London sherry-parties. That he wrote only when he was drunk, and that when drunk he was given to throwing the furniture about, even at his best friends. That he wrote best with the drink in him he did not deny; particularly French drink. But he had no recollection of ever throwing furniture except once in a Bloomsbury pub when a certain male reviewer 'swept in like the queen-mother', as he had declared at the time, and taking exception to such queenliness he had picked up a table and flung it, but only that once. . . . But that, of course, was how legends grew up. He had the reputation of being a wife-beater, which again was nonsense, and arose out of the fact that once at a party at which he was very bored he had thrown a tiresome female down the stairs. Females who wore collars and ties and cropped their hair like a man's and staged jealousy acts over their girl friends the moment a man looked at them were, in his opinion, much better thrown downstairs—any stairs, any time, anywhere. As to reviewers, most of them should have been smothered at birth. Altogether, in a world of great pro-vocation, in which jockeys won the races they ought not to have won, and left unwon the races they ought to have won, and most reviewing was so much vomit, and most women whores on horseback, he considered himself a remarkably forbearing man. Most men of any spirit, for one thing, would have murdered Kitty Shann within the first six months of marriage. . . .

He was attractive to women, with his tall, spare figure, his red hair, brilliantly blue eyes, and small pointed beard, but he was in fact much less readily attracted to them than reputation credited him with being. It was not so much that Kitty had left him bitter as wary—he had too great a zest for life, and too strong a sense of humour, for bitterness. But Kitty had fooled him, and he was not to be caught napping twice. He had never wanted marriage. That had been her idea; she had had a notion that it would be romantic to be married to 'Michael Harrigan, the novelist', and live at Ballyrannon Castle. And because she had been lovely enough and spark-ling enough to make a man dizzy he had, a little ruefully, allowed her to have her way. 'Pretty, witty Kitty'. Like a lovely naughty child. Well, well. She sat a horse better than any woman he had ever seen before or since. No doubt in heaven it would be accounted to her credit. Her ghost walked at times, but by a combination of rye whisky and cynicism it could be laid. But anyone who suggested that Mike Harrigan drank to drown his sorrow was asking to be hit over the head. He drank, by God, because it gave a kick to life, and a man of his capacities needed all the kick available. . . .

2

Flynn's earliest recollections were of Tante Emma, wrapped summer and winter in her black shawl; of the smell of burning turf, the smell of stables, the feel of a pony under him, the instinct to grip with the knees, the terror and excitement; of the baby that was Bridie; of plunging down through golden waves of daffodils to the lake; of learning to swim in its icy waters. Then, later, the incident of the Black and Tans, and the thrill of pride in his father; and the first time he saw the electric blue flash of kingfishers over the lake, with Bridie, five years old, at the bottom of the boat, and Cousin Kate, three years older than himself, resting on the heavy wooden oars, black hair blown across her face.

At that time he lived in an endless fantasy of chivalrous and romantic episodes with his cousin; in these fantasies the boat upset and he kept her afloat and swam with her to shore; her pony bolted and he raced on his own to her rescue . . . in fact she was a stronger swimmer than he was, and there was no horse in the Harrigan stables at that time. He was eight years old, and Tante Emma was too old, and Bridie still too young, to satisfy his emotional need. It was Kate who organised everything they did together, and he was content to follow her leadership.

Tante Emma disliked and disapproved of 'the O'Donal girl'. She regarded her as a 'showing-off' child, with all her dressing-up and her play-acting and her talk of going on the stage when she was older. The darling of her heart was Bridie, and when Kate was there she would keep the child with her, protectively, muttering about 'That One and her black ways', deliberately inciting Bridie's jealousy over Flynn.

"Ah, that bold Flynn," she would murmur, "small use he has for his little sister, or anyone else, when That One's about, but what should we two be caring, alanna?"

Bridie's jealousy of Cousin Kate, fostered by Tante Emma, intensified as she grew older. Flynn was the whole of her world. Anyone who intruded upon it could only be an invading enemy. When they were alone together she was completely happy. It did not matter what they did so long as they did it together. She loved him with the whole of her being. There were moments when she had the feeling that he was her being. She would look at him and it was as though she stood outside of herself and he was her physical self. They were physically alike, with their mother's fair hair with a suggestion of the Harrigan red in it, and their father's brilliantly blue eyes, but whereas his were deep-set theirs were wide, with a narrowing and slight lift towards the temples which gave their faces a dreaming 'lost' look. They had the same high cheekbones and sombreness of expression when not smiling, the same shy, curiously gentle smile, never more devastatingly charming than when they were bored, as they invariably were when their father, in one of his fits of revolt against the monotony of life at Ballyrannon, invited people at random to the castle—people met at hunt-balls and small-town dances, people picked up in pubs, a raggle-taggle of impoverished gentry and local tradesmen. When they had gone—because there was nothing left to drink—Mike would run a hand through his red hair and exclaim, "God, what a rabble!"

His children on these occasions were always very puritanical and severe. They came close in their disapproval; it cemented their world. In that world was no endless adult babble, no reek of whisky, no fumes of cigar and pipe and cigarette smoke, no loud lewd laughter. It was a world in which dreams and realities fused, inhabited by wild unspoken loves and sword-bright unacted chivalries, by the whirring spread of swans' wings over the lake, the creak of rowlocks, and the plash of water under dipping oars, the mewing of curlews, the leap of fish to the taut rod. A world in which blossom broke like sea-foam over crumbling walls, and yellow irises grew in fairy-rings in the green, wet meadows.   A world of strewn boulders and treeless perspectives and blue untrodden hills. Of black peat-stacks and brown bog-water.   Of banshees and leprechauns.   Of Jesus and Mary, and the holy flowering thorn.   Priests and nuns and Franciscan brothers, and corner-boys and old women in black shawls, moved across their landscape as the rain-heavy clouds moved across the sky.   In autumn and winter the damp came out in the walls in great fungus-like patches alike in the whitewashed cabins and in Ballyrannon Castle.   Then the wind blew the smoke down the chimneys, and doors banged and gates flapped, and the hills vanished in grey mists.   In that world of wind and rain was complete isolation from any outside world.   It drove Mike Harrigan to drink, and his children deeper into their fantasy world, so that in winter they lived out their lives under eternally blossoming boughs, to a rhythm of endlessly unwritten poems. Sometimes for Flynn something would get caught on paper, but he never finished anything, and Bridie, whose head was full of chants out of the wind and the soughing trees, and the lapping waters, had no desire to write any-thing down.   Sometimes words came to her lips and she shaped a tune to them, but she never remembered words or tune afterwards, and what Flynn wrote down he showed to no one.   No one at all.

II

FLYNN was educated by 'the Brothers' at the monastery at the other end of the lake.   There was a school-house on the road that ran out from the lake to Ballyrannon itself, but it was too far out of the town for the children to come in wild weather, and gradually it fell into disuse.   Children threw stones in at its windows, and the wind and rain took the tiles off its roof, and in time it served no other purpose than a derelict hoarding upon which to chalk political slogans—'Up Dev', 'Up Cosgrave', 'To Hell with Britain', ''Ware I.R.A.', 'Up the I.R.A'. Eventually the authorities had the inspiration of opening a school actually in Ballyrannon, but that was too far for Flynn, and Tante Emma considered the monastery more 'suitable' for the heir of Ballyrannon Castle. . . .

Bridie went to 'the nuns' in the town, living at the convent as a boarder. For a long time the three miles dividing the castle and the convent seemed a very great distance.

It was not Aunt Christabel's idea as to how Mike's children should be educated, but it was better than nothing, and during Mike's especially 'broke' periods she came to the rescue with the fees.   But for her brother's stubbornness she would have done much more—taken the children back to Dublin with her and had them educated 'properly' . . . and incidentally, said Mike, drained all the originality out of them.

At fifteen Flynn finished at the monastery, and it was time, Aunt Chris declared, for him to decide upon a career, and his further education arranged accordingly.   What did he want to be?

"Perhaps he just wants to be?" Mike suggested.

"If the Harrigans were still making whisky, or were the landed gentry they used to set themselves up to be, well and good," his sister retorted. "As it is, you know as well as I do the boy will have to earn his living."

"That," said Mike, "is something he will no doubt discover for himself."

"And that he has no qualifications!"

"He has looks, intelligence, and a pair of hands."

"You're incorrigible, Mike!"

She tried the boy himself.

"Now you've finished with the schooling, Flynn, what do you want to do —I mean do you want to be a writer, or study for Trinity, or what?"

"I'd like to own a racehorse and train it and ride it myself in the Galway races." His eyes were bright as he said it.

"Darling, yes, but I mean about earning a living—your father can't afford to give you an income——"

"The racehorse would win money for us—thousands of pounds——"

Christabel gave it up, to the great relief of both father and son. Christabel was a darling, but she fussed too much. She could never see that there was always 'time enough' . . . which was odd, considering that in the management of her own life she had always lived according to the philosophy of sufficient unto the day. Which was, in Mike Harrigan's opinion, the only possible working philosophy.

At fifteen Flynn began to be aware of his father as a writer. He did not read his novels, but he read the reviews of the latest one, out of curiosity, and found himself much impressed. He had had no idea his father was such an important writer. But he was puzzled; reading all that was said about Mr. Michael Harrigan's work you would think that he was a very different sort of person. Was he really so sensitive, witty, and all the rest of it, and such a poet? He seemed to Flynn so coarse, insensitive, unimaginative. Yet the excerpts quoted by reviewers from this new book seemed to him very fine, undeniably fine, full of poetry and feeling and a kind of wild beauty, full of sadness and excitement and a shouting on the wind. Only, somehow, not to be associated with his father shuffling about in a dirty old camel-hair dressing-gown, or swaying home from Ballyrannon, arm in arm with someone as drunk as himself, his battered hat on the back of his head, and dirty from rolling in the road, and singing fit to wake the dead. Or his father lying in the narrow iron bed, late into the day, letters and books and papers and press-cuttings strewn over a counterpane that had been white but was now grey and stained, with brown burns from cigarette ends, and on a kitchen chair beside the bed a candle in a grease-corroded enamel holder, a saucer full of cigarette stubs and ash, a half empty bottle of whisky, a thick tumbler, matches, a crumpled packet of cigarettes. He would be aware of his father's nicotine-stained fingers, the pouches under his eyes, the blotchiness of his complexion, which he knew was from the drink. Drunk or sober, Flynn would think, there was something gross about him, about both his body and his mind. In a good humour he would be cynical and coarse, derisive of everybody and everything; in a bad temper he was derisive still, but without being amused or amusing; or so it seemed to his son.

Every day Mike would lie in bed till about mid-day, waiting and watching for the postman to turn in on his bicycle—a rusty, clanking affair that needed no bell to warn of its approach—up the avenue of dark ilex trees. Occasionally there would be no letters for the castle, and then Mike would be too disgusted to get up till the evening. Then he would pull on trousers over his pyjamas, and a coat if needed, thrust his bare feet into down-at-heel handmade shoes, finish up any whisky left in the house, and, whatever the weather, tramp the three miles into Ballyrannon in search of what he would call, bitterly, 'the pleasures of the town'. If any of the people with whom he drank happened to have a car he would as likely as not finish up the night fifty miles or more from home, and it would sometimes be a week before he would reappear at the castle, wild of eye and unrepentant of spirit.

Flynn was very well aware of all this, and he found it difficult as he grew older to reconcile it with the things his father wrote and that were said about him. It seemed to him that this man who wrote so finely of the springs of feeling of eternal things demeaned himself by soaking himself in whisky and consorting with ignorant and degraded people with whom he had nothing in common save debauch. Drunk, his father was either malicious and abusive, or morose. After a bout of drinking he was usually irritable and depressed. Sometimes sober he was so cynical and sardonic that Flynn would find himself preferring him drunk. Yet this man could write, so the critics said, with passion and tenderness, with wit and poetry and pity.

He came half drunk into the library one day and found Flynn reading a cutting of a long review of his new book by a very distinguished English critic. It was a very flattering review, giving Michael Harrigan direct spiritual descendency from Synge. Mike, when he had read it, had roared with laughter, read it out to the totally uncomprehending Tante Emma, and demanded of her if it didn't 'beat the band'. He regarded his son now with amusement, then flung himself down into an old leather armchair whose entrails had burst through the canvas of its underside, and demanded, "Discovering what a great man your da is, eh?"

Flynn smelt the drink on his father's breath and observed the alcoholic flush on his cheekbones, and the admiration the review had aroused in him was smothered in a distaste that bordered on disgust.

"When you're sober you seem to be able to write," he said.

Mike pushed his hat to the back of his head and grinned.

"Isn't it the perfect little prig I've raised up, now?"

He groped in an inner pocket for his cigarettes, and as he did so quoted in a loud, sonorous chant—

> "For men at times are sober,
> And think, by fits and starts,
> And when they think they fasten
> Their hands upon their hearts."

Flynn never hated his father so much as when he was in this mocking mood. His heart beat fast, and he went a little pale. He said, violently, trying to keep his voice steady and not quite succeeding, "I don't believe it's true what they say about your books! I don't believe a dirty rotten drunkard can write beautiful things! If you do write them it's all lies and humbug."

Mike, who had lurched over to a cupboard and was pouring himself out

a drink, looked up, amused by the boy's intensity, aware of the tremor in his
voice.

"So that's what you think, is it, little one? You think bad man bad
art, eh, good man nice, pure, good, sweet art—fine, noble, uplifting art?
You think all great artists were faithful to their wives and never touched a
drop? You didn't know about a dirty rotten drunkard called Kit Marlowe,
I suppose, or a fornicating play-actor called Bill Shakespeare?"

He leaned with his back against the cupboard and his blue eyes blazed at
his son.

"You think a man rises 'pure from the night and splendid for the day' and
produces great art, do you? You think it all comes out of the head, like
water out of a tap—that a man can produce something out of nothing, eh?
My God!"

The boy said, stubbornly, "I don't see how getting drunk and beastly
helps!"

Mike finished off his drink in one gulp, then shoved the glass back into
the cupboard.

"Ah, get out," he said, "you make me tired!"

When Flynn had gone, sullenly, out into the bright day, Mike sank down
again into the sagging chair and passed his hand across his face, down over
his forehead and nose and mouth, brushing away invisible cobwebs. He
always found the border-land between drunkenness and soberness depressing.

He sat and stared out of the dirt-filmed windows, across the crumbling
terraces, gay with wild flowers and weeds, to the lake, blue-grey under a
mistily blue sky heavy with heat to come. He was a fool; what was the use
of trying to explain the creative urge to virgin youth? You came bang up
against the innate puritanism of youth. The boy had plenty of romantic
imaginativeness, but there was that puritanism of inexperience. He had to
come through emotional initiation to the realisation of art as an expression of
life, an affair of the emotions, not of the intellect, the red stuff of the blood,
not the grey matter of the brain, derived direct from the basic realities,
straight out of the belly, bowels, genitals. He'd come to it in time, God
help him, he'd come to it. Easy enough to take life neat when you were
young and only taking it in small doses. As you got older, and covered the
grass a bit, it was your drink you had to take neat, in order to make the
grade. But with a little spirit in you you could put an edge on the dulled
blade of living, by God. You could find a way to cut clean through the
pallid proprieties to the hidden core of ecstasy, then. The inner vision was
kindled, the approach to the realities of truth made plain. But you couldn't
explain that to a boy of fifteen. Jesu, Mary and Joseph, you couldn't
explain it to the wall-faced, bowler-hatted millions, the stolid, cloth-capped
millions, running round in circles so busy earning their livings they had no
time to live. You could ask God to have pity on them. But you had to be
a little drunk before you could yourself have pity. Then you could have
pity out of your sense of the vast luxury of living; then you could feel com-
passion, and get the pity and terror of life in the aggregate down on to paper.
And pale, puffy critics, beefy, red-faced critics, over-fed and under-sexed, thin,
withered, constipated critics, little tin gods of prancing pansy critics, all the
hacks and whores of Fleet Street, wrote of your 'sensitive handling', your

'poetic imaginativeness', your 'delicate awareness', with an oh-so-literary slant on 'Irish genius', and if they saw their Irish genius reeling out of the dark dirty little pub on the corner they'd turn away in disgust, because the approach at second-hand to the reality of truth was one thing, and the truth itself quite another.   They and their press-fed public wanted the man and the artist kept separate.   They wanted something called art, and they wanted it immaculately conceived, all nicely in the mind, and it couldn't be done. From Beethoven with syphilis, Van Gogh hacking off his ear for a prostitute, Robert Greene running wild from tavern to tavern, Francis Thompson in his laudanum-dimmed squalor, not to mention Mike Harrigan reaching for the stars through a haze of rye-whisky, they would run a mile. . . .

Art be damned ! All that self-conscious muck about the sacredness of art, the 'vocation' of 'the artist', the writer or the painter as something special, something holy and apart. You expressed yourself in the way natural to you, and it might or might not turn out a good job of work ; there was nothing you could do about it, either way. If you were Mike Angelo you knocked up masterpieces. If you were Mike Harrigan you knocked up a living. Whatever you spawned might be cockeyed, a poor thing, but your own. You invited the world to take it or leave it, and thereby preserved a certain integrity—drunk or sober. Leave it at that, man dear, leave it at that.

He laughed, suddenly, and got up and poured himself out another drink.

III

AFTER the scene with his father Flynn went out through the French window and slowly down the weed-grown terraces to the lake. The dew still lay on the grass like a light frost and the air was warm and still. In the distance the blue hills were misty with impending heat. . It was going to be a grand day. It stretched ahead of Flynn like a golden unexplored country. The anger and hate he felt for his father only made the day seem more beautiful. From the blackness in your heart you could turn to the day with love and relief. The day was all peace and beauty and blessedness. All that was ugly and hateful was behind in a dingy room that smelled stalely of tobacco smoke ; a room to which the June morning did not penetrate.

There was a shrub whose name he did not know ; it seemed to spread like a weed. It had round soft greyish-green leaves, and a tiny pink flower in summer and white berries in the autumn, and it held a lush green smell that seemed to leap out at him as he passed. The soft greenery tumbled out over the broken steps and he stopped to touch it, as though it were a dog or a horse nuzzling up to him. He was filled with love, touching the soft leaves and feeling the warm still air lave round him. He stood a moment looking out across the garden to the lake. A heron paddled about on its long slender legs on the foreshore. His mother came into his mind. He thought of her rowing out to the island to plant the daffodils. 'A wild lovely craythur', Tante Emma called her, and would not hear a word against her, for all she had gone off and left her babes. Since they had been able to ask questions

at all he and Bridie had asked Tante Emma endlessly about their mother;
she had unearthed old photographs to show them, faded, yellowing things,
but, to the boy and girl who gazed at them, full of beauty in their strangeness,
and that increasingly as they grew older.   One day, Flynn was convinced, he
would meet her, the wild beautiful craythur.   They would meet in a city
street and he would know her at once.   Bridie did not share this fantasy;
she would never forgive their mother for her desertion.   Her face always
darkened with the thought of her.   That she was beautiful did not excuse
her; if anything, it somehow made her sin the blacker.

Flynn thought of her now with a deep longing.   Strange that she should
be moving somewhere about the world, living her life, and they living out
theirs at the castle, as it might be on another planet.   If she were here now
they would go out in the boat together, he and she and Bridie; they would go
out to the island and take their lunch, and she would tell them about the
days when she was young.   They would laugh and sing and make up stories.
Two swans whirred up suddenly from the lake's edge, filling the air with the
beating of their wings and their strange cries.   The spell was broken.   The
soft shrub slid away under his hands and he went on down to the water.

There was a low wall bounding the castle grounds where they touched the
lake's narrow beach.   Now it was little more than a straggling heap of
stones with weeds and wild flowers thrusting up between.   He clambered
over and dropped down on to the beach, where white and grey feathers blew
lightly over the shingle and there were the markings of birds' feet in the soft
mud.   He went along till he came to the point where the boat was moored.
Various pleasant possibilities were in his mind.   He might row down the
lake and out to the sea, in search of Patrick Doyle, who would almost
certainly be pottering about in his boat looking to his lobster-pots.   If he
failed to find Patrick he could row out to Bream Island and pass the time
chatting with Mrs. Doyle; he might hoe the potato patch and do any such
small jobs that wanted doing; he might go down to the Sound with two or
three of the younger Doyle children; he might take them in his boat and
bring them back to the castle.   On the other hand he might turn his back
on the sea and row across the lake to the dark green woods on the other side,
tie up and go part of the way along the road to meet Bridie on her way back
from the town.   She had gone in on her bicycle on some domestic shopping
for Tante Emma.   They could leave the bicycle with the boat and spend the
day lazing in the woods and pottering round the lake's edge.   Or he could
spend the morning at the monastery, helping in the garden, cleaning out the
hens; perhaps Brother Francis, his ex-tutor, whom he greatly loved, would
want some errands running, a letter posted, a message taken somewhere.
He might help with the scything of the long grass.   He might polish the chapel
brasses.   He might spend some hours in the library transcribing the ancient
Gaelic poems that had so great a fascination for him.   When Bridie came he
might borrow her bicycle, to save going back home for his own, and go into
Ballyrannon and see if anyone was about.

He untied the boat and pushed it out a little way, the cold water of the
lake pouring into his broken shoes, then jumped in and unshipped the oars.
He rowed gently out to the lake island, turning over in his mind the day's
potentialities.   When he reached the island he tied up and climbed up over

the rocks, then sat down amongst the heather and looked back at the castle
and at the monastery and thought how much more beautiful the monastery
was than the castle, how much more gracious, with its white façade and its
clock tower and its hayfields flowing down to hawthorns and hazels and
willows at the lake's edge.   Then he turned round the other way, rolling
over so that he lay face downwards, and looked towards the woods and the
range of blue hills beyond, and he thought of Cousin Kate who was always
wanting to climb those hills, though she was always being told that that was
something no one ever did or even thought of doing.   But that, she had
declared, was a very good reason for doing it.

  Kate was eighteen now and had already had small parts on the Dublin
stage, at the Gate, which was then still new enough to be exciting.   But
Flynn had never been to a theatre and he could not imagine this grown-up
Kate, Miss Katherine O'Donal.   He could only see her as he had always
known her, with bare legs and feet and tumbled black hair, always ready for
adventure, full of vivacity and gaiety.   "Flynn darlin'," he could hear her
strong clear voice, calling him, coaxing him; and, when he had pleased her in
some small way, the softly laughing note, the sing-song inflection, "Isn't it
very nice you are now?"   He had the feeling of something happening in his
blood when he thought of her, a warming, a quickening, and everything in
him answering the image of her, darling, darling Kate.   One day, he promised
himself, he would go to Dublin and see her on the stage ; only that would be a
little frightening, because it would be a Kate he did not know, moving in a
world of which he had no experience.   Yet it would be wonderful to see her,
and all the people looking at her and admiring, and he holding proudly in his
obscure person the secret of their relationship.

  He lay on his face amongst the heather, and the water lapped softly
against the rock, darkly green, and he could see the black shadowiness of
fish.   Curlews cried, and the monastery clock chimed with a slow sleepiness,
small ripples of sound sliding over the sunny surface of the air.   The
clatter of a donkey-cart along the road carried over the water.   The world of
motor-cars and buses to which Kate belonged seemed utterly remote.   Something in him insisted that she didn't belong there ; that she belonged here, in
Ballyrannon, to the lake, and the blue hills, and the green and brown bog-
land.   She should be here now in the flesh, sharing the golden day.   Suddenly he was filled with a great longing.   It swept through his blood like a
fever.   He buried his face in his arms.   If she were here now they would
pull the boat in under the shade of the trees at the far side of the lake ; they
would lie together in the boat, or in the deepness of the wood, and he would
kiss her like it said in the poem, 'kiss her until she be wearied out'. . . .   She
would twine her bare brown arms round his neck and draw him down to
her.   'Flynn darlin',' she would say, 'Darlin', darlin' Flynn. . . .'

  So after all there was nothing more perfect to do with the day than lie
islanded in the middle of the lake dreaming of a love wild and bright as a
seagull's wing in sunlight, sweet as the song of a blackbird on a blossoming
bough.

IV

IN Ballyrannon it was fair-day, and Bridie moved amongst the lowing black cattle and the huddled frightened sheep, and her heart was light because of the feeling of movement and happening. For six weeks now she was free of the convent. In contemplation it seemed all summer stretched ahead. In August Aunt Chris would come for them to take them back to Dublin for the Horse Show; in August, too, there would be the Ballyrannon races, that important local event which outshone even the Galway races, and somehow or other she and Flynn would contrive to ride in it. Last year it had rained for a week beforehand and on the day itself, and the course was a sea of mud, with people and horses sinking into it; but it had been a wonderful day all the same. Bridie smiled, recalling it. Conal O'Shea had been so angry at the sight of Charlie O'Brien bumping and boring his way to the winning-post, and he with half-a-crown on the horse behind, that he had potted at him with his gun, and had missed and shot old Mrs. Reilly leaning on the rail instead. She had screamed that she was murdered, but she was alive to this day, and, whatever anyone might say, it had really been very funny. . . . There was always excitement of one kind or another at the local races.

Bridie skirted the groups of sheep and cattle and picked her way amongst their droppings, and came to the open space where the two wide streets, flanked by shabby old houses and dark little shops, converged. The two streets, with a few odd houses straggling up a bit of a hillside behind, and down 'the sea road' where the lake ran out to the sea, and the tiny railway station about a mile out the other way, was all there was of Ballyrannon. But it was generally considered 'a fair, sizable town', and why should anyone be wanting anything bigger? It had a fine large Catholic church set upon a hill, and a small, dingy Protestant church half hidden in a wood. It had a guards' house and a school-house, and a convent, and on the road out to Lough Head a monastery and a castle. It had three commercial hotels with aspidistras on bamboo tables in the ground floor windows, long lace curtains, and on the floor polished linoleum. The largest and grandest was the Railway, which had a pillared porch with seats each side. It had ten public-houses, but many more if you counted the bar at the back of the petrol-station, the bicycle shop, the ironmonger's, the chandler's, and other places. There was a train out to Galway every mid-day, and a train in every evening, and if you had nothing better to do you strolled down to the station in the evening to see was there a stranger got off the train; or just for the sake of seeing the train come in, which, after all, had a certain excitement in itself. There was a harbour, but it was long ago silted up, and the tall ware-houses along it long ago fallen into ruins. There was a crumbling squash court, left by the English. . . . Some of the houses had also fallen into ruins, from lack of occupation, and standing between occupied shops and houses were like so many decayed teeth in a mouth.

Where the two roads converged, the small open space served as a market-place, and once a week old women in black shawls, and men in dark jerseys and cloth caps, come in from Bream Island mostly, stood guard over fish laid out on pieces of sacking on the ground, and donkeys were tethered round the white-washed walls of a urinal in the centre. Joe Foyle, whose grocery stores—with bar at back—was opposite, at the corner of the main street, was much offended by the urinal. He had the biggest business and the most progressive mind in the place, and he would have liked a bandstand where the urinal stood, for, he urged, wouldn't such a thing attract visitors to the place in the summer months, and wouldn't it lend an air of distinction to the town? He saw it in his mind's eyes painted a nice green, with baskets of geraniums suspended between its pillars, and a fine array of Galway musical talent assembled under its roof; but the inhabitants of Ballyrannon were generally of the opinion that a urinal was more useful.

On fair-days a motor-van from Galway parked itself in the market-place and displayed cheap ready-made clothes, gents' black cloth suits for Sundays, ladies' blouses and jumpers, and clothes for children. On fair-days, too, the shops brought all manner of things out from their dark interiors and displayed them on trestles set out on the pavement or propped up against the walls—piles of cracked and chipped plates and cups and dishes, pieces of meat, barrels of salted fish, zinc pails in all sizes, corneted inside each other with the prices painted on each in bright blue, coils of rope and twine, spades and shovels, brushes and brooms—nothing frivolous, but everything needful and handy, and all at guaranteed bargain prices.

The sheep and cattle brought in to Ballyrannon on fair-days were bought by farmers from the richer pasture-lands inland, away from the stony wastes of Connaught, and were taken back by them to be fattened up for slaughter. The fair-days were only once a month, so if the local farmer or smallholder did not sell his stock on the day it was a serious matter in many cases. Some of them drove their sheep and cattle a good many miles along the rough roads to Ballyrannon, only to drive them back again in the evening in a forlorn procession.

But Bridie Harrigan, brushing her bare legs against the flanks of sheep, and rubbing shoulders with the bullocks, and tripping amongst pigs that seemed to dart in all directions at once, was aware only of the exciting sense of movement and event, of summer, and her personal freedom. When she had done Tante Emma's errands she would collect her bicycle from Farrell-the-weaver's, the last house out of the town on the Lough Head road, then she would ride like the wind back to the castle and find Flynn, and they would take out the boat and picnic on the island and look for gulls' nests, and swim, and lie in the sun like seals; or they would row over to the woods and Flynn would shoot pigeons, or wild duck in the swamp beyond—whatever they did would be lovely, because they did it together, and there was the whole long golden day ahead. . . .

The shops were full of old, patient women in black shawls, and it took a long time to get served, but Bridie pilfered an apple here, a sweet biscuit there, and various people she knew spoke to her, and one gave her an orange, and another a few sweets, and the time passed pleasantly enough.

When she got back to Farrell-the-weaver's she saw a ladder against the cherry-tree by the near gable of the house, which was the usual low white-washed cabin with a roof of ragged thatch, and was aware of a commotion that was more than birds in the green branches. A pair of feet in broken shoes were just visible on the ladder, and then branches were parted and Patrick Doyle's face emerged, grinning, and with ear-rings of white cherries over each ear.

He invited her, "Come and get some cherries."

Mrs. O'Farrell came to the door of the cottage. "We're after getting them before the blackbirds take them all," she explained.

"Are you paying Patrick by the hour or by the stone, Mrs. O'Farrell?" Bridie inquired, loud enough for him to hear. "For if you're paying him by the hour they'll be expensive cherries, I'm thinking!"

Patrick spat a cherry-stone down at her.

"Ah, sure, 'tis all for love he's doing it," Mrs. O'Farrell told her, laughing, adding, "and he the biggest blackbird of the lot! Will I have him bring some down for yourself, now?"

"Let her come and get them!" Patrick insisted.

"Isn't he the disrespectful one?" Mrs. O'Farrell complained, and called up to Patrick, "Is that the way to speak to a young lady, at all?"

Bridie tossed her head. "None of the Doyles have any manners. Wait till I go up and make him apologise!" She began swarming up the ladder. Patrick sat on a branch and waited. He was a tall slender youth of seventeen, with a thin eager face, thick dark hair, and startlingly blue eyes that laughed easily. Flynn Harrigan was his greatest friend, and Bridie his unchanging dream. One of these days she would be his girl; there was time enough; he could wait. . . .

At the top of the ladder Bridie pushed her red-gold head through the dark green foliage and the pale cherries, and demanded, her eyes flashing, "Will you say you're sorry for your rudeness, Patrick Doyle, or will I push you out of the tree?"

Patrick laughed. "There's nothing to be sorry about. Have some cherries?"

He held a handful out to her. Bridie's mouth watered, but she was determined to put Patrick in his place, once and for all. She had old scores to settle. There had been whole days when Flynn had been out fishing with Patrick. He was one of the enemy, like Cousin Kate.

"I will take what I want when you are gone," she said, and hurled herself on to him, violently, in an attempt to dislodge him.

Patrick laughed, lost his balance, clutched at a branch, swung from it a moment, then dropped to the ground. Bridie climbed triumphantly up into his place and peered down at him through the leaves.

"That will teach you manners!" she said, severely.

He looked up at her. "Aren't you the strong one?" he mocked her, then walked over to the ladder and took it away, leaning it up against the house.

"Will I let them know at the castle Miss Bridie will be sleeping in the tree tonight?" He winked at Mrs. O'Farrell, but she refused to be reassured.

"Patrick, now, put the ladder back this instant—this instant now——"

"When she's apologised," Patrick said, and looked up at Bridie.

"Aren't you very sorry?" he demanded, and ducked, laughing, as she spat a cherry-stone down at him.

"You can keep your old ladder," she said, and turned round on the branch looking for a way down.

"You can't do it," Patrick said, suddenly anxious. "It's too big a drop. You'll have to stay there till you're good."

He watched her move along a branch, cautiously, like a cat. Then to his dismay saw her grip the branch, lower herself from it, and prepare to drop. He ran under the branch and caught her as she fell.

"Mercy!" Mrs. O'Farrell screamed, but Patrick steadied himself and looked up over the top of Bridie's golden head and smiled.

"Cats always fall on their feet," he said. "She's not hurt."

"Let me go!" Bridie gasped, crushed against him.

He laughed, his grip tightening. His heart was beating very fast. He looked down into her angry eyes, blue as his own. He said, quietly, "You needn't say you're sorry, Bridie, because I'm not."

He let her go.

"That bold Patrick!" Mrs. O'Farrell scolded.

Bridie gave herself a little shake.

"He thinks he's clever," she said, and walked over to the gable to fetch her bicycle. Patrick had placed the ladder in front of it and she could not extricate it. He came to her rescue, moving the ladder.

"We're friends, aren't we, Bridie?" he urged, in a voice too low for Mrs. O'Farrell to hear.

Bridie, still shaken from her fall, and from the strangeness of being held in Patrick's arms, did not answer.

"Sure, I was only teasing," he coaxed. "Wait, now, while I get you some cherries—the fine big ripe ones from the top branches!"

He seized the ladder and carried it back to the tree. Bridie stood leaning on her bicycle, torn between pride and a weakness for fat ripe cherries . . . and something she could not quite explain; something that had to do with the sensation of Patrick's arms round her, gripping her tight, and an awareness of the quick loud beating of his heart.

She stood watching him climbing the ladder, clambering up into the tree, raising himself up in a fork of branches, holding on with one hand and with the other reaching out his full length along the laden upper boughs. She had a curious sense of excitement, like walking through the streets of Ballyrannon on fair-day.

Then Patrick was back at her side with a ragged cap full of cherries, each faintly pink, not like the hard greenish yellow cherries of the lower boughs. He poured them into the shopping-bag hung from the handlebars of her bicycle, and pulled handfuls out of his pockets, eagerly, filling up the gaps in the shopping-bag, finding room for more in the little black satchel on the carrier, insisting that they were the pick of the tree, and plenty more where those came from, till she had to stop him, laughing. Then, because she laughed, everything was all right between them, and more than all right—different. . . .

"Come out with Flynn and me in my boat this afternoon," he urged. "We can go round to the other side of the island, where the seals are."

She shook her head. "Flynn and I are doing something else."

"Tomorrow, then. I'll come for you——"

"No. We'll come out sometime."

He had to be content with that. He wheeled her bicycle out on to the road for her and they parted. Patrick went back to the cherry-tree and picked cherries, blindly, seeing only red-gold hair between the leaves as his fingers pulled at the pale fruit. Bridie pedalled furiously back to the castle; because she was already late; because she had to find Flynn before he went off and did something else.

When she got back and had delivered the shopping to Tante Emma she searched for him in all the likely places, and then went down to the beach and found the boat gone. She looked out across the lake and saw it tied up at the island, and putting her hands to her mouth called to him across the water.

"Fly-nn! Fly-nn-n!"

The sound carried to Flynn lying dreaming amongst the heather. At first, confusedly, he thought that it was a flight of wild duck going over; then it came again, long-drawn and echoing, with a strange mournfulness.

"Fly-nn! Fly-nn-n!"

He sprang up, then, a crazy thought flashing to him that Cousin Kate had got back and had come to find him. His heart pounded heavily. Then he saw the small childish figure of Bridie waving from the beach, and for a moment could have wept with disappointment. He waved and went down to the boat. The air still seemed to vibrate with the call; he had a sense of feeling it in his body, vibrating in his blood.

He untied the boat, pushed off, rowing mechanically. The shore came nearer, bringing Bridie with it. The boat's keel rasped on the beach and Bridie was scrambling into the boat, her hands full of cherries, cherries dangling from her ears and from her mouth. Then she was sitting in the bottom of the boat, her lap full of them, and shooting the stones out between her lips into the water, and laughing, and chattering to him about Patrick and his 'boldness' at Farrell-the-weaver's.

Flynn listened and smiled, and Bridie was happy because she was with him, her darling brother; but for him none of it had reality; he was still wrapped in his dreams, not present in his body, his spirit shaken, still, by a soft, troubling wind of enchantment.

V

THAT year Flynn began to take an interest in growing things. For some years he had helped Tante Emma with the potato patch which flourished like an oasis in the weed-choked wilderness of the kitchen-garden. Tante Emma had kept this patch going because it was unthinkable that the Harrigans should not be able at least to keep themselves in potatoes, and they with a hundred acres or more. For a time, too, she gathered the gooseberries and blackcurrants and bottled them and made them into jam; but after a time she got beyond it, and the crops, in any case, became less good as the bushes became more and more choked with the weeds, so that it ceased to be worth while, even if she had had the energy. The children brought in the apples from the few trees that survived the Atlantic gales and the lichen slowly creeping along their branches.

When he was quite a small boy Flynn liked helping the old woman plant the seed potatoes, and, later, hoe the furrows, and in due course dig the new potatoes up; and even as a child it seemed to him wasteful that the fruit-bushes should have been allowed to become choked up. Whilst he was attending the monastery he wanted his spare time for his own affairs, except for his help with the potatoes, but when he had finished with what his father was pleased to call his 'schooling', he began to need something to do. It was not always the right weather to go fishing, or paddling about on the lake, and you did not always want to be shooting things. Or reading books. Or pottering about over at Bream Island with Patrick. He began to amuse himself extricating the currant and the gooseberry bushes from the weeds, and burning the grass off the whole garden preparatory to digging it up and re-planting it. When this was done he conceived the idea of enlarging the chicken-run, and instead of 'cooling off' the broody hens sitting them— which Tante Emma had never done because it involved too much work when the young chicks hatched out. But Flynn was fired by the idea that the Harrigans should be at least as self-supporting as the Doyles. He persuaded his father to allow him to buy a young sow at the next fair-day. As soon as she was in season he knew where to take her, and in due course there would be young pigs for the market, and for fattening for home use. It would be fine to see a side of bacon hanging up in the kitchen—Tante Emma said there always had been in the old days.

Mike produced the money for the sow, and for garden implements which Flynn said he needed, but he could not raise any interest in his son's schemes. They had managed well enough all these years without turning the place into a smallholding or a farm. Flynn urged that there was 'money in pigs'. When asked what he would do with the money he replied 'Buy more stock'. Mike very nearly did not give him the money for the sow after that.

"If you had said you intended drinking it, or going abroad with it, or spending it on women, or even books—but *stock*!"

"Isn't it the sensible thing to be doing with it?" Flynn demanded, impatiently.

"That's just what I complain of!" his father roared at him. "It's the horrible sensibleness of the whole idea that I can't stomach! By God, if ye didn't look like a Harrigan I'd swear your mother had betrayed me with an English stockbroker!"

Flynn's own blood was up by then. "If there was a little more sensible-ness up and down the country Ireland wouldn't be as poverty-stricken as she is today! It's people like you who help to keep Ireland shiftless and poor!"

Up till then Mike had been merely ironically amused. Suddenly he was as violently angry as Flynn. He no longer roared; he spoke in a low hard voice which for Flynn somehow matched the ice-coldness of his eyes.

"Let me tell you something, son. It's people like me who help to keep the spirit of Easter Week alive in this country! And that, let me tell you, is the soul of this country! When men stop being crazy and shiftless and reckless and letting tomorrow take care of itself they become a nation of shopkeepers—like the English! In all the things that matter, let me tell you, this is the richest country in the world!"

Flynn was silent. He had an intense sense of injustice. He recognised the truth in his father's words. He knew Irish history. It was the one thing he did know. His blood stirred with the names of Tone and Emmet, Mitchel and O'Brien, and the heroes of Easter Week, Casement, and the sixteen who were shot. And no episode in history, and no line of any poem he had ever read, thrilled him like Connolly's words to his men in the Post Office when surrendering to the English—'*We are going out to be slaughtered, but has it not been a full life, and is not this a good end?*'

His father could tell him nothing about the 'soul' of Ireland. But his father, it seemed to him, was a romantic, though it was probably the last thing in the world he would have thought of himself as being. He was always insisting that Man did not live by bread alone, but all the same you had to have bread; you could not live by fine words and brave gestures alone. And if Ireland lived in the heroic sense because nobody bothered, except when the fight for freedom was involved, they also starved for the same reason. Or so it seemed to Flynn, in those years when he was beginning to observe and to think. His father was always very fierce and contemptuous of people who romanticised the Irish, picturesque Paddy, all 'Faith' and 'Begorrah', but it seemed to Flynn that he romanticised them in another way, with his Republican insistence on the spirit of Easter Week, and his poet's indifference to the problems of daily bread. What Connolly had written of the Young Irelanders seemed to him true of his father, 'While the people perished the Young Irelanders talked, and their talk was very beautiful, thoroughly grammatical, nicely polished, and the proper amount of passion introduced always at the proper psychological moment. But still the people perished.' It was not enough that Ireland should liberate herself from the English yoke and become a free Republic of thirty-two counties. It had to be a Republic of the common people; what Connolly called a workers' republic—but in this, he knew, his father was not interested. He was not interested in the reasons-why of things. As they were, so he accepted them, and wrote of them. He was not concerned with the economic factors behind the Dublin slums, or why the people in the whitewashed cabins of Connemara lived mainly on tea and potatoes. His interest was in effects, not causes. He was not even interested in his own children, Flynn thought bitterly, until such time as he might perhaps find them useful material to write about. When he had any money he went off to Dublin, London, Paris, leaving them to manage as best they could. And now when he, Flynn, was trying to contrive that they should manage a little better he strutted in the role of happy-go-lucky, irresponsible Irishman, taking no heed for the morrow and despising those who did. . . .

He let his father have the last word in the matter, but his resentment against him deepened. He was glad when he went away and he did not care if he never returned. As to Bridie, she barely noticed that he had gone. Tante Emma said, "Wouldn't ye think, now, the divil himself was at his heels, the way he's always runnin' and racin' from one side of the counthry to the other, and no rest in him at all?"

Flynn thought less and less about August and the Horse Show and Cousin Kate, as he became increasingly preoccupied with the work he had taken upon himself. It was as though he had to assume an extra load of responsibility to make up for his father's lack of it. When her rheumatism was not too bad Tante Emma hobbled about the grounds waiting on him, admiring, advising, constantly exclaiming that the castle was "comin' to itself at last, glory be to God!" On Sundays, after Mass, people walked in from Ballyrannon especially to view the 'renovations'. Flynn had hacked down some alders and thorn-bushes and exposed an aspect of the castle that had not been visible for years, and had cleared the avenue and painted the iron gates, "the way you'd think her ladyship was expected back, or there was a marrying on the wind".

Hacking, sawing, painting, digging, Flynn gradually began to develop the idea of not merely making a kitchen-garden and raising enough stock to keep the castle in bacon, milk, eggs, poultry, but of restoring the flower-gardens. Whilst he worked he would be immersed in an endless reverie of his mother. It was not so much that he thought of her as that she came into his mind, like stepping into a room. Every morning when he went out into the grounds to continue his work it was as though he kept a tryst with her. Under her direction Ballyrannon Castle gardens had been the talk of the countryside; when she had gone their wonder had faded, and finally disappeared altogether; now it should be restored—like a monument to the memory of her. . . . But of this he said nothing to anyone, or that he cherished this dream of making the gardens flower again.

When Aunt Chris came, near the end of July, to spend a week, she was both astonished and approving.

"You'll be glad of a holiday after so much hard work," she said.

"I can't take a holiday this year," Flynn told her. "There's too much to do. I've ducks and hens sitting, and I can't leave them to Tante Emma—it'd be too much for her, and she's so forgetful these days, and I'm expecting Biddy to come into season any day now—and you know what it is with sows!"

Christabel O'Donal laughed. "I can't say I do—why should I?"

"Well, anyway," Flynn said, lamely, disconcerted, and reddening a little, "You have to watch out. And I've one goat in kid and two in milk, and a whole lot of land to turn up yet for the autumn sowing——"

"So it's to be a farm, after all, and not a racehorse?"

He saw that she was amused and felt that she was a little mocking, and suddenly that he did not want to discuss any of it any more with her.

He made what his aunt considered an extraordinarily ambiguous, if not downright stupid, answer.

"Och—I don't know, I'm sure!" he said. And it was true; he quite simply did not know. He only knew that anyhow for the time being there was this deep compulsion to create an oasis of orderliness and approach to good living in the confused and confusing wilderness of Ballyrannon Castle. That it was a protest against his father, and a tribute to his mother, and a response to an urge within himself—but none of it to be discussed with Aunt Chris, whose eyes laughed at him, and whose words probed his secrets, without understanding.

He had always admired her—her vivid red-haired beauty, her gaiety and vitality, but he had always been a little afraid of her. Other people entered a room; she always seemed to sweep into it, like a wind—a warm, scented wind, but none the less a wind that had a way of sweeping everything before it.

She always somehow contrived to make the journey across Ireland, and the last exhausting fifty miles out from Galway, and look as immaculate as though she had just stepped out of Grafton Street. Even in a damp and bare and draughty ruin of a castle amongst the stones of Connemara, she was somehow always completely 'Christabel O'Donal, the actress', parading before invisible footlights, bowing to unheard applause. At forty-five she could still look thirty-five off the stage and twenty-five on it. She had a speaking voice that, when she liked, would melt the heart. If she over-dressed, bringing Grafton Street to Connemara, she never over-acted. She was quick-tempered, generous, impatient, in love with life, passionately devoted to the theatre, and her 'impossible' brother. She could never find it in her heart to forgive Kitty her desertion of him and of their children. If she had had her way she would have taken the children and brought them up herself; it had always seemed preposterous to her that they should have been left to be brought up by the old woman they called Tante Emma. Flynn's fear of her had a good deal to do with the fact that as far back as he could remember she had been wanting to tear him and Bridie away from Bally-rannon and Tante Emma and have them 'brought up properly'. She was beautiful, she was warm-hearted, but it was impossible to feel safe with her; there was no safety until she had gone, returned to her own world, then there was the feeling of having escaped for a little while longer. It seemed impossible to convince her that he and Bridie were all right as they were; that they did not want the good education she was always harping on, or the careers, or 'polish'—whatever that might mean. If Ballyrannon Castle was, as she so often declared, a pig-sty, well, they liked it that way. If they all went about looking like tramps, what did it matter in Connemara? They always tidied themselves up when they went into Galway, or on the annual holiday to Dublin. And it was no *use* brushing Bridie's hair or putting her on a clean dress . . . and if even the nuns couldn't cure her of pilfering, why should Aunt Chris think it could be done in Dublin? It wasn't, anyhow, such a very black sin, that he could see; she wasn't, surely, going to be kept out of heaven at the end because of a few oranges and sweets and lead-pencils?

That summer Aunt Chris took him to task very severely over Bridie. It all arose out of the fact that when she learned that Flynn wasn't going to Dublin Bridie said that she too didn't want to go. It was no use Aunt Chris coaxing, saying that it would be lovely, that they would go to the Horse Show, go to the theatre and see Cousin Kate act, go out to Glendalough in the car and picnic beside the lake, buy some nice new summer dresses and shoes, the way nobody would be knowing her when she got back. Bridie merely looked out between the straggling wisps of her red-gold hair, her blue eyes bright with suspicion, like a wild animal that refuses to be coaxed to nibble from the human hand held out so friendlily, and insisted, with an unnatural politeness, Thank you very much, but she'd rather not. . . .

Aunt Chris complained to Flynn, "I don't know what your father's thinking of to let that child run wild the way she is, and you are old enough now to have some authority over her."

"But if she doesn't want to go to Dublin without me——" Flynn protested.

"Ah, sure, it isn't only that, and you know it. Look at her, now—gone thirteen, and running wild like a gipsy! And picking and stealing like one, too!

"No!" Flynn cried, distressed. "'Tisn't like that at all, truly, Aunt Chris! I promise you! Even Father Faherty doesn't think so badly of her."

"You're not going to tell me his reverence considers it no more than a childish ailment, like measles!"

"He has spoken to her about it at Sunday school—only last Sunday, and she has promised never to do it again."

This was completely untrue. Father Faherty was not even aware of Bridie's little weakness, since she never confessed to it, but Flynn had somehow to persuade Aunt Chris to leave the matter alone, to convince her that Bridie's spiritual welfare was being looked after by someone competent for the task.

"I must have a word with his reverence before I leave." There was no end to the menace Aunt Chris represented. Flynn could only do his utmost to avert that catastrophe.

"Father Faherty doesn't like outside interference when he's trying to help anyone," he said, desperately, and further slandered that most tolerant and easy-going of priests by adding, wildly, "and he's terribly down on actresses!"

"Horrible man! You really are living two hundred years behind the times out here! I shall write to your father."

The danger was averted once more, but Flynn did not feel safe until Aunt Chris had climbed into her rakish-looking car, and complaining bitterly about the state of the roads, set out on the long drive back to 'civilisation'. . . .

Closing the newly painted gates after her, he touched a part not quite dry and some paint came off on his fingers.

"Damn!" He pulled a dock leaf and began rubbing.

Bridie said, "Use this," and pushed a handkerchief into his hand.

"You with a hanky, Bridie! Wonders will never cease!" Then suddenly he noticed the 'C' embroidered in a corner.

He looked at her. "Where did you get this?"

"I took it. Out of her drawer. She's got dozens."

Flynn frowned. "Don't you know that's stealing?"

"It's nothing much. I could have taken a pound note if I'd liked."

Flynn insisted, "Big or small, it's all stealing. You're always doing it. What's going to happen to you, at all? You'll come to a bad end—in a reformatory or something." He spoke violently. Coming on top of Aunt Chris's lecture, Bridie's latest delinquency seemed too much. He had this new sense of responsibility, and the burden of it seemed suddenly too heavy.

Bridie said, stubbornly, "I wouldn't steal money, or anything big. I wouldn't take anything of yours or Tante Emma's."

"That's not the point. It's wrong to steal from anyone. And Aunt Chris has been so kind. She brought you that lovely dress all the way from Dublin, and that big box of chocolates for us both, and she's kind to us in lots of ways, and then you steal from her. It's mean!"

Bridie made no answer and they went on up the drive together in silence. Flynn felt thoroughly miserable. He had no idea what to do about Bridie. Until then her petty pilferings hadn't seemed to matter, but Aunt Chris had somehow given them importance, and then to find Bridie had taken something of hers . . .

He said at last, desperately, "You will have to go away—right away, to a school in Dublin. I shall write to Aunt Chris and tell her to get round our father."

In a tense, strangled sort of voice, Bridie said, "I'd run away!"

Then suddenly she had darted away from him and stood with an arm against a tree-trunk, and her face against her arm, and was crying, wildly.

It was more than Flynn could bear. He was beside her instantly, pulling her round to him, so that she faced into his breast, into his heart.

"I didn't mean it, darlin'! Don't cry, darlin'! Bridie darlin', don't cry! I love you! I swear it! No harm shall come to you, ever. I'll look after you, always. Everything will be all right . . . You'll see."

He wiped her face with the stolen handkerchief, which he still carried, and then he laughed, though he was nearly crying himself. "There, now, isn't it a good thing you took it, after all, or we'd have nothing to mop you up with!"

She snatched the handkerchief from him and blew hard into it.

"Making me cry!" she said.

But when they went on together she put an arm round his waist, holding tight on to his coat.

"I'm glad we're not going to Dublin," she said, firmly.

"We'll make up for it," he promised her, recklessly. "We'll go to the Galway races by our two selves! We'll have a grand time—just the two of us. . . ."

Bridie smiled and leaned her head against his shoulder, contentedly.

"A grand, glorious time," she affirmed, and having successfully got round him wished now that she had taken the pound note as well, so that they could have had it to spend.

VI

FLYNN had too many preparations to make for the few days away from home to worry any more about Bridie, and their aunt's lecture. Arrangements had to be made for a niece of Tante Emma's to come over from Letterfrack to stay. She was 'good with' sitting hens, and knew a sow in season when she saw one, and could milk goats. She was to arrive the day before Flynn and Bridie left, so that he could instruct her in everything.

In the midst of this business he received a telegram from his father in Paris congratulating him on his sixteenth birthday—he himself had no idea it was his birthday till then, not because he did not know the date but because he did not keep count of the days, and as often as not did not know the day of the week until Tante Emma reminded him that tomorrow was Sunday and to get up in time for Mass, and put on a clean shirt. It seemed to him odd that his father who took so little interest in him when he was there should think fit to send him a telegram all the way from Paris because it happened to be his birthday. He found himself wondering if somewhere in the world his mother was remembering that on that day sixteen years ago she had given birth to her first child. . . . If *she* had sent a telegram, now, that would have been something to light up the day! Or if Cousin Kate had—but why should she remember?

When Tante Emma knew that it was Flynn's birthday she insisted that there must be a celebration. The neck of a hen past laying had to be wrung, and by boiling it for the greater part of the afternoon, and roasting it in the evening, she guaranteed that it would 'eat sweet as a spring chicken'.

Then of course there must be some guests; you could not have a celebration without guests. Her niece must be wired for to come at once, and no doubt he would be wishing to ask young Patrick Doyle, and wasn't there anyone Bridie would be asking?

Bridie said at once, "I think it's nicest if it's just ourselves, but your niece could come, as she's coming anyway." She looked at her brother, anxiously, adding, a little forlornly, "But it's for Flynn to say—it's his birthday."

Flynn would have liked not merely Patrick but his sister Maureen, because then there would have been dancing, but then perhaps Bridie would have sulked, and it was better not.

"I think we'll just ask Molly," he said.

So Bridie went in on her bicycle to Ballyrannon to send the telegram, and whilst she was there she bought a highly ornate coloured birthday-card for Flynn, and because it was his birthday resisted the temptation to steal an indiarubber that all but came into her hand without effort on her part, and so, full of virtue, returned to the castle.

As it was a celebration it was decided to serve the supper in the dining-room, a fine oak-panelled room with a parquet floor, which had not been opened for years. Flynn had already cut the ivy back from the windows as part of his 'restoration' program, and when the French windows were opened out on to the terrace their broken panes of glass were not noticeable, and when the floor was swept, and a long oak table imported from the library and placed in the centre of the room, and some cream cluster roses arranged in a glass jam-jar placed in the centre of that, it looked a very fine room indeed, and fit for a banquet.

Bridie was so delighted with her decorations that she went all round the grounds gathering all the flowers she could find. The rhododendrons were finished, but their foliage filled up the empty fireplace effectively, and tall yellow wild irises in jam-jars on the floor in the corners of the room relieved the general bareness. Bay willow herb flamed above the mantelpiece in a flamboyant display of ragged purple, and jam-jars of red roses at either end completed the table decorations. The tall straight-backed chair in which Mike Harrigan did his writing was brought from the library and placed at the head of the table for Flynn, and candles stuck into empty whisky bottles were ranged round the centre-piece. Flynn pointed out that it would be broad daylight when they ate, but both Bridie and Tante Emma insisted that you could no more do without candles at a feast than at a wake. . . .

Tante Emma's niece, Molly Murphy, arrived in the afternoon. She was a plump, good-natured looking girl who smiled easily, and having been summoned for a feast had had the forethought to bring with her some home-made raisin cake, a piece of bacon for boiling, and 'a few peas from the garden'.

At the last minute Tante Emma decided that it was not a proper feast unless there was some drink, and she cajoled her niece—"Pop along, now, on yer bicycle, there's a good girl, and ask in O'Connor's will they let ye have a bottle of whisky, and to put it down to Mr. Michael Harrigan. If they're after making any trouble at all tell them we've had word this very day himself will be back any moment now, and not a drop of drink in the place. And call in at Maggie Jameson's and ask her will she lend me her Paisley shawl, and her ould green velvet blouse that should have been in the rag-bag long ago, for we're celebratin' Master Flynn's birthday and I've not a dacent rag to me back. And hurry now!"

Molly went off on these errands and returned with them well and truly accomplished, and did not think it worth spoiling the festiveness of the occasion by conveying Mr. O'Connor's message, which was that that was the last item he would book to Mr. Harrigan till he had had something on account for what was owing already, nor Maggie Jameson's indignant, "Did ye ever hear the like of that now? Haven't some people the greatest impudence?"

When Bridie saw Tante Emma arrayed in the old green velvet blouse, and her best skirt, the one with the flounce at the bottom which she wore to Mass and for funerals, and the brightly patterned shawl ready to be put on when the cooking was done, she became herself infected with the dressing-up spirit and voluntarily changed into the new dress Aunt Chris had given her, and actually invited Molly—to whom she had taken a fancy—to brush and comb her hair and find a piece of ribbon with which to tie it. The dress was a simple green cotton thing, but to Bridie, because it was new and clean, it seemed very grand. She pinned a bunch of cluster roses into the middle of the bodice, and tucked more into her hair, under the piece of grubby tape which was all Molly had been able to find for a bandeau. Flynn was startled by the transformation in her appearance. He had never thought of her even as pretty before, but the combination of excitement, roses, and the new dress and brushed hair made her, he thought, quite lovely—he felt that he would always remember her so, with the green dress, and bright hair, and the yellow roses.

"You look like the queen of the fairies!" he told her, and Bridie felt herself take on new beauty with his words, till it seemed to her that even the vivid Aunt Chris couldn't rival her.

Flynn changed into his one suit and a clean white shirt, and selected one of his father's ties—a broad grey silk affair from the Rue de Rivoli, chosen for him by a woman and despised by him, and never worn, but Flynn did not know this; it was very elegant, but a little odd in conjunction with the rough homespun tweed. When he had brushed his hair and flattened it down with water, and dug some of the garden dirt out from under his nails, Flynn felt that he could do no more, and that in any case he was by then grand enough for the grandest hotel in Dublin. But Bridie insisted that he must have a buttonhole, and broke him off one of her own cream roses, then similarly decorated Tante Emma and Molly.

"Now we all look like lords and ladies," she declared, and strutted, trailing an imaginary train—from a photograph of her mother in ball dress.

As everything had to be done 'properly' that evening, when the meal was ready for the table, instead of being carried in on an old tin tray, with the potatoes in a saucepan, the serving-hatch had to be forced open, dislodging a good deal of dust, and the food passed in from the kitchen by Tante Emma and carried to the table by Molly, with the potatoes 'decanted', as Flynn called it, into a cracked vegetable dish without a lid.

When the candles were lighted Tante Emma had the sudden thought that the table looked like a bier, and crossed herself, hurriedly. But the three young people were entranced, because except for the altar at the Easter Mass, with its white flowers and lighted candles, they had never seen anything so beautiful. That it was like an altar occurred to all of them. And thinking of the Mass, Flynn thought that this, too, was a kind of sacrament—to sit down to a feast with those who were near and dear, and the thought filled him with love and happiness and the feeling of something holy in it all.

Bridie found herself thinking of the altars she had helped to dress in the convent garden for the Feast of Corpus Christi. She had liked best the one with tall blue spikes of delphiniums reaching up between the golden candlesticks to the blue robes of Our Lady, and she with the Infant Jesus in her arms, and on her head a little crown of golden stars. Flynn had been one of the choirboys in a red cassock and lace-edged surplice, and with his bare shining head he had looked, she thought, like something out of a stained-glass window, but she had never told him this, because boys did not like to be told such things, and she was not sure, for another thing, whether it wasn't blasphemous. The choirboys had marched behind Father Faherty—very fine in red and lace and gold—swinging censers, and she had worn a white dress and veil like the other girls, and a wreath of pink rosebuds holding the veil in place, and had scattered rose-petals, and the nuns and the lay-sisters had moved dark and close together, like a flock of birds. But the high peak of it all was the blue and gold altar she had helped to dress, as now the high peak of everything was the table with its roses and candles, and Flynn looking down between the candles, his eyes shining with the great wonder of it all.

"Isn't it the most beautiful sight?" Molly breathed, and there were tears in her eyes, because it all seemed so beautiful, and she was so happy.

But Tante Emma was preoccupied with corporal things.

"Ah, will ye hould ye wisht now, and be passin' the plates," she commanded.

When everyone was served, and a few mouthfuls eaten, she poured the whisky. Molly and Flynn were a little dismayed, but Bridie was delighted.

"Will we all get tipsy?" she demanded, excitedly. Then she sniffed the tiny drop at the bottom of her glass and made a face.

"It's like medicine," she said.

Tante Emma filled the glass up with water, and passed the water to Molly and Flynn, but kept her own whisky neat.

She raised her glass to Flynn. "Here's lookin' at ye, Flynn me darlin'—may yer shadder never be less!"

Molly raised her glass, shyly. "Best wishes," she murmured.

Bridie looked from one to the other, uncertain what to do.

"Raise yer glass now and drink to yer brother," Tante Emma commanded.

"What will I say?" Bridie inquired.

"Ah, sure, say whatever ye've a mind to say——"

So Bridie said, firmly, "I hope you will have a long life—and everything you want!" and took a long drink and tried not to shudder.

Flynn laughed. "First of all I've got to know what I want," he said, and tasted the whisky. It was curious, he thought, so sweet, and it seemed to go straight into your blood. Perhaps when he had drunk a little more he would know what his father got out of it that he couldn't get any other way.

"You want a horse," Bridie said, "that's one thing."

"Perhaps he wants a sweetheart," Molly said, emboldened by the whisky.

"There's time enough for that," Tante Emma observed, drily, and filled her glass up again.

Bridie passed her plate for a second helping.

"We don't go in for sweethearts in our family," she said, frowning.

Molly giggled. "It sounds awful dull!"

Bridie waved an invisible fan. She said, loftily, "On the contrary we are very gay. Isn't that so, Tante Emma?"

The old woman, mellowed with the whisky, chuckled. "Ah, sure, the gaiety at Ballyrannon Castle would put Dublin Castle itself to shame, so it would! Isn't the place fallin' to rack and ruin with the people dancin' themselves through the floorboards year in and year out?"

Flynn regarded Molly solemnly. "You have no idea," he affirmed. "We entertain the strangest guests," and as if in confirmation of it a rat scampered in the skirting. "We had a couple of cows in the drawing-room only the other afternoon."

Molly giggled again, helplessly. "What a way to talk!"

Said Bridie, emulating Aunt Chris, "Oh my dear, it was quite like being in Dublin, I assure you!"

They talked and laughed and the candles spluttered down into the necks of the bottles. The evening was airless and sultry and the roses wilted in the heat and dropped their petals. Flynn grew a little flushed with the whisky, and excitement and sadness, and indefinable longing, stirred in him. He had a fantasy in which Cousin Kate remembered his birthday and came to him across all Ireland. The hot still evening would give her up just as the dusk closed in full of bats' wings and the last lost sad cries of sea-birds over the lake. "Flynn darlin'," she would say, in her deep warm voice, "I had to come. . . ."

He flirted a little with Molly because she seemed to expect it of him, and because of the stir of excitement in himself; he gathered up the fallen rose-petals and rained them on her hair. She giggled and was coy, but he was hardly aware of her. His mind ran with wild sad songs and his blood with a wild sad longing.

The meal came to an end, and the old woman brought out a clay pipe and began to fill it. "Let us tell stories," she said.

"The old grey shawl," Flynn said quickly.

"It's so sad," Molly protested, "it'll have us all cryin'!"

"All the best stories are sad," Flynn insisted.

"It's Flynn's birthday so he must choose," said Bridie, with a wave of the fan.

The old woman got her pipe going, then wrapped the shawl round her in spite of the heat, and sat a moment puffing at the pipe and rocking herself to and fro. Then she took the pipe from her mouth and her sunken faded blue eyes looked beyond the guttering candles and the intent, flushed faces of the young people, and she said, "Glory be to God, there are stories will live in Ireland till the end of time, and one of them is the story of Tommy Whelan, God rest his soul. People are coming all the time from all parts, all the way to Connacht, to Mrs. Whelan's cabin, to hear the story, and not one goes in but comes out with eyes streamin', and not a mother in Ireland but would be proud to call the Whelan lad her son. Walking along the railway line he was when the Black and Tans came up with him and began their questionings about the shooting of the British agents. But, God help him, he could not tell what he did not know—though they'd have got nothing out of him if he had known. . . ."

"Don't tell what they did to try and make him tell," Bridie beseeched, crumbling rose-petals in her fingers like bread, her eyes bright with dread, her face flushed.

The old woman said, sternly, "Cover your ears with your hands, then, for tell it I will. Would ye be havin' me lave out the half of the story?"

Bridie looked wildly from Tante Emma to Flynn, who smiled at her, and reached out and took her hand.

" 'Tis all over and done with now," he sought to comfort her.

"Over, but not done with," Tante Emma said, firmly, and continued, "They tore his finger-nails out one by one, and when his mother came to visit him in Mountjoy prison he kept his hands behind his back so that she should not be seein' what they had done to him, but when she was lavin' him he turned away, and she looked back, God help her, and then she saw what they had done to her son, but she gave no sign. Whilst he was in prison he was always after whistlin' and singin' 'The Shawl of Galway Grey', and when his mother got back to Galway, after they had hanged him with other lads in Mountjoy, the crowd came round her singin' this same song, and pluckin' at the fringes of her shawl till there was scarce a thread left bordering it. But they had to have souvenirs, God help them, and they with the tears streamin' down their faces for the death of an innocent lad. . . ."

Molly wept unashamedly, and Tante Emma wiped the tears from her own face on the ends of the borrowed shawl. Bridie stared hard into the heart of a candle, and Flynn snuffed out with his fingers a candle that had guttered down, the wick spluttering in a mess of melted grease.

" 'Tis a fine brave story," he said, carefully controlling the tendency to tremor in his voice, "I should be proud to live and die as bravely."

The old woman nodded and muttered. "Aye, aye. Isn't there the whole great story of Ireland in it?" She tapped out her pipe against the leg of the table and for a few moments they brooded, staring at the candles, then suddenly their heads jerked up at the sound of wheels on gravel.

Tante Emma whipped the whisky-bottle off the table and hid it in her shawl.

"Mother of God, if it isn't himself back from Paris without a breath o' warnin'!"

But Flynn knew; even before he had reached the window and seen the whiteness of her blouse as she stepped out of the ramshackle cab, he knew that it was Cousin Kate, come all across Ireland because she had remembered. . . .

He was through the French window and out on to the terrace, leaping the low crumbling brick walls and bounding down through the jungles of weeds towards the avenue, before any thought had shaped itself. Then he was running under the dark ilex trees and the cab was clip-clopping away and she was standing in the middle of the avenue waiting for him, hatless, smiling, a small dressing-case at her feet.

She laughed as he came up with her, stumbling in his eagerness.

"One would think you were a hare with the hounds on its heels," she said, and her voice went through him as always.

He caught at her hands, gripping them so that the knuckles whitened. He did not know what he was saying; his words tumbled over each other in his exultation.

"But this is a miracle," he was crying. "All the evening I was wanting this to happen! When I heard the cab I knew it was you!"

"The play finished last night," she told him, "I knew a week ago that it would, but I wanted it to be a surprise. I must go back tomorrow."

In his present excitement that made no sense; that she was there was the only reality.

He picked up the dressing-case.

"We were having a wee party," he told her. "We opened up the dining-room—in honour."

"Who's there?"

"Only ourselves and a niece of Tante Emma's—Bridie and I are going to the Galway races, and she's come to look after things while we're gone." But he did not want to talk of such things, but only to savour her presence. He took her hand and conducted her the short way to the house, through the weeds, and she thought, 'It'll ruin my stockings,' and did not care. Her mother had declared her crazy when she announced that morning that she was catching the mid-day train to Galway, and when she was on the train, trundling slowly across Ireland, she herself had wondered, and on the little train out from Galway, when the train seemed to crawl. People did not make such journeys merely to spend a night in a place—not unless they were in love. . . .

Then Flynn was standing before her, tall and slim and eager, and somehow heart-breakingly young, and she knew that it had been the kind of craziness that is the only sanity . . . and that it was true that people only did this sort of thing when they were in love.

On the terrace she turned to look back for a minute at the lake.

"It's so beautiful," she said, "It's always more beautiful than one has remembered," and her heart added, "And you too, my darling, you too!"

Flynn was too excited to think what might be Bridie's and Tante Emma's reaction to Cousin Kate's arrival. He led her triumphantly into the dining-room, but the candles were extinguished and the room was empty, and lonely with dusk.

"Look who's here!" he had cried, and the empty room, with its reek of recently snuffed-out candles, mocked him. He was momentarily dismayed, then angry. What right had they to do this? He groped in his pockets for matches. She came to his rescue with a lighter.

He relit such candles as were still lightable and saw with relief that there was some food left.

He went to the hatch and jerked it up, but the kitchen was in darkness.

"They've all gone to bed, it seems—I can't think why."

She smiled. "As a protest against my arrival, no doubt. Tante Emma never liked me, and Bridie is jealous—you know that."

Did he know it? It was something he had not wanted to have to acknowledge. Even now he had to excuse her. "She's only a kid. Sit you here now, while I get you a clean plate." He led her to the big chair and removed his own used plate.

She sat down and leaned her head against the high back of the chair and smiled at him.

"Bring two glasses," she said, "and in my case you'll find some champagne, and something I brought for you for a present."

He brought the case to her. "I would sooner you opened it," he said, and went out.

When he came back from the kitchen with two glasses, a clean plate and knife and fork, she sat with a bottle of champagne in front of her, and in her lap a small grey book. He set the plate and cutlery before her, and she handed him the book. It was Dr. Hyde's translations from the Gaelic of *The Love Songs of Connacht*.

"I was fortunate to find it," she said. "There were only three hundred copies printed, in 1904."

He handled the book, wonderingly. "I don't know what to say—to thank you." Then he turned a page and saw that she had written, simply, 'For Flynn from Katherine', but the sight of their two names gave him a curious pleasure, and his heart quickened a little.

"It's a lovely book," he murmured.

"The paper's hand-made," she informed him, and the satisfaction in her voice made him want to laugh, it was so like what Bridie might have said. But he only said, gravely, and with the utmost sincerity, "If I live to be a hundred I shall never have anything I shall value more than this."

He laid aside the book and began hacking off for her the remains of the chicken, and cut a slice of the bacon, then at her request opened the champagne. It frothed up and splashed over the roses, and they laughed, excitedly. He was caught between a sudden wish that the others had been there, particularly Bridie, to share it with them, and an elated sense of the luck of having Cousin Kate to himself.

She raised her glass to him. "Here's all you wish yourself, Flynn darlin'."

He asked her about the play, and what she was going into next, and they sat a long time. He fetched fresh candles from the kitchen, and outside the last light drained imperceptibly from the sky.

They were both a little drunk when the door opened and Bridie did not so much walk as glide in, in a long white nightgown, withered roses still clinging to her tumbled hair, her eyes closed.

They both stared at the apparition for a moment, then Katherine murmured, "Miss Bridie Harrigan as Lady Macbeth!"

"She's asleep," Flynn said, "I've never known her do that before! It must have been all the excitement this evening."

He got up and went over to her. "Bridie," he said softly, "Bridie," and took her hand.

She started, opened her eyes, and stared at him.

"What is it? Where am I?" She clung to him.

He said, soothingly, "It's all right. Come back to bed."

He put an arm round her shoulder and led her out of the room.

When the door had closed on them Bridie leaned against him. "I'm so tired," she said, "so sleepy," and yawned.

"I'll carry you." He slipped an arm under her knees and lifted her. She leaned her head against his shoulder and her eyes closed again.

He carried her up the broad bare sweep of the stairs and along the wide dark corridor, lighted only by the glimmer from the uncurtained windows and into her room, where he laid her on the bed and pulled the covers over her, then kissed her forehead.

She murmured, drowsily, "Your breath smells funny."

"Cousin Kate brought some champagne."

"I'm thirsty—I want some."

"I'll save you some for tomorrow—it wouldn't be good for you to have any now."

She repeated, "I'm thirsty—I want some now."

"Just half a glass then."

"A whole glass."

He went out of the room and when she was alone Bridie sat up and groped for the candle on the chair beside the bed and lighted it. She had been a little scared creeping along the corridor and down the stairs, but it had all gone off very well, she thought; there was a girl at the convent who used to walk in her sleep, and she had often watched her, fascinated. She had startled them, she thought; she had felt them staring at her when she had glided in; it had been a great effort not to open her eyes.

When Flynn re-entered the dining-room Katherine smiled.

"That child was no more sleep-walking than you are," she informed him, "but it was a good act. Tell her I said so."

"An act? But why should she?"

"Just to see what we were up to—just to cause a diversion. I don't blame her. I did the same thing myself when I was about her age and my mother was giving a party."

Flynn sighed. "What will I do with her at all? She wants a glass of champagne now."

"It's you she wants, not the champagne—to get you away from me. If she wants anything else you'd better tell her to come and get it!"

When he got back Flynn sat down on the edge of Bridie's bed and watched her whilst she sipped the champagne. She looked very small and childish and innocent in the old-fashioned nightgown and with the wilted yellow rose in her hair.

"Why did Cousin Kate want to come and spoil everything?" she demanded after a few minutes.

"But for Cousin Kate you wouldn't be drinking champagne at this moment," he pointed out.

"All the same, we don't want her. How long will she be staying?"

"She's going tomorrow—more's the pity."

He got up, feeling that he had indulged her already more than enough, and she said quickly, "Don't go! Stay with me. I think I feel sick—I'm going to be sick——"

. Flynn said, "All right, be sick! But any more trouble from you tonight and we don't go to Galway. If you're ill I'll fetch Tante Emma—she knows where the castor-oil is——"

"No, no, I won't be sick. I promise. I won't stir from this bed. Only don't go—stay with me—let's tell stories—happy ones—about Ossian and Grania and the Fianna——"

"I've had enough of you," he said, and went out—followed by the immediate sound of noisy sobbing. His lips tightened; one act a night was enough, he thought, grimly.

Downstairs he found his cousin standing by the French window. She turned as he entered, and smiled.

"It's cooler now," she said, "a little wind has got up."

He went over to her and she reached out and took his hand and drew him a little to her.

"Don't frown, Flynn darlin'. Look, the moon's coming up. Let's do a crazy thing and take the boat out——"

To do a crazy thing with her was to do a lovely thing. All that was troubled in him subsided. He went out with her into a soft warm darkness that smelled faintly of roses and strongly of the sea. A bird called mournfully over the lake, a long-drawn cry that might have been a signal—to a gunman on the run, or men who waited in ambush. He said this to her as they plunged, hand in hand, down through the wilderness to the lake's edge, and because he did not know it she told him the story of Yeats' *Cathleen Ni Houlihan*, and when she chanted the lines—

> "They shall be remembered for ever,
> They shall be alive for ever,"

he knew again the authentic spinal shiver of inspired utterance.

When they were in the boat, cleaving water of the soft brightness of a heron's wing under the rising moon, they went on talking, Katherine of the Abbey Theatre and parts she would like to play, Flynn of things he never told to anyone.

"It's no use your mother, or anyone, asking me what I want to do," he tried to explain. "If I could say I wanted to study law or medicine or go into business or become a writer, it would be easy. But I don't want anything like that. First I want to make something of Ballyrannon, and then I don't know. I'd like to have been with Connolly and the others in the Post Office during Easter Week. I'd like to have been with De Valera in Boland's Mill. I'd like that sort of chance." He added, finally, because it was possible to say it out there on the lake, in the moonlight, with Cousin Kate, to say outloud what he had long held in his heart, heard upon the wind and in the cries of curlews, and felt in every breath of bog and burning turf, "I'd like to serve—Cathleen Ni Houlihan."

She thought, with both elation and sadness, "We shall never be as young as this again!"

And Flynn was sixteen, but he knew, even then, that whatever might or might not have significance in the years to come, this night would have significance. That all his life he would remember the table with its flowers and candles, like an altar, and the feeling of sacrament; and Katherine waiting under the dark ilex trees, and that moment of invitation into the waiting stillness of the summer night, and the release of thought and feeling, the sense of dreams crystallised at last into words, as they moved together over the shadowy waters of the lake.

They tied up at the islet, and sat for a time watching the play of moonlight on the water. There were no words for it, Flynn thought, you could never capture it in any poem, but there could never be anything in the world as beautiful as moonlight on the lake at Ballyrannon.

"Isn't it strange," Katherine said after a while, "to think of people lying asleep in their beds, with all this shut out from them? Let's not go to bed all night! The night's too beautiful to sleep it away!"

Flynn said, laughing, "I feel as though I shall never sleep again—but it all feels like a dream for all that!"

"I think I shall go for a swim," Katherine announced. "The water's so warm." She trailed a hand over the side of the boat, then sprang out and ran over the heather. A few minutes later he heard a splash, and he began to strip off his own clothes.

She laughed as he came up with her through the moon-silvered moor. "Think of the good brothers sleeping in their beds in the monastery there, and the two of us naked in the water, right under their holy windows!"

"As it's all happening in a dream it doesn't matter," Flynn said, and knew that tomorrow, with Katherine gone, he would ask himself if any of it happened at all. But she had given him *The Love Songs of Connacht*, and by that token he would know. . . .

Her naked breast lifted out of the water as she swam was as impersonal for him then as the breast of a gull, and as beautiful; something for a poem or a song, but no relation to his noontide dreams of her in absence. Even the cool impact of the water on his own naked flesh had a curious unreality.

When she clutched at a rock to pull herself up on to the island he swam on round to the boat. He had no thought of her fully naked in the moonlight, but only that in a few minutes she would be seated opposite him again in the boat, and the strange lovely dream would move on to its next stage.

He dressed and waited for her in the boat, and when she came she announced that she was 'ravenous', and that they must return immediately and 'forage for food'. And if Bridie hadn't got at it there was some champagne left in the bottle. . . .

The castle in the moonlight looked quite preposterously romantic; like something in an opera, Katherine said, and one day they must do a play on the terrace. One would never guess, she said, that there were rats in the skirting, bats in the attics, a wasps' nest in the drawing-room, and apples spread out all over the floor.

"Your mother always says it's a cross between a ruin and a slum," Flynn told her.

"It's a darlin' place, all the same," Katherine insisted, all their shared childhood summers flooding her, and was suddenly sad because childhood was over, and now she was in love with him, and the three years between them that had mattered so little then now seemed enormous. She was his darling Cousin Kate, but she felt that he did not yet know what it was to be in love, for all his love of her. He was a boy still, 'shut up in dreams, a shadow-catcher'; all the romanticism of his youth flowed out to Cathleen Ni Houlihan, not to Katherine O'Donal, and the thought made her feel old, and worldly, enclosed in her worldliness, unable to reach out to him wrapped in the unrealities of his dreams . . . or so it seemed to her, looking at his rapt face in the moonlight.

Flynn knew no such analysis of thought and emotion ; that she was there beside him was perfection.

At the castle he kindled a small turf fire in the library, the only room in which they could sit with any comfort ; in spite of the warmth outside it was chilly indoors, and the fire, in addition, gave life and intimacy to the shabby, ramshackle room. He pulled his father's sagging leather armchair up to the fire for Katherine, and sat himself on a rag rug at her feet. They finished the champagne, gnawed chicken bones, and ate raisin cake, laughed and talked, and were gay and serious in turn. For a while the champagne and a sense of adventure kept them awake, but presently the silences became longer, and in one silence Flynn drifted into sleep, his arm thrown out across her lap, his head against her knee.

When she was sure he slept she reached a hand down and slid it over his hair in a caress full of tenderness, and when she too fell asleep her hand came to rest at the nape of his neck.

VII

WALKING to Ballyrannon with Katherine in the morning, to catch the one train of the day, Flynn was still held by the sense of unreality. Not until the train was steaming out of the little station, and she was waving from the window, did he realise that she had come and gone, and all his impulse was to run wildly after the train, to shout to it to stop. She had come and gone and nothing of importance had been said. He had longed for her so madly, and when she had come all they had done was to eat and drink, and row and swim, talk of plays and poetry, and Cathleen ni Houlihan, and lose the precious hours in sleep. Then he had carried her dressing-case to the station, and they had made casual conversation on the way, and not even kissed goodbye, and but for the reality of the grey-covered book it might none of it have happened.

For the few days before he and Bridie left for Galway he was in what Tante Emma called one of his 'black moods'. He was, in fact, wildly miserable, completely possessed by Katherine, to the point of exhaustion, physical, mental, and emotional. Sixteen seemed to him a horrible age to be ; no one took you seriously at that age. You were no longer a child, but you were also no adult, at least in the eyes of older people. He was filled with mistrust ; Cousin Kate was sweet to him and had come all across Ireland just to spend a few hours with him on his birthday, but she could not possibly be expected to be more than fond of him. She was used to experienced young men older than herself ; what use could she have for a callow youth who spent his life at the back of beyond hoeing potatoes and grubbing in the earth? It was just her natural goodness of heart that had brought her out to Ballyrannon, and she probably thought that a book of old love-songs for his birthday might help to educate him a bit, wake him up. To her, no doubt, he lived in a coma, he thought, bitterly.

Both he and Bridie rode in the local races, but without distinction, their mounts being merely shaggy ponies taken out of turf carts, and Bridie had created a diversion by trying to make her pony jump a ginger-beer stall and only succeeding in overturning it, with the result that all the bottles went rolling out over the course, to be swooped upon by eager children. The owner of the stall was for making Flynn pay, and Bridie seemed to think the whole episode funny. . . .

There was a dance at the town hall in the evening—it was the town hall not in any civic sense, but simply in that it was the hall at which local events, such as an occasional film, dance, or concert, was held. The 'band' consisted of an accordion, a fiddle, and a drum, and its repertoire consisted of exactly six tunes, which it repeated monotonously, from seven in the evening till two in the morning. Patrick Doyle persisted in 'Paul Joneses' till at last Bridie fell to him, and after that gave her little rest. But all the time Bridie was straining to see where Flynn was, with whom he was dancing, and her only happy moments were when he was dancing with her.

Whilst the band was out quenching its thirst, local talent was invited to contribute an impromptu program, and after a number of rather bashful songs and recitations, and a few self-conscious jigs and step-dances, Bridie, to Flynn's astonishment, suddenly ran out into the centre of the hall and began throwing somersaults with remarkable ease and rapidity, and a sensational display of brief red knickers which Tante Emma had run up for her from an old petticoat. When she had completed the length of the hall she bowed, gravely, then flung herself down into the nearest chair, flushed, breathless, and defiant. What little applause there was came from the batch of 'corner-boys' who huddled together by the door when not dancing and were continually slipping out for drinks.

Flynn heard the exclamations and comments of disgust and dismay all round him, and was himself shocked and angry. That Bridie Harrigan had upset the ginger-beer stall at the races in the afternoon, and turned catherine-wheels at the dance in the evening, would be the scandal of Ballyrannon for weeks—until, in fact, something else happened to take the local mind off it. Mother of God, what could one do with a sister like that?

He felt a hand on his shoulder and turned to face Patrick Doyle, who was laughing.

"What came over her at all?" Patrick inquired.

Flynn replied, angrily, "You'd better ask her, Patrick, she'll not heed me. She'll have to go away—she's getting to be more than I can manage!"

Patrick's dark eager face clouded. "No," he said, quickly, "let her come and stay a while with us, rather, if folks do be talking."

"It might be an idea," Flynn said. "I'll take her home now, before she decides to stand on her head, or do a trapeze act from the electric lights!"

"Ah, don't be hard on her, now," Patrick pleaded. "Sure, 'tis only a child she is!"

"She's rising thirteen," Flynn said, violently, "and what's to happen to her, the road she's going?"

He strode off down the hall, his face flushed with anger, and aware that people nudged each other and whispered as he passed.

He found Bridie with a group of giggling girls.

She grinned as he approached her. "That shook them, didn't it?"

Flynn scowled. "I've a very good mind to shake you!" he told her. "Come along, now, we're going home."

She stared at him for a moment, on the point of defiance, but something in his manner compelled her. It would never do to quarrel with Flynn now, for tomorrow they were to leave for Galway and the great and glorious annual event of the West.

Outside, in the bright white moonlight, she said in a small voice, "I'm sorry if I did a wrong thing, Flynn darling."

He said, savagely, "Don't be darlinging me! You're going to be sent away—right away! That's what's going to happen to you, till you get cured of thieving and play-acting and making exhibitions of yourself in public, and being a nuisance to everyone generally!"

Bridie was silent, all feeling concentrated in a stubborn resistance. To send her away they would have to carry her bodily to the train, and to keep her in the train they would have to bind her with ropes. She did not know why she had suddenly had the crazy notion of turning somersaults at the dance; it had 'come over' her that it would be fun to do so, because it would startle everyone so, and everything up till then had been so boring, except the dances with Flynn. It had come into her head; it was just the devilment of it; surely Flynn could understand that? As for the incident at the races, how was she to know that that fool of a pony couldn't even take a small jump like that? No one could say with truth that it had been her fault, and there had been no need for old Moriarty to have made such a fuss about a few old bottles of ginger-pop. . . .

She trudged along beside her brother, silently, but for the clip-clop of her downtrodden shoes. Once she excused herself from him to go behind a stone wall, then had to run to catch up with him. She slipped a hand into his, then.

"Flynn," she said, softly, ingratiatingly, and when he did not answer, more loudly, "Flynn—don't be angry!"

He snatched his hand away. "Ah, don't be trying to get round me! You'd best be thinking up what to say to Father Faherty when he calls round tomorrow."

"With any luck we'll have left before he comes," Bridie suggested, hopefully.

"I've no heart for the races now. What's the use? You'll probably go and throw a hand-stand in the paddock, and get caught stealing things from the shops!"

Bridie made no comment, and they went the rest of the way in silence.

When they got in Flynn went straight up to his room in the tower, lit the candle, and flung himself down on the bed. What sort of life was this at all, with a father who spent most of his time in Paris, indifferent to his family, and who when at home was drunk more often than sober, and a mother who was God knows where, and a sister who by the looks of it ought to be in a reformatory? What was the good of anything, with this deep dissatisfaction at the heart of it all? He had to be father and mother all in one to Bridie, and it was too much for him. He would have to get away from Ballyrannon before he, too, became part of its general slow deterioration and decay. He rolled over on to his face and gave himself up to a fantasy in which he ran away to Dublin, and turned up at the O'Donal house, and Cousin Kate opened the door to him and he stepped straight into her arms . . . which went round him, blessedly. Had she really been there only a day or two ago? Had they really touched hands, and had he really seen her naked breast white upon the water?

He did not hear Bridie creep into the room, and was unaware of her till she bent over and laid her face against his.

"Flynn," she said, "Flynn," and he knew that now she was not coaxing or play-acting. He recognised the desperation in her voice. He knew very well how it was with her; she was feeling lonely, and frightened of her sins. Ahead of her was the confessional. He put out an arm and drew her down to him on the bed.

"It's all right, Bridie," he said, and turned on his pillow and smiled into her small troubled face. Whatever happened, she would always be the little sister, needing his love, and commanding it.

"I'll make it all right with Father Faherty—and all of them," he promised her. "We'll get down to the station early in the morning and perhaps his reverence won't be about so soon, and then for three whole days we won't think about Ballyrannon at all. Now you must go to bed—it's getting late."

She did not move. There was a thing to say.

"I didn't mean to make you miserable, Flynn. I won't do it again—I promise!"

He pinched her cheek. "It's rash to make promises, Bridie."

She could smile now, because he was on her side after all.

"What did Patrick say?" she demanded.

"He thought it might be a good idea for you to go and stay with them on Bream Island till it had all blown over."

She tossed her head. "Why should I? We're going to Galway."

He sat up on the bed and looked at her, and she flung herself on him in a throttling embrace.

"I love you and love you and love you!" she declared, kissing him violently with each declaration.

When Flynn had extricated himself from the stranglehold he pleaded, laughing, "Then prove it by going to bed, there's a good wee girl."

She scrambled to her feet, swept him a low curtsey, holding out her grubby nightgown, blew a kiss from the door, and was gone. Flynn sat watching the candle flame wavering in a light wind, and he thought, 'In three or four years Bridie could marry and settle down. She could marry Patrick.' It seemed the obvious solution. But at sixteen three or four years represent eternity.

He sighed and began to undress, and then, because there was no sleep in him, sat down again on the edge of the unmade bed—Tante Emma complained that she could not toil up into the tower, and Flynn himself could not be bothered—and began turning the pages of the book Cousin Kate had given him.

He came upon a verse in *The Red Man's Wife* which answered his mood—

> 'There grows a tree in the garden
>   With blossoms that tremble and shake,
> I lay my hand on its bark
>   And I feel that my heart must break.'

He felt that he did not as yet know the name of the tree, but that in the morning he had parted from Katherine he had already laid his hand upon its bark.

2

In Galway city his mood lightened. There was never yet born the Irishman who went to the races or a horse show with anything but the uplifted heart. Flynn Harrigan and his sister were to be seen at the races on the two successive days, the Wednesday and the Thursday, and though they lost money had more than their money's worth of pleasure and excitement. Between races they hung round the paddock, not merely to assess 'form', but for what was for them the intense joy of watching thoroughbred horses moving in sunlight. Apart from the pleasures of the paddock and the thrill of the actual races, both enjoyed the atmosphere of a race-meeting, the fair-day feel of the crowd, the diversions of the side-shows, the gipsies and the tipsters, the quacks and the rogues, who were part of it all.

At the close of the second day they both looked wistfully at gay posters announcing the Limerick Junction races, to which most people, it seemed, were going on, but there was no more money to spare, and Flynn was anxious to get back to his livestock and his gardens. They spent their last day wandering about the town. They went down to the Bay and looked across to the Aran Islands, misty in the distance. They visited a cinema and saw things which made very little sense to them ; and afterwards Flynn found a bookshop in which they spent a lot of time and in which, out of sheer boredom, Bridie pilfered a pocket-diary, a pencil, and a few postcards. She hid the things away in her handbag so that Flynn should not see, but it oppressed her conscience as another sin that she was now not merely a thief but a deceiver. She had the feeling that however many Hail Marys and Our Fathers and I Believes Father Faherty gave her as a penance after her next confession it would never absolve her. . . .

But when they left the bookshop they went to a commercial hotel off the market-place, up shiny, linoleum-covered stairs and into a large pseudo-modern dining-room, where modern lighting was combined with ferns in brass-bound oak tubs balanced on pedestals, and plain, rough-surfaced, cream wallpaper broke out into delphiniums and hollyhocks reaching up from skirting to picture-rail in the corners. Here they had an enormous high-tea and Bridie forgot her sins in a new pleasure. She felt grown-up and mportant pouring out the tea, and remembered not to wipe her mouth on the back of her hand, and was careful to remove the spoon from the cup after stirring and to place it in the saucer. She would have liked to have stayed the night in that hotel, so that they might have breakfast amongst the alabaster electric light bowls and the wallpaper delphiniums and hollyhocks, but Flynn preferred a little public-house down by the quays. It was a dingy, flyblown place, but he liked it because it looked out to the islands, and because of the faded blues and greys and rose colours of the harbour, with its shabby old houses, its fishing-boats and barges, and its old men who leaned against capstans and did nothing all day but smoke and spit and yarn and stare out to sea.

Galway city was for Flynn firstly the road to Ballybrit and the races, and the gateway to Dublin, and then the faded colours of the harbour, and old men leaning, with time flowing past them like the tides. And, pervading all, the smell of seaweed and porter and turf, and a pale evening light that seemed to come up out of the sea, and a sense of age and changelessness, and the ghosts of Spanish ships with wine in their holds, and of shipwrecked sailors fugitive from the English soldiery. On a summer evening, after a day of diffused sunshine, the sea would be colourless, as though all its strength had been drained up into the pale gold sky. Then the white and pink-washed old houses would seem strangely luminous in the soft light, and a tremendous sadness creep down over everything. You felt then, if you were Flynn Harrigan, you could die for love of Cathleen ni Houlihan, and were filled with a happy sadness. The light in Galway city seemed somehow different from anywhere else, he would think, and when he tried to find a word for it 'unearthly' was the one that came to him.

He liked to walk with Bridie along the sea-wall and out to Salthill, and there lie in the coarse sandy grass and look out to the misty islands and dream of the gentle, noble Sir Philip Sidney, making that same walk, planning the book that was a plea for justice for an oppressed country, but which left the English unmoved. With Bridie in the grass at his side, dreaming her own dreams, he would come close to her in the spirit; then he need not worry about her, feeling her part of himself.

"Next year," he promised her, "we will go on to Limerick and Dublin."

Dublin for Bridie meant the Horse Show. For him it meant Cousin Kate. And for them both a year was a lifetime.

VIII

THAT was the pattern of their lives in those early years. There were the wild wet months of autumn and winter and early spring, with all the brown undulating bog-land they called 'mountain' running with water, and the ditches overflowing at the sides of the roads, day after day of grey mists of rain swirling out of a grey sky, and great gales sweeping in from the Atlantic, and the lake whipped up till it became a shoreless sea, the hills behind it completely obliterated in the mist.

There was April with the new softness on the air, and the waves of daffodils flowing down over the terraces of the castle to the lake, and gathering in clumps on the boggy land in front of the low whitewashed cabins huddled under their winter-ravaged thatch—the leafless, almost imperceptible Conne-mara spring that was yet so insidious. Then May, when the bog came alive with the turf-cutters, the rich black earth, with its strong good smell, laid open to the drying wind and sun ; and after that the slow sweet tide of summer and the fuchsias flaming along the bog-roads and beside the ancient stone walls, the hills darkly blue and hazy, and the bog flecked with small bright flowers and the white cotton-wool wisps of the bog-cotton, and purple smears of heather. Summer and the local races, and the Galway races, and Limerick Junction, and the Dublin Horse Show. Summer and Aunt Chris coming to stay, and Mike Harrigan back from Paris with the manuscript of a new book in his battered, label-plastered suitcase.

There was the occasional local dance and film. There were fair-days, and Bream Island, and the Doyles. And always, behind everything, the regular rhythm of religious devotions, welding the haphazard days to-gether, imposing discipline upon wildness, ritual on formlessness. Bridie might gabble her penances, impatient to have done with them and escape into the outer air, keeping careful count of them lest she repeat one prayer too many, but she never had any wish to evade them, and never went any-thing but willingly to her religious duties. And Flynn would no more have thought of questioning the faith to which he had been brought up, and the expression of it, than he would the sequence and manifestations of the seasons. Sometimes he and Bridie went into Ballyrannon for the rosary ; at other times Tante Emma gathered them in the castle kitchen and said it ; but they never missed it. · In their drifting lives the Church represented order and meaning. It was the one thing static.

Not that either Flynn or Bridie ever thought of their lives as drifting and aimless. When Bridie at fifteen finished at the convent she had no sense of time hanging heavily on her hands. She worked with Flynn in the garden ; she helped with the livestock ; she was always ready to help Tante Emma bake bread, bottle fruit, pluck a chicken ; she was always rushing into Bally-rannon on her bicycle, shopping, or on other errands, and sometimes for her own amusement—to find someone with whom to gossip, to visit the sisters at the convent. She rowed and swam, alone and with Flynn ; she visited the Doyles, and occasionally, with the utmost condescension, allowed Patrick to take her out in his curagh when he was inspecting his lobster-pots.

To Aunt Chris's frequently reiterated, "But what does the child find to *do* all day ?" she could hardly have answered straight off, but the days never dragged, and so long as all was well between her and Flynn she was happy.

She was sixteen in the election year of 1932 and Aunt Chris was anxious to give a party for her. She would have liked Bridie to have spent a month or two with her ; she would never become 'civilised' so long as she went on running wild in Connemara. She had looks if she was dressed properly, and she was bright and quick ; something could be made of her ; she might even show some aptitude for the theatre. . . . But Bridie would not stay so much as a week without Flynn, and Flynn would not leave his livestock and his spring-sowing for more than a few days at a time.

Mike had come home for the election and was drunk for a week in celebration of the defeat—at long last—of the Cosgrave government. The release of the I.R.A. prisoners from the Arbour Hill military prison was for

him the crowning peak of the De Valera victory. That Bridie's birthday
came just at that time offered the perfect opportunity for celebrations on a
scale his sister had not dreamed of when she had first proposed a little birthday party for Bridie at the Shelbourne. He had a little money that winter
and had intended paying off a few debts, buying Bridie a pony for her birthday, and giving Flynn a cheque to spend at the next fair-day. He had had
all these good intentions, but now it seemed a great deal more important that
the champagne should flow freely at the party, that Flynn should have a
dinner-jacket, Bridie a long dress, himself new dress-clothes, and that the
Harrigans generally should do honour to the Fianna Fail triumph.

When Chris realised the scale on which Mike proposed to give the party
she suggested transferring it to her own house; instead of a dinner-party
there could be a nine o'clock party, with music and champagne and whisky
and a buffet supper. It would be cheaper, she urged, and he could then ask
all the people he wanted. But Mike would not hear of it. There had to be
a dinner-party at the Shelbourne, with a cake with sixteen candles for his
beautiful daughter—he had suddenly discovered that she was, anyhow in-
cipiently, a beauty—and it should be seen that though the Harrigans had not
now that strength which in old days moved Dublin and Connemara, they
still knew how to entertain in the grand manner.

"It will cost the earth," his sister pointed out.

But Mike Harrigan had two hundred pounds to spend, and he was quite
prepared to spend it all in one night if need be. . . . Never should it be
said that the Harrigans did not know how to spend.

Bridie would a great deal sooner have had the pony than the celebrations,
and Flynn was appalled by the thought of it all. A little dinner-party with
Aunt Chris and Cousin Kate, and himself and Bridie and their father, and
perhaps one or two other people if Aunt Chris thought fit to ask them, might
have been fun, he thought, but the kind of party it was now proposed to give
would be not Bridie's birthday party, but Mr. Michael Harrigan, the novelist,
entertaining at the Shelbourne on his return from Paris. . . .

His own sixteenth birthday party had had beauty and significance;
Bridie's would be merely a social occasion. The one compensating feature
of the whole thing was that he would see Cousin Kate.

He had seen her only once since his sixteenth birthday, and then not
alone. He and Bridie had gone to Dublin the following year and had stayed
in a small hotel along the quays, because the O'Donal house was already full
of summer visitors come for the Horse Show. Aunt Chris had given them
lunch at an expensive restaurant off Grafton Street, and Katherine had been
there. She had had to go away immediately after the lunch to the theatre.
In the evening they had seen her play at a small studio theatre. She had
played the street-girl in *The Plough and the Stars*, and it made no sense for
either Flynn or Bridie. Everything in Flynn insisted that that hard-eyed,
hard-voiced creature with the great red gash of a mouth was not Cousin
Kate, and that she had nothing to bring to the part. She was, in fact, as the
critics were agreed, quite unsuited to it.

At the luncheon she had been lively and gay, and in that role also she
had been unreal for Flynn; she was being theatrical, artificial. It was because she was nervous, but Flynn could not know this. He wanted to meet

again the girl who had caught his hand and invited him to do lovely crazy things on a warm summer night; he had nothing in common with the young woman with the smart hat and the lipsticked mouth and the affected manners who was Miss Katherine O'Donal, the young Gate Theatre actress.

Afterwards, at the Horse Show, walking with Bridie under sun-golden trees and between flower-beds gay with summer flowers, he had been unhappy, thinking that he had waited a year to see Cousin Kate again and when at last it had happened it hadn't counted.

His eighteenth birthday had been spent on Bream Island in the Doyles' cabin. There had been story-telling, and singing and dancing, and he had been happy. He enjoyed the jigs and reels on the earth-floor, to the scrape of a fiddle wildly played by a wild-looking old man, far more than the fox-trots and waltzes and one-steps of the local dances. To clasp some girl in your arms and hurtle round the floor with her in an intimate embrace seemed to him both grotesque and indecent. He felt that he understood very well why Father Faherty frowned on that kind of dancing, and the streak of puritanism in himself endorsed the priest's attitude—in conflict with another part of himself which could and did plunge recklessly into that kind of dancing and, at the time, enjoy it, though a sense of guilt made the memory uneasy. But no such misgivings attached to the old dances; they were fun, and with a little poteen in you you could dance like mad till daylight, and instead of growing tired as the night wore on—as you always did with the modern dances—feel an exciting, growing power. . . .

There had been no trip to Dublin that year; Aunt Chris had not invited them, being occupied with rehearsals for a new play, and they had no money with which to go uninvited. They had gone again to Galway, instead, and looked for no further excitement till the following summer. But in February of the next year there had been the excitement of the general election, and Flynn and Bridie had gone round chalking 'Up Dev' on every available fence and wall, and even across the roads. . . .

2

The Shelbourne dinner-party was a dazzling affair, a literary and theatrical Who's Who, which Mike and Chris and Katherine enjoyed immensely, and in which Flynn and Bridie were completely submerged. For Flynn it was the same sort of ordeal that the luncheon-party of the summer before last had been. On this occasion he met Katherine O'Donal, very striking in a red evening gown which made her seem, somehow, much more naked than when she had swum naked in the lake; but not all the evening did he so much as glimpse Cousin Kate.

He sat with Bridie, looking, in her long white dress, rather like a wild fairy, on his right, and a vivacious young actress on his left. He thought the actress very beautiful, and was sure she was clever, but he had no idea how to talk to her, or how to answer most of her questions, since he had not read the books or seen the plays of which she spoke, and she concluded that in spite of his good looks he was a very dull young man, and after a time abandoned him, to concentrate on the elderly but amusing author-poet on her other side.

Across the table from his son, Michael Harrigan, on the other hand, was having an almost riotous success, keeping the ladies on either side of him laughing till their eye-black ran. He was being Michael Harrigan at his most entertaining, and, watching him, Flynn and Bridie drew together in the old instinctive alliance, with the old upsurge of slightly puritanical disapproval. Mike was full of bawdy limericks and verse and racy stories, full of wittily malicious gossip, and enjoying himself enormously. In the odd moments in which he had time to notice them he decided all over again that his children were damned young bores. The girl had looks and spirit, like her mother; might make something of her later. The boy had brains, but he was still sound asleep; needed a gal—'a nice gal, a decent gal, one of the rakish kind'. . . . A pity this wasn't Montparnasse instead of Dublin. In Dublin's fair city the girls were so pretty—but damned strait-laced. Look at that perennial virgin, Katherine O'Donal. . . . Well, look at her. Attractive enough in her red dress, and coquetting like mad with the men on either side of her, and it didn't mean a thing. He had written somewhere that the curse —one of the several curses—of this country was that the females were either virgins or married women, and the widows wedded to the Church. . . .

With the coffee the air became hot and smoky, and, the champagne having done its work, the talk was in full spate. Flynn thought of the quietness and coolness of Stephen's Green across the road, and of March moonlight silvering the river and the shabby old houses along the quays, and suddenly leaned over to Bridie and whispered urgently, "I can't stand much more of this, can you?"

She tossed her hair back from her face. "It's so hot," she complained.

"Let's go. Pretend you're going out to the 'Ladies', then get your wrap and I'll join you in the lounge in a few minutes. Nobody will miss us— they're all far too busy with themselves, and are half tight, anyhow." He added, viciously, because of his ache for her, "Even Cousin Kate!"

From that moment everything was perfect for Bridie. The smile she turned on her brother was radiant. She swept out proudly, with a wave of invisible plumes about her red-gold head.

A little later they were seated together in a fusty-smelling horse-cab and clattering away down Grafton Street, Flynn curiously 'caged' in his boiled shirt and new dinner-jacket, Bridie strangely grown-up in the long white dress, and a white fur cape which made her feel like a princess, and which was a present from her father.

As they came down to College Green a cold wind blew up from the river; they lifted their flushed faces to it, gratefully, drinking in the clean air. They held hands and laughed over their 'escape', and were happy for the first time that night.

Afterwards, what they chiefly remembered about Bridie's sixteenth birthday party was how they had leaned on the parapet of the O'Connell bridge at midnight and looked at the moonlight on the Liffey and thought and talked of Ballyrannon.

IX

1932 was altogether a year of triumph for Michael Harrigan, for in the summer he sold the film rights of an early novel and received through his agents a thousand pounds on account. It seemed to him such a fabulous sum that he delcared his intention of photographing the cheque and having the photograph framed. Fifty pounds was a comprehensible sum; and a hundred pounds, though a large sum, was still realisable; but a thousand pounds was as astronomical figure; you couldn't even *begin* to drink such a sum. . . You could be roaring drunk for a week—which he was—and make no impression on it.

For a few weeks he talked a good deal about going to Hollywood to work on the script of the film and walk in Danae showers of dollars. After all, as he airily declared in every bar in Ballyrannon, every author of any repute at all went to Hollywood, eventually. There was not yet born, he declared, the author whose soul could not be bought if a sufficient number of dollars were forthcoming. He could not think why he had not put his own up for auction long ago. As a result of all this the story went round that Mr. Michael Harrigan had been offered a fortune to go to Hollywood and become a film star, and everyone to whom he owed a few shillings or a few pounds sent in their bills.

When the first excitement had worn off Mike decided that perhaps the money would last longer and be better spent in Paris and Antibes—it would be time enough to think of Hollywood when he was broke again.

That year Flynn and Bridie were taken to both the Galway and the Limerick Junction races, and on to the Dublin Horse Show, by their father. Mike planned to go to Paris via London, from Dublin. After the Horse Show there was nothing to stop in Dublin for. He was in high spirits and in luck; at the races he plunged wildly—and backed winner after winner. It was as though he could not lose. 'The Midas touch at last, by God!' he thought. He had seen that sort of thing happen on the tables at Cannes and Monte Carlo, fantastic runs of luck that almost led one to believe in a fool-proof system, a cheating of chance, or a superstitious faith in a spell of personal infallibility. At the tables it usually ended in the spell breaking just at that point at which everything was staked, so that the entire winnings were lost on the one throw too many. He had never had any luck at the tables, but all his life plenty with horses—though he would insist that it was not luck which put the money into your pocket at race-meetings instead of into the bookies', but knowing your subject, which meant knowing more than horses, but jockeys and trainers, and the games they were up to. . . .

Whatever it was, luck or knowledge, the Harrigans swept across Ireland that summer flushed with triumph, travelling first-class, staying at the Shelbourne, taking taxis everywhere, eating in expensive restaurants. Mike insisted that Bridie must have some clothes. But Bridie said, boldly, that if he wanted to spend any of his money on her she would sooner have the pony she was cheated out of on her birthday. Mike laughed, indulgently. Cheated, was it? But didn't she have the grandest party in the town? "You did," Bridie told him. "Flynn and I were non-starters, scratched on the day!" Ah, to hell with all that, Mike said, but she should have a pony. They would find one at the Show, and no one should say he was not the world's most indulgent parent.

Bridie gave him a bright ironical look and murmured that some people had the *queerest* notions of themselves. . . .

There were plenty of good hacks and hunters up for auction in the show-yard that would have suited Bridie; she pored eagerly over the catalogue and marked several and was all excitement, but as it turned out she did not even stay to see them brought in, because she saw the look on Flynn's face when a light chestnut Arab filly was led into the yard.

He gripped Bridie's arm. "Heavens!" he whispered. "Will ye look at that now! Look at that head!"

Mike said, indifferently, "Pretty enough, but too light for hunting. What Bridie needs is a good sturdy cob." He smiled down at her and pinched her cheek. "Isn't that so, little one?"

But she was not listening to what he said. Her heart was beating very fast from the battle going on inside her. Flynn wanted that horse more than he had ever wanted anything; she knew that quite certainly. And with the same deep certainty she knew that she could induce their father to get it for him if she abandoned the idea of a horse for herself.

A runner trotted the filly up and down, and Flynn, watching every movement, said softly, "Look at that action, now! Did ye ever see the like of it?"

His cheeks were a little flushed, and his eyes were shining. He had lost awareness of his father and sister and the people pressing about him; he stood, his whole spirit aflame, in a world which held only himself and the strong delicate grace of the little mare.

Bridie felt sick with excitement as the battle in her neared its peak. She had this supreme opportunity to do something for her beloved, darling Flynn. It was her chance to atone for all her sins. Expiation through renunciation, as the nuns taught. The one thing Flynn had always wanted, and it was in her power to make it possible. Cousin Kate, whom he thought so wonderful, could not do this for him. The most she could do for him was to cross Ireland for him to spend a few hours with him on his birthday; but she had only done it once, and if it had seemed a big thing at the time it was not really so very much. She could not through any sacrifice of hers make possible for him the thing he wanted most in all the world—secure for him this world's wonder of a horse. And this was for Bridie, somehow, even more important than absolution for her sins.

She touched her father's arm.

"It's the horse for Flynn," she said quickly, her heart seeming to pound in her throat. "If she didn't fetch too high a price, that is. I don't need a pony all to myself—if we had the mare we could share her." But she knew that if they had the mare she would be Flynn's.

"She'll fetch at least five hundred guineas," Mike said, but excitement was beginning to stir in him too. The more he looked at the filly the more he liked the idea of her in the Harrigan stables that had been so empty for so long. It would be almost like bringing home a bride! A somewhat exotic bride, more suited to drinking the desert wind than the wet west wind of Connemara; about as unsuitable, for all practical purposes, in fact, as the bride he had once brought home. He took a perverse pleasure in the thought. If you were a Harrigan you could be relied upon to do the different, the un-suitable, the magnificently unpractical thing. A thoroughbred Irish horse, a good hunter, was the obvious sensible thing, but the sensible thing was the negation of poetry and adventure; and the sun shone, and Mike Harrigan had had enough double whiskies to make him feel pleasantly reckless and in the mood for the poetic, the imaginative, gesture. The filly could be a twenty-first birthday present from Mike Harrigan to the son he thought a bore. True, Flynn wasn't twenty-one till the summer after next, but in two years' time he mightn't have the money for anything so spectacular. Supposing it did cost him five hundred guineas? That was half his film money; well, what of it? Money was made to be spent, and, by God, they should see once again that when he had any money Mike Harrigan knew how to spend it! They'd be coming from fifty miles and more around the countryside to see a flashy filly like that. A pity Kitty wasn't still about to ride her.

He had no thought of Flynn as he began bidding, and that Bridie had made any sacrifice he was quite unaware. To bid for an expensive, unusual little filly like that was a gesture after his own heart. Who rode her, whether Flynn or Bridie, once she had been acquired for the Harrigan stables, hardly mattered.

The bidding rose quickly to three hundred pounds, then hung fire a little. Bridie clung to Flynn's arm. She felt suffocated from the heavy beating of her heart. The most important thing in life now was that their father should not be outbid. If he was she thought she would die. The whole thing was an agony to her.

Comments buzzed all round her, distractingly, every favourable remark a menace,

"Plenty of bone, that little mare!"

"A fine shoulder."

"Beautiful action."

"Nice little head."

It was a relief to hear someone say, "That sort of thing's all right in a circus or for showing, but she's too light for hunting, and for a good hack give me an Irish blood-horse every time! Ye can't bate it!"

There was an acutely anxious moment when someone stepped forward and looked at the filly's mouth, then bent down and felt her legs. The crowd stood watching, smiling, commenting. The auctioneer grew restive at the lull. He caught the eye of the runner.

"Run her up again, Paddy," he commanded, then turned to the crowd. "Come on, ladies and gentlemen, now! Ye'll not be getting the chance of a little mare like this every day! Surely someone will bid me three hundred guineas?"

He looked round almost beseechingly, blue eyes searching from a brick-red face, bowler hat pushed to the back of his head. He pulled a red and yellow silk handkerchief out of his breast pocket and mopped his face and neck, then suddenly focussed his attention on a point at the back of the crowd, and exclaimed, "Ah, thank you, sir—gentleman over there bidding three hundred guineas."

Someone behind Bridie muttered sardonically, "He knows he's safe—there's probably a reserve of at least five hundred guineas on that filly!"

"Three hundred and fifty guineas," someone said, and Mike followed with four hundred pounds; then there was another pause. Flynn hardly realised what was happening. His father, he thought, was bidding for devilment, to show off, knowing quite well that eventually he must be outbid and drop off. They had come to the auction to find a horse for Bridie; a strong serviceable hunter was what would go back to Ballyrannon with them, not any living poem of an Arab mare. But in the meantime he could feast his eyes, and his imagination, on her.

The bidding ceased at four hundred and fifty guineas, in spite of the auctioneer's efforts to bring it up to a round five hundred, and Mr. Michael Harrigan was the owner of Jameel, by Sununu out of Emiri.

Mike laughed, excitedly. "Well, Flynn, she's yours—you'd better say how-do to her!"

Flynn stepped forward, wonderingly, and took the bridle in a dream. He was completely bewildered. It none of it made any sense. These things didn't happen. Bridie was clinging to him, laughing, the tears streaming down her face.

"She's yours, Flynn darlin'!" she was crying, excitedly. "Yours!"

"Your twenty-first birthday present well in advance," his father said, carelessly, and then they were walking out of the yard and the runner was saying that Jameel meant beautiful, and that she was sired by 'the swallow' out of the 'princess', and insisting that you couldn't beat an Arab for hacking; that he'd had experience of them in the East, and anyone who'd had anything to do with an Arab wouldn't look at any other breed of horse. You got everything in an Arab—intelligence, hardiness, character, looks. . . .

It all flowed over Flynn meaninglessly. He felt dazed, as though he were walking in a trance. All that remained in his mind of the groom's chatter was the name, Jameel, which meant beautiful. . . .

Then he was sitting at a little table under trees, with his father and Bridie, and they were drinking champagne. People were talking and laughing all round; there were the gold necks of champagne bottles slanting in silver buckets, beds of scarlet flowers, very hot-looking in the bright sunshine, blazing up from striped lawns, the sheen on the coats of horses moving in sunlight, a floweriness of women's summer dresses, the red roof of the grandstand gabled across the deep clear blue of the sky.

His father and sister talked of nothing but the mare. They might breed from her presently. And show her next summer. In the hack class, anyhow, if not in the jumping. . . .

Flynn tried to realise that the horse they were talking about was his; that his father had spent half his thousand pounds windfall on buying it for him. It didn't make sense, for why should his father, who didn't even like him, do anything of the kind?

Then he remembered Bridie clinging to him, looking up at him, laughing and crying together, and she was looking at him now, with her face alight, and suddenly something in him shouted that, by God, it was true! There was a little Arab filly called Jameel, and she belonged to him, Flynn Harrigan. . . .

He looked at his father and asked him, "Why did you do it?"

"Do what? Buy the filly?"

"Yes."

Mike looked at his daughter. "Why did I do it, Bridie? You tell him!"

Bridie finished her glass of champagne, tossed back her hair, and laughed,

"Sure, you did it for the glory of the Harrigans!" she said, and hiccupped loudly.

Mike refilled their glasses, chuckling delightedly. "I knew there must be some good reason," he observed. "But I didn't know it was as good a one as that!"

Flynn recognised the old mockery in his father's voice. He wanted to thank him for what was for him a quite incredibly wonderful gift, but the mockery was a barrier he could not pass. It came to him, suddenly, that this magnificently generous gesture was in fact not generosity at all; Mike Harrigan had merely gratified his own vanity. There was no bitterness in the thought; it afforded him a curious satisfaction, since it at least spared him the necessity for gratitude.

2

The acquisition of the mare took the edge off his disappointment over his cousin. The girl who had obeyed an impulse and crossed Ireland just to spend a few hours with him on his sixteenth birthday seemed to have gone for good, swallowed up in Katherine O'Donal. This Katherine O'Donal was a smart, striking-looking young woman who came to lunch, and once to supper at the Shelbourne, and was nothing whatever to do with him. He sat by her side but felt that he never got anywhere near her. She remained as impersonal for him as the actress who had sat next to him at Bridie's birthday party. She asked him about the Show, about the morning auctions, the afternoon jumping; she talked about the play she was in, and not once did she mention Ballyrannon. When, excitedly, Bridie told her about the mare he thought he caught for a moment a flash of Cousin Kate. But it was a flash only.

"How old is she?" she demanded.

"Rising three. Broken in, but still very green."

Mike put in, "All the same, she's a surprisingly nice-mannered creature for one so young."

Bridie said critically, "She's all right once you're up, but she doesn't stand yet—she wants a lot of schooling. 'Specially if Flynn's going to show her."

"She'll be small, of course," Katherine said.

"Fifteen hands," Flynn told her, and Bridie added, eagerly, "But she rides bigger."

"What's her name?"

"Jameel." Flynn spoke the name like poetry.

Katherine repeated it after him. "It's a curious name," she said.

"It means beautiful," Bridie said, proudly, and Flynn smiled.

For a moment Katherine's eyes were soft as they rested on him.

"Is she very beautiful?" she asked, softly.

He assured her, "I've never seen anything so beautiful!" He wanted to add, "Except you, the night you came out to Ballyrannon and waited under the ilex trees!" But his father was there, and Bridie, and Aunt Chris.

Bridie said, with a touch of grinning malice, "She's the colour of weak tea and has a behind like a hippopotamus, and Flynn is madly in love with her! Aren't you, Flynn darlin'?"

Flynn, meeting his cousin's vacant smile, knew that the flash was already extinguished. It was Katherine O'Donal, not Cousin Kate, who murmured vaguely, "I must see her—she sounds a wonder." Flynn knew that it was just one of the things people say, the way they said, 'You must come and see me sometime,' without suggesting any day, and it didn't mean a thing. Sophisticated conversation, he thought, was largely made up of insincerities.

He said, desperately, because it was their last day and he would not be seeing her tomorrow before they went off, their father to Kingstown, he and Bridie back to Galway, "Will you ever come to Ballyrannon again? It's three years now since you were there."

"How can I say? It depends what I'm playing in, and when, and where. In the theatre it's almost impossible to plan ahead."

"Between plays," he urged.

"Between plays one is rehearsing—or hopes to be."

"If ever you shouldn't be——" He smiled, but his heart was despairing.

"Yes," she said doubtfully. "Yes, of course——"

She was troubled; all over again she told herself it was simply no use being in love with Flynn Harrigan. At nineteen he seemed as remote, as shut up in dreams, as he had been at sixteen. Not once had he written her since she had been to Ballyrannon, and not once when they had met in Dublin had he shown any more than a kind of brotherly affection; if anything, she thought, he was more reserved than he had been at sixteen. He had had at least a quality of boyish impulsiveness then; the way he had come running to her down over the castle terraces and up the drive, like a hare with the hounds on its heels. Now he seemed completely withdrawn, and hardly looked at her, even. He was difficult to talk to, too, being so out of the world, knowing nothing of current books and plays, and people who wrote and acted. And when he had a chance to meet interesting and amusing people, as on Bridie's birthday a few months ago, he walked out on them.

She told herself all this, but was troubled all the same. It was one thing to criticise Flynn, but quite another to root him out of your heart. It was with her feeling for Flynn much as it was with her feeling for Ballyrannon; you could tell yourself it was a deadly place, a dying place, the end of everything, just a heap of stones, a wilderness, like the rest of Connemara, and it was all true, but it didn't stop you remembering—with an at times almost intolerable nostalgia—the cry of curlews over the lake, the flash of kingfishers' wings, electric blue, above the sedges, the clouds going over the dark blue mountains, and the strong sweet smell of burning turf. Your mind was one thing, it seemed, and your heart quite another. There were plenty of young men in Dublin ready to make love to her at the slightest encouragement, young men who had thought her 'ravishing' that night at the Shelbourne—when Flynn Harrigan had been so indifferent, so bored, even, that he had walked out of the place with his sister. What was the use of eating your heart out over a young man like that?

Besides, she had something better to do; she had her career to think of. She had, she told herself, a little defiantly, a little proudly, her art. Her defiance was directed at Mike. Spelling art with a capital A, he would call it, she knew. He was always jibing at what he called self-consciousness in art. "Well, Katie, how's Miss O'Donal the artist?" he would mock her.

"What is it this time, *The Shadow of a Gunman*, or *Deirdre of the Sorrows*? Revolutionary realism or Celtic Twilight ?"

All the same, he was himself a considerable artist—though he would all but hit you over the head for saying it. Art, he would insist, is simply a job of work well done. Inspiration be damned. You gave out what was in you. The Gaelic revival was a bore, coupled with the name of Willie Yeats. Ireland herself was a bore, throwing rotten eggs at the Abbey stage when the *Playboy* was first done, unable to laugh at herself, unable to stand a breath of criticism, and driving her authors to England to get published, and banning them at home.

All the same, who had got drunker than Mike Harrigan when Fianna Fail entered the Dail, and when Dev came into his own ? Who was it who hung out the green and white and gold when Casement was executed, and made an annual pilgrimage to the grave of Wolfe Tone ? Strange, she would think, that Mike Harrigan should be Flynn's father, the one so vehement and worldly, the other so lost and shut up in dreams, so much off the earth. Now it seemed as though Flynn would love this Arab mare more than he was ever likely to love any woman. With which thought Katherine turned back to the theatre, because that was something she understood, and the problems with which it presented her at least of the kind she knew how to handle. Perhaps it was true, as one critic had so unkindly said, that she could never hope to find a place in the gallery of great Irish actresses—Maureen Delaney, Maire O'Neill, Sara Allgood, Christabel O'Donal—but that she had some-thing to contribute to art through the Irish theatre she was convinced. She had a great deal to learn, she acknowledged that, but she was prepared to learn.

"You need experience, darling," her mother was always telling her. "If you'd stop mooning, now, after Cousin Flynn, and get yourself a real young man—know what it was to be in love and madly happy and madly un-happy ! I never did anything worth calling acting till I married your father, and it wasn't till he was dead, God rest him, that I could play the mother in *Riders to the Sea*. I didn't know till then what it was to suffer bereavement —I hadn't been close to death. That wonderful line—'There isn't anything more the sea can do to me now'—you have to know what it is to have suffered to be able to give real feeling to it."

Katherine had answered, a little sulkily, "I can't just go out and get experience like buying a hat !"

"You could at least make yourself vulnerable to it !" her mother had flashed back.

That was all very well for brilliant, spectacular people like Christabel O'Donal, Katherine had thought, resentfully, but she was her father's daughter rather than her mother's. She resembled him both in appearance, in her darkness, and in spirit, in her essential seriousness. He had been a musician, and a very good one ; he had been full of warmth and brightness and humour, but he had none of that volatileness which characterised Chris, and which she seemed to regard as essential to the artist. He had died from an appendix operation when Katherine was six years old, and she had only dim memories of him, but enough to keep alive in her the feeling of belonging more to him than to her mother.

Uncle Mike and her mother were very much alike, she thought, physically and in all ways. They were essentially the same kind of people ; they were Harrigans, and Bridie was, too, full of wildness and a curious kind of heartlessness underlying gaiety and generosity. Their attitude to life was that of mockery—Bridie was still too young for it to be manifested in her, but it was there, she was convinced of it ; the way she had of looking at you under her gipsy hair, as though she both despised you and was amused by you. They had charm, when they liked, those Harrigans, but they could be ruthless. But not Flynn. Flynn was the reaction against all that. Flynn was a poet, even if he never published, or even wrote, a line of poetry. The thought of him made her emotional ; if a producer could have found for her a play in which she could portray a frustrated romantic love she might have been found to be a great actress. She should have played in *The Cherry Orchard* or the *Three Sisters*. But nobody had yet discovered that.

There was something lacking in her, Mike would think, watching her on the stage in the minor parts that were all that were allotted to her even after four years. It was not lack of vitality, or even of feeling. It was as though she offered sincerity, but could bring no personal knowledge to illumine her sympathy. It ran round Dublin for a while that Michael Harrigan referred to his niece as 'the virgin of the Gate'.

On the whole he considered her a tiresome young woman ; but then the young, in general, were tiresome, with their intensity, their bright-eyed, deadly earnestness, their ghastly idealism, their boring aspirations, their inability to be serious without being solemn—Flynn with his Gaelic Revivalism, Katherine with her romantic realism, that pendulum of exclusive Irishness swinging monotonously between *Deirdre of the Sorrows* and *The Plough and the Stars*.

He had more hope of Bridie. He was beginning to be amused by her, her regular attendance at Mass, and her incorrigible wildness in between. She was growing into a beauty, too, he thought, with a good deal of Kitty about her, and to see her ride was pure joy, a demonstration of poetry in motion. It was a gift she had inherited from her mother, beyond all doubt. It was she who should have had the mare, not Flynn, who rode well enough, to be sure, but who never looked as though he were anything but a man on a horse, whereas Bridie—like her mother—in the saddle became one with the horse, all flowing harmony and rhythm.

By giving Flynn the mare he had cleared his conscience regarding him. Now he need do no more for him, surely to God. He had given him the one thing he had always wanted, and he had set him up in what seemed to him the extraordinary business of turning Ballyrannon Castle into a smallholding. All past neglect was atoned for. Even Chris conceded that he had done handsomely by Flynn—at last. Now he could go to Paris and stay indefinitely with a clear conscience. About Bridie he did not worry. She would almost certainly marry eventually.

X

THE story ran round Ballyrannon that Michael Harrigan had bought a 'racehorse' for his son at the Dublin Show, and for a week, in the evenings, people walked in the three miles from the town and up the castle drive, nearly another mile, and across the weed-grown courtyard to the stables to see this world's wonder of a horse. Tante Emma would come out to fetch in some washing and find small groups of people gathered round the loose-box, oblivious of the shirts and bloomers and nightgowns flapping round their ears, for all the world, as she declared, indignantly, as though they had never set eyes on a horse before, and they trespassing on private property, as brazen as a cartload of monkeys.

Flynn had numerous offers of service from would-be grooms, and a 'special offer' from Charlie O'Brien, the horse-coper, to buy the filly for two hundred guineas. There was a great deal of speculation as to what Mike had paid for her.

After a week the excitement died down and Flynn could feel that Jameel belonged exclusively to him and not to all Ballyrannon. Grooming and exercising and schooling her he was happy in a way he had never known before. He gave her all his spare time, and more than he could spare, and his patience with her was inexhaustible. He loved her intensely, and she looked at him with soft liquid eyes and he thought that she began to understand and to love him. Bridie pestered him continually about showing her next summer at Galway, urging him to find out about hacking-classes and entrance fees. When he told her, repeatedly, that there was 'time enough' on all that, she sulked, and had fits of being as jealous of Jameel as of Cousin Kate. It was one thing to do an act of expiation and make a dream come true for Flynn, and another to discover that in practice her grand sacrifice instead of bringing Flynn closer to her shut her out from him. For two hours every day he was out on Jameel; when he was not riding her he seemed to Bridie to be every minute in the stables with her, grooming her, till her golden coat shone like satin. "It brings her muscles up," he said, but Bridie grumbled, "What's the use of all that if you're not going to show her? What good is she at all, except to eat her head off and cast her shoes and cost money?"

To which Flynn replied angrily that the upkeep of Jameel was his affair. It was his labour, after all, which kept the place going nowadays—the few rents that still came in were negligible. If he was prepared to sweat his guts out for Jameel if need be—and he was—it was his business, entirely.

His first ride on her was a revelation. He had not known that a horse could be like that, responsive to the lightest pressure, having hitherto only had experience of farm-horses and ponies out of turf-carts, hard-mouthed, mishandled by too many people. With Jameel he felt that the reins were a living part of her sensitive mouth, and his joy and pride in her had a quality of tenderness. It gave him almost as much pleasure to see Bridie ride her as to ride her himself, because then he could watch her beautiful sweeping action, the proud, gay lift of her head and tail, her small, hard, polished feet 'daisy-clipping' over the 'mountain', soft and springy and dry with summer. His heart would swell, then, with love and pride. He always visited her last thing at night, and in time she came to wait for him, and he would hear her high excited whinny as he crossed the yard, Jameel, the beautiful one. . . .

2

In her jealousy of Jameel Bridie condescended a little to Patrick that summer. For a long time, it seemed to him, she had been lost to him, and he never passed Farrell-the-weaver's cherry-tree in June without recalling the child who had jumped from it into his arms, and whom he had held for a moment against his plunging heart.

Since then she had become rather 'grand', with her Dublin parties. He heard from Flynn how beautiful she looked in the white evening dress, with the white fur cape, and silver shoes on her feet, but he could not imagine her like that; the wild girl throwing catherine-wheels at the local dance, with a display of red flannel knickers, was much more real to him; Bridie with her hair in her eyes and the devil in her heart. His heart would quicken with the sight of her rowing up the Sound in Flynn's boat, her hair lifted on the wind, and he would have a sense of his blood running to meet her.

When she came into the rocky creek, the boat's keel scraping on the beach, shipping her oars, he would wade into the water, steadying the boat for her to climb out, and there would be for a moment her hand on his; then he would pull the boat up and they would stand together laved by the deep silence of the island, and if she frowned a little—because she despised herself for coming, which he knew—it did not matter, since nothing mattered except that she was there.

For weeks and sometimes months at a time she did not come, and though he was frequently over on the mainland he was a long way from Ballyrannon Castle, and they did not meet. Occasionally he would see her in the town; sometimes she would merely wave to him as she passed on her bicycle, and he would know a contraction of the heart; sometimes she would encounter him in the market-place as she handled fish or looked thoughtfully at the clothing displayed on the motor-van from Galway, or he would run into her coming out of a shop, and he would have a chance to speak to her, but she seemed always anxious to get away from him as quickly as she could. On the whole he preferred not to have these chance encounters in the town; they unsettled him, destroyed the fantasies he wove about her. It was better to wait without seeing her till she came to the island again, deliberately seeking him, if a little sullenly.

It was generally accepted in Bream Island, if nowhere else, that Patrick Doyle was courting Bridie Harrigan, and there was a certain amount of heartburning amongst the island girls, for why should he be overlooking them, who were to hand, and willing, for. That One who was so high and mighty she only came out to see him once in a blue moon, and he too proud to be going after her? Besides though the Harrigans were poor enough, they were landed gentry, and what were they to do with island folk living on dried fish and potatoes? Did Patrick really think she would ever marry him and come to live that kind of life? Or did he deceive himself with grand notions that marrying her he would move into the castle? But the Doyles themselves were proud that their Patrick was courting the young lady from the castle, and that she came to see them at all did them great honour. They gave her a warm welcome when she came, and she herself felt happy and at home amongst them. For Patrick, next to watching her rowing up the Sound there was no finer sight than to see her seated on a little stool beside the turf fire in his own home, and his family gathered about her, his mother on one side of her, his sister Maureen on the other, his two brothers, Stephen and Michael, leaning at the door, full of shy admiration, and the two young children, Seamus and Sheila, crowding at her knees, and his father coming in, a gaunt, weather-beaten man with curiously fierce blue eyes blazing out of a mapped brown face, and presenting her with the biggest lobster of the week's yield, and assuring her that she was welcome as the flowers in May. If it was a cold wet day he would bring out a bottle of poteen from a hiding-place in the chimney-corner and pour a little into a cracked cup for Bridie, the rest of them taking swigs from the bottle itself, and when it flowed warmly in their veins they would fall to telling stories. First Bridie would tell of Dublin gaieties and adventures—mostly fictitious, or so slightly founded on fact as to be virtually fictitious—and going on to older and wilder stories, of Devorgilla riding away with her lover, the King of Leinster, whilst her husband, the King of the West, was away making penance at Lough Derg; of Queen Maev, she of the big bladder, who marched across Ireland to take up the challenge that her fine white Connacht bull was second to the brown Ulster bull of Cooley; of Grania O'Malley, the great Granuaile, who slept in a castle by the sea with a boat's hawser tied to the end of her bed, the way it would be tugging on a windy night fit to drag the bed out into the sea; of the king's daughter from across the waves, who rode over the sea on a white horse to ask the Fianna, camped on the Western shores, for Ossian for a lover. Of how Ossian rode away with her and forgot all else, and all was happiness until the waves washed up a branch that was from Ireland. Then the great longing came on Ossian to see his own country again. He begged to be allowed to go, promising but to set eyes on Ireland and return. Niav, his mistress, gave him her consent and lent him her fairy horse for the journey, but insisted that he must on no account set foot on the shore. Ossian promised and rode away and came to the shores of Ireland, but the Fianna had gone long ago, and the peasants working along the shore looked poor and mean. He was about to ride back over the sea when he saw four men struggling to lift a sack of sand. Ossian stooped from his saddle to help them, and bursting the saddle-girth fell to the ground, and immediately the stiffness and aches of age were upon him, he who had been the shining golden one, and he was an old man. . . . Always, it seemed to Bridie, the best stories were sad. But it was not such a sad story after all, said Maureen, who told the story, for his own people brought him to the blessed Saint Patrick, who made a Christian of him. But Niav, Bridie insisted, wasn't it very sad for her, looking out over the sea for the white horse that did not return with Ossian? Niav was a fairy, Maureen said, and fairies are faithless and do not suffer as humans do.

But when the sun shone they did not sit over the fire drinking poteen or telling stories; then Patrick would take Bridie across the stony treeless little island, sectioned by grey stone walls, and dotted with low white cabins, and the black lumps of peat stacks, to a sandy cove where the curaghs of the islanders lay upturned like black seals, and here they would sit, skimming pebbles out over the sea, telling of small things, Patrick of wakes and weddings in the island, of the letter they had had from his sister in America, Bridie of

Flynn and his latest activities, the letter they had had from their father, who had left Paris for the South, or the latest flying visit from Aunt Chris, who was still pestering them to 'smarten the place up' and take in paying-guests.

Patrick had already heard about the mare when Bridie visited Bream after that last triumphant Dublin visit, but he had not realised how much the filly meant to Flynn until he sensed Bridie's jealousy. He understood, then, that she had come to him because she was jealous, as shut off from her brother by his preoccupation with his horse as she had been as a child by his pre-occupation with Cousin Kate.

Patrick was emboldened to say that summer, as they lay on the sand between the curaghs, "Why don't the two of us be weddin' and makin' our own lives?" He smiled at her and added, even more daringly, "Aye, and raisin' up sons to the glory of Ireland?"

Bridie, lying face downwards in the sand, drove a shell deep into it and said, vehemently, "Because I've no wish to be marrying—you or anyone at all!"

Patrick said, "I shall ask you again in a year's time—unless you tell me you're after changin' your mind before then."

She drove another shell into the sand. "If Flynn were not my brother I would marry him. But since he is my brother I shall not marry any-one!"

She tossed her hair back from her face and looked at him, defiantly.

His smile faded. " 'Tis unnatural," he said, and frowned. He added, "One of these days Flynn will marry—then what will you do?"

"Drown myself in the lake, probably. Or else jump from the tower."

Patrick was angry then. " 'Tis no way to be talkin'! What would Flynn say if he heard such talk? Isn't it very selfish you are?"

"Perhaps. But that's how it is. I think I've always known it in my heart, ever since Flynn and Cousin Kate and I played together and I always felt left out; but I didn't realise it, somehow, till we got back this time."

Patrick said bitterly, "Then you could even be jealous of his horse!"

She got up and stood looking down at him, her blue eyes burning, and she said, no less bitterly, "Yes, even of his horse!"

She began walking away, back over the sand and up the low cliff with its tufts of coarse grass. He went after her, and when he came up with her took her hand.

"Ah, let's not quarrel," he said softly. " 'Tis only natural that with no mother and no father to speak of you should look for everything in your brother. But there's my love, too, Bridie, any time you'd be wantin' it."

She persisted, walking fast, "I could never leave Flynn."

"There'd be no need. I could come and live at Ballyrannon too, perhaps."

"I mean so long as he has no one else I couldn't have anyone either."

"But if ever he does get anyone else?"

"I don't want to think about it. I can't imagine it. It makes everything seem—dark. I fill up with black thoughts—black feelings——"

They went the rest of the way across the island, and down to where the boat was tied up, in silence. She scrambled in and he untied; before pushing the boat out he said, "You'll come again soon?"

To his surprise and delight she promised him, "A week from today. Wet or fine." She smiled, faintly.

He watched her rowing back down the Sound, and not till she was out of sight did he turn and climb up over the rocks to the headland. He felt within himself the risen heart, because of her promise. She was only sixteen. Much might happen in a year or two. . . .

The seed of what was to happen was already germinating, as it happened, in another conversation that afternoon between two people lying on another stretch of summer sand ; but in this case the sand was imported for the season for that particular fashionable strip of the Côte d'Azur. Above them was a striped sun-umbrella ; all around them half-naked bodies lay prone, female backs and male torsos frying, covered in oil, in the sun. It was a very crowded beach, full of wealthy Jews, English and American social celebrities, divorcees, gossip-writers, and the literary and artistic combings of Montparnasse, of whom Michael Harrigan was one. He was telling a good-looking American woman in a white bathing costume about Ireland and his castle in the West. He was assuring her that he was the uncrowned King of Ireland, and that any time she thought of going over she need only ask for him when she got off the boat at Kingstown ; and she was looking at him with wide-eyed wonder and exclaiming that Gee, she had always wanted to visit Ireland ; it must be so ro-*man*-tic ; all those bogs, and Mr. Yeats and everything, and she'd always wanted to live in a cass-ell. . . .

But that was where Mike Harrigan began to be bored. He had met a woman once before who had always wanted to live in a castle, though not with that accent. In Ireland, he told her, when people lived in castles it was usually because they couldn't afford to live anywhere else. At which she laughed and said wasn't that cute. . . .

Mike said hadn't they better be moving if they were going up to Sunflower Joe's for a drink before dinner.

When they sat at a blue-painted table under yet another striped sun-umbrella, sipping champagne cocktails and eating thin pointed French olives, he had a sudden vision of the great patches of damp coming through the walls of the castle in the wet weather, and the little growths of mould that appeared above the skirtings, and the rivulets of moisture running down the banisters. Thinking of it he could almost smell the apples laid out on the drawing-room floor, and feel upon his eyes the smart of the smoke blown back down the chinney when the wind was in the wrong direction, and had a sudden longing for the taste of rye whisky on his lips.

Ah, sure, Ireland was cute all right, he said, and knew a sadistic longing to set her down, in all her chic American sophistication, in the midst of it all.

XI

ON a rainy afternoon in September, when Flynn was up in his room in the tower, aimlessly turning the pages of books, and sifting through tattered manuscripts of poems, for the most part unfinished, and Bridie was sitting on the floor of the unfurnished drawing-room, her back against the lintel of an open French window, dangling a piece of string for the amusement f a kitten, and Tante Emma was asleep in the kitchen, and Jameel was looking sad-eyed out over the half-door of her loose-box . . . briskly invading all this indolent afternoon inactivity, a car turned in at the castle drive and followed the avenue round to the stretch of weed-grown gravel of the main entrance.

Bridie stopped playing with the kitten and stared in amazement. Flynn came to the window of the tower and leaned out. When their father was at home dilapidated cars of ancient make occasionally drove up to the castle with various hard-riding and hard-drinking friends from round about. But this was not that sort of car. It was bright and shining and very respectable-looking. It stopped immediately opposite where Bridie sat, and a red-faced man with a bristly little grey moustache thrust his head out and in a very English voice asked if this was Ballyrannon Castle. Bridie replied, laconically, "It is." Beyond the man she could see a homely-looking middle-aged woman with a dark felt hat and horn-rimmed spectacles.

The man switched off the engine and addressed Bridie again. "Is Mr. Michael Harrigan at home?" he demanded.

"He is not," said Bridie.

"Ah, a pity." The man fingered his moustache. "When do you expect him?"

"In about six months' time," Bridie said, carelessly, and continued dangling the string for the kitten. Now that they knew her father was not expected back for some time they would surely go away. . . .

The man laughed, and the woman at his side smiled and leaned forward.

"Are you his daughter, by any chance?" she inquired, in the tone of one anxious to propitiate the wild native.

"I am, for my sins," Bridie told her, without returning the smile.

The man and the woman exchanged amused glances. They were prepared to be amused by almost any utterance from an Irish person, so convinced were they of innate Irish wit.

"We were sent here by your aunt," the woman explained. "Your father's sister, you know—Miss Christabel O'Donal, the actress. We were introduced to her in the Green Room at the Abbey. We know someone in the cast, you know. It was a great thrill—meeting Miss O'Donal, I mean. We told her we were spending a motoring holiday in the Emerald Isle and going out to the West, and she told us to be sure to call here and ask if you would have us as paying-guests. We should simply love it, of course, and we should be no trouble. I mean we should of course make our own beds, and we can eat anything. There's just the three of us, Mr. Pocock and myself, and our daughter Frieda—about your own age——" She turned to the back seat. "Frieda—where are you, dear?"

Whilst her mother had been talking, a tall thin girl of about fourteen had climbed out at the back of the car and stood staring at Bridie. She was an unattractive child, with mousey hair done into two tight thin plaits which rested on her shoulders, and she had a freckled face and a wide mouth with projecting teeth. She stood with her feet well apart, sticks of legs terminating in large sandals, and her expression was truculent.

Not seeing her in the back of the car, Mrs. Pocock climbed out herself.

"Oh, there you are, dear! Don't get wet, will you, dear, it's raining quite hard. Run in under that tree, there——"

Frieda turned and ran in the opposite direction along the terrace, darting into some bamboo.

Mrs. Pocock looked about her, admiringly, blinking a little as the rain spattered her glasses.

"Isn't this the most romantic place?" she demanded, of no one in particular.

At this point Mr. Pocock also left the car and began gazing about him with a knowing air.

"Fine old place," he observed. "Twelfth century, I should say. Drat this rain! Worst of this country. Coming down heavier than ever now." He turned up his coat-collar. "Fine old tower. Neglected, of course. They never restore anything in this country."

Mrs. Pocock gazed respectfully at the tower, then she exclaimed, apologetically, with a nervous glance at Bridie, "But oh dear, we shouldn't be staring—there's someone up there!"

"So there is!" Mr. Pocock, eager to show friendliness in this wild territory, smiled up at the figure leaning out of the tower window.

"That's my brother," Bridie said, getting up. "We keep him shut up there because he's stark raving mad."

She stood at the top of the steps looking down into the three startled English faces.

"I wonder my aunt didn't tell you," she said. "It's why we live out here in this lonely place. Father won't have him put away."

Mrs. Pocock said, uneasily, "I suppose he's harmless?"

"He's very violent," Bridie said, gravely. "We have to have a keeper for him."

"Doesn't your aunt know about this?" Mr. Pocock demanded, indignantly.

"Sure. Why wouldn't she?"

"Sending us here! I mean to say——"

"Some people don't mind loonies," Bridie said, indifferently, thrusting out a foot in a dirty canvas shoe for the kitten to play with.

"The poor things can't help it, of course," Mrs. Pocock said, and looked apprehensively up at the tower again, but Flynn had withdrawn his head and was on his way down to see what was happening.

"Oh dear, he's not there now. You don't suppose he's got out, do you? Frieda—Frieda—where are you, dear? We're going. Come along at once!"

Mrs. Pocock began darting about like an agitated hen, running a little way towards the end of the terrace and the bamboo clumps, then back again to the car, looking fearfully at the castle. "Daddy, you call her!" she beseeched.

Mr. Pocock got back into the car and blew several loud blasts on the horn, then started up the engine. Mrs. Pocock stood by the bonnet, getting very wet.

"Better get into the car, Bessie," her husband advised.

"Oh dear," Mrs. Pocock whimpered, and called again, "Frieda—Frieda—will you come this minute——"

At that moment Flynn appeared at the French window. He looked extremely wild; his hair was on end, he had not shaved for three days, and he wore only a ragged shirt and a pair of very dirty old flannel trousers; his feet were bare.

Mrs. Pocock glanced up and saw him and gave a little shriek, then ran round to the car door and clambered in.

Flynn looked inquiringly at his sister.

"They've lost their little girl in the bamboo," Bridie said. "You'd better go and find her."

"Really!" said Flynn. "In this rain! What is their brat doing in our bamboo, anyway?"

"She probably wanted to go somewhere," Bridie suggested.

"Mother of God," Flynn cried, "with the whole of County Galway spread out before her why must the brat choose to go somewhere—in our bamboo and then get lost in it?"

He turned up his coat collar and came out on to the top of the steps, shrugged at the first impact of the rain, then came down the steps. Instantly Mrs. Pocock leapt out of the car and rushed towards him.

"It's all right, it's all right," she cried wildly. "You'll go back into the house. Shoo! Back indoors—understand?"

Flynn looked at her blankly. Mrs. Pocock faced him, as she was afterwards fond of recounting to her friends at English suburban tea-parties, with the courage of desperation. "Shoo!" she said again, and swung out her handbag on its long black handles towards him.

Mr. Pocock leaned out of the car window and called irritably to Bridie, "Can't you do something, Miss? Where's his attendant?"

"Are you both crazy?" Flynn demanded, and turned and strode back to the house. At that moment the child came scrambling up the terrace, very wet, and clutching a bedraggled bunch of leaves and berries which she had gathered in the garden below. Both parents called to her, angrily, to come on for goodness' sake, to hurry. When she came up to the car Mrs. Pocock darted forward and boxed her ears.

"Keeping us waiting about!" she exclaimed.

With a loud howl Frieda climbed into the back of the car, and when Mrs. Pocock had bounced into the front seat and slammed the door, Mr. Pocock started up the engine again and then swung the car round on the gravel so violently that to Bridie's great delight he nearly went over the edge of the terrace.

"What on earth——" said Flynn, leaning with Bridie against the French window and watching the car hurtling back down the avenue.

"They wanted to stay here," Bridie explained, "and their name is Pocock, if you ever heard such a thing!" She giggled.

Flynn smiled. "Why should they want to stay here, for goodness' sake?"

"Aunt Chris sent them from Dublin. She thought we'd like to have them as paying-guests. They thought it ever such a good idea, and the castle ever such a romantic place—'genuine twelfth century, you know'——" she mimicked the English accent. "Then they saw you looking out from the tower, and after that they couldn't get away fast enough!"

"God be praised for that, but what was so terrifying about me looking out from the tower?"

"I told them you were starko, God forgive me."

"Starko?"

"You know——" She indicated with her forefingers at her temples.

Flynn laughed. "Well I'm damned! That's why the old girl shooed me and the old boy wanted to know where my attendant was! Aren't you the bold one, Bridie?" He stood chuckling for a moment, then was suddenly serious. "But look here, you know, we can't have Aunt Chris doing this on us. I shall write and tell her. Your trick worked this time, but I can't always guarantee to be up in the tower when the brutes she sends us call!"

A week later they had a letter from Aunt Chris saying that she hoped they had liked and were getting on with 'the nice English family' she had sent them; she was sure they were very homely and nice, for all they were English, and Black Protestants at that, and that they would take everything as they found it and be no trouble at all, and it really was time they began to act on the suggestion she had been making for years that they should take paying-guests—particularly now that they had 'that absurd horse' to keep as well as themselves. . . .

The reference to Jameel infuriated Flynn, and he who never wrote letters if he could avoid doing so wrote a very violent one to Christabel O'Donal. In writing which sprawled all over the page in his anger he informed her that he was 'heartily sick' of her persistent attempts to interfere in his and Bridie's private lives. She could note once and for all that they had not the smallest intention of turning the castle into an hotel, but if they had ever contemplated anything of the kind they would not have dreamed of accepting horrors like the English family with the unpleasant name she had seen fit to sick on them. There was quite enough of that kind of vomit spewed over the West of Ireland during the holiday season, without her directing it to Ballyrannon. As to that absurd horse, as she knew nothing whatever about horses he was not prepared to discuss the matter with her; it was not her business, anyhow, and he would thank her to get on with her play-acting and leave people who were leading real lives alone, from this out. . . .

He felt much better when he had written that letter. He read it aloud to Bridie and Tante Emma. Bridie declared that it was all right as far as it went, but that it didn't go far enough; she wanted to add a postscript, 'If you want to talk about something really absurd, what about yourself in your last play?' But Flynn said that there was no need to descend to petty spite. Tante Emma had no criticisms to offer; she thought it a beautiful letter, with a fine spirit to it, the way her ladyship would not be after havin' to read it twice to get its manin' clear. . . .

When Christabel O'Donal read the letter her first reaction was one of surprise. She had had no idea that the quiet, 'dreamy' Flynn had such violence in him. He was his father's son after all. Then she was amused; it seemed such a great weight of violence pitched against so little. She handed the letter to Katherine.

"Your little cousin is growing up, it seems," she said.

Anger leapt up in Katherine as she read. How dared he write like that? She could not know that she was merely finding an excuse to be angry with Flynn because of her deep, secret grudges against him.

"How perfectly disgraceful!" she exclaimed. "I hope you'll send him a postcard telling him he wants his bottom smacked!"

Chris smiled. "Ah no, why bother about it at all? Though what is going to happen to those two, God knows!"

Katherine said nothing to her mother, but when she was alone she wrote to Flynn, beginning the letter coldly, '*My dear Flynn*'. She wrote, '*I have seen your abominable letter to my mother, who has always been so kind to you and Bridie, though you have neither of you ever shown the slightest sign of appreciating it. I can only hope that when your filthy temper has died down at least you will have the decency to apologise. Otherwise, if we ever meet again you must not expect it to be as friends. You talk of people leading real lives—do you really for a moment imagine that that is what you are doing out there in your wilderness of stones, cut off from everybody and everything? One of these days perhaps you will realise that when you wrote that letter—and perhaps for a long time after—you did not know one single thing of real life.*'

She signed this letter simply, '*K*'.

When she had written it anger ebbed from her. She felt a little afraid. Perhaps he would write her a violent letter back, and she felt she could not bear that. She had never had a letter from Flynn, for all her longing. That he had a drawer full of unfinished poems all bound up with the thought and memory and dream of her she could not know. The ebb-tide of anger left her stranded on a desolate shore, along which her spirit fled weeping. Flynn, her heart cried, Flynn darlin', you shouldn't have written like that, but I am young and inexperienced, too, and I know what it feels like to be told perpetually how to conduct one's life. I know so well how false and artificial and unreal life here in the city must seem to you beside your wild and lovely lake. Oh Flynn, I do know, and no one will ever know it better than I, that for you, the only living reality, ever, will be the dream within yourself. . . .

Nevertheless, she posted the letter she had written.

2

When Flynn realised that it was Cousin Kate's handwriting on the envelope he was momentarily filled with joy, and then frightened. Supposing she should have sided with her mother? The Cousin Kate he had once known, to whom he had shown the kingfishers on the lake in sunlight, with whom he had swum naked in moonlight, would be on his side; but Katherine O'Donal would quite certainly write only to reproach him for his angry letter. How could he know which of them had written?

"Open it! Open it!" Bridie cried, excitedly. "Let's see what she says!"

But Flynn thrust it into his pocket. "I don't suppose it's much," he muttered.

He carried the letter round with him all the afternoon. He took Jameel out; they made the circuit of the lake and came back. He unsaddled her and rubbed her down, watered and fed her, made up her bedding for the night; shut up his ducks and hens; milked his goats; came in for the rosary.

Then when he saw Bridie racing into Ballyrannon on her bicycle, because Tante Emma was of a mind to fry some fish for supper and had just realised that there was no fat for the purpose, he went up to his room in the tower.

C

He closed the door, sat down on the unmade bed, and pulled the letter out of his tweed riding-jacket and turned it over in his fingers. His heart was beating heavily. He finally tore the flap of the envelope along jaggedly, and took out the folded sheet of blue notepaper with Katherine's heavy, masculine writing marching across it in firm, even lines—so unlike his own wild sprawl.

From the opening words, 'My dear Flynn', he knew that it was Katherine who had written, and not Cousin Kate.

'You do not know one single thing of real life.'

He sat for a long time with those words repeating themselves in his brain, in endless accusation.

Presently he replaced the letter in its envelope, got up and thrust it into the drawer with his manuscripts. Then he stood leaning on the window-sill and watching the clouds, heavy with rain, moving over hills become darkly blue and very near.

Life was a matter of experience, but of what did experience consist? Being born at all, living itself, was an experience. He had lived intensely the summer evening he had run to meet Cousin Kate under the ilex trees, and drunk champagne and laughed and talked with her, and taken out a boat with her in the moonlight. There had been all that experience on the physical plane, but there had been also the intense spiritual experience of that moment in which he had seen the birthday supper-table as a kind of altar, and the meal itself as a kind of sacrament. That moment had been real, and no amount of worldliness on Katherine O'Donal's or anyone's else part could lessen its reality.

Experience was suffering, mental and physical; life as his father understood it, the impact of its variety and complexity; it was love and hate and struggle. But it was also the impact of spirit upon dream, and the resultant torment and ecstasy, delight and fear. It was the heart eternally remembering in winter the blossoming boughs of spring, and in spring the trembling of the hand upon the living bark. And this, everything within him insisted, was as much reality as getting drunk or sleeping with women or any other physical experience.

He did not reply to his cousin's letter, except in a poem he called 'The Blossoming Bough', which it could never have occurred to him to send her. The next day, when he was out exercising Jameel, Bridie, searching, found and read both the letter and the poem.

XII

FLYNN carried Katherine's letter like a bruise on his heart for months, through all the gales and storms of autumn, and the mild, wet, windy winter. Grooming Jameel, riding her, running up hen-houses, mixing pig-swill, turning the earth, what Katherine had written was at the back of all else; she had indicated the penance he must make, and he had not made it, and so there was no absolution. Now if they met it would not be as friends. He tried to imagine such a meeting, in which she turned coldly away from him, and he could not visualise it. He wanted to destroy the letter, but somehow could not bring himself to do so.

At Christmas he cut branches from some firs in the castle's belt of trees, for decorating the monastery chapel. He had begun going again to the monastery that winter, reviving his friendship with the gentle, scholarly Brother Francis. In contemplation of the lives of the blessed saints, and in discussion of the Gaelic songs and legends, as ancient as the stones of Connacht, in the difficult translation of ancient manuscripts, Flynn found that he could lose the ache within him for a little while. Deeply he envied Brother Francis his tranquillity, his ability to confine experience to the spiritual, adventure to the intellectual. Deeply he envied the ecstasies of the saints, who knew only the white, incense-smelling boughs of heavenly vision, and nothing of the heady perfumes of earthly blossomings. By December he believed that he was recovering from the wound on his heart, but, to his dismay, at the Christmas Mass the thought of Katherine kneeling in church at the same moment in Dublin came between him and his prayers, and pain and the sense of sin were fused together.

He was silent and moody during those months, and Bridie, full of her secret knowledge of the reason why, tried by her love and good behaviour, and the determination not to be jealous of Jameel, to compensate him for his disappointment over Katherine. Now, she could feel, Cousin Kate was out of the picture, and Flynn would not go on moping for ever. Once Christmas was past it was soon spring again, with the new shoots pushing up excitingly at the base of the fuchsias, and the deepening of the green on the 'mountain', and the rain, that all autumn and winter had seemed unceasing, broken now by spells of sunshine.

In the early spring Mike returned unexpectedly from Paris.

"For the next few weeks we are going to be very busy," he informed his son and daughter, "because in May we are going to entertain paying-guests. Two ladies . . ."

Flynn and Bridie stared at him aghast.

"We turned down an English family Aunt Chris sent out to us last September," Flynn told him.

"These ladies are American," Mike said, "and rich. At least, one of them is—the other is her companion."

"We can't entertain rich Americans," Flynn protested. "Americans like comfort—not merely hot water but central heating, and we can't even offer them running water and inside sanitation! Besides, where will they sleep?"

"I ordered some furniture on the way through Galway," Mike said, carelessly, "and we'll open up one of the big front bedrooms."

"The one with the ceiling down, or the one with the hole in the floor? Or the one with the wasps' nest in the chimney?" Flynn demanded, grimly.

Mike made a gesture of impatience. "Ah, will ye stop yer blathering? Is there anything wrong with mending a ceiling and burning out a wasps' nest?"

"Nothing at all," Flynn retorted. "It will make Harrigan history! But you'll have to count me out on the interior decorations—I've every minute of the day filled as it is. But who are these females, and how long are they proposing to stay, for goodness' sake?"

"Mrs. Stephanie Paul, and her companion, Miss Bryce—Miss Philippa Bryce. Mrs. Paul is probably about forty-five but manages to look thirty-five—thirty with her back to the light. The other one is about twenty-five,

I imagine, but she's one of those born spinsters who reach an uncertain age and then stop there."

"It sounds frightful," Bridie murmured. "What will they do with themselves all day, and do they know we've no bath except the tub in the kitchen?"

"I propose to fix up a bathroom," Mike said, grandly. "It's only a matter of pumping the water up a certain height into a cistern and connecting it by a pipe with the house."

"That's all," Flynn muttered.

"It won't be hot, even then," Bridie pointed out.

"Who wants a hot bath in the summer?" Mike demanded, impatiently.

"Americans, most probably," Bridie insisted, "Otherwise they might as well use the lake—it'll be lake water, anyhow.   I don't see the point of bringing the lake upstairs and pouring it into a tub! . . ."

"Americans like to do what they call 'take a bath' "—he pronounced it with the short 'a'—"and that means turning on taps.   Very well, then, there shall be taps."

"Americans also like plugs to pull, no doubt," said Bridie. "What do we do about that?"

"We accustom them to the back-to-nature habits of rural Ireland.   It's what Americans call the simple life; it's a great deal more complicated than what they're used to, but as they haven't got to endure it for ever they find it what they call 'kind of cute'."

"You seem to know an awful lot about Americans," said Bridie.

"I've known these two American ladies for nearly eight months," Mike replied, sedately. "I met them in the South and we travelled back to Paris together."

"I suppose Mrs. What's-'er-name's a fan?" Flynn said, caustically.

His father smiled.   "Dear boy, how bitter you are!   Mrs. Paul is what is called a voracious reader and has read everything your distinguished father has ever written.   What is more, she retains what she has read—a kind of literary camel, you know."

"Well, anyway, why do we have to have her?" Flynn asked, irritably.

"Because she is rich enough to make it worth our while—and because, money apart, the idea amuses me."

"It means, of course, that Bridie and Tante Emma will do all the work, all the extra cooking and cleaning, and you will rake in the cash and have all the fun!"

Mike regarded his son's flushed, angry face for a moment, then he said, "I see you are still a prig and a bore!" and turning his back on his children he slouched across the room to the cupboard in which he kept his drinks and poured himself out a whisky.

Flynn and Bridie exchanged glances, then went out, to discuss with Tante Emma in the kitchen as to how the invaders might be defeated, if possible, before even they had crossed the threshold.   It was no use doing the mad brother act again, they pointed out, as obviously it wouldn't 'wash' in this case; their father would be sure to have told all about them.   But what *could* they do?

"Ah, sure, don't be worryin'," Tante Emma said, "sure we'll make it so depressin' for them they won't be wantin' to stay."

Bridie turned various possibilities over in her mind, from rat poison in the food the first night, to frightening them away with ghost stories of haunted rooms. She laughed softly, wickedly.

"Daddy will never forgive us," she said.

"God will!" said Tante Emma, with conviction.

"Even if they only stay a week we shall hate every moment of it!" Flynn predicted, gloomily.

"Ah, not at all!" Tante Emma made a gesture of waving away any such idea. "We'll be after havin' the greatest sport," she promised them, then added, "Did I tell ye about the time when I was in New York City as a young girl, now?"

"You did, then, many times," Flynn said, firmly. "What we've got to discuss now is not your invasion of America, but the American invasion of Ballyrannon, God help us."

"He will, He will," Tante Emma assured them.

"It'll be an experience," Bridie said, thoughtfully, and added, "The O'Donals are always saying we're cut off from everyone and everything out here—now perhaps we shall be able to catch up. . . ."

Flynn's face clouded again. "Ah, leave them out of it!" he exclaimed, violently.

He was still suffering, then, Bridie thought—a little pityingly, but more triumphantly.

2

Mike borrowed Flynn's bicycle and made a succession of visits to Ballyrannon, from which he returned on each occasion with cans of paint and distemper swinging from his handlebars, and brushes and sandpaper and bags of plaster-of-Paris strapped on to the carrier. After one such expedition he returned with workmen—an old man called John O'Hara, the leading carpenter of Ballyrannon, and Farrell-the-weaver's eldest son, a weedy, sandy-haired youth with some pretensions to a knowledge of the decorating and building trade. Mike installed his workmen in the big room over the porch, imported bottles of stout and whisky, and the work was in progress . . . with himself as foreman.

For days a tremendous scraping and sawing went on. O'Hara's contribution was to make a fine large cupboard, with space for hanging one side, and shelves the other. The furniture which Mike had bought in Galway consisted merely of a couple of cheap oak beds, some cheap bedding, a second-hand and very threadbare dark red carpet, a shabby leather armchair, and a plain deal table which he proposed to paint dark red to match the carpet. He had also bought a dilapidated second-hand settee with which to 'furnish' the drawing-room.

It was said of O'Hara in Ballyrannon that he had a large family—there were ten children—a large heart and a large thirst, also that he would talk you black in the face and argue the hind-leg off a donkey. . . . For some reason he was considered a good carpenter, though every shelf he put up had a whiskered underside, and he had a rough-and-ready way with hammer and nails. He had never in his life made a door that fitted or a drawer that pulled out except with a series of jerks, but as he was always so loud in his own admiration of his handiwork he had succeeded in creating for himself this legend of his good workmanship.

He was, Flynn declared, a spoiler of good wood at exorbitant prices, but he never knocked-up a shelf but what, when the job was done, he would stand back and exclaim, admiringly, "Ah, it's a beautiful piece of furniture, so it is!" and proceed to reckon up the incredible number of hours he had taken in doing the job and charging accordingly. A great deal of the time charged for was occupied with talking. He liked to hold forth about the days when there was no means of getting to Galway except by the bog-road, and when poor folks had no windows to their houses, and tea was a luxury; and always the moral of it all was that folks were happier then than now, un-settled as they were by all the excitement—a train to Galway once a day, and a film once a fortnight, and everyone pampered with windows to their houses and shoes to their feet, and drinkin' tay and thinkin' nothing of it. . . .

Mike found the old man's chatter entertaining, and as to his workman-ship, well, nobody in their senses expected the same standard in the wilds of Connacht as in Paris or London or even Dublin. Young Farrell was as silent as O'Hara was garrulous; he only came vocally to life to point out to Mike holes in the walls he had omitted to fill in with plaster before distem-pering, and to insist that he was using the distemper too thick. In attempt-ing to replaster the ceiling he succeeded in scraping further holes into it, but eventually everything was filled up with plaster-of-Paris, which cracked as it dried, and was altogether a very doubtful-looking job. Mike distempered the walls a pale cream, and painted the woodwork red, and when all was done O'Hara proclaimed it 'a beautiful piece of work'. Farrell looked anxiously at his ceiling, from which loose pieces were already threatening to break away. The lady's bed, he said, had best not be going immediately under 'the bad part'. But Mike said it would have to, to cover up the huge patch of damp which no amount of distempering would obliterate in the wall. Americans, he said, were fussy about damp, for some reason. They would far rather be killed in their beds by falling plaster than come across a patch of damp no bigger than your hand. . . .

When the big room was finished a smaller room next door had to be repaired and decorated for Mrs. Paul's companion, but by the time this room was reached Mike had lost interest in all that part of the work and was doing Herculean things with a plumber-builder imported from Galway to 'fix up' a bathroom. The bath itself was second-hand and needed re-enamelling. It was deep and narrow, and discouragingly black where the paint had worn away. It had claw feet at each corner, and spinsterish-looking taps. When the water was finally connected and the taps turned on there were the most agonising noises in the pipes, but the lake came gushing green and cold out of the taps, and Ballyrannon Castle could be said to possess a bathroom. . . .
The day the water was pumped up into the bathroom O'Hara threw down his saw, and Farrell his brushes, and came running to witness the performance, and they were agreed that it was a fine sight, and that there wouldn't be anything the like of it in any house or habitation for miles around. . . .

O'Hara and Farrell contrived to make their part of the work last for some weeks after the bathroom was finished, and when Mike protested

O'Hara reproached him, "Ah, sure, your honour, but isn't there only the two of us working now?" And when Mike pointed out that the two of them were working on a room half the size, O'Hara replied, even more reproachfully, but wasn't there twice the amount of work in it, what with the wasps' nests in the chimney, and the rat-holes in the floor, the way there was hardly a board but wanted renewing, and it slow work with only the one pair of skilled hands. . . .

Tante Emma, inspecting the work when it was finally completed, stared at the red woodwork and demanded, "Will ye be *lavin*' it that colour?"

Bridie looked at the worn red carpet on the floor and the oak head to the bed, and the strips of white muslin which she herself had stitched floating at the windows—the broken panes neatly 'repaired' with slats of wood left over from the carpentering—and thought, the Shelbourne Hotel apart, of course, that it was the grandest room she had ever seen, even though the ceiling did look as though it were liable to fall smack on the bed at any moment . . . which, with a little connivance with Flynn, could no doubt be arranged to take place at an early opportunity when the bed was occupied.

XIII

MIKE was out fishing at the far side of the lake on the cloudy May afternoon on which Mrs. Paul and her companion arrived. He had not forgotten that they were due that day, but he had expected them on the evening train; instead of which they had spent the night in Galway and come out by car the next day. Mike had taken the boat, rod and line, a jam-jar full of daddy-long-legs, several bottles of Guinness, bread and cheese, and gone out for the day, 'dapping' for trout. If he caught any they would be excellent for supper; if he caught nothing he would nevertheless have had a pleasant day. You were not always in the mood to sit in a boat and contemplate water and wait for fish to rise; but when you were it was one of the great joys of life.

Flynn was also out, schooling Jameel; he had arranged a series of furze jumps of varying heights in one of the unlet fields and was taking her over them. Bridie was mooning about, restless as always when Flynn was away. She was hanging out of her bedroom window when the car containing the visitors turned in at the avenue. She watched it bumping over the ruts and pot-holes for a few moments, then something like panic seized her, and she rushed out of the room, along the long corridor, down the bare wide sweep of the stairs, along another corridor and into the smoky whitewashed vault of the kitchen where Tante Emma sat nodding beside a smouldering turf fire.

"Wake up!" Bridie cried, wildly, as she burst in. "Wake up! They've come!"

The old woman jerked into wakefulness.

"Glory be to God!" she exclaimed. "What is it, at all? And me dreamin' I was a girl again, and himself courtin' me!"

"It's the Americans!" Bridie cried, despairingly. "They're coming up the avenue this minute, the two of them! What shall we do? There's only you and me here!"

"Ah, will ye stop blatherin' now, and be answerin' the door to them and speakin' civilly, the way they can see ye've been dacently brought up! Let them be freshenin' themselves after the journey, in the fine new bathroom, and I'll be after bringin' the kettle to the boil and makin' a cup o' tay for the craythurs. Be off wid ye, now!"

Bridie, who had hoped wildly for a few moments that Tante Emma would at least agree to barricading the front door and holding the fort till Flynn returned, went sulkily out of the kitchen. She went slowly back along the corridor, across the hall, and out through the open front door and on to the pillared porch, with its broken steps down to the terrace.

The visitors had already paid off the cab and stood gazing about them, surrounded by suitcases covered by innumerable coloured labels of foreign hotels. They had their backs to the castle and did not hear Bridie, in her soggy, rubber-soled canvas shoes, until she came out through the porch and on to the top of the steps. Then they turned and saw a quite ferociously scowling young girl with untidy red-gold hair, bare brown legs, a grubby cotton frock, and hostile blue eyes. The older of the two women smiled.

Bridie stared back very hard because she had never seen anything in the least like Mrs. Paul. The other woman she saw as merely an ordinary, youngish, horn-rimmed, rather clumsy-looking person in rough tweeds. But Mrs. Paul was something from another world entirely. She was small and slim, and possessed of an elegance which Bridie had hitherto known only in racehorses. Mrs. Paul was a quite typical chic Paris-American, but Bridie could not know this; she only knew that she had never seen a suit which fitted as that black suit fitted that slim figure; hitherto she had always associated black with funerals, but there was nothing funereal about black as Mrs. Paul wore it, with what seemed to Bridie the whitest blouse in the world. She recognised at once that this American woman was very good-looking; not pretty, like the young actress who had sat next to Flynn at the Shelbourne dinner, or beautiful like Aunt Chris, with her flowers and feathers and sparkle; but something quite different; something very cool and clear-cut; something that was all one with the black suit and the immaculate blouse. . . .

Mrs. Paul smiled. She had very good even teeth.

"Hullo," she said. "You're Bridie, I guess. I'm Mrs. Paul, and this is my companion, Miss Bryce. Your father got my letter saying we were arriving today?"

"We were expecting you," Bridie said, and her heart beat very fast, because it seemed to her that she stood alone to resist the force of the invasion, and if the invasion were to be driven back it was necessary to act then and there. "We were expecting you," she said, "but truly I don't think you'd like it here!" She wrung her hands together distractedly, looking wildly about her, hoping Flynn would return to reinforce her.

Mrs. Paul went on smiling. She said soft y, in her sing-song American, "I don't know why you should say tha-at. I think we're going to like it here vurry, vurry much!"

"I think my father misled you," Bridie said, desperately. "We've no conveniences of any kind—no running water, no plugs to pull—we haven't even a drain——"

"But that's fine," Mrs. Paul said, "no drains, no bad smells, and after Paris that'll be swell!"

Bridie stood her ground firmly at the top of the steps. If only Flynn would come to relieve the beleaguered fortress!

"It's all a mistake," she insisted. "We don't take paying-guests. There's a hotel in Ballyrannon where you can stay—the Railway, it's called. They've got running water and everything. Mr. De Valera himself stayed there once. You'd like it there, for sure."

"Sure, we'll like it here," Mrs. Paul assured her, and at that point her companion came to life.

"Supposing we cut the cackle and take the baggage in, as there seems no one about to do it for us," she said, curtly, and swooped down on two large suitcases. "You take those two light ones," she commanded her employer, and to Bridie, "It would be more to the point if you gave a hand instead of keeping us standing here!"

She marched up the steps and pushing past Bridie dumped the suitcases in the porch. Then she looked about her. In a big bare room across the hall she saw bales of hay, and apples laid out on newspapers on the floor. In a smaller room—Tante Emma's—she saw an iron bedstead, sagging in the middle, covered with an old patchwork quilt, and under the bed an enamel chamber-pot. Tante Emma always left all doors open during the daytime. She said that it aired the rooms, without the trouble of opening windows.

"What sort of a dump is this, anyway?" Miss Bryce demanded.

"It's much worse upstairs!" Bridie assured her, eagerly. "Rats in the skirtings, bats flying in and out of the windows——"

Mrs. Paul, who had followed Miss Bryce into the hall, laughed.

"It sounds just simply full of local colour!" she said.

Then, to Bridie's great relief, there was the sound of horse's hooves.

"My brother!" she exclaimed, and rushed out on to the porch.

"Let's hope the brother's a little more civilised!" Miss Bryce observed, drily. "We might get him to give us a hand with the rest of the baggage, since there don't seem to be any servants."

Mrs. Paul agreed that that was 'an idea', and they went out together. They wandered along the terrace, Mrs. Paul exclaiming all over again about the view and that she had never seen anything like it, and coming out at the head of the drive found themselves with the stable-yard ahead. Flynn was standing beside his horse whilst Bridie poured out, excitedly, the story of the 'invasion'. She broke off, abruptly, as the two women approached. Mrs. Paul regarded Flynn with interest. The same high cheekbones, brilliantly blue eyes, and untidy reddish fair hair; tidied up, he might be quite an attractive boy. He had a vurry good figure in his riding clothes. . . .

She smiled, and asked in her soft drawl, "Are you Flynn? I am Mrs. Paul, and this is Miss Bryce. We wondered if you could spare a minute to give us a hand with our baggage——"

The smile and the voice broke down Flynn's defences immediately. "Sure!" He handed the reins to Bridie. "Throw a rug over her," he said, "she's a little warm."

"Your little sister did her best to persuade us we wouldn't like it here," Mrs. Paul told him, laughing, as they walked away together.

"You probably won't," Flynn said. "We live a barbarian kind of life here."

Curiously, he did not feel in the least hostile to Mrs. Paul. He had always pictured her as large and angular and loud, and she was none of these things; her voice was the softest he had ever heard. Because, like Bridie, he had never seen anyone in the least like Mrs. Paul, he was hardly aware of her companion; she was merely a rather frowsy female in a tweed suit. Mrs. Paul, he thought, was like a heron in her slender neatness.

He collected the rest of the baggage and carried it upstairs to their rooms for them.

"We had the rooms done over for you, specially," he said, in sudden pride, pushing open the door of the big room, which still smelt of paint and distemper.

Mrs. Paul went straight to the window and looked out.

"It's just the grandest view," she said.

Miss Bryce merely gazed disapprovingly at the threadbare carpet, the unevenly slapped-on distemper, the cardboard and wood slats where panes of glass should be. Was Paulo really going to sleep in this appalling servant's bedroom in her exquisite satin nightgowns from the Rue Faubourg St. Honoré? Would her Numero Cinque ever succeed in overcoming the smell of paint? Was she really expected to unpack pink feather mules and place them on that revolting carpet, hang a marabout négligé over that squalid chair?

"The best view is from the tower," Flynn told her, eagerly. "You can see the whole of the Twelve Pins. It's why I chose that room——"

She turned dark animated eyes to him, their lids blue-shadowed.

"I'd love to see it," she said, softly. "Are you coming, Philly?"

But Philippa answered dourly, bending over the lock of a suitcase, "I guess I've had enough scenery for one day, thanks!"

So Flynn took Mrs. Paul alone up the steep stairs to his room in the tower, and as he came into it was suddenly ashamed of the unmade bed and the grey-white sheets.

"I'm afraid it's rather untidy," he murmured. "It's too much for Tante Emma, the old woman who looks after us, to toil up here, and Bridie and I always seem to have so many things to do——"

Mrs. Paul smiled. "You've a lovely lot of books," she said, and began to examine them. But they meant nothing to her, being mostly in the Gaelic, and those that were not were devotional works and lives of the saints. She straightened herself and saw the crucifix above his bed, the pair of torn and dirty flannels hanging at the foot, the old and grimy canvas shoes lying under it, scattered as he had kicked them off. Above a rickety-looking chest of drawers a reproduction of a chalk drawing of Da Vinci's head of St. Anne looked down, infinitely tender, fastened to the blue-washed wall with drawing-pins. Flynn prized it greatly, both aesthetically and sentimentally. He had admired it in a Dublin shop-window, and Bridie had bought it for him for a birthday present, out of some pocket-money their father had given her to spend 'in the town'. Mrs. Paul alighted on it eagerly. She recognised Culture when she saw it.

"Ah, the Mona Lisa!" she cried, and turned rapturously to Flynn. "I always think it so lovely," she said.

"It's Saint Anne," Flynn told her.

But Mrs. Paul had not studied Culture for nothing. "It was probably the same model," she said, lightly. "They always painted their mistresses, of course. All those beautiful Madonnas were somebody's mistresses. Though I believe Da Vinci was homosexual, wasn't he?"

But Flynn had not the slightest idea what she was talking about, never having heard of homosexuality under that or any other name. He smiled, vaguely, and murmured that he did not know.

The poor boy was probably horribly shocked, Mrs. Paul thought, but it was very good for him. She would hope to educate him quite a lot whilst she was here. This frightful bondage to the Catholic Church . . . she must try and emancipate him from that.

Flynn was, however, not in the least shocked by the suggestion that the old masters painted their mistresses as Madonnas, because 'mistress' to him suggested something noble and romantic, such as Ossian and his fairy mistress, Niav. There would be nothing wrong in painting anyone so strange and beautiful as that as Our Lady. Whoever the original of St. Anne might have been she must have been good, or she could not have had so sweet and gentle an expression.

Mrs. Paul's attention was next arrested by *The Love Songs of Connacht*. She murmured the title aloud, then looked at him and smiled. "That should be in-er-esting," she said.

"It is," he said, but suddenly he did not want her to touch it, and he directed her attention to the view.

"When the hills look dark purple like that, and very near, it means there's rain about," he told her.

She stood leaning on the window-sill, and he stood behind her and thought how tiny she was, and was aware of her perfume, which was like nothing he had ever known.

She was intensely conscious of him standing behind her, so close in that small space that the rough tweed of his riding-jacket brushed her, and of the smell of stables on him. She wondered if he had a girl, and what a woman meant to him, if anything. He had the makings of a poet in him, Mike had told her, but he was 'asleep' still.

She turned and smiled up at him. "It's so peaceful here," she said, in her soft sing-song.

Was it? He hadn't thought of that. You weren't peaceful because a place was quiet and still, or unpeaceful because it was noisy like the Dublin streets. Peace, as Brother Francis had once told him, was within you, like the Kingdom of God. He could have put all this into a poem, but not into words for Mrs. Paul, so he said only, "Perhaps we had better go down—you'll be wanting to unpack, and some tea after your journey, and I must get back to the stables."

When they got down from the tower Flynn left Mrs. Paul at the door of her room and went on downstairs. Philippa came along the passage.

"There's a bathroom," she announced, "with the most goddam awful-looking old iron tub you ever set eyes on, and of course the water's stone cold and is full of livestock into the bargain."

Mrs. Paul smiled. "We'll go down to the kitchen and find out about the hot-water system," she said, soothingly, "They probably don't light the boiler till the evening."

She took off her hat and sitting down on the bed opened her handbag and brought out a gold cigarette-case and extracted a cigarette. Philippa was immediately at her side with a lighter.

"I'll go and find out about the boiler and bring tea up," she said. "You rest."

She pulled out the pillow and folded it over, and Mrs. Paul arranged herself against it but was unable to make herself comfortable.

"I'll bring the pillow from my room," Philippa said, and went out.

When she had finally settled Mrs. Paul against the two pillows she regarded her, sombrely.

"You'll never stick it here, Paulo."

"Darling, it's an *experience* ! Remember the cockroaches in the hotel at Moscow, and the private bathroom in which we couldn't bath because there was no water, and even if there had been water there was no stopper to the bath ! How horrified we were at the time, and how we laughed about it afterwards ! One just doesn't have to bring the same standards to bear in places like Russia and Ireland !"

Philippa sighed. "Of course, you're wunner-ful, Paulo !"

She had been thinking Stephanie Paul 'wunnerful' for eight years now, ever since they had met in a Greenwich Village café. Life had been very drab for Philippa Bryce until then, studying art and getting nowhere with it —because of her bad sight, of course, not from any lack of natural ability. It was just too bad that her bad sight interfered with her 'vocation' for art. At nineteen she was already a man-hater. That is to say she realised that she did not attract the opposite sex. She did not attract her own sex, either. Or children, or stray dogs. She had never attracted anyone until that wunnerful night when Mrs. Paul had come with a party of people in evening dress to see the 'artistic' life of Greenwich Village, and Philippa was one of the 'art students' on show, and with whom she got into conversation, just to show how 'democratic' and 'vie Bohême' it all was. Mrs. Paul, who had had a good many bootleg drinks before going out to Greenwich Village, had confided to Philippa, holding her hand, how lonely she was ; she had just divorced her husband, and there was no one—temporarily, but that was something Philippa was to discover later—in her life ; no one at all. Philippa was also onely ; she had never been anything else, even as a child, so they had got on fine, and Mrs. Paul had ended up by taking Philippa back to her apartment on Park Avenue, and they had had more 'bootleg hooch', and a good cry together over their loneliness, and then it had been too late for Philippa to go back to her own dreary apartment down-town ; she had stayed the night, and she had never looked back from that day. Mrs. Paul was wanting a 'secretary', it seemed. So they went to Europe together. London, Paris, Vienna, Antibes, Moscow, Salzburg—for the Music Festival—Florence—they had a villa up at Fiesole for a time—they went everywhere, and if only Mrs. Paul, her darling Paulo, had been content to settle down snugly in their cosy, beautiful friendship, it would all have been perfect. As it was, there was always 'some man' sharing Paulo's affections, and though she accepted it, Philippa never got used to it. In Paris and the South this time there had been the Irish novelist, Michael Harrigan, for whose works Paulo had a passion. Paulo swore that they were not lovers—'worse luck', but it was really almost as bad as if they were, because she could never get Paulo to herself; she was always going off to have cocktails with him, to lunch with him, to dine with him, and at Juan-les-Pins to lie about on the plage with him. And now they had to come and live for the whole summer—unless Paulo couldn't stand it that long—in this horrible ruin of a castle, where the water came ice-cold and full of newts out of the hot tap, and the beds were like boards . . . and there was a tall romantic-looking young man with blue eyes and a dreamy manner whom Paulo was pretty certain to fall for. . . .

Her darling Paulo, who was so wunnerful, so generous to everyone—even with her person, alas—and so *brave*. . . . But they'd never stayed anywhere, not even in Bolshevik Russia, quite as barbaric as this Irish castle. Goodness only knew what the *food* would be like. They would probably be expected to live on potatoes.

'Goodness knows what she would do without *me*!' Philippa thought, on her way down to the kitchen. It was the thought which always came to her, and comforted her, whenever she and Paulo found themselves in what she called 'grimy' situations—such as when they had inadvertently taken rooms in a *bordel* in Toulon, and when they had had bed-bugs in Leningrad, and a little trouble with the police over their visas in Majorca, owing to the riff-raff of dope-addicts, dipsomaniacs, homosexuals, crooks, with whom poor darling Paula managed to get herself mixed up. . . . They had only very narrowly averted being asked to leave the island, along with a bunch of other Americans and English, and Paulo had her, Philippa, to thank for the avoidance of that humiliation. But then no one could talk with Philippa Bryce for five minutes without realising that she was a thoroughly serious person. It was her grim boast, "There's no nonsense about me!"

Now here they were in the wilds of Connemara, the back of beyond, the so-called glamorous West, and they hadn't been inside the house ten minutes before Paulo had somehow inveigled herself up into the boy's bedroom on the pretext of admiring the view. Paulo had looked at so many views, all over Europe. And here there was nothing *but* scenery. . . .

Philippa sighed upon the reflection; then, in her serious, sensible manner, braced herself for a long, exhausting, and difficult summer, telling herself, resolutely, that every cloud has a silver lining, that it's always darkest before the dawn, and it's a long road that has no turning. Which, in practice, meant hoping for the best whilst preparing, mentally, spiritually and physically, for the worst.

XIV

THE rain set in, as though by arrangement, on the visitors' first morning, and continued almost daily for the rest of the month and most of June, a fine, soft, sad rain from clouds that seemed to rest heavily upon the tops of the few trees and swathed the hills in grey mists. An occasional heavy shower was a break in the monotony of the steady, unremitting endlessness of the small rain.

At first the visitors accepted it philosophically, telling themselves that after all when you came to Ireland, particularly to the West, they said, you expected rain. Like Wales, and the English Lakes, you know. They put on elegant macintoshes and hoods and overboots and went out into it, resolutely. They walked into Ballyrannon and bought the papers, and had whiskies at the hotel. They walked round the lake. They tramped between broken stone walls along endless bog-roads and out to the sea, where the kelp-gathering went on in the rain, and, with the water running down her face, Mrs. Paul talked bravely of the wunnerful colours you got in the West of Ireland even on grey days, and Philippa stared dutifully at the indicated yellow seaweed covering brown rocks and grey boulders, and observed the dark shadows of clouds on the heaving grey-green sea, and the clouds breaking on the grey-blue hills, and the green and brown bog running with brackish water, and thought that it was as though the sun had gone forever, but she had her own kind of courage—a grey courage, not multi-coloured like Mrs. Paul's—and kept this dreariness to herself. To her ever-lasting credit it should be recorded that not once all that boring, monotonous, rain-swept Irish summer did she suggest that they should go, or complain because they were there. When Paulo wanted to do a thing, hers not to reason why; hers merely to hold on and try to make life as tolerable as possible for them both.

And in spite of the rain and the boredom and the monotony Stephanie had no wish to be anywhere else. She liked to think that in the very strangeness of the life she was experiencing something of profound significance. It was, she said to Philippa, a spiritual going into retreat. She talked a good deal in that strain on the numerous wet afternoons when they sat in the lace-curtained lounge of the Railway Hotel, looking out on to the wide street awash with the rain, and drinking rye-whiskies. The more whiskies she had the more profound became the significance of the whole experience. Then Philippa's heart would swell with love for her darling Paulo who felt things so deeply and expressed them so beautifully, and she would want to cry, and sometimes did. *Vino tinto* in Majorca, Pernod in Paris, vodka in Moscow, had the same effect on them both. Mike called it their *de profundis* act. . . . Philippa had never forgiven him because once, at Juan-les-Pins, when, after several champagne cocktails at Sunflower Joe's, Paulo had asked him didn't he think life was just one great long make-believe, he had replied, solemnly, "Life—shall I tell you what life is? Life is just a water-closet!"

They saw a great deal less of Mike at Ballyrannon than they had at Juan-les-Pins and Paris. He went out fishing for whole days at a time, and they could hardly fail to observe that he had some curious private life from which he was apt to return with his hat on the back of his head and singing "Stand, boys, stand together," supported by the most extraordinary-looking people with whom he appeared to be on the terms of the greatest intimacy, so that Mrs. Paul was forced to conclude that they had some qualities not apparent to her in her ignorance of Irish life, for Michael Harrigan would surely never consort with 'rubbishy' people?

She once invited herself out fishing with him, but only the once. It was excessively boring; there was none of the brilliant, racy, 'typically Irish' talk she had anticipated in the tête-à-tête, nor any of the gay intimacy they had known in Paris and the South.   Mike sat silently in the boat, puffing at his pipe, staring at the water, and to all intents and purposes oblivious of her. There was only Guinness, which she disliked, to drink, and the cheese was dry and the bread damp, and it rained on and off, with an uncomfortably chilly little wind, and she got very wet and cold and discouraged.   She was not to know that Mike had resolved to cure her, once and for all, of any wish to accompany him fishing.   Something in life had to be kept inviolate, and for him it was fishing.   Besides, she bored him.   He had been cynically amused by her in France, but in her conscientious adaptation to Irish life she was of little interest.   In bewildered, despairing, defeated conflict with it she would have interested him enormously ; as it was, she was so painstakingly adaptable that having established the fact that she could 'cope' with the lack of plumbing, the weather, and Tante Emma's erratic meals, plus the complete absence of anything to do, he could not understand why she did not go.   He had made it quite clear to her that he had no intention of becoming her lover, and if she had hopes of the boy she had better settle down for a couple of years at least.   He had watched Flynn's reaction to her with some interest, but not even the fascinating Mrs. Paul, it seemed, could compete with the attractions of Jameel. . . .

There were times when Mrs. Paul felt this herself, though she always told herself that that of course was absurd, that in his preoccupation with the mare Flynn was merely 'sublimating' his natural impulses.   Horses, politics, and the Catholic Church between them accounted for 'a whole lot' of sublimation amongst the male population of Ireland, she decided—generalising as always from the particular.

Partly from lack of anything better to do, and partly because she was determined that Flynn should become more acutely aware of her, she began going down to the field in which he put Jameel through her paces.   He was to be found there every afternoon, wet or fine.   She tried very hard to be interested, but as she had no idea what he was trying to make the mare do, or not do, it was difficult.   And Flynn was as completely absorbed in his horse as Mike was in his fishing ; even when he cantered right past her he did not appear to see her resting wistfully on the gate and trying to look intelligently interested.   It was always very much the same.   He would canter the mare very slowly down the field, with soft words of encouragement, bring her to a standstill in her own length, back her a few yards, then start her off again in another slow, sedate canter.   When the performance was to his satisfaction—but it always looked the same to Stephanie—he would dismount, pat the mare's neck, fondle her soft nose, feed her a carrot from his pocket.   Then it would start all over again, and Stephanie found it quite extraordinarily boring to watch—though Mike and Bridie, she had observed, were capable of leaning on the gate and watching for an hour or more, with expressions of the most rapt or the most lively interest.   She couldn't think why Flynn didn't just go for a good long ride and have done with it. . . .

The only occasion when she felt in the least interested was one afternoon when she and Philippa were returning from a desperate walk in the rain and, passing the field on the way up to the castle, were astonished to see the three Harrigans performing the most extraordinary circus tricks with the mare. Mike stood in the middle of the field long-reining the mare round in a wide circle at a slow canter, and Mike and Bridie ran round the inside of the circle taking it in turns to vault up on to her bare back, standing with folded arms and a triumphant expression. They were obviously, in Stephanie's language, 'having fun', but it all looked extremely dangerous to her. As soon as Bridie was up Flynn would try to come up in front of her, usually knocking her off. Or if it was not Flynn who dislodged her as he flung his leg over, the mare would break into a trot, and she would come off—only to pick herself up, laughing, push her hair back out of her eyes, and start running round again. Once she dislodged Flynn, and when the mare slowed down to a walk called out excitedly, "Wait while I throw a handstand !" and to the on-lookers' amazement proceeded to stand on her hands and maintain her balance for a few moments until Jameel broke into a trot again, when she came off once more.

"My !" Mrs. Paul exclaimed, admiringly. "My !"

"I wonder they don't call themselves Harrigans' Circus and have done with it," Philippa observed, caustically, as, discouraged by the Harrigans' complete unawareness of their audience, they went on. Mrs. Paul began to talk, a little wistfully, of happy, sunny mornings watching the high-school riding in the Spanish Riding School in Vienna. Then they both thought of sunshine in the Ring Boulevards, café-terraces under trees, coffee with a froth of thick cream on the top, and cocktails at Sacher's Bar in the evenings . . . and the more they recalled all that the colder and wetter they felt, and the more incredible it seemed that anyone should wish to spend hours, hat-less, in a sodden field fooling with a horse. But, as Mrs. Paul pointed out, if you were going to *live* in Ireland—and it should be remembered that some people had to—you simply *had* to learn to ignore the weather.

But after a month of it even Mrs. Paul could not go on pretending not to mind the everlasting small sad rain. Instead of resolutely getting up and going out into it, as at first, she took to remaining in bed till mid-day, and if it was still raining in the afternoon, as it usually was, they stayed indoors, playing cards, listening to the radio Mrs. Paul had imported from Bally-rannon at the end of the first week—because otherwise, she said, you felt so cut off—drinking rye-whisky, talking, reading—something cultural, on art or philosophy—and waiting for the clouds to break, when they would go for a short walk.

It had been the longest month either of them had ever lived through, but Philippa knew that equally long months stretched ahead, and that if a spell of good weather should by any chance come in the fall they would probably stay on . . . so long as Flynn Harrigan was there. Mrs. Paul did not acknowledge it to Philippa, but she did not attempt to deny to herself that her stubborn refusal to be defeated by the rain and the monotony of the days was entirely because of her interest in Flynn. But that she thought of him as a potential lover was of course absurd. . . .

Morning after morning she lay, in a satin nightgown, between the coarse cotton sheets of her hard bed, staring at the bulging patch in the ceiling and wondering how soon it would fall on her, looking out at the rain, and listening to the wind, and to the hoary brown tendrils of the ivy tapping against the broken windows, and then Flynn would come into her thoughts, a golden youth, curiously 'untouchable', with his shy, charming smile, and that sense she had of him of tentative approach immediately withdrawn the moment he realised her awareness of it. There was no doubt that he was *vurry* attractive. Something really quite *unusual* about him. In Montparnasse and Greenwich Village any unusual-looking young man generally turned out to be 'homo', she had observed, but the Irish apparently didn't run to that. In fact, as she generalised to Philippa, they didn't seem to run much even to normal sex. She seemed to remember reading somewhere that it was because they were essentially a fighting race. Take their poetry, she said. It was much more concerned with Cathleen ni Houlihan and the Dark Rosaleen than any real flesh-and-blood woman. Take their plays, she said. The real heroine was always Ireland—the bedroom scene invariably concerned with gunmen on the run, Free-Staters and Republicans shooting each other up. You had your choice between nationalist realism at the Gate and Celtic Twilight at the Abbey. Nothing between *The Shadow of a Gunman* and *Deirdre of the Shadows*. Of course it was all very in-er-esting, and in its own way it was ro-mantic, but when you got a boy like Flynn Harrigan it seemed a pity, for—she said to Philippa—there you got the poetic, sensitive, passionate type, and you kind of felt all his emotions and energy were drained away into nationalist fervour on the one hand and the Catholic Church on the other. And—but this she did not say to Philippa—if you were Stephanie Paul you did not reckon to have to compete with *institutions*. . . . The thing, of course, was to 'draw the boy out'.

She worked quite hard at this. She would lean against the half-door of the loose-box and chat to him whilst he was grooming his horse. Jameel was the one subject on which he talked easily and freely. With Flynn it was clearly a case of love-me-love-my-mare. She found herself regretting that she did not ride and knew so little of horses and was, in truth, a little scared of them, though Flynn assured her that for all her spiritedness Jameel was the gentlest of creatures. The difficulty, of course, was getting Flynn alone. Bridie was almost like his shadow. It was sheer desperation which sent Mrs. Paul up the dark spiral stone staircase of the turret late one night after all the goodnights had been said, ostensibly to borrow a book. She debated with herself for some time as to whether she would visit him in her dressing-gown or not, but finally decided against it. It would be better not—for a first visit, anyhow. She found him in bed, reading by the light of the candle on the chair beside the bed. He had heard footsteps on the stairs and expecting to see Bridie was startled when Stephanie came in carrying a guttering candle. She smiled at him over the small bending flame. His pyjamas with their broad stripes were, she thought, quite hideous, and they appeared to be made of some frightful flannelly material. . . .

"I hope I'm not disturbing you," she said, "but I just can't sleep, and thought maybe you'd lend me a book."

"Sure," Flynn said, "help yourself," and was glad that he had the book that Katherine had given him in his hands. He would have had to refuse her that had she wanted it.

She pulled out the first intelligible title from the row of books that stood along the chest-of-drawers, under the picture of St. Anne, supported at either end by heavy stones brought in from a broken wall. It was Synge's *Aran Islands*.

"I've always wanted to read Singe," she said.

The pronunciation jarred on him, but he let it go. It was somehow strange seeing her there in his room by candlelight. The collar of her white silk shirt was fastened by a large diamond brooch, which flashed as she moved like some brilliant night-moth.

She came and sat down on his bed, fingering the book, then looked about her, smiling, with a lift of her sleek head that reminded Flynn of Jameel.

"Don't you find it kind of eerie up here at nights?" she demanded.

"I like it," Flynn told her. "I moved up here when I was fifteen——"

"Taking up imaginary drawbridges after you?"

"Yes—perhaps." He smiled, faintly, not quite sure of her meaning. It was somehow difficult to talk to her without Jameel nuzzling between them, or Bridie seated opposite.

Stephanie groped about in her mind for another suitable opening to intimate chat such as she had visualised. It was rather late at night to start 'debunking' the Catholic Church, she thought, after a glance at the crucifix above the bed; besides, something less controversial was called for. But some time she must get on to him about all that.

"What are you reading?" she asked, hoping it was not some Catholic devotional work or the biography of a saint.

He told her, *The Love Songs of Connacht*, and she reached forward to take it from him, then sat turning the pages over, staring at them but, he knew, taking nothing in. He had seen people do it at Aunt Chris's in Dublin, taking books from the shelves, flapping the pages over, replacing them, pointlessly. It was like the meaningless things people said. . . .

"I must borrow it some time," she said. He was silent, and after turning a few more pages she returned the book to him, fully aware that he had not said, 'Yes, do; take it now.' She had the feeling that he waited for her to go, and she got up. If he had only been a little more helpful and followed up the cues she gave him they might have had a cosy little chat on love-poetry. She had been going to ask him if he had read *The Song of Songs*, then decided that perhaps being a Catholic he wouldn't have read the Old Testament. She had been prepared to quote him some of the more candid lines from *The Passionate Pilgrim* if he had taken his cue and said yes to her suggestion that she should borrow the Irish poems. But what could you do with a young man who just didn't co-operate in the getting-acquainted game?

Lying in bed on wild wet windy mornings she would recall this sleeveless errand of a visit, and wonder whether it was worth trying again. She had been altogether too tentative, she thought; on any subsequent occasion all the initiative would have to come from her. There would have to be direct frontal attack, no skirmishing. To break through the shell in which he enclosed himself it was necessary to have as much patience with him, she told herself, as he had with his horse, and Philippa had with her. Given patience it should be possible to waken him eventually to a sense of the Realities of Life. She did not define these Realities. Definition had—had it not?—a way of destroying the subtleties of thought. It was important to preserve the balance between 'a shepherd simplicity' on the one hand and the delicate nuances of spiritual experience on the other. . . . She tried this profundity out on Philippa, who murmured that she guessed that was 'vurry true'.

Flynn no doubt believed that the sum of spiritual experience was confined to the Catholic Church and Gaelic poetry, though this she did not say to Philippa; from all such limiting belief he had to be emancipated, and she, Stephanie Paul, was resolved to do it, if it took all summer, even though it rained every day. . . .

2

After that nocturnal visit to him in the tower Flynn found it impossible to get Mrs. Paul out of his head. Even before then she had filled a great part of his thoughts, and only concentration on schooling Jameel could eliminate her. Now every night he lay listening for her step on the stair, and he would be filled with an almost intolerable longing for the door to open and her neat dark figure to enter, her brilliant dark eyes smiling at him over a candle-flame bending in the draught. There were times when he wished, passionately, that she would go; at other times something like panic filled him with the realisation that one day she would inevitably go, and that after that he would in all probability never see her again. 'Possessed' by her, as he was, night and day, he no longer carried Katherine's letter like a bruise on his heart, and because this was so felt in some curious, undefined fashion that he was 'revenged' on her. All his frustrated love for the girl who had been Cousin Kate flowed out now into this new channel, with all its excitement of strangeness.

He began slipping away to his rooms in the afternoons, when he could evade Bridie's watchful eye, in the hope that Mrs. Paul would find an excuse to come to him there. Several times she did come, to lend him a book, or borrow one, or return one. She would lean against the window-sill and say how beautiful the view was, or sit on the bed and smoke a cigarette and talk about poetry. He hardly knew what she said, because of the strangeness and wonder of her there intimately in his room like that. Afterwards he would think that she must have thought him very stupid in his inarticulateness.

He did not know whether he thought her beautiful or not. He only knew that she was 'different'. Beauty was Cousin Kate with black hair lifted on the wind and eyes full of laughter; it was Bridie in a long white dress sweeping proudly out of the Shelbourne; it was the tender face of St. Anne in the Da Vinci picture; it was Jameel daisy-clipping over the summer-dry 'mountain'. Beauty was something you did not merely see with your eyes; it was something that caught at your heart.

And there was nothing of this about Stephanie Paul. She had a certain aura of worldliness and self-assurance that ruled out tenderness in connection with her, and tenderness entered strongly into his conception of beauty. He had never heard of the sense of tears behind all beauty, but he understood very well what Francis Thompson meant by

'Whatso looks lovelily
Is but the rainbow on life's weeping rain.'

Mrs. Paul did not come into that category. She was too sophisticated, though Flynn could not have defined it in those terms, the word 'sophistication' being not then in his vocabulary. He only knew that Mrs. Paul, like

Katherine O'Donal 'the young actress', belonged to a world of which he had no knowledge. His world was of wind and rain, earth and sky; beauty for him must always have an element of wildness; everything he loved had wildness in it—the stones and waters of Connemara, Bridie of the changing moods, the warmth of Cousin Kate, the desert fieriness of Jameel, the rhythm and sorrow of Gaelic poetry, the proud, passionate spirit of Ireland herself. There was no wildness in Mrs. Paul. It was impossible to imagine her windblown, or anything but elegant; she even came in out of the rain looking elegant in her white macintosh. He did not know the expression 'wellgroomed' in connection with people, but Mrs. Paul always reminded him of a racehorse newly groomed. There was a tendency to masculinity in her clothes, and she wore her thick dark hair, with a streak of white in it, cropped like a man's, yet, strangely it seemed to Flynn, she never ceased to be feminine. The network of fine lines under her eyes seemed to him only to accentuate their dark aliveness, and he liked the slight hollowness under the cheekbones and the lines the years had drawn from nose to mouth; they made her face interesting, he thought. That she looked a great deal younger than her actual years was of no interest to him; she seemed to him ageless, and some quality of her personality and her physical presence stirred his blood and troubled his spirit. But it was all as secret as his drawer full of poems— and as little of a secret to Bridie.

Bridie had been fully aware of the look on her brother's face when he had first set eyes on Mrs. Paul, and she had seen it on his face many times since— a look of wonder, of fascination. Bridie's jealousy intensified her perceptiveness, and she knew intuitively that Mrs. Paul only remained on, in the face of the bad weather, and all the inconveniences and discomforts, because of Flynn. She was aware that Mrs. Paul was always trying to get him alone, to establish some sort of intimate understanding between them. She always knew when Mrs. Paul had been 'hanging round' Flynn in the stables, because of her perfume clinging to the mare. Flynn, too, was always aware of the perfume clinging to Jameel after Mrs. Paul had handled her, which she liked to do, to ingratiate herself with Flynn, laying her face against the mare's silky neck, kissing her wide forehead, stroking and fondling her, and it stirred something in his blood, so that he felt almost guilty before Bridie's accusation, "That woman's been hanging round here! Jameel stinks of her!" Similarly she knew when Mrs. Paul had been up in Flynn's room; even the smell of her Egyptian cigarette did not quell the subtle yet insistent smell of her Numero Cinque. Her own room carried the scent strongly, over-riding the smell of damp and paint and distemper, and floating out into the corridor when the door was opened—to the great disgust of Tante Emma, who called it both immoral and heathen, and went marching through it with an onward-Christian-soldiers air, flapping her apron about before her face to drive it away.

Bridie hated Mrs. Paul with passionate intensity. She was jealous of Cousin Kate, and resented her, but she was not completely intolerable to her as Mrs. Paul was, so that she found it impossible to be civil to her. She never spoke either to Mrs. Paul or to Philippa if she could possibly avoid it, and by insisting on taking her meals in the kitchen she contrived to avoid it fairly effectively. Flynn made excuses for her by saying that she had always liked to eat with Tante Emma, and that when they were alone they both always ate with her in the kitchen, which was true. Mike listened in silence to Flynn's embarrassed explanations and was sardonically amused. His sympathies were entirely with Bridie; he did not hate Mrs. Paul, but she bored him increasingly. At first he had amused himself by baiting Philippa, whose complete lack of humour fascinated him, but after a time the novelty of that wore off and he ignored her as completely as Bridie ignored Mrs. Paul.

Flynn was always uncomfortable in Philippa's presence; he felt her dislike for him, and her complete disapproval of the whole place. She and Tante Emma hated each other fiercely, and after the first week the old woman refused to have her set foot in the kitchen. It meant that the only people who found any satisfaction in the existing arrangements at the castle were Flynn and Stephanie. It had originally amused Mike to inveigle the two women into a visit to Ballyrannon; he had had a malicious desire to cure Stephanie of her sentimental romanticism over Ireland and the Irish and to watch her Paris-American sophistication in reaction to what he called, ironically, 'wild life in the West', but she had cheated him by her adaptability; and as for Philippa, she was born to suffer uncomplainingly in the cause of devotion. He knew very well that Stephanie must be hating a number of things, but she was so determined to find Ireland and the Irish romantic that she tolerated everything, the livestock in the cold bathwater, Tante Emma's atrocious cooking, the damp running like tears down the banisters and breaking out in a kind of fungus on the walls, the crude sanitary arrangements, the colossal boredom, accepting it all as part of the 'peasant simplicity' of Connemara existence. He was forced to give her a kind of grudging admiration; but after a month he wished to God she would go. He proposed to stay himself only for the summer; he wanted to see the races and the Horse Show round again, and then he would go on from Dublin to London and back to Paris. Stephanie was also keen on seeing the Galway and the Limerick Junction races, and going to Dublin for the Horse Show. She, also, would probably go back to Paris after that via London. Well, Mike had no objection to offer to that; Paris was big enough to hold them both—Ballyrannon was another matter.

It was altogether a wild wet summer; July had less rain than June, but the days for the most part were grey and heavy with clouds, with only fitful sunshine, and that always with the threat of rain behind it. A mid-July dance in Ballyrannon broke the monotony of the days. Stephanie looked forward to this with the utmost eagerness; for one thing it should enable her to make considerable progress with Flynn; there was nothing like the intimacy of dancing together—the 'imitative copulative article', Aldous Huxley had called it, hadn't he? Well, never mind. It was useful all the same. And there was, of course, the Cultural side. She understood that a return to the old national dances was part of the Celtic Revival, and looked forward to all manner of wild jigs and reels. Bridie also looked forward to the dance; she would be able to wear her long white dress again, and in Ballyrannon it should cause a sensation. Patrick, too, would almost certainly be there. She had not seen him, except for chance meetings in the town, and at Mass, since the previous summer when they had lain on the sand between the curaghs and he had asked her why didn't they marry and raise up sons to the glory of

Ireland. . . . She had always remembered those words, and she thought of them now, with a curious stirring of excitement in her, though of course she would never marry, Patrick or anyone else—never. The reflection that Patrick loved her and no one else, and that she could marry him if she had a mind to, was nevertheless very comforting, surrounded as she was by the enemy aliens, and Flynn making calf's eyes at the blackest of them. . . .

Other years when they had gone to the local dance Flynn and Bridie had walked into Ballyrannon, meeting other young people at the cross-roads and stopping to dance with them, in accordance with custom, but this year, as Bridie was wearing her long dress, and the high-heeled silver shoes that went with it, and as 'the ladies' were also in evening dress, they hired a car from Foyne's combined garage, radio shop, and bar, a dilapidated, musty-smelling vehicle chiefly employed to bring summer visitors up from the railway station to the Railway Hotel, a matter of a couple of miles. Stephanie and Philippa had arrived at the castle in it, though they had hoped for a 'jaunting-car'. . . . The Irish could be disappointing at times.

For Bridie, Mr. Foyne's shabby, ill-sprung car was the utmost luxury and excitement, but this time the rare pleasure of riding in it was spoilt by the presence of Mrs. Paul. She sat in front with Mr. Foyne in order to have her back to her.

She had pinned some late yellow roses from the garden to one shoulder of her dress, the way she had seen it done by fashionable ladies in the Shelbourne Hotel. They were the wrong colour for her hair, Stephanie thought, and anyway the child should know that you cannot just pull flowers from a garden and pin them to your dress like that, fastening them with an unsightly safety-pin. . . . But of course it was no use trying to help or advise such an extremely unpleasant little girl.

Her father and brother, however, thought that Bridie looked fine, the world's wonder, and that there was great beauty in her small piquant face when her hair was brushed and combed and bound with a ribbon, and her eyes were alight and eager, and no frown darkening her golden brows.

The yellow roses reminded Flynn of his sixteenth birthday party, and a great longing for Cousin Kate swept over him with the memory, and he filled with sadness. Had she really gone for good, she of the Dear Dark Head, she who was Cathleen ni Houlihan made living and real in the flesh? He was as silent as Bridie as they drove in to Ballyrannon.

Stephanie, aware of his sombre mood, asked him, "Don't you like dancing, Flynn?" She wondered why he hadn't put on a dinner-jacket; he must surely have one, as Mike had spoken of parties at the Shelbourne; the Harrigans were, after all, the local gentry. . . .

Bridie came out of a reverie that was all of Patrick to inform her, "He only likes dancing with Cousin Kate and me!"

Stephanie knew that Bridie was trying to ruffle her, so she smiled sweetly and murmured that that was 'just too bad', and turned hopefully to Mike.

"You're not going to tell me you only like dancing with Tante Emma?" she said.

"I don't dance," Mike told her. "Not in this country, anyhow. The Biguines and the Bal Négre in Paris—that's another matter. Here I just look in for a few minutes to show there's no ill-feeling, and then beat it to

Murphy's Bar. Sorry, sister! Flynn will take care of you all right, I guess!''
He used the Americanisms deliberately; they had, he always thought, a
brutalising effect on speech. . . .

Flynn did not at all want to dance with Stephanie that night, though
almost any other night he would have found the idea exciting. There was
only one woman he wanted to hold in his arms in that mood, and that was
Cousin Kate. If he had to dance he wanted to dance only with Bridie, and
for everything to be as it used to be, before some horrible English people
called Pocock had invaded them, and he had written that letter to Aunt
Chris which had provoked from Katherine the rebuke which once again lay
like a bruise on his heart. He felt that he would give years of his life to see
Cousin Kate come into the hall and make her way towards him, crying, her
eyes alight, "Flynn darlin'! Darlin' Flynn!" Sometimes miracles happened
even outside Holy Church; once he had known a miracle on a summer night
—why should it not happen again?

A miracle did happen that night, but it had nothing to do with Cousin
Kate.

XV

WHEN they reached the town hall Patrick Doyle stepped forward from the
crowd gathered at the door and claimed Bridie immediately. He was a little
shy, despite his eagerness, because she was such a grand lady with her long
dress and elegant fur cape, Miss Bridie of Ballyrannon Castle. But she laid
aside her grandeur with the white fur, and as soon as they were on the floor
the music got into them both, so that they began trying out all manner of
complicated steps, laughing a good deal, their heads together as they looked
down at their feet, and Bridie's hair escaping its ribbon and a lock of it
falling over her face, so that she was herself again, the wild one, quite capable
of throwing a handstand even in a grown-up dress. . . . For a while she
could forget the hateful Mrs. Paul, and her deep jealousy. When Flynn
passed her with 'the enemy' in his arms she saw the set expression on his face
and knew that he was not in the mood, and that in that mood only Cousin
Kate arriving suddenly would lift his heart, let the music into his blood. So
that it did not matter how often he danced with Mrs. Paul, and she could give
herself up to enjoyment with Patrick.

Flynn danced badly, because he had no desire to dance at all. He held
his partner stiffly, and well away from him, and occasionally, because he was
not hearing the music, he stumbled on her toes and muttered apology, and
behaved altogether, Stephanie thought, like the clumsiest kind of corner-boy.
Being herself a good dancer she suffered quite acutely. The boy seemed to
have no sense of rhythm whatever; with his graceful figure he ought to be
a good dancer, but there it was, unfortunately, and at the end of one dance she
had had quite enough and was anxious to evade the encore.

"I think maybe this isn't a vurry good tune," she said, tactfully, dis-
engaging herself from Flynn.

He told her, with a rueful smile, "I'm sorry; I'm afraid you're being polite.
'Tis a perfectly good tune, but I'm in a bad mood.''

"Poor darling!" She pressed his hand, and suggested, "Why don't we slip out to the Railway Hotel and have a few drinks? It would do you good."

It seemed to Flynn a good idea; it might help to put Cousin Kate out of his mind. He glanced round the hall and saw that Bridie was still happy with Patrick, and that Philippa was talking to his father. He and Mrs. Paul could slip out unobserved.

In the linoleum-covered lounge of the Railway they drank rye-whiskies, and after his revulsion over the sweetish taste of the first he found that the second tasted much less sweet and that he was already beginning to feel a good deal better.

"Of course, what you need is a change," Stephanie told him, and as they had by then had three whiskies, and there was no one else in the lounge, she took his hand. "At your age," she said, "you ought to be moving about—going places, London, Paris, Vienna. You ought," she added, firmly, "to be having love-affairs."

He told her, "I am in love with someone, but it's no good."

"Having love-affairs, I said, not just being in love. Leave out the word love, if you like. *Affaires*."

"'Tis an ugly word," he said. He added, after a moment, in which she watched his troubled face intently, "Even if I didn't think so it would be impossible here, in Ireland."

He smiled at her, suddenly. "We are very strait-laced! Priest-ridden, you'll probably say."

"It's just terrible," she said, in her soft drawl. "I don't know why it should be like that here—France is a Catholic country, but people manage to enjoy themselves!"

"Perhaps we take our Catholicism more seriously," he suggested.

"Maybe you'd see things differently if you got out of the country for a while," she counter-suggested. "Take your father—his Catholicism doesn't prevent him from amusing himself!"

Flynn frowned, and said, sharply, "There are good and bad Catholics."

"I see; and you're a good one, is that it?" She laughed. "Isn't that just kind of a little bit self-righteous?"

The troubled look came back to his face. "I'm not good, of course I'm not—it's obvious. I only mean that some people just don't care——"

"And you do care—you'd like to be a good Catholic and live a strait-laced life and miss everything all along the line? Live all your life out here in the wilderness and never know one single thing about real life—is that it?"

He stared at her. "That's what Cousin Kate said—almost her very words! About not knowing anything——"

"Cousin Kate—is that the girl you're in love with?"

"Yes."

She smiled. "Anyone who cares for you and who knows anything would tell you the same."

She had a sense of everything in him sheering away from the impact of unorthodox ideas.

He said, troubled, "I could never get away from here—there's only me to run the place. But for me it would be more of a ruin than it is. And until Bridie marries she needs me."

"You mean you don't really want to get away!"

He raised his head and looked at her, suddenly defiant.

"I mean that, too. I don't really want to get away—I love Ireland." He drew his hand away from hers. "We ought to be getting back," he added.

"I guess so." There was, she knew, no further headway to be made at that point.

They returned to the hall in time for a highly unpopular interlude of national dances. Stephanie's delight at having got back 'in time' was short-lived; only a few enthusiasts formed themselves into sets, and for one reel no one came out on to the floor at all, and the band was obliged to change the tune. There was a solo performance by a young man with an intensely serious, almost angry, expression. He held his arms loosely at his side and his body very rigid; his feet in heavy boots kicked and stamped, and medals flew up and down on the lapel of his jacket; he performed this one brief, very rapid, number, then, with the same angry look, ran off the floor. He received mild applause which Stephanie did her frantic best to intensify and prolong, but it was no good; the angry-looking young man was not prepared to repeat the performance, and no one but Stephanie wanted him to. When, to the general relief, the band struck up a popular fox-trot which it had already thumped out a dozen times that evening, and the floor filled up again, Flynn looked round for Bridie, but she was with Patrick. He saw Philippa 'bumping and boring' through the crowd in the arms of the red-faced Charlie-the-horse-coper, and wanted to laugh; her expression was one of resigned suffering, and Charlie as he passed winked boldly over her drooping shoulder.

Flynn turned to Stephanie. "I hardly like to ask you to dance this with me——"

She smiled and stepped confidently into his arms, and this time, as she had known, he found that he could dance. He felt, now, as alight and alive as previously he had felt dead. He held her close to him, keenly aware of her body in the long, tight-fitting black dress, and of the momentary brush of her smooth hair against his cheek. It was the first time he had seen her in anything but a mannishly tailored suit, and he was startled now by her femininity. The dress, with its square-cut bodice and the long tight sleeves, made her look, he thought, like something out of a mediaeval painting. It was a very clever dress, designed by a very eminent Paris designer, and it had, in Stephanie's language, 'cost the earth'; it had had a good deal of success at parties in Paris, London, Vienna, and a number of quite distinguished artistic people had complimented her on it, but it was a great disappointment to Ballyrannon, which had looked for something much more sensational. By Ballyrannon, festive in coloured lace and art silk, it was considered 'very plain', and what sort of colour, at all, was black for an evening dress? And if the craythur had to have sleeves for an evening dress wouldn't you have thought, now, she'd have had them stop short at her elbow, instead of creeping right down over her wrists and half covering her hands? Miss Bridie, now, in her white dress, like a bride, with silver shoes to her feet, and flowers on her shoulder, and a ribbon in her hair, was elegance itself, and next to her for smartness came—it was generally agreed—old Mrs. Flaherty's niece Molly, come in from Letterfrack, and a fine sight in a green dress of shining satin, bright as grass in spring.

There was a certain amount of disapproval both of Mrs. Paul and her companion in Ballyrannon—disapproval of something strange and new. Both women had painted lips and had been seen smoking cigarettes in the street, and they thought nothing of going into a public bar for a drink. Their clothes were strange, and their clear, self-confident voices, and their accents, and their unself-conscious manners, and their complete indifference to being stared at. Brazen was the word Ballyrannon used about them in discussing them, which it did, endlessly, humorously and quite without malice tearing their characters to shreds.

Neither Flynn nor Mrs. Paul herself was aware of the attention they attracted when they danced together that second time, or of the ripples of disapproval in the human stream that ebbed and flowed and surged about them.

Once Stephanie smiled up at him, and murmured, "I knew you could dance !"

He made no comment, but laughed, a low, excited laugh, and drew her closer to him.

They remained on the floor for the encore, and at the end, she said, "It's getting hot in here, and this band is kind of monotonous. Why don't we go back and sit in your room and talk ? It should be ro-mantic up there in the tower when the moon's up. We could send the car back for the others."

His blood quickened anew at the suggestion. It was an effort to say carelessly, "We could, then. We can slip away without being noticed, but I must come back for Bridie. I can say that I took you back early because you were tired."

"The driver won't mind waiting ?"

"Ah, no. Sure, he's been doing little else the best part of his life !"

He was suddenly gay and excited, as on the night when Cousin Kate had suggested taking the boat out in the moonlight. This, too, was a summer night, and the moon riding high in the sky.

In the darkness of the car she took his hand, came closer to him, leaning her head against his shoulder, and it was like the first time he had been aware of her perfume on Jameel, the same sense of being momentarily engulfed in a dark tidal wave of sensual excitement.

When they reached the castle she waited for him in the dark hall whilst he groped about with a candle in the library for whisky for Mr. Foyne, then he came back to her and took her hand and they went up the wide staircase together and along the long, broad corridor at the top, where the curtainless windows threw black and silver moon-shadows on the bare boards of the floor. Narrowing away into the darkness where the tower stairs spiralled up to the turret room, the corridor had the vistaed endlessness of a dream, a perspective telescoping into eternity. Once there had been the moonlit unreality of a silent lake, and a girl's bare breast like a gull upon the water ; but at the core of this unreality was a flame, and in this dream the senses wide awake.

They climbed up through the darkness of the turret and into the small circular room bright with moonlight.

Flynn set the candle down on the chest-of-drawers, and Stephanie immediately blew it out.

"The moonlight's better," she said, softly, and turned to him.

He stood behind her, and in that close space when she turned she was against his breast, and then somehow naturally in his arms.

It was, after all, as easy as all that.

But for Flynn a miracle beyond all understanding.

XVI

THE journey back into Ballyrannon, and the return with Bridie and Philippa, continued the sense of unreality for Flynn. He had the feeling of his body performing certain actions, but of his essential self being left behind in the turret with a woman whose arms had wound about him in the moonlight, and with whom he had travelled mindlessly to the end of the night. . . .

The dance was already over by the time he got back, and Bridie and Philippa were standing at the door of the hall, with a crowd of other people engaged in final gossip, in saying goodnight, or waiting whilst others went off to bring round motor-cars, jaunting-cars, pony-traps. Bridie and Philippa had waited only a few minutes, but they were full of indignation at Flynn's neglect—Mike had disappeared from the dance early in the evening and had not returned, and Patrick, who had gone in search of Mr. Foyne's shabby old car, had reported that it was nowhere to be seen. As Mrs. Paul and Flynn were also nowhere to be seen, and had not been for some time, the deduction was obvious, so that it was a very tight-lipped pair that Flynn came to collect. He murmured something about having taken Mrs. Paul back early as she had had a headache, and both of them were aware of his absent manner and the smell of Numero Cinque on his tweed coat.

"I'll never forgive you for this!" Bridie hissed at him, as she picked up her dress and climbed into the car, which also held the hated perfume.

"I'm sorry," Flynn murmured, absently, "I'm sorry you had to wait."

No one spoke on the drive back, but Flynn was unaware of the silence, and Bridie knew that nothing either of them could say could make him present in his body.

When they reached the castle Philippa said a curt goodnight and went straight upstairs. Bridie announced that she was 'starving' and was going to the kitchen to find something to eat.

"Come with me in case there's a rat," she commanded.

They went along the dark passageway and into the kitchen, where the moonlight lay barred across the table and a faint glow came from the fire, the turfs carefully raked together by Tante Emma to last till the morning. Flynn lit the lamp and turned up the wick, and Bridie went to the cupboard and cut herself a thick slice of bread and smeared it with butter. Deliberately she did not inquire if Flynn wanted anything to eat, but he did not notice; his only desire was to be alone, given over to the spell that held him. Bridie closed the cupboard door and stood with her back against it and drove her teeth hungrily into the bread.

"If there's nothing else you want, why not take it upstairs?" Flynn suggested.

Bridie went on eating for a moment, then, ignoring his suggestion, said,

"You and that woman came back here because you wanted to be alone together."

Flynn met her challenging eyes. He said, quietly, "If you're proposing to stage one of your jealousy acts I'm going to bed."

Bridie methodically licked the butter off each finger.

She said, carelessly, "Wouldn't it be a great pity, now, if a stone should be coming through her bedroom window some fine night, and the two of us safely in our beds and knowing nothing of it?"

He stared at her. "What, exactly, do you mean?"

"I was thinking of those two who stayed down at the Railway Hotel one summer, giving it out they were man and wife, and then the story went round they were nothing of the kind, and one night a shower of stones went through their bedroom window, and in the morning they were gone."

His heart quickened a little. "What has that to do with Mrs. Paul?"

She flicked crumbs from the bosom of her dress. "Only that 'twould be a pity if anything of the kind should happen through any talk about you and her."

Flynn said, violently, "If anything happens to Mrs. Paul you will be packed off to a convent at the other side of the country, even if we have to put you in a strait-jacket to get you there!"

He turned round and stalked out, followed by Bridie's mocking, "Isn't it very easy to talk, now?"

In his room Flynn sat on the narrow bed and looked at the imprint of Stephanie's head upon the pillow and felt her perfume all about him, and the angry beating of his heart subsided as he filled again with the memory of her. He leaned forward and lay with his face buried in the pillow, his arms encircling it, and presently he slept.

2

Philippa told herself that if dear Paulo had a headache it was her duty to 'look in' on her before going to bed.

She opened the door of Stephanie's room very gently and peeped round. Stephanie had some time ago extinguished the candle, but the moonlight fell full across the bed and it was a relief—which she would not have admitted—to Philippa to see her there.

She said, softly, "Are you all right, darling? I was worried when I missed you."

She came into the room and sat down on the bed.

"Have you taken some aspirin?" she added.

Stephanie yawned. "I was sound asleep," she lied. "Have you just got back? It was kind of boring, I guess——"

"It was more or less what I expected," Philippa said. "But I'm worried about you. Can I heat you some milk, with a drop of whisky in it?"

"No, thank you, darling. I had some drinks with Flynn."

It gave Philippa the cue she wanted. "You know, honey," she said, "you wanna be careful in a place like this—you don't wanna get *talked* about with that boy. It was kind of indiscreet the way you went off together tonight. This isn't Paris. . . ."

Stephanie yawned again. "Darling, don't start in being profound at this time of the night, there's a honey-lamb. Little Paulo can't cope . . . Nightie-night."

Philippa stood a moment staring down at her, full of unsaid things, resentment burning in her, and all the time the wild effort to pretend to herself that she really believed that Flynn had brought Paulo home because she had a headache. And the disloyal thought that she was making better headway with the son than she ever had with the father, and that it probably meant that they would be staying in this goddam hole for months now—unless Paulo decided to take the boy back with them to Paris, which God forbid. But he would never leave his frightful little sister, and that goddam horse, even if Paulo succeeded in beating the Catholic Church. . . .

She bent down and kissed her. "Nightie-night," she said. "Sleep well," and kissing her could have sworn—though of course it was the merest imagination, she told herself afterwards—that she smelt the peaty smell of homespun tweed on Paulo's hair,

After Philippa had left her, Stephanie lay a little while staring at the moonlight and thinking of Flynn, and her lips smiled faintly. He really was rather sweet, and provided he didn't get a violent reaction in the morning due to guilt-complex—she had read her Freud—the experience would be quite valuable for him. . . . She felt tender and indulgent towards him, but it did not for a moment cross her mind to take him back to Paris with her, or on his account to stay a day longer in Ballyrannon than she had planned.

She slipped into sleep with a pleasant sense of satisfaction and tiredness, and seemed to have been asleep for only a minute when she wakened with a start and a sense of the roof falling in on her. Hardly aware of what she was doing, she leapt out of bed ; something had struck her forehead and the room seemed to be full of dust. . . . Then the door burst open and Philippa rushed in in her pyjamas, with loud exclamations and inquiries which Stephanie only heard confusedly.

Then Philippa had her arms round her shoulders, was inquiring if she was hurt, was groping for the candlestick and matches on the chair beside the bed.

When she had lit the candle it was immediately revealed that the plaster-of-Paris patch on the ceiling had come down, and lumps of the plaster lay on Stephanie's pillow and scattered over the bed and the floor.

Stephanie laughed, a little shakily. "I knew it would happen one day," she said, "but I always hoped it would be in the daytime. A lump caught me on the forehead——" She put a hand up to her forehead and felt blood. Philippa held the candle up and examined the injury, anxiously.

"It's only a graze," she said, "but it might have caught your eye or anything. I'll bathe it for you . . . Why do we stay in this goddam place?"

Stephanie sat down on the bed, and Philippa padded over to the washstand and poured cold water into the basin and threw in some antiseptic from amongst Stephanie's collection of toilet articles.

Stephanie said, removing some of the plaster from the bed, "It's a question I've often asked myself."

"Let's go," Philippa urged, dipping a piece of cottonwool into the disinfected water.

"And cut out the Galway and Limerick races?"

"What does it matter? We can take in the Dublin Horse Show and amuse ourselves well enough in Dublin for the next fortnight before it comes off——"

"It's an idea, certainly," Stephanie said, thoughtfully.

Whilst Philippa was bathing Stephanie's forehead, and the two of them were debating early departure, Bridie was tip-toeing out of the empty room above, her silver shoes in her hand, her long white dress lifted, and an expression of the utmost satisfaction on her small face. She had hurt her bare feet a little, jumping so violently on the bare boards, but the magnificent thump she had produced, and the noise of the crashing plaster, Mrs. Paul's startled cry, and the sound of Philippa rushing in, had been more than adequate compensation. . . .

XVII

BRIDIE indignantly denied to Flynn any knowledge of the fall of the plaster in Mrs. Paul's room. It was true she had once proposed jumping in the room overhead to bring it down, but if she had wanted to do it she would have done it long ago, for, she said, she had no more reason to hate Mrs. Paul now than when she first set foot in the place. Flynn was not convinced; the fall of the plaster the same night as Bridie's speech about stones through the window was too much of a coincidence, but it was no use, he knew, arguing with her; having told her lie she would stick to it even in the face of eternal damnation. As it was, she would confess it in church, gabble the prescribed prayers, and forget about it. Every time he looked at the graze on Stephanie's forehead he felt violently angry and bitter.

In the morning the sun shone, the lake sparkled, and there was such a feeling of lightness and gaiety in the rain-washed air that, to Philippa's disgust, Stephanie decided that perhaps after all they would stay on at least till the end of the month. Things were, after all, only just beginning to be interesting—though she did not say this to Philippa . . . who was well aware of it.

At mid-day, when she came downstairs, she went immediately in search of Flynn. Not finding him in the stables she crossed the yard, opened a rickety door in the wall, and let herself into the walled kitchen garden. Flynn was hoeing potatoes, and as usual when the sun shone he worked in only a pair of very old and stained shorts; it was the first time Stephanie had seen him like that, and she was startled by the brownness of his body. She thought all over again that he really was 'vurry sweet'. She smiled at him.

He was so full of her that when she stood before him in the flesh, cool and immaculate as ever in the inevitable dark suit and white blouse, he could not be certain for a moment whether she was reality or a mirage of his obsession. Even when she said good morning he could not be sure, for he had been hearing her voice all the morning. Then he saw the graze on her forehead and knew that she was real. He had already heard about the fall of the ceiling from Philippa and received Bridie's denial of any knowledge of it. He threw down his hoe and strode over to her, his face troubled.

"Were you badly hurt?" he demanded, anxiously.

She laughed and put up a hand and fingered the medallion of St. Christopher on the thin chain round his neck, and his blood stirred at the touch of her cool fingers against his bare flesh.

"Does it look like it?" she asked.

"I'm terribly sorry about it," he said. "It's the way things are done here—nothing ever seems to get done properly. Miss Bryce said something about your going earlier than you intended—you won't do that, will you? Not now——" He seized the hand that fingered the medallion and kissed the palm.

"I love you," he said wildly.

She smiled. "That was something I waited for you to say last night, but you didn't——"

"Last night everything was unreal. You see—I'd never even kissed anyone before, except Bridie. Promise me you won't go away sooner than you intended——"

She was flattered, rather than touched, by his urgency.

"Darling, of course I won't. Listen, honey—I was thinking, couldn't you let your sister exercise Jameel this afternoon and the two of us spend the afternoon together? It's the first really summer day we've had since I've been here. . . ."

He said, eagerly, "It's a wonderful idea. We might go out in the boat—if you'd like that——"

Stephanie had envisaged an amorous afternoon in the turret, with Bridie safely out of the way with Jameel, but perhaps it would be more discreet to go out in the boat; it would at least avoid giving Philippa further excuse to lecture her.

Bridie was always so glad of an opportunity to ride Jameel that it had not occurred to Flynn that she might refuse to take her that afternoon. But to his casual, "Would you like to take Jameel out this afternoon?" she demanded, with instant suspicion, "Why—what are you going to do?"

"I wanted to paint the boat," he told her.

Bridie flicked her hair back off her face.

"I don't think I feel like riding today."

Flynn smiled. "People sometimes do things for other people whether they feel like it or not," he pointed out.

"All the same, I don't feel like it." Her heart was beating very fast. That Flynn should have found something in his life more important than Jameel was frightening. He might conceivably neglect Jameel for Cousin Kate, but that he should do so when Cousin Kate was not involved . . . Her mind resisted the idea that it might be for Mrs. Paul, but emotionally she knew, beyond any doubt.

He read the challenge in her eyes, knew that from then out the war was on between him and Bridie. He had lost Cousin Kate and now he had lost the little sister who lay beside him in the sandy grass of Salthill and dreamed her dreams with him, and whom he had loved in spite of everything, and who had loved him. He had the feeling of a core of hardness shaping deep down in him. Very well, then, the war was on with Bridie, as it was with Katherine, since she wanted it that way. . . .

He turned away. "It doesn't matter," he said, "It won't hurt Jameel to stop in for once."

During lunch he boldly asked his father, "Would you like to exercise Jameel for me this afternoon? I've promised to take Mrs. Paul out in the boat."

Mike raised his eyebrows. "I had intended trying to sleep off the world's biggest hangover," he said.

"Maybe you could ride it off instead?" Stephanie suggested, a little archly.

He looked at her, curiously, a moment, and then at his son.

"Maybe I could. Might I suggest, however, that it's not an afternoon for fishing?"

Philippa said, with sudden bitterness, "Fishing isn't the only reason for going out in a boat."

Mike grinned. "Neither it is. I'd forgotten that. It shows how old I'm getting."

"It's an afternoon for picnicking on the island," Flynn told him with that same startling candour. A strange new defiance was working in him—up from that slowly forming core of hardness—demanding why should he lie and pretend?

"So it is." Mike smiled pleasantly from one to the other of them. "So it is." The look on Philippa's face gave him immense pleasure. He liked to think of her spending the afternoon sitting on the terrace, or at the window of her room, watching the boat being rowed out to the island; she would see her darling Paulo stepping ashore with her young man, and the two of them climbing up through the heather . . . then if they had any sense they would cross the island and go down the other side out of sight.

Which is precisely what they did. But Philippa did not sit and watch; she went up to her room and, having locked the door, lay on her bed, her face buried in the pillow, her hands clutching at the top of her head, and she was startled to hear the words coming out loud from her mouth, "O God! O God! O God!"

2

Deep in the heather at the far side of the island Stephanie lay on her back looking up at the pale blue silk of the sky, and Flynn supported himself on his elbows and looked down into her face. Sometimes he put out a hand to touch the curve of her chin, a wave of her hair, the finely pencilled lines of her plucked eyebrows.

She smiled at him after a long, intent silence, and asked him, "What are you thinking?"

He told her, simply, "I was thinking that I never dreamed I could be so happy. I was happy once before, on my sixteenth birthday, but it was all wild and strange; there was no peace in it, like this."

"You were happy last night?" she suggested.

He shook his head. "That was a storm taking place in a dream," he told her. "Real happiness has peace in it—I know it now. I've never known peace before."

It crossed her mind that that was all very easily explained, but if the boy wanted to see it that way, romantically, why destroy the illusion with biological exactitudes? This tender, poetic, youthful love-making was really rather charming—and a little touching.

"I never thought I'd be able to feel tenderness for you," he told her. "You always seemed so—so self-contained. I was a little afraid of you."

He bent and kissed the hollow of her throat. "And now you seem not at all frightening, but very small, and very sweet, and I love you so much my heart beats it all the time. . . ."

She laughed and sat up. "Well, if that isn't quite a speech!"

She brushed his hair back from his forehead with a little caressive gesture, then said, "Pass my jacket over, honey, I want my cigarette-case out of the pocket. There are too many dam' midges on this island of yours!" .

The enchantment held, in spite of that.

3

Leading Jameel out of the yard Mike saw his daughter leaning against a pillar of the porch and looking, he thought, oddly like a child who has been put into a corner and told to stop there until it is good.

He smiled at her. "Coming with me? We might go down to the field and do some long-reining and circus tricks."

He waited, and she sauntered over to him and stroked Jameel's velvety nose. She was silent for a moment, then she said with a kind of half-suppressed violence, "Why don't you send Mrs. Paul away? She and Flynn have got a crush on each other!"

Mike said, drily, adjusting a stirrup, "I'm very glad to hear Flynn has got a crush on someone at last!"

"Flynn had a crush on Cousin Kate long ago."

"Ah, yes, but that was purely romantic. Mrs. Paul wouldn't stand for any nonsense of that kind."

The colour rushed up into Bridie's face, and she demanded, her eyes flashing, "Aren't you ashamed to be talking like that of your own son, and that woman old enough to be his mother?"

Mike hoisted himself up into the saddle. "When you've got a crush on someone yourself, little one, we can discuss these matters; until then it's useless. For the last time, are you coming? If so, hop up behind and look sharp about it. . . ." He bent forward and patted the mare's neck. "Aisy now, girl, aisy! Dancin' about like a cat on hot bricks!"

Bridie told him with a choking violence, "I wouldn't come with you if you were the last person left alive in the whole wide world!" and turned and walked away.

Mike laughed and gave Jameel her head. The child was like her mother; she had a power of beauty in her when her eyes flashed with rage and the fine wild tide of colour beat up in her cheeks. . . .

When Bridie got back to the porch she could just make out the boat tied up to the island. There was no sign of its occupants.

A few minutes later she was cycling like mad down the avenue and out on to the Ballyrannon road. She rode into the town and out the other side

D

and along the 'sea-road' until she was opposite Bream Island. Then she
jumped off the bicycle, propped it up against the stone wall, and scrambled
down a low bank covered with grass and brambles to the shingly strand
below. Here she pulled off her shoes and dress and pushed them under a
dead, sea-whitened thorn-bush, then in her vest and knickers picked her way
across the stones and waded out into the water and began to swim.

There was a fairly heavy sea running, and by the time she reached the
island she was at the point of exhaustion. She pulled herself up on to the
rocks and lay there panting for a little while. Some children came along the
top of the low cliff and she called to them.

"Go up to Mrs. Doyle's house, quickly, and tell them Bridie Harrigan's
here and half dead from the sea, and to bring a shawl."

A few minutes later the children came back with several added to their
number, and with them Mrs. Doyle and Maureen and Patrick. Patrick
reached her first; he swooped down on her like a hawk on its prey and
lifted her up in his arms, crying wild distraught things to her, calling her his
bride and his darling and his dear, dear love, and she clung to him, turning
her face into his shoulder like a child, and burst suddenly into hysterical
weeping. His mother wrapped a shawl round her whilst he held her close
to him, and then he carried her up to the cabin, followed by his mother
and sister, and a procession of children and dogs and hissing geese.

When they had dried her, and wrung the water out of her hair, dressed
her in Maureen's clothes, and given her a sip or two of poteen to revive her,
and she sat in the sun outside the cabin, with Patrick at her side, holding her
hand, Bridie no longer felt anger or jealousy, or that curious, indefinable
fear which had sent her rushing in a frenzy to Patrick, as though for re
assurance and protection. It was very pleasant sitting there in the sun
warmed with the poteen, the centre of attraction, with the faithful, patient
Patrick gazing at her in loving anxiety, and she began to enjoy herself. She
told a pathetic story of her loneliness and unhappiness at the castle, her
brother preoccupied with his horse, her father with his writing, herself over
burdened with all the extra work she had to do for the paying-guests, and how
she had felt that she could not bear it any longer, and that if she did not get
to those who loved her she felt that her heart must surely break.

Mrs. Doyle's eyes filled with tears as she listened. "Poor wee childeen,"
she murmured, and Maureen declared that it was 'a terrible thing' to trea
a young girl so, and her the only daughter, and motherless, and why wouldn'
she be laving them all and coming to live with dacent folks, with hearts in
their breasts. . . .

Patrick watched Bridie's face, and listened to her, and wondered, and the
more he pondered the matter the less he was deceived. Bridie was putting
on an act now, but her wild weeping when he had picked her up had been
real enough. Something was working in her. He would never forget the
look on her face at the dance when she had missed Flynn and Mrs. Paul
It was as though all the blood had drained away from her heart. He, too
had been shocked and distressed by Flynn's disappearance with That One
and he was not prepared to stand by and see Bridie made unhappy in a
worthless cause. Connemara, after all, had stones and to spare. . . .

When he rowed her back up the Sound in the evening she told him

"Flynn and Mrs. Paul spent the afternoon on the island. It was why I had to swim out to you—they had the boat. I asked Daddy to send her away, but he doesn't care that she and Flynn have a crush on each other. They were going at the end of the month, but now they may never go !''

He said softly, "Ah, don't yez be worryin' yerself, Bridie, sure they'll go. We'll get rid of them. Lave it to me."

They looked at each other and smiled, and understood one another.

XVIII

THE following day, as soon as he had milked the goats and seen to the live-stock generally, Flynn raced into Ballyrannon on his bicycle and bought a large tin of bright blue paint and a small tin of white, and spent the rest of the morning down by the lake painting the boat. Until then it had never had a name; now he called it the *Kingfisher*, because the previous day he and Stephanie had seen the kingfishers along the lake and she had declared that their flashing brilliance against the dark sedge was something she would never forget. When the boat was painted blue as a kingfisher Stephanie should name it and launch it, and they would go again to the island. Now he had a sense of the summer stretched endlessly ahead, filled with happiness. He did not ask himself whether Stephanie loved him; it was sufficient that he loved her, and that all beauty and delight were concentrated in her; it was as though rousing his senses to active life she had completely drugged his intellect. Now when he went to lock Jameel up for the night nothing stirred in him at her eager whinny as he crossed the yard; where once he had gone to her to say goodnight, now he merely shut her up as he did the hens and ducks and goats. He caressed her velvety nose perfunctorily, impatient to have done with her, because every moment that he spent with her was so much time away from Stephanie. He no longer groomed her to excess to bring her muscles up; he no longer worked on the land for the satisfaction of it; he did now only what was strictly necessary, and even that he did with a sense of impatience. The fine weather continued, and it was as though the summer, long withheld, had suddenly broken into flower.

Philippa suffered intensely, as she suffered every time her darling Paulo became involved in a new love-affair, but this time her sufferings were intensified by her sense of Ballyrannon Castle as a prison. There was nothing to do and no one to talk to. She would take a book and go to some part of the gardens from which it was impossible to see the lake, and the blue-painted boat cleaving the dark green water, or tied up at the island, but it was never any good; she could not concentrate; between her and the written word came, always, the tormenting thought of Paulo and 'the Harrigan boy'. In any civilised part of the world she could have found forgetfulness at the pictures, or found relief in talking to people; but what could you do in this wilderness of stones and water ? If only Mike had been more human; but he was, she was well aware, merely cynically amused by what was happening. She had heard him assert so often in Paris and the South that any kind of experience was better than none, and that it was better to suffer than to feel nothing at all. She could only tell herself, resolutely, that nothing lasted for ever, or even long, and that one day they would arrive back at the Gare du Nord and know again the smell of strong French cigarettes, and garlic, and coffee, and drains, and know that they had come 'home' once more. In the meantime she struggled with Mr. Gerald Heard's *Social Substance of Religion*, and the more arid and obscure it seemed to her the greater the satisfaction in the struggle. As she wrote, grimly, in her diary at that time, the preservation of one's personal integrity was all that left to one. When dear foolish Paulo was satiated with this new, and alas worthless, romance, she should find her best friend, Philippa Bryce, unchanged by the chaotic interlude, but quietly pursuing intellectual and spiritual adventure. . . .

There was a day when Stephanie declared that she really must give Philippa some attention; she had neglected the poor girl for a week. Some nuns from a convent a little way out were having a sale of work at the Railway Hotel and she proposed to take Philippa down to it, and they would stay on and take their evening meal down there; it would be a change for everyone—and it was time, wasn't it, that Flynn took Jameel out himself. . . . He agreed, reluctantly, that she was right, but she must promise to come to him at night.

Stephanie laughed. "Wouldn't it be a good thing to make it a day of complete abstinence?" she said.

He said, firmly, "It would not."

She persisted, "But there'll be no moon tonight——"

"We don't need the moon. Promise me you'll come."

She promised. He had grown up a lot in these last few days, she thought, and the thought stirred her a little.

She kept her promise, and discovered that she no longer had a diffident, dreaming boy to deal with. She was late, because she had waited for Philippa to 'settle down' before slipping out of her room—but even so Philippa heard her go—and she had expected to find him full of romantic sadness and youthful yearning, instead of which she found him impatient and *intransigeant*. It was not at all how she had visualised their relationship; as she had seen it, he was always grateful, undemanding, and altogether manageable. You cannot confer favours upon someone who reproaches you for being late—instead of being grateful that you have come at all—or be magnanimous to someone who declares, almost brutally, that in another few minutes he would have given up waiting and descended upon you.

"Why, Flynn——" she cried, half laughing, half protesting. "What has come over you?"

He said, violently, "You have come over me!" and his mouth on hers prohibited argument.

Later, when she was leaving, she observed, suddenly, "Where is the picture of St. Anne?"

He told her, a little grimly, "She's face downwards in the drawer."

She smiled. "But you left the crucifix over the bed!"

He was startled. "What has that to do with it?"

It was her turn to be puzzled. "Everything, I should have thought. I should have expected to find it gone before the picture."

He said, simply, "I don't know what you mean. I took the picture down for two reasons—one, that it was given me by Bridie, and two, that it reminds me of someone I once loved."

"Your cousin?"

"Who else? There was never anyone but her."

"You're not in love with her any more?"

"One can't be in love with two people at a time."

He bent and kissed her lips, softly, and was suddenly filled with a terrible sadness. Until he had spoken the words aloud he had not realised what blasphemy there was in denying Cousin Kate.

When Stephanie had gone he went to the drawer and took out the picture and looked at it, steadily, for a long time, till his eyes were blinded by tears and he could no longer see it, and he had the sense of his heart swelling until it finally burst its bonds and broke, leaving him utterly disintegrated, with nothing but the chaos of his passion for Stephanie Paul storming within him.

2

Stephanie had barely entered her room, carrying her candle, before a shower of small stones suddenly rained through the open window, spattering to the floor like a heavy hail; several struck the glass, and one whizzed past her face and narrowly missed her. She gave a little scream and rushed from the room, and in that same moment Philippa rushed out of hers, so that they met in the corridor.

Thoroughly shaken, Stephanie flung herself into Philippa's arms. She was trembling violently. ·

"Stones!" she cried, on the edge of hysteria. "Someone is throwing stones in through the window—someone out there in the darkness—stoning me!"

The door of Mike's room opened and he came out carrying a small oil-lamp. He was wearing his old dressing-gown; his red hair stood on end, his blue eyes were bleary with sleep and confusion.

"What the divil is going on?" he demanded.

"Someone is throwing stones through Stephanie's window!" Philippa cried.

"The divil they are! Wait while I get my gun!"

He turned to go back into his room and then halted as Flynn came hurtling down the stairs.

"This is Bridie's work!" he shouted, "and, by God, I'll not stand for it! I'll put a bullet through every one of them! This is something she'd wish she'd never started!"

Mike stepped forward and blocked his way. "Ah, don't be a fool!" he commanded. "Sure, they're half a mile away by this time. There's nothing we can do."

Flynn was in such a fury that he was hardly aware that his father spoke. "Where's Bridie?" he stormed. "She's probably out there with them!"

He rushed down the corridor to her room and burst open the door.

Bridie had been lying trembling in her bed for the last hour or more, and when she heard the stones come through the window had buried her head under the clothes. She had seen Patrick in the town that morning and he had told her he had been waiting for the moon to wane and that she might expect 'a little disturbance' that night. She had listened with a plunging heart to the commotion that followed Mrs. Paul's scream and her flight from her room. She heard Flynn's accusation. Then there was the terrible moment when the door opened and he rushed into the room, blundered through the darkness to her bed, groped and found her and dragged her out.

"You'll pay for this!" he cried, and pulled her out into the dim light of the corridor, where their father still stood holding the oil-lamp, and Mrs. Paul in oyster satin clung to Philippa in camel-hair.

Bridie kicked and scratched and bit.

"Leave me alone!" she cried. "Leave me alone, I tell you! I don't know anything about it! You're hurting me!"

When she saw the others she struggled more wildly than ever to free herself.

"Make him leave me alone!" She began to sob, hysterically.

Mike stepped forward. "Leave her be," he urged, "leave her be!"

Flynn's eyes were blazing. "I'll not leave her be!" he shouted. "It's all her work, the same as the ceiling the other night! She wants to get Mrs. Paul out of the house, but, by God, it's herself will be going out!"

Mike handed the lamp to Philippa and went over to Flynn.

"Give over," he said sharply, and gripped Flynn's wrists. For a moment Flynn stood rigid with resistance; there was that momentary struggle of his own will against his father's, and Mike's won. Flynn had a sudden sense of everything in himself sagging; he loosed his grip on Bridie and leaned weakly against the wall. His face was grey, and wet with sweat.

Stephanie said, weakly, "I guess there's no point in us all standing here. We might as well get back to bed. I'll finish the night in with you, Philippa——"

"We'll all go down to the library and have a drink first," Mike said. "You all go on down—I'll see Bridie back to bed."

Bridie clung to him, burying her face in his dressing-gown.

"You'll all sit down there plotting to send me away!" she cried, "but I won't go, I tell you—I won't go!"

Mike, an arm round her shoulders, hugged her to him. "I promise you we'll do nothing of the kind."

Stephanie said in a hard voice, "There'll be no need, because we two will be going. Bridie wins, I guess!"

"Go on down, now," Mike urged. "We'll talk it over——"

He turned away with Bridie, and Stephanie looked at Flynn and gave him a wan smile and held out her hand to him.

"Let's go and have that drink," she said. "You look all washed-up——"

Flynn did not move. "I'd like to talk to you alone," he said. He regarded Philippa steadily. "D'you mind?" he said, and there was something so deadly in his tone that Philippa, already overwrought, crumpled up.

"If I'm not wanted," she almost whimpered, and looked appealingly at Stephanie.

Stephanie said, gently, "I think maybe Mike and Flynn and I had better have this out together," she said. "I'll be along presently——"

Flynn took the lamp from Philippa, and he and Stephanie went down the stairs and across the hall and into the library.

Stephanie flung herself down into the shabby arm-chair, leaning her head against the back and drawing her feet, in their absurd befeathered mules, up on to the seat.

"Oh, gee, what a night! Listen, honey, before your father gets back— Philippa and I will have to go. They'll be stoning us in the street next! What do you think started all this? Maybe we caused a scandal leaving the dance that night?"

He sat down on the table beside her chair, his hands hanging limply down between his knees.

"'Tis all Bridie's doing," he told her. "She threatened this the night we got back from the dance, but I didn't take her seriously——"

"But who did it? She wasn't out there——"

"There's a boy who's in love with her—she probably put him up to it. There were probably several of them——" He buried his face in his hands for a moment. "I'm so terribly, terribly sorry," he said. "Everything has been so wonderful, and now suddenly all this ugliness——"

She reached out a hand from folds of satin that seemed to him the colour of moonlight and laid it on his knee.

"Don't fret, honey," she said, softly. "Philippa and I will go, but why shouldn't you join us in a more civilised place—in Paris?"

He looked up, startled, stared at her a moment, incredulously, then demanded, a little breathlessly, "D'you mean that?"

She smiled. "Why not?" That soft provocative sing-song . . .

He said, with sudden bitterness, "I never thought I should want to leave Ireland. I never thought I could hate Ireland. . . ."

The door opened and Mike said, "Didn't you, by God? Then it's time you did!"

Stephanie said, "I was suggesting that he should join Philippa and me in Paris—in a week or two's time. It would do him good—complete his education."

Mike gave her a quick look, and the old sardonic smile.

"Yes," he said. "Sure, it would do that!"

But the first wonder was already ebbing from Flynn on a cold tide of practicalities.

"It's no use talking about it," he said. "In the first place I've no money, and in the second place I couldn't leave everything here—who would look after things? There's the kitchen garden and the livestock and Jameel——"

Mike went over to the cupboard and brought out whisky and glasses.

"There are some people," he observed, "who if you offered them the keys of heaven on a golden plate would suddenly remember they had to wait for the washing to come back. . . ."

He poured out the whisky and handed round the glasses, then came and sat on the table next to Flynn.

"As to the money," he went on, "you've got a couple of goats in kid, and a fine litter of young pigs, and next week you've got the August fair coming along and the chance of good prices."

"And Bridie would look after Jameel," Stephanie suggested.

"Of course." Mike drained his glass, and refilled it. He added, "By the way, Bridie swears she knows nothing about tonight's little affair, but I suppose she does?"

Flynn said violently, "Of course she does! She hinted at something of the kind the night of the dance. She's jealous of Mrs. Paul the same as she was jealous of Cousin Kate, and then of Jameel!"

Mike looked thoughtfully at his glass. "'Twould be better for her if you went away for a wee while," he said.

Flynn protested, "But what's to happen to her? You were talking of going abroad again yourself after the Dublin Show—we can't leave her here with no one but old Tante Emma."

"She can go to your Aunt Chris."

"And Jameel?"

"Ah, sure, she can go to Dublin too! Aren't there plenty of stables will take her at livery?"

"And have her hacked to pieces—her mouth ruined!"

Mike said, patiently, "We can put her at full livery at some dacent place and have Katie keep an eye on her. There's Freda Moran's—there'd be no one riding her then except Freda herself, and Katie on Sundays if she'd a mind to——"

"I'll have to think about it," Flynn said.

Stephanie crossed one slender leg over the other, smoothing the folds of moonlight satin along her thigh. "Does it take so much thinking over, honey?" she drawled. "Because if it does, then maybe it's not worth thinking about at all."

Flynn looked at her, despairingly. "I want to go—of course I want to go, but I can't suddenly uproot myself—not care about anything here any more——"

Mike gave a short laugh. "It's the only way, I assure you!" He refilled Stephanie's glass. "It might be best if you and Philippa went off tomorrow," he told her. "We don't want any more trouble. I don't know who's behind this night's work, but if it's anything to do with Bridie then it's Pat Doyle—that young feller you saw her dancing with—and they're a pretty tough lot, those Bream Islanders. If you stay on they'll be at it again, and that'll mean Flynn and meself out after them with guns, and the guards up here, and the divil's own business." He smiled at her. "You wouldn't like it, lady," he assured her.

"I'd hate it," Stephanie agreed. "I never did care for all that Wild West stuff."

"Well, but this is the Wild West," Mike said, "so it might be a good thing if you and Philippa took a car right through to Galway tomorrow to avoid any kind of a send-off from here. Flynn could follow in about a fortnight—he'll have to arrange things here and wait for the August fair."

He filled up his glass again. "Stoned out is what you are, lady. So much for the romantic Celtic Twilight and the glamour of the West, eh?"

"You get hooliganism everywhere, I guess," Stephanie said, resolutely.

Mike swallowed his drink at one gulp. "This isn't hooliganism, lady, it's Jansenism! But not being a student of religion you'd not know about that."

Flynn said, impatiently, in reply to Stephanie's questioning look from one to the other of them, "He means that the Catholic Church had its Calvin—Jansen—and that the moral narrowness of the Irish is not Catholic but Jansenist——"

"And you'll gather from the young man's tone that he doesn't support this view! Personally I'm not debating it now. I'm going to bed! You two had better leave Jansenism alone and talk over what you're going to do. God bless!"

He shuffled over to the door in his trodden-down slippers and went out.

When the door had closed on his father Flynn came and sat on the arm of Stephanie's chair and said in a low, urgent voice, "You know how much I want to join you in Paris, darling. But the moment I begin to think about it all sorts of things begin tearing at me, the way you'd think they had hands! This place was a wilderness when I took it over a few years ago, and if I go away now it'll all go back. I set out to do something, and to go would be leaving it unfinished—'twould be a sort of betrayal. . . ."

He got up and poured himself out another drink. It was easier to talk when the drink worked in you. He swallowed the neat whisky at a gulp, and his head swam a little, but the words seemed to slip easily out of that lightness in his brain.

He came back and sat on the arm of the chair again. "I never told you, but it was my mother who made everything here. When she was here the gardens of Ballyrannon Castle were the wonder for miles around. She had the daffodils planted on the island, and fairy-rings of wild iris in the estate fields. The daffodils and the irises are the only things that have been true to her; they come up year after year. I wanted to get everything looking again as she had had it—as a sort of memorial. I had a fantasy that one day she might come back." He paused a moment, then added, "She was very beautiful."

Stephanie took his hand and smiled at him. "Darling, I'm sure she was, but isn't it time you were through with all that mother-complex? She isn't likely to come back after all these years—you don't even know if she's still alive! And you're much too busy with your goats and pigs and hens to keep the gardens as she kept them—they probably had a whole fleet of gardeners in those days! And this fantasy gets you nowhere—whereas Paris would get you a whole lot further along the road of real living. You remember that talk we had the night of the dance?"

"I do. There isn't anything I could ever forget about that night."

She put up a hand and brushed back the lock of hair from his forehead with the familiar caressive gesture. She said, softly, "You can't stay here eating your heart out when I'm gone——"

He took her hand and kissed the palm.

"I can't imagine life without you, any more."

"Well then—I guess it's settled."

He laughed suddenly, and pulled her up out of the chair and into his arms.

"I guess it is!"

She had a way of making everything very simple at the last.

XIX

THERE was no communal breakfast at the castle, and no fixed breakfast hour. Mike invariably lay in bed till the post came, and it depended on the state of his health whether he broke his fast with a cup of black coffee, a cup of tea, or a 'prairie oyster'. When Tante Emma brought up the mail—or came up to report that the postman had passed, or had called but there was nothing for him—she took his instructions as to his requirements. Flynn was always the first up; he would rake down the kitchen fire, bring in fresh turf, build the fire up, take a couple of large buckets to the spring for fresh water, fill the large black kettle and balance it amongst the glowing turfs, then attend to his livestock, let out the hens and ducks, milk the goats. When he got back he usually found Tante Emma about, making herself some tea, impatiently blowing at the fire with bellows. Bridie came down at all hours, sometimes soon after Flynn, sometimes long after Tante Emma, and helped herself to whatever tea was left in the pot, however long it had been made, whether it was black as night from long brewing, or pale as ditchwater from having been filled up several times already. 'The ladies' had their breakfast on a tray in Mrs. Paul's room. At first Philippa prepared it herself, cutting the bread-and-butter wafer-thin, lightly boiling the eggs, carefully timing them by her wrist-watch, making coffee—procured by post from Dublin—and generally 'riling' Tante Emma so much with her fussings and refinements that she finally revolted and refused to allow her to set foot in the kitchen. After that Philippa was forced to announce outside the kitchen door when she and her lady were ready to break their fast, and Tante Emma would stump upstairs with it in her own time, the tea stewed, the eggs hard as rocks, the bread cut in chunks. If Flynn happened to be about when it was ready he would take up the tray, but he was usually out on the land or grooming Jameel by the time Philippa came down.

But the morning after the stone-throwing episode everything was different. Mike got up 'in the middle of the night', that is to say at eight o'clock, and shuffled along the corridor in his old dressing-gown and his slippers like dried red fish, and first got Tante Emma up and then Bridie.

He stood at the foot of his daughter's bed and looked down at her as she struggled up out of sleep. The little divil, his heart approved her, the pretty wicked little divil. She sat up with her bright hair all over the place and her young pointed breasts thrusting through the ugly calico nightgown, and her small fine brown hands—so like Kitty's, the lightest hands that ever held reins—clutching the grubby bedclothes, and something in himself flowed out to her.

When she was finally free of the cobwebs of sleep, she stared at him a moment, then grinned.

"You look like Old Nick," she said.

He bowed. "Thanks for the compliment, little one, but I am in fact an angel of annunciation. The ladies are leaving Ballyrannon as soon as they can get out of it. If you were to get up and get dressed and go on your bicycle, now, you'd catch Mr. Foyne at home, maybe, and wouldn't it be a fine thing if he took them all the way to Galway and saw them safely into the Dublin train this very day?"

Bridie's eyes sparkled. "Are they going for sure?"

"For sure if you can find a car to transport them in!"

She flung off the clothes and leapt out of bed.

"I'll find a car if I have to cycle all over County Galway!"

When her father had gone she tore off her nightgown, pulled on knickers and dress, thrust her feet into her old flattened rubber shoes, scraped a comb through her hair, then rushed out of the room and down the stairs. That the enemy were on the run was too good to be true. Her heart was like a singing bird in her breast.

She burst into the kitchen, then stopped short. Flynn was leaning against the table with a mug of tea in his hand. He gave her one glance, then went out, taking his tea with him. Bridie made a face at his back. Tante Emma, kneeling beside the fire and puffing at it with a decrepit pair of bellows, looked up.

"It seems the ladies are for lavin' us this very day," she observed.

Bridie took a mug off the dresser and helped herself to tea. "I'm going in for Foyne's car in a minute," she said, and then, "Did Flynn say anything about last night?"

"Ah, he did then, and whoever threw them stones last night into her lady-ship's room, God help him when Flynn Harrigan does be findin' him!"

"Just a few corner-boys," Bridie said, hacking bread, "and wouldn't you think Flynn would be glad we'll be having the place to ourselves at last, after all these months?"

The old woman went on working the bellows. "He's a young man," she said, "and she's not young, That One, but neither would anyone be calling her old, and maybe there's a power of fascination for a young man in a woman like that."

Bridie tossed her head. "I call her skinny!"

"Maybe, but 'tis not always beauty puts a spell upon a man."

"What is it then?" Bridie stuffed her mouth with bread-and-butter.

"Ah, sure, 'tis something in a person—a person's smile, maybe, or way of walking, or sitting quiet. Maybe with That One 'tis her soft sing-songy way of speaking, or the cool look she has to her, the way you'd think on a hot day, or in wind and rain, she was straight out of a silk-lined box! And isn't it a terrible thing that anyone should be stonin' the craythur out of the place?"

Bridie jumped up, brushing the crumbs from her lap.

"Don't be pretending, Tante Emma. You're as glad as I am that she's going! You know you hate the sight of her, and of the other one even more!"

"God forgive me, so I do, but all the same 'tis a terrible thing, and Master Flynn's heart turned to a stone itself, God help him!"

Bridie said, lightly, "He'll get over it."

The old woman abandoned the bellows and came to the table. She said, reaching for the loaf and tucking it under her arm to cut a slice from it, "Sure he'll get over it. In time we all get over everything, even our days on this earth——"

Bridie went out, her own heart singing like a cageful of linnets, and they with their eyes blinded.

Stephanie left Philippa to finish packing and went out in search of Flynn. She found him, as she had expected, in the stables, grooming Jameel. He looked up at the sound of her step in the yard and ceased his energetic brushing and hissing and pushed open the half-door to admit her.

He was very pale, she noticed ; it made him look grey under his tan.

She smiled, and said softly, "It's not goodbye, honey. We'll be together again in a week or two. In Paris—think of that !"

His shirt was open at the neck, and she put up a hand and fingered the blessed medallion lying below the hollow of his throat, but this time he did not seize her hand to kiss the palm. Strongly upon him was the feeling that from now until they met again everything would be merely something happening in a bad dream. There was this terrible greyness and numbness . . .

It was no use, he knew, trying to tell her—It's terrible for me to go from here ; everything in me belongs here ; but terrible for me to remain without you.

He could only say, greyly, "I can't think of anything except that tonight your room will be empty, and that I'll never again listen for your step on the turret stair."

"Don't be morbid, darling. There are stairs in Paris, too."

She brought sugar cubes out of her jacket pocket and fed them to Jameel, then stood leaning against the mare's warm flank. Flynn sighed, and was silent for a moment, then asked, "What time are you leaving ?"

"Any minute now, I guess. Your father sent Bridie in for Mr. Foyne's car half an hour ago. I must go back and help Philippa finish packing."

Flynn said, "I'll not come round when the car comes. We'll say goodbye here. Only I daren't kiss you in that fine white blouse and me in these dirty old clothes smelling of stables and covered with horsehair !"

Stephanie had, in fact, been pondering that very problem, but a gesture was called for, so she laughed and flung her arms round his neck and pressed her mouth to his. To her astonishment there was no answer in him, and when she had kissed him he turned away, leaning against Jameel, one arm flung out over her back. There was a smear of lipstick across his mouth.

He said, helplessly, "You'll write from Dublin——"

"Of course, darling, and from London, and you have my address in Paris." She hesitated, then added, "You won't be unhappy, will you ?"

He straightened himself with a sudden abrupt gesture, picked up his brushes from a table littered with harness.

"I won't be anything till I'm with you again."

She hesitated for a second more. His deadness defeated her. She had visualised a wild, impassioned farewell, full of a delicious exciting sadness. She was a little piqued, and there was nothing left to say but, "Well—I guess I'll be going."

When the half-door swung to behind her she looked back, but he had already resumed his brushing and hissing.

He did not know whether it was a long or a short time after that that he heard the car come up the drive and swing round on to the gravel before the main entrance.

He heard his father's voice, and Tante Emma's, and Philippa's nasal twang, and if there was Stephanie's musical sing-song in the confusion of voices and slamming doors he did not know. He only knew that when the car turned and drove back down the avenue its wheels ran over his heart.

He did not come into the house at mid-day ; he had no desire to eat, and a great desire not to see Bridie. In the afternoon he took Jameel out over the springy turf of the bog towards the blue range of the Twelve Pins. He rode her at a gentle canter, and the even rhythm set something flowing in him again, pride and pleasure in the sensitive responsiveness of his horse, aware-ness of the dense blueness of the hills, the rich blackness of the peat stacks, the luminous whiteness of the cabins in the soft diffused sunlight of late summer, the toning of golden seaweed on brown rock, and the old deep love of Connacht released in him.

It was evening when he rode back along the Lough Head road ; the west was an arc of gold, as though the day-long sunshine, retreating from the earth, had been drawn up into the sky, invading it like a gold fire. The belt of trees at the far end of the lake was black and strange, and wild duck flew over with a sundown urgency in their wild cries and rushing wings. The bog-pools reflected the sky's amber, and fuchsia hedges, darkly crimson all day, were a bright clear scarlet in the fading light. There was that brief interval in which everything stood out in a new intensity before the dusk closed in and blurred outlines and colours. You could paint it, Flynn thought, but you could not capture its essential quality in words, that sense of the light intensified with the withdrawal of the sun, and of every rock and stone and flower and tree, all colours and all contours, made luminous in a brilliant twilight. You could make a poem of your awareness of it, but not of that strange soft brilliance itself.

Back at the castle, he rode Jameel over to the water-trough in the stable-yard, then dismounted. As he did so Bridie came staggering out of the forage shed with a truss of hay, only her clasping arms and her old white canvas shoes visible. He relieved her with a curt, "Here, I'll take that."

She said, as they crossed the yard together, "I thought I'd lend a hand as it's getting late."

He mumbled into the hay, "There's no need."

She followed him into the loose-box, but he deposited the hay and came out without speaking to her again. When he returned with Jameel she was forking over the straw, bedding-down for the night.

"I've done the milking," she told him.

Unsaddling, he said, "Nothing you can say or do now can make any difference. I'm going from here after the August fair."

She rested on her fork and stared at him.

"Where are you going?"

"To Paris—at Mrs. Paul's invitation."

He saw the colour drain out of her face, and knew a sense of exultation. This round, at least, was to him.

She said after a moment, in a half-whisper, "You wouldn't dare !"

He carried the saddle over to a saddle-horse. "You'll see," he said.

Bridie went on forking the straw. She said, with an effort, "I'll leave you to make up the feed. We'll wait to say the rosary till you have it finished out here."

She went out into the warm dusk of the yard, walking slowly because of the heavy, painful beating of her heart. Over and over again she said to herself, "He'd never dare! He'd never dare!"

2

After that Bridie made no more attempts to reinstate herself with Flynn. They all three ate now in the kitchen with Tante Emma, but there was none of the old easy-going family talk. Flynn was silent and morose, never speaking unless he was spoken to, and then replying as briefly as possible. Tante Emma abandoned her first bantering efforts to close the breach between brother and sister, and when Mike was there he took refuge in the *Irish Press* or in his mail. It was a relief when Flynn did not come in for meals. He sometimes ate outside at mid-day, on the pretext that he did not want to stop for lunch, and he took to going out in the evenings. He usually went on his bicycle in the direction of Ballyrannon, and it was assumed that he spent his evenings in various bars, but in point of fact they were mostly occupied discussing market prices of livestock with farmers and smallholders.

At other times he went no further afield than the monastery, where he sat in talk with Brother Francis in the common-room, pored over old Gaelic books in the library, or sat in meditation in the tiny chapel, his spirit heavy with the weight of sin which he felt himself unable to confess. Bridie, her small sins confessed, could go triumphantly up to the altar for Holy Communion—or did she consider that she had no need of confession? He who had every need, both spiritual and emotional, knelt with the unconfessed, and sat for long hours prayerless in the monastery chapel, laved about by a peace he could no longer receive.

When the young moon hung low in the sky he took the boat out, bright in its gay blue paint, newly painted in Stephanie's honour. "And name you *Kingfisher*," he could hear her say, as he pushed the boat out into the water, and almost feel the vibration of her low husky laugh on the still air.

He would rest on his oars and let the boat drift, and his thoughts with it —that were not so much thoughts as an endless reverie. The burnished gold of the young moon above the lake, and the lost cry of a night-bird skimming low over the water, moved him as always with the sense of sadness in beauty, but now the sadness was intensified, because though his physical self remained, in spirit he had already left it all. In arranging for the disposal of his livestock he had said goodbye to Connacht, and soon the weeds would spring again on the land he had tended with such love for so long. He would not see the silver splendour of the full moon on the lake, that great silver flood that made the castle romantic as something in an opera, and the monastery white and mysterious as a Spanish villa. It would all lie dreaming there in the milk-soft light, the castle, the monastery, the lake, the distant hills, the bogs and boulders, the broken stone walls and the little twisted roads, and he would see the moon, but not its light upon all that he loved . . . but only upon the face of the woman who was drawing him away from it all, as she drew him from the peace and anchorage of Holy Church. There should be exultation in that thought of moonlight on the sleeping face of the beloved, but he knew only the sense of inner weeping and inevitability.

He would leave behind, unfinished, everything that he had begun—even Jameel, the beautiful, with her quick intelligence, her sensitive response, her gay spiritedness; even his work with her would be left unfinished. He had, strongly, the feeling that once he had gone he would never return. He could not have said why he felt this; it had nothing to do with reason or any vision of the future; he only knew that he had, deeply, this sense of final farewell, of the complete sacrifice of everything he had ever loved or known to the spell that was upon him, and its relentless compulsion. He could not see into the future; he could not imagine a city called Paris, or any kind of life he might lead there. He only knew that he had to go, and that at the end of the journey was a peace he could find nowhere else and which alone could make life tolerable. So much had fallen away, it seemed to him now—Cousin Kate, Bridie, the fine sweep of that first creative urge dedicated to the memory of his mother—who, too, had gone away and never returned. . . . So much had fallen away, like last spring's blossoms, and all the yesterdays of childhood summers and the first wild sweet dreams of idealised love; it all fell away, but it went on swirling round you, like dead leaves round your feet, so that in whatever happened after you never quite got clear, and there was sadness in it.

One morning in the town he came upon Patrick standing in the market-place with other island fishermen, pollock laid out on a strip of sacking on the ground at his feet. He went up to him, and Patrick smiled his warm friendly smile.

But Flynn did not smile. He said, "I want to know—had you any hand in that stoning affair at the castle the other night?"

Patrick said, still smiling, "And why should I have had any hand in it, man dear?"

"Because you're in love with Bridie, and you know that Bridie hated Mrs. Paul and wanted her to go."

"Sure that would be a very good reason, so it would, but faith it never came into me mind at all, and herself must be thinking the less of me because of it!"

Flynn said, "You're a good liar, Patrick, as good a liar as Bridie herself, and that's saying something! Last week if I'd had my gun with me when we met I'd have put a bullet through you, but now it doesn't matter any more, because I'm going away—and that'll mean you'll not be seeing Bridie either, for she'll be going too, though not with me, thank God."

Patrick no longer smiled. "For any wrong I've done you, Flynn, God forgive me. Some might say that to rid a man of something evil in his life was not to sin against him."

Flynn said violently, " 'Twas nothing to do with you!"

Patrick replied equally violently, his colour rising, " 'Twas everything to do with me when it was making Bridie miserable, the way she wasn't sleeping at nights, and coming out to us weeping and crying, and washed up from the sea like a piece of wreckage, with wild talk on her!"

"It's the end of friendship between us," Flynn said, "and a black curse on you from this out!"

He turned and strode away, his heart beating furiously. One of the Bream Island fishermen standing by Patrick called out after him, "And a curse on you, Flynn Harrigan—bad cess to ye!"

Patrick crossed himself, and prayed wildly, "Mother of God, don't let them send Bridie away—don't let them send her away !''

Because nothing more was said about Flynn's departure Bridie believed that he had been merely making threats.   A letter came for him from Dublin, and by the scent of it it could only be from Mrs. Paul.   Bridie was for steaming it open before giving it to him, but Tante Emma would not hear of it, and delivered it herself into Flynn's hands.   He went a little pale when she handed it to him, and did not open it until he was up in his room.

It was written on Shelbourne Hotel notepaper and it began, 'My own darling Flynn'.   It was somehow more than he had dared to hope for, and his head reeled for a moment.   The letter itself was not particularly personal ; she and Philippa were having a swell time in Dublin ; they had been to the Abbey and the Gate and had seen his cousin in *The Silver Tassie*, which they hadn't cared for ; his cousin hadn't had much to do and hadn't done it particularly effectively.   They were looking forward to the Horse Show next week.   They had had some pleasant picnics out at Glendalough and in the Wicklow Hills, where half the literary and artistic set appeared to have cottages or shacks of some kind.   They proposed only to pass through London, as they were homesick for Paris.   She would write him from there. She concluded with a line from *Antony and Cleopatra*, 'I hold you to my heart and give you to the gods' ; and then there was a large straggling S and a wavy line straggling from it for her signature.

He had a sense of desolation, momentarily, then consoled himself with the thought that the mere fact that she had written was proof that she thought of him.   She had written 'My own darling', and 'I hold you to my heart', and that she loved him was clearly implicit in this.   Her perfume on the notepaper was an emanation of her presence once more in the turret room, quickening his heart, flooding flesh and spirit with an intolerable urgency. After a week her room still held this perfume, and her bed was as she had last left it, for Tante Emma saw no reason to attend to a bed that was not wanted.   It would be time enough to 'see to it' when it was next wanted, which, if God were good, would not be for a very long time.   The room had no intimate memories for Flynn, and after Stephanie had gone he had no urge to go into it until the perfume on her letter sent him there, pursuing the fading scent as an evocation of her spirit.   He took to slipping in during the afternoons, when Bridie was out of the way, and last thing at night, on his way up to bed.   He never stayed more than a minute or two ; he would stand with his back against the door and his eyes closed, breathing the atmosphere of the room, that was wholly of her, his whole being given to her, as the spirit is given in prayer.

On fair-day he hired a donkey-cart to transport his ducks and hens to the town, and not until Bridie saw the crates being loaded up did she realise that he was serious about going away.   She stood in the yard watching, and all the colour drained out of her face.   When Flynn took the donkey's bridle, and drove the goats and the sow before him, she stood watching the procession going down the avenue, and when it was out of sight, beyond the dark patch of the ilex trees, she rushed indoors and flung herself into Tante Emma's lap.

"He means it !" she cried wildly, "He means it !   He's after taking every single thing to the market !"

The old woman laid her hands on the girl's head.

"Aye, he manes it, God help him!" she said, sorrowfully, "and there isn't anything anyone could say could stop him now, not even if Katherine O'Donal herself were to come walking in at that door with a smile bright as the morning! 'Twould make no more difference than a cup of water on a burnin' furze bush!"

Bridie looked up suddenly, and there was a wild light in her eyes.

"If Cousin Kate were to walk in now, and she smiling, he would forget That One as though he had never set eyes on her!"

She sprang up. "He'll not go!" she cried. "You'll see—he'll not be going!"

"Wisht now, alanna," the old woman pleaded. "Ye'll be up to no more mischief. There's been trouble enough. His mind is made up now, and Mr. Foyne's car is ordered to take him to the railway station in the morning."

"You'll see," Bridie repeated, and though Tante Emma called after her, she ran out.

She could not see clearly ahead. She could see only that unless something happened to stop him Flynn would leave for Dublin in the morning. If Cousin Kate were suddenly to arrive she was convinced he would not go. . . . But Cousin Kate had quarrelled with him, and in any case she could not leave the theatre. But if she were to send a telegram saying that she was in Galway and was coming out to Ballyrannon the next day, then he would wait for her. It ought to be possible to get a telegram sent from Galway in her name. Beyond that Bridie could not think. Mr. Foyne's car was ordered for Flynn in the morning, and unless something happened between now and then he would go away in it. If only he could be stopped from leaving in the morning, after that anything might happen, and there was only this one thing would stop him. . . . She hurtled down the avenue on her bicycle and out on to the Ballyrannon road.

It was impossible to cycle right into the town on fair-days, the streets being blocked with cattle and sheep, and she left her bicycle at Farrell-the weaver's and continued on foot up the road and over the low stone-walled bridge into the broad market-street. Just beyond the bridge she saw Flynn standing with the goats, but he was deep in conversation with an old woman and he did not see her. She manœuvred her way through the congested street, rubbing shoulders with the little black Connemara bullocks, dodging between frightened sheep that ran in all directions, skidding in trampled cow-dung, saying good-morning to the various people who greeted her and agreeing that it was a grand day, and finally came to the post-office. As always on fair-day, it was full of old shawled women drawing pensions and cashing postal orders, Bridie pushed her way through and got to the writing-place with the row of telegram-form boxes above it. She extracted a form, picked up the blunt stump of pencil fastened with a chain and wrote out a wire to Flynn Harrigan, Ballyrannon, Co. Galway. Then she wrote the message already composed in her mind:

Arrived Galway today coming Ballyrannon tomorrow evening.

She signed it 'Kate'.

When she left the post-office she went up behind the town by an alley-way and along the backs of the houses to avoid being seen on her way to the station. She arrived half an hour before the Galway train was due to leave, but there were plenty of people waiting, and on the platform crates of live hens and young pigs and a great squawking and squealing. She hung about round the booking-office listening for a suitable person to ask for a ticket to Galway. Everyone seemed to be going to places along the line—Recess, Oughterard, Marm Cross, and no one right through. Then a young priest asked for a ticket to Galway, but she did not feel she could ask him, nor the rolling, red-faced man who was the next to ask for a through ticket. For one reason or another the few who were going right through were unsuitable for Bridie's purpose, and the train was already standing steaming in the station before she summoned up the courage to ask a tall gaunt-looking man who wore a shiny blue suit and a dusty bowler hat and carried a shabby suitcase. She approached him as he left the booking-office.

"Excuse me, but I wonder would you do me a small favour in Galway City?"

He looked down at her and asked doubtfully, "Is it a letter you're wanting posting there?"

" 'Tis a telegram I'm wanting sending," she told him.

"Sure, there's a telegraph office in this town itself," he pointed out.

Bridie reddened, but persisted, " 'Tis very important it should be sent from Galway, and here is half a crown will cover the cost of it and buy your honour a drink for your trouble."

She thrust the telegram form and the half-crown into his hand.

"God's blessing on you if you will do this service for one in great trouble," she said earnestly.

Her small face was so anxious in its pleading that Mr. Doherty, who had had a bad day in Ballyrannon, unable to interest any of the shops in any of his 'lines', and was wondering where the next drink was coming from, and he with a thirst on him enough for a dozen men, accepted the half-crown gratefully and gave his solemn promise that the wire should be sent immediately on his arrival in Galway City, 'and let not yourself be worrying'.

Nevertheless Bridie worried for the rest of the day and could not sleep at night for worrying. Over and over again she worked it out in her mind that the train would get in about six o'clock, and if the wire was sent off immediately, say at six-thirty, it would probably be received at Ballyrannon post-office after they had closed at seven o'clock. Then it should be sent up first thing in the morning. As it was sure to be known that Flynn had ordered Foyne's car to take him to the station, the telegram would probably be sent up by Mr. Foyne himself—unless anyone else was going out along the Lough Head road before then. . . . Her thoughts went round in circles. Supposing the wire did not arrive in time, and Flynn left . . . But if it arrived in time, and he waited, and the Galway train came in in the evening, and Cousin Kate not on it, what then? Wild thoughts of telephoning Aunt Chris and telling her that Flynn was going to Dublin en route for Paris, and that he must be stopped, and that this could only be done by Cousin Kate coming out at once, went round and round in her head.

When she finally slept she dreamed that Mr. Foyne arrived with the car and she ran out on to the porch and he got out from his driver's seat and said, "I've brought your cousin." Then he opened the other door of the car and helped someone out, but it was not Cousin Kate but Stephanie. She came towards Bridie smiling, but it was not any smile that she had ever seen on Mrs. Paul's face, but something quite horrible, utterly evil, so that Bridie wanted to cry out, but the sounds choked in her throat and no words would come, and she wanted to turn and run, but was rooted to the spot. . . . She wakened sobbing and crying, her heart pounding, and her body wet with sweat.

It was night still, and the moon stared in at the window. She sat up in bed, trying to shake off her dream, but the nightmare sense of evil clung to her. Still sobbing, she knelt up on her pillow and took the crucifix down off the wall above her bed and locking her fingers round it began to pray. . . .

XX

THE telegram arrived in the morning, not by Mr. Foyne, but by a small boy on a very large and heavy and rusty bicycle. As he came clanking up the avenue Flynn crossed the stable-yard, having, as he believed, just finished grooming Jameel for the last time.

When he took the telegram and saw that it was addressed to him he had a sense of the blood rushing to his head. It could only be from Stephanie. Perhaps it was to ask him if he could join her at once in Dublin. If that was so they would be together that night. . . .

When he read the wire he felt stunned. He fumbled in his jacket pocket and gave the waiting boy a few coppers, then read the wire again. Cousin Kate had been so remote from his thoughts lately that the thought of her in Galway and coming out to Ballyrannon in the evening of that very day was a shock; he had to accustom himself to the idea. His heart quickened. Would he run to meet her waiting in the dark shadow of the ilex trees as before? Would she smile her forgiveness and take his hand and say in her warm lovely voice, full of a soft laughter, "Flynn darlin'—darlin' Flynn!"?

He crushed the telegram into his pocket. That he would send Mr. Foyne and his car away when they arrived went without saying. One did not go from a place when Cousin Kate was coming into it. His heart felt suddenly light and gay. He ran into the house and into the kitchen where Tante Emma and Bridie were breakfasting. His face was alight.

"Cousin Kate is in Galway and she's coming here this evening!" he cried.

The colour rushed into Bridie's face and she bent down and untied and retied the lace of her canvas shoe. Tante Emma heaved herself up out of her chair and went over to the fire to place on it sods it had no need of.

"Glory be to God," she muttered. "I thought 'twas in Dublin itself she was!"

"Perhaps the company's come out to Galway," Flynn said. "Whatever it is, isn't it the most wonderful news? When Mr. Foyne comes I'll tell him to meet the Galway train this evening and bring her here. I wonder would we be able to find a nice chicken for supper?" He looked eagerly from one to the other. " 'Tis only a week off my birthday, and we'll make a party of it like we did last time!''

He sat down at the table and Tante Emma put the teapot in front of him and threw some slices of bacon into the pan and balanced it on the fire.

Flynn poured himself out tea and said thoughtfully, as he stirred, "Wouldn't it have been a terrible thing if the telegram had come after I'd left for Dublin? If she's going to be staying in Galway I shall put off going whilst she's there. We could all go in and see her act, and perhaps she'll be able to come out here again. . . ."

The kitchen filled with the good smell of the frying bacon, and Bridie stood opposite Tante Emma and watched the rashers sizzling, and her mind went round and round like a rat in a trap. Something had to happen by the evening. But what? Perhaps another telegram from Cousin Kate saying that she had been held up and couldn't get away till the end of the week. But how—how? Perhaps if she put this to Flynn in the evening, that Cousin Kate had been held up, he would stay on, waiting. If he could be kept waiting long enough for Cousin Kate perhaps That One would get tired of waiting for him in Paris?

Tante Emma put the bacon on a plate and set it in front of Flynn. He said, spreading mustard along the edge of the plate, "We must have some roses on the table this evening, like we did before—yellow roses, and some candles. . . . Cousin Kate hasn't seen Jameel yet. Perhaps we'll do our circus act for her benefit, eh, Bridie?"

"Perhaps." Bridie turned away from the fire. "Perhaps she won't be able to get away from the theatre after all."

"Won't be able to get away? What on earth gives you that idea? Why would she be sending us a telegram if she couldn't get away? If that's what you're hoping for I'm afraid you're going to be disappointed."

Bridie tossed her head and went out. Tante Emma poured herself out another cup of tea and let it get cold at her elbow. She sat staring at the fire, so troubled of spirit that it took all her concentration not to rock to and fro and groan aloud. Jesu, Mary and Joseph, what was to happen now? She could see no way out of the tangle Bridie had created.

When he had breakfasted Flynn went out on Jameel, his heart singing because the evening of that day held the promise of Cousin Kate, and because she had given him this sweet sign of forgiveness.

He came in at mid-day and joined Tante Emma and Bridie in the kitchen for the mid-day meal. Half-way through the meal Mike came down in his dressing-gown. He carried the *Irish Press* and his opened letters. He was unshaven and bleary-eyed. There was always heavy drinking in the town on fair-days, and as usual he had, in his own words, been 'in at the death'.

He said now, cheerfully, "I've changed my mind, Tante Emma, I think maybe I could eat something after all——''

He sat down, and Flynn announced, "Cousin Kate is in Galway— I had a wire this morning. She's coming out here this evening! It's why I'm not gone to Dublin."

Mike regarded his son with an effort, the hangover still pressing heavily down over his eyes.

"Sure, I was forgetting you were going at all! What was it you were saying about your Cousin Kate?"

"She's coming here this evening, from Galway. She must be playing there—or going to."

Mike said, "Perhaps it's having such an outsize in hangovers, but I don't see how she can broadcast from the Gate Theatre tonight in *The Silver Tassie* if she's to be here——"

"Who says she's going to broadcast tonight?"

"There's a letter from your Aunt Chris telling me the hour and minute and bidding us beg, borrow or steal a wireless set so that we can listen to the great genius of Katherine O'Donal, and it's in the day's paper——"

Bridie said quickly, "Perhaps it's her understudy will be broadcasting —maybe she left for Galway after Aunt Chris wrote——"

Mike held his head in his hands. "Maybe. If anyone's interested, Mrs. Paul's radio hasn't gone back to Foyne's yet . . . Och, it's a hair of the dog I'm needing, and nothing to eat after all——"

He got up and shuffled out, leaving his mail and the paper on the table.

Flynn picked up the paper and opened it.

"Why would she be coming to Galway when she's announced to broadcast from Dublin?" he demanded.

Neither Tante Emma nor Bridie had any suggestions to offer. Flynn laid aside the paper and looked from one to the other, and was suddenly aware that the eyes of both of them held the same strained look, and that Bridie was curiously pale. Both looked away, and suddenly he was on his feet, his own eyes blazing.

"Mother of God," he shouted, "you thought you could keep me here by a trick like this—'twas you who sent that telegram, Bridie—you with the devil in your black soul!"

Bridie sprang up, crying wildly, "It's a lie! How would I send a telegram from Galway? Why would I wish to do such a thing?"

"A lie, is it? Maybe Mr. Patrick Doyle took it into Galway for you— as easily as he arranged the stoning party! You thought you could keep me here, didn't you?" He was as white as Bridie herself, and trembling with fury. His words tumbled over each other and he was hardly aware of what he was saying. "You didn't think I meant it when I said I was going to join Mrs. Paul in Paris, did you?"

Tante Emma came round the table and laid a hand on his arm.

"Aisy now, aisy. Sure, there's been a little mistake somewhere——"

He shook her off. "Sure there's been a mistake! Bridie's mistake! Tonight when Cousin Kate wouldn't be coming off the Galway train Bridie had her little speech all ready, the one she rehearsed this morning—about maybe she'd got held up! Maybe she'd got some more telegrams from Galway arranged for me, to keep me here! But that's where you're making a mistake, because I'm not stopping here one minute longer—not one minute, see?"

He rushed blindly out of the kitchen, and when the door had slammed on him Bridie still stood staring at Tante Emma, then suddenly she gave a little scream.

"Jameel! He'll get away on Jameel!"

She was across the room and out of the door before the old woman had realized what was happening. She rounded the corner of the stable-yard just as Flynn was finishing saddling-up—he had not known that he could do it so quickly.

"Flynn!" Bridie cried. "Don't go—I want to tell you something——"

He responded by hoisting himself up into the saddle and heading Jameel off towards the avenue. Bridie ran forward and hurled herself at the mare's head; Flynn swerved, evading the wild grab at the bridle by a matter of inches.

Bridie stumbled, righted herself, then screamed after him, "Flynn! Flyn-nn!"

Flynn's answer was to lean forward over Jameel's neck and urge her into a gallop.

Bridie watched till he was out of sight, then she broke into a wild cry like a keen and ran back to the house and collapsed in Tante Emma's arms.

The old woman did her best to comfort her. "He'll come back," she promised her. "Sure, 'tis only the Harrigan temper taking its course. He'll ride the mare into a sweat, and then he'll come to his senses. Rest aisy now, rest aisy, alanna. He'll be back in time for the rosary. . . ."

Bridie spent the afternoon sitting on the steps of the porch, leaning her head against a pillar, her eyes never leaving the narrow road that skirted the lake down below. A good deal of the time Tante Emma sat with her, shelling peas, stalking red currants. Bridie made no effort to help; she sat with her hands in her lap, straining her eyes down over the terraces to the twisting grey snake of stone wall that indicated the road. Tante Emma went in and made tea and brought it out on the old tin tray.

"Take a sup o' tay now," she urged, " 'twill do ye good."

Bridie drank the tea, but refused anything to eat.

Presently Mike came out with a fishing-rod and looked up at the sky, hopefully.

Bridie said, in a low voice, without looking at him, "I sent Flynn that wire saying Cousin Kate was coming, and after you'd said about her broadcasting he guessed 'twas me that sent it, and now he's gone off on Jameel, in a towering rage. . . ."

Mike leaned the rod against a pillar and brought a tin of flies out of his pocket and proceeded to examine the contents, thoughtfully.

"Aren't you very foolish, now?" he said casually.

Bridie did not answer, and Tante Emma said, firmly, "He'll be back before we say the rosary. He'll ride his temper down."

Mike closed the tin and replaced it in his pocket.

"He probably thought to cut across the bog and pick up the train at Recess. He could probably make it if he didn't lose his way——"

Bridie began to cry again, pressing an already sodden handkerchief to her eyes. The old woman gave her a quick glance.

"Ah, don't be heedin' him at all, alanna. After all the rain that's drownded us this summer for him to be talkin' of cuttin' across the bog, and it runnin' with water the way anyone would be wantin' a boat to cross it!"

Mike shrugged, picked up his rod, and went on down the steps.

He paused on the terrace to say, "If I meet him I'll tell him you're waiting the rosary and supper for him, and hurry him up."

He did meet his son along the Lough Head road, but he gave him no message. In the amber evening light a turf-cart came clattering towards him with a flash of red-painted spokes in blue wheels. He was for passing with an evening greeting when the man reined in and touched his cap.

"Mr. Harrigan, your honour. 'Tis Master Flynn met with an accident out by Recess. Ridin' like the wind, he was, and headin' straight for a wall, drivin' the mare on with a stick. She got her forelegs up on the wall and came down head over heels—a complete somersault, your honour, and when we came up we found her stone dead, with her neck broke, and Master Flynn a few yards off without a breath o' life in him seemingly, but his heart still batin', glory be to God, and we thought it best to put him in the cart and bring him straight back . . ."

XXI

WHEN the turf-cart drove up on to the castle terrace Bridie and Tante Emma were still sitting on the steps. Mike jumped out as the man reined-in and said curtly, "Get on your bicycle, Bridie, and go for a doctor. Flynn's met with an accident."

Bridie sprang to her feet, her face white. She looked fearfully at the cart, with its gay red and blue sides that hid her brother from her.

"Is he badly hurt?" She could not make the words more than a half-whisper, because of the terrible sickness rising in her.

"Till we get the doctor we don't know. He's unconscious. Get along with you now."

He turned to the owner of the cart. "Help me bring him into the house."

Bridie rushed off in the direction of the yard to fetch her bicycle, and in a few minutes was hurtling down the avenue and out on to the Ballyrannon road. She rode like the wind, completely possessed by the urgency of getting the doctor. Not until she was on her way back, and the doctor's car had already passed her on the road, did it occur to her to wonder what had become of Jameel.

Flynn made use of Mr. Foyne's car after all that day. The doctor took him back into Ballyrannon in his own car after examining him, and Mike and Bridie went with him. Mr. Foyne was sent for from the doctor's house, and the still unconscious Flynn was transferred to his car. His father and sister went with him into Galway and Mr. Foyne went back empty to Ballyrannon. It was late by the time Flynn was settled into the hospital, and Mike took rooms for himself and Bridie in the hotel in the market-place at which she had once longed to stay.

Now she was hardly aware that it was the same place. She was utterly exhausted. She had never loved her father or felt close to him; now she clung to him, and he knew again that curious, only half-acknowledged, feeling of tenderness she could evoke in him.

They sat in the lounge of the hotel drinking whiskies—a double one for himself, a small one for Bridie—and he tried to comfort her. "Concussion isn't serious. They're sometimes unconscious for a day or two——"

"How long will he be in hospital?" she asked, fearfully.

"Some weeks, the sister said."

"Will we stay here till he comes out?"

"I don't know about all the time—we'll stay for a few days, anyhow." She slumped in her chair. "I'm so tired I could die of it."

"I'm pretty tired myself."

They sat in silence for a few minutes, then Bridie forced herself to ask, "What happened to Jameel—was she hurt?"

He wondered momentarily whether she could stand another shock, then decided that there was no way of breaking the news gently, and he said briefly, "She broke her neck."

To his astonishment Bridie gave a little gasp, then began to cry—the first tears she had shed since the accident.

"It's all my fault," she wept. "Flynn will never forgive me—never, never!"

"You can thank God it wasn't Flynn himself!"

"I do, I do. But he'll never get over it. He'll never forgive me. . . ."

Mike got up and went over to her and put an arm round her.

"Get along to bed, childeen," he urged. "It'll all look better in the morning, and maybe Flynn will have come round and they'll let us see him for a wee while."

They went along to the hospital in the morning, but Flynn had not come round, nor that afternoon, nor that evening, nor by the evening of the next day. He regained consciousness on his third day in hospital, but he was not allowed to see anyone. It was over a month before Bridie saw him. The doctor took Mike aside and explained to him that Flynn had recurrent bouts of delirium in which he alternately threatened to murder Bridie and refused ever to set eyes on her again. He asked a good deal for someone called Stephanie, but it was most essential that he should be kept quiet, and not desirable that he should see anyone at all until he had regained normality, and then, in the doctor's opinion, some time should elapse before he saw his sister. Mike had placed all the facts before the doctor—Bridie's jealousy where her brother was concerned, her ruse to try and prevent him from going away to join the woman with whom he was in love, his rushing off on the wild ride, the disaster to his beloved mare. . . .

"When he comes home and sees the empty stables—what then?" Mike asked.

"He must be told before he goes home," the doctor said, and added, "But it will be a long time before he is ready for that news. In the meantime I would suggest sending his sister away. It would be better she should not be there when he returns home."

It was, Mike thought, the very divil. It was useless to suggest to Bridie that she go and stay in Dublin with the O'Donals.

He explained to her that Flynn had to be kept very quiet and not see anyone, and that there was therefore no point in either of them remaining longer in Galway. Flynn was likely to be in the hospital for some weeks. Bridie begged wildly to be allowed to see Flynn 'just for a minute' before they left, but Mike finally succeeded in convincing her that to do so would do him actual harm. "You don't want to do that?" he urged. She shook her head and said, stonily, "I've done him all the harm in the world already."

As soon as she was convinced that in no circumstances would she be allowed to see Flynn she was impatient to get back to Ballyrannon and Tante Emma. She ran to her immediately on arrival, and seeing them with their arms about each other, both of them with tears running down their faces, it suddenly came to Mike that when Flynn was coming back he might send Bridie away with the old woman. They could stay with the old woman's relations at Letterfrack, and the niece, Molly, could perhaps come to Ballyrannon for a time. But there was time enough in which to break it to Bridie that she was not to be there to welcome her brother back. . . .

2

Flynn had lost all sense of time, and of reality. He had lucid intervals in which he was aware that he was in bed in a small cell-like room with white walls, and in those intervals he had confused recollections of a quarrel with Bridie, of riding Jameel like mad, of forcing her, desperately, to take a wall, but when he tried to recall the reasons for it all his head began to ache intolerably and everything would fade away into a phantasmagoria which closed in on him till he shouted and beat the air in a delirious frenzy of fear, anger, confusion . . . from which he emerged trembling, sometimes sobbing, shivering, sweating, hands gripping his wrists, and a serene face surrounded by a white coif looking down on him. Then a quiet voice would pierce through the fog that swirled round inside his head and before his gaze, and behind the voice the compulsion of a will imposed, resolutely, on his own disintegration. He felt the impact of this will like a cold compress on his forehead, and something in him would relax; he would sigh and his rigid body go limp, after which he would slip into sleep as easily as though yielding to an anaesthetising drug. It was a long time before the quiet voice and the serene face and the resolute will unified in the person of a nurse. For weeks before that his spirit wandered in a cloudy world of shrouded figures which, turning, terrifyingly revealed only a black absence of face, or, strangely luminous, were possessed of faces he knew that yet had no resemblance to those faces. Thus a face would be Bridie's and yet not Bridie's, Stephanie's and yet not Stephanie's, but distorted as in death, or with malignancy. He would hear a whinnying and try to leave his bed to go to Jameel, and fight violently with hands that tried to hold him down in the bed, and all the time there would be a thudding of hooves beating about his ears. Then, as the frenzy abated, the hooves would gallop away into the distance, and the shrouded figures melt into mist and vanish into air, and the thudding would be in his own body, and it would be the thunderous beating of his heart, and the quiet voice would be saying, "Steady, now. You're all right," and there would be that strong impact of a will imposed upon him.

It went on for weeks, though he did not know this, and the lucid intervals became longer, till there was a night when he slept without waking in a fever of hallucination. He wakened during the night, but his mind was quiet as a pool. He opened his eyes and met the gaze of a nurse sitting in the corner opposite his bed.   She smiled and came over to him.   He smiled at her as she stood with her fingers on his pulse and a watch in her other hand.   When she released his wrist he asked her the time.   She told him it was three in the morning.   He asked if he might have the blind up so that he could see the sky.   She turned away and pulled a cord and the blind flew up over the deep window.   He saw a blue-black sky sparkling with stars, and a cool wind came in, and he smelt the sea.

"What is this place?" he asked her.

"Galway Hospital."

"How long have I been here?"

"Just over three weeks."

"When am I going home?"

"Very soon now, if you go on being good and quiet like this."   She came back to him.   "Will you try to sleep again now?"

"If you'll answer one more question."

"What is it?"

"I had an accident, riding, didn't I?"

"You did."

He closed his eyes and the night nurse went back to her corner and the novelette she had been reading by a dim light.

Flynn lay feeling the night wind on his face and smelling the sea, and through his mind ran an endless blood-red ribbon of wild fuchsia luminous in evening light, and the golden rhythm that was Jameel with her head and tail held proudly and every nerve and muscle in her sensitive body strained as she took the wall, the other side of which was oblivion. . . .

When the night nurse made out her report before going off duty she wrote that the patient had spent a quiet night, waking at three a.m. for a few minutes; he was quite rational, and soon went to sleep again.   His pulse was normal.   He was sound asleep when she went off duty at six.   His sleep was restful, except once when he murmured something confusedly about 'Cousin Kate'—which was a new name in the history of his illness—but he showed no symptoms of distress.

A few days later his father came to see him.   Flynn was sitting in a chair by the window when Mike entered.   Flynn stared at him as though he were a complete stranger, and Mike was disconcerted.

He said, with an attempt at casualness, "Hullo, Flynn."

Flynn replied, laconically, "Hullo."

Mike drew up a chair.   "How are you feeling now?" he inquired.

"Weak," Flynn said.   "Weak as water."   He looked out of the window, and whilst Mike was pondering what to say next, Flynn said, without turning his head, "I want to know what happened to Jameel."

Mike recognised that the moment he had been dreading had come. He hesitated, his mind groping for suitable words, and before he had assembled them Flynn had said in the same flat tone, "I suppose you had to have her put down."

Mike told him, "We were spared that.   She broke her neck."

He looked at his son's averted face and added, awkwardly, "I'm sorry. She was a pretty little mare.   But thanks be to God it wasn't yourself."

Flynn said, flatly, curiously without bitterness, "It might as well have been."

He turned his head and looked at his father then. "I am dead. My body's still alive, but everything that was me is as dead as Jameel."

"Ah, sure, it's only because you're weak," Mike suggested. "When you get about again you'll come to yourself—youth is very resilient."

Flynn did not answer, and they sat in a silence which Mike found acutely uncomfortable, but which Flynn appeared not to notice. It was a relief to Mike when a nurse came and asked him to conclude the visit. He was glad to go, but he was worried, and before leaving the hospital he had a word with the sister.

"My son asked me about his horse and I broke the news to him. He seemed completely indifferent—though he had thought the world of that little mare. His manner was altogether not normal. It set me wondering—is the concussion going to affect him mentally?"

"He'll be all right in time," the sister assured him. "It's quite common in these cases for everything to seem a bit unreal to them for a while. It takes time to get over a thing like this."

Mike hated anything to do with illness and hospitals. The only illness he knew anything about and for which he could really raise imaginative sympathy was a hangover. Flynn's illness had been a bore, more than anything else, and, since it involved the death of Jameel, a crashing waste of money. Anyone else would have had a mare like that insured, but he could never be bothered with these business affairs—insurance policies, making your will, keeping accounts, investments, it was all a bore. If you had money you spent it, and that was all there was to it; when you hadn't any you borrowed, you got advances, you persuaded some fool of an editor or publisher to buy something, to advance something; somehow you scraped a few pounds together to tide you over. To have to think about money at all was squalid; life was experience—zest, elation, emotion—not £ s. d. You could not be a *bon vivant*—and he was that—and reduce life to such sordid economic terms. Flynn's accident had tied him to Connemara when he was impatient to get back to Paris; it had robbed him of the Dublin Horse Show, though he had managed to fit in the Galway races, combining it with visits to the hospital. He had offered to take Bridie with him to the races, but she had had no heart for it. She took the boat out a good deal during these weeks—he did not know that she took it, usually, to Bream Island, that Patrick and Tante Emma were, between them, all her comfort now.

It broke her heart to be sent away just when Flynn was coming home, but Mike convinced her that the doctor had insisted very strongly that Flynn must be kept quiet for some time, and that his sister's presence—in view of all that had happened—would disturb him and might even have a disastrous effect on him. Father Faherty, to whom she took her trouble, urged upon her that she must regard her banishment as a penance for the wrong she had done her brother by her wicked jealousy and deceit.

The priest had been much exercised over the Harrigan family since the arrival of the American women. His attention had been drawn to Flynn's disappearance from the dance with Mrs. Paul, and there had been general gossip, culminating in the stone-throwing episode, of which he had also heard, indirectly. Then there had been the accident, and Bridie's confession of jealousy and the faked telegram. He had noticed, too, that since the night of the dance Flynn had ceased to be a communicant.

When Mike was back in Ballyrannon, therefore, after the few days in Galway, he had gone to see him—ostensibly to inquire after Flynn, but in fact to look into Harrigan morals generally. He had chosen, unwittingly, a bad day, for Mike had a hangover and was not up—it was barely past noon. When Tante Emma had come up to his room to inform him that his reverence had called he had said, irritably, that if his reverence wanted to see him he had better come up, but she had better warn him that he had chosen the wrong day for soul-saving. . . .

Father Faherty had found Mike sitting up in bed in his grimy dressing-gown, his face blotched, his eyes bleary, as always after heavy drinking, the bed strewn with galley-proofs which he had felt too ill to deal with, a nearly empty whisky-bottle on the floor beside the bed. The atmosphere reeked of damp walls and stale tobacco and spirits.

"I'm sorry to find you indisposed, my son," the priest had said.

Mike had swept some proofs and papers and a soggy packet of cigarettes off the chair beside the bed.

"Take a seat, Father. I'm not indisposed—I've got a hangover, that's all. In any case I never reckon to get up till the streets are aired."

Father Faherty had made no comment on this, and had inquired, "How is your son? I heard he was taken to hospital following a riding accident."

"He has concussion and will be in hospital for some weeks."

After expressing his sympathy, Father Faherty had added, "I have been meaning for some time to have a word with you concerning stories which have been circulating about Flynn and the American lady—nothing but boyish infatuation, no doubt, but a pity, none the less——"

Mike had clamped a hand to his throbbing forehead. "Look here, Father—you've probably never had a hangover in your life, so you don't know what it is, but let me tell you that when a man is suffering from one it's no time to start moralising with him! What is more, the Harrigans have never in all their disreputable and glorious history permitted themselves to become priest-ridden, and they don't propose to begin doing so now !"

Having said which, he had reached over the side of the bed for the whisky-bottle and held it up to the light.

"Be the Holy Powers, there's enough left for a hair of the dog !" He had raised the bottle to his lips and drained it, and Father Faherty had risen to his feet and said, mildly enough, " 'Twould be better to continue this discussion when you are in a more reasonable frame of mind. I'll be going along now, and we'll talk it over another time."

"We'll do nothing of the kind !" Mike had roared at him, and whirled the empty bottle above his head, then, remembering in time that this was not a Bloomsbury party, hurled it instead through the closed window. . . .

The following Sunday Father Faherty had preached on 'the sin of intemperance', with special reference to 'the demon of evil here in our very midst, and in the very place in which an example of Christian temperance should rightly have been found'. Father Burke himself had never preached more eloquently on the subject. Mike sat through it, smiling and amused, but when he came out of the church a tremendous nostalgia for Paris seized him—Paris and all that it stood for of wider worlds and personal freedom. Here, however rebelliously, one lived, inescapably, in the shadow of the parish priest.

XXII

MIKE recalled the priest's visit, and the ensuing sermon, when he set out to bring Flynn home a week after his visit to him. He felt a little anxious; it wouldn't do for Father Faherty to come pestering Flynn if he was to be kept quiet. Perhaps he could persuade him to go to Dublin—as a jumping-off ground for Paris when he felt equal to the journey? He had wired Stephanie of the accident, and there was a letter from her for Flynn—he had it locked up in his desk to avoid tempting Bridie. It seemed odd that Flynn should have asked about Jameel and not mentioned Stephanie. Perhaps when you'd been unconscious for several days, and had weeks of not being yourself, it took time to catch up on things. . . . He sent Tante Emma and Bridie off to Letterfrack the day before Flynn was to come home, and then on the way to the hospital made a detour to call for the old woman and take her with him—in a sudden panic that he was not equal to handling Flynn alone. He had found him difficult enough before his accident, but this post-concussion strangeness was positively unnerving. He told Tante Emma, "He hasn't come to himself, yet, and you understand him better than I do."

"Faith, you've never understood either of them, or tried to," the old woman told him, severely. "You that's the great understanding writer, with yer name to a whole row of books, and letters full of praise and flatthery from all parts of the world!"

Mike accepted the rebuke humbly. It was true enough, he thought. She understood these strange difficult children of his because she loved them—and they were 'open' to her because they loved her, and were, inversely, 'closed' to him. He had the feeling that if Flynn were raving mad the situation would still present no difficulties for Tante Emma. The moment she set eyes on Flynn waiting in the entrance hall of the hospital, in charge of a nurse, she rushed across to him and flung her arms round him, and Mike was relieved to observe that Flynn laughed and returned her embraces.

He was silent in the train, but it hardly mattered, since she kept up a running commentary on things seen from the window, and detailed the births, deaths, marriages, and scandals which had given life interest in Ballyrannon since he had gone away. She did not mention Bridie, and he did not ask after her, but it occurred to Mike that something had better be said before they reached the castle. As they approached Ballyrannon he said, casually, "By the way, Bridie is away at Letterfrack on a little holiday. Tante Emma is going there tomorrow and Mollie will come over and look after us."

Flynn said, looking out of the window at the river cascading over the stones, "I suppose you mean that Bridie was sent away—tactfully?"

Mike admitted, "We thought you might not be too pleased to see her—she idn't want to go, I assure you!"

"Ah, let her come back—it makes no difference at all."

Tante Emma patted his knee. "Ah, sure, there's time enough for the two of yez to start quarrellin' again !"

"We'll not quarrel. It takes energy to quarrel, and I haven't any."

"That'll wear off," Mike muttered, but Flynn made no further comment.

At Ballyrannon station there was the usual crowd come to meet the train and see was there a new face come off it. Everyone knew that Flynn Harrigan was returning from hospital that day, and a small crowd gathered round him as he stepped out of the compartment, shaking him by the hand, inquiring after his health, welcoming him home.

Flynn smiled at them and answered them normally enough, and they were all as unreal as the figures on a cinema screen.

In the car Mike told him, "I let Stephanie know about your accident, and there's a letter for you from Paris—it came a week ago."

Tante Emma put in quickly, "Ah, sure, he'll not be thinking any more about all that—'tis all over and done with, please God." She pressed Flynn's hand and gazed anxiously at him, but he said nothing.

Mike tried to make casual conversation. "The fuchsia's going over," he said, looking out of the car window, and, "We had a terrible fair-day last week—it rained all day and there were no buyers ; they were all driving their stock back by mid-day," and "Joyce's sheep keeping getting into our place, we'll have to get some more wire up."

It was a relief when they reached the castle.

"There's a beautiful bit of cold bacon for yer supper," Tante Emma informed him, patting his knee as she climbed out of the car, "and some Guinness yer Da brought in specially. . . ."

Flynn smiled and climbed out after her. "Come into the library and I'll give you that letter," Mike said.

Flynn followed his father into the library, and Mike unlocked his desk and took out the letter and handed it to Flynn, then went over to his cupboard and poured himself out a whisky. Flynn went out of the room and slowly up the broad staircase and along the corridor, then climbed the steep stone stairs to the turret. He felt quite incredibly tired by the time he reached his room.

He sat down on the bed and tore open the envelope with the French stamp and Stephanie's sprawling writing. There was no wild plunging of the heart when he unfolded the sheet of paper ; he was as dead and grey as on the day she had gone away.

Flynn darling [she wrote],

I did not write before as I gathered from your father you were not in a state to receive letters, but now I hear you are shortly coming home, so this is to welcome you back to Ballyrannon, and to say that Paris is as lovely as ever and still awaits your visit when you feel able to make it. I like to think of you reading this in the turret room and feeling me as close to you as you read it as I feel in writing it. Write to me when you feel able. The chestnuts are already yellowing in the gardens of the Luxembourg, where I have so often dreamed of our walking together hand in hand. As they say in your country, please God we shall be together before the trees are bare. My love to you, Sweetheart,
                                                                                    S.

Flynn read the letter only once, then folded it and put it into his pocket and went back down the stairs to the kitchen, where Tante Emma laid the table for supper.

He was silent during the meal and Mike looked at him a little anxiously. "News all right from Paris ?"

"I'm still invited, if that's what you mean."

"Do you good to get a change and get away as soon as you're fit enough," Mike muttered. He added, "We'll keep Bridie under control this time."

Flynn said, "Bridie should come back. There's no sense in keeping her away." He turned to Tante Emma. "When you go there tomorrow tell her I was asking for her."

"I will, but if you could send a forgiving word 'twould ease her feeling of guilt and sin——"

He said, impatiently, "Forgiveness, is it ? Sure, she has it—she has it !"

Tante Emma paused in the slicing of cold bacon to exclaim, fervently, "God's blessing on you for that ! She'll be flyin' back now like a bird to its nest !"

2

Bridie returned the following afternoon. Flynn was in the kitchen garden when she arrived, taking stock of the month's neglect. She came through the door in the wall, her face eager, the sun gilding her thick bright mane of hair. He smiled, faintly, and instantly she came running down the rough grassy path and hurled herself against him. His arms went round her and she was crying against his breast, "Oh, Flynn, I'm glad you're back, and I'm so terribly sorry about everything. . . ."

He said, "It's all right, alanna," and they left the garden with their arms about each other's waists.

She was keyed-up and excited and chattered incessantly, and he found himself recalling the day, years ago, when she had come down to the edge of the lake and called him, her hands full of cherries, and almost as though she read his thought she said, suddenly, "Let's take the boat out to the island— I'll do the rowing. We could take our tea——"

It was a soft warm September afternoon, all diffused mellow sunshine and stillness. The Twelve Pins had a grape-bloom haze on them that deepened to a shadowy purple in their folds. The bog was golden and brown, and in that light the beehive-shaped turf stacks almost black. When a curlew went crying mournfully over the lake Flynn had a sense of the bird's movement and cry in his own body, far more real than Bridie's eager face or Stephanie's letter. The bird was reality in an unreal world, and he stood looking after it with a curious sense of affinity, his quickened spirit vibrating to the rhythm of its wings and echoing its wild, lost cry.

The creak of the rowlocks as Bridie pulled the boat out across the lake to the island seemed to fill the afternoon and accentuate its deep, golden, summer's-end stillness. When they reached the island he helped her pull the boat up on to the narrow beach and then they scrambled up through the heather, Bridie plucking ripe blackberries from the brambles sprawling over the boulders as she went. They came to the piece of level ground where he had picnicked with Stephanie, and he recognised the spot, and remembered the occasion, without emotion. On the belt of trees at the marshy head of the lake there was a smear of autumn yellow, and he remembered Stephanie's words about the chestnuts of the Luxembourg, but it was all infinitely remote. As remote as the memory of a little golden mare, Jameel the Beautiful.

Bridie poured out tea from a flask into enamel mugs, passed sandwiches, and alternated chatter with contented silences. It was like the times they had spent lounging in the sandy grass at Salthill, she said, and next summer they would go again. His birthday had passed unnoticed this year, but next year they would make up for it. Mike had impressed upon her that on no account must she say anything that would distress her brother, so she carefully did not mention Jameel or Mrs. Paul. Flynn's silence did not trouble her ; he had forgiven her ; they were doing something together again, and there was nothing and no one to come between them. All the conditions for happiness were therefore fulfilled, and because she so intensely wished it she had come to believe that Mrs. Paul was a closed and finished episode.

Flynn lay on his back and looked at the sky and let Bridie's chatter flow over him like the humming of bees and the movement of clouds. Lake and hills and bog, the warm, afternoon smell of heather, the crushed-out pungency of bracken, the fretful, quarrelling cries of gulls, the boom of a bittern over the marsh beyond the thin woods, the plaint of a curlew, the clatter of a cart along the boreen, all these things had reality for him, but not Stephanie and Paris, or the little golden filly called Jameel, or Bridie talking common-places and eating jam sandwiches amongst the heather. To think was too much effort, all memory infinitely remote, and all feeling numbed except this deep love of country, which flowed in him like the flow of his blood, and which was in some indefinable fashion a part of it.

In his room that night he replaced the picture of St. Anne upon the wall, and lay a long time in bed looking at it before blowing out the candle, but Cousin Kate in Dublin was as remote as Stephanie in Paris ; St. Anne was more real, and the spiritual communion with Our Lady through prayer more real than any communion of speech in the physical world.

XXIII

FLYNN found his way back to reality through the earth that he loved. As his strength slowly returned he worked increasingly to repair the month's neglect of his gardens. The sight of the soil turned by the fork, cleaned of weeds, gave him a strong pleasure, a deep satisfaction. He had a notion that the earth was grateful to him for cleansing it, loosening it, breaking it up so that it could breathe in the wind and sun ; he enjoyed the sight of green growing things freed from choking, strangulating weeds, and standing up freely and proudly in their own right. He surveyed the hoed potato furrows with pride, savouring the rhythm of their clean lines. The tomato plants he had put in before he had decided to go away had been staked up by Tante Emma in his absence and bore heavy green clusters ripening in the sun. When he was not working in the kitchen garden he was on his hands and knees weeding the terraces, or plunging in amongst the dead summer flowers, cutting them down to their already new-springing bases.

Bridie worked with him, at first with an eager persistence, then more fitfully; but even when she had reached the fitful stage a day never passed but she came out to him and spent some hours with him—if it was only to sit on a step or a grassy bank and watch him working. . . .

But there were bad times, especially at night, in bed, when he lived again, in a mental agony which made his body sweat, those moments in which he rode the mare at the wall, sensing her misgiving and forcing her on with a stick, his whole will, and every nerve and muscle in his body, concentrated on getting her over. Then a moment of triumph as she braced herself and jumped, and in the next instant the cancelling flash of realization that it was only her forelegs that topped the wall . . . then the confusion and darkness following the flash.

It was something to know that she had broken her neck in the somer-sault of her fall and had not had to be put down. But there was a hell of torment in the realisation that it was he who had killed Jameel the Beautiful. All his love and care, all his patient schooling and gentleness, all the tenderness he had felt for the little mare, had all culminated in the blind, cruel selfishness which had impelled him to ride her at a jump beyond her powers, even to the extent of taking the stick to her to force her to his will.

There had been those first agonised moments of realisation in hospital, then the deadness invading him as a defence against pain, a form of self-anaesthetising, so that his mind merely said 'Jameel is dead', and he no longer felt anything. Back at the castle he passed her empty loose-box daily and his mind registered the fact that he no longer had a horse, and sometimes it said, 'I killed her myself', but there was no emotional reaction. He never heard her eager whinnying in the evenings when he came to shut her up for the night, or saw her cantering along the boreen, head and tail proudly lifted, stepping out as though she owned the earth, as he had in hospital. There had been a little Arab filly, pretty as a picture, with an action that was poetry in motion, the world's wonder of a horse, but she had belonged to a Flynn Harrigan who was as dead as she now was herself.

Then in the slow thaw of return to normal, pain stirred in him, and a terrible grieving, and he avoided the stables. With this return of the sense of reality of the physical world Stephanie came back into his thoughts, dimly at first, then with increasing clarity, until once again he could hear her drawling sing-song, her throaty laugh. There was a day when he saw her so clearly that he stopped work, gazing at the gate in the wall, seeing her standing there, cool in her black and white, the grey streak in her hair almost white in the sunlight, and he knew again the touch of her fingers toying with the medallion below the hollow of his throat, and with that thought his blood quickened, and the smear of autumn yellow on the trees beside the lake sent his imagination racing to the gardens of the Luxembourg, and he knew that he must get there before the leaves fell.

But this time there must be no trouble with Bridie; he would not tell her he was going; only his father should know, and Bridie should not be told until he had already boarded the Dublin train at Galway. As soon as his mind was made up he discussed the matter with his father.

Mike was intensely relieved. He had been invited to go to Hollywood to work on the film production of his book; he would like to get away by the

E

end of October at the latest; Bridie should have her choice of going to Letterfrack with Tante Emma, or to Dublin to stay with the O'Donals, but it was agreed that nothing should be discussed with her until Flynn was safely away. They might get someone to rent the castle—some enthusiastic American with romantic notions concerning Celtic Twilight and the Glamour of the West, perhaps. If not it could stand empty and Tante Emma could come over occasionally to put down a fire. . . . It was no use fussing over domestic details; they could take care of themselves.

"How long do you think you'll stay abroad?" Mike asked.

Flynn replied, simply, that he had no idea. He resisted, now, the idea that he might never return . . . But once again he found it impossible to think beyond the immediate future.

He wrote to Stephanie in the evening of the day he discussed the matter with his father. It was his first letter to her, and his first love-letter to any-one, and when he came to write it it seemed to him that it called either for a poem or for the barest essential minimum; anything in between must seem hackneyed and trite. So he wrote, simply:

Stephanie,

> *I am better now and I want to come to you. I had thought of leaving here on the first of October. Please tell me if this is all right. Nothing shall stop me this time if you still want me. I had your letter when I came home two weeks ago, but I was not ready to write before now. I love you.*

Flynn.

He posted the letter in the pillar-box in the monastery wall and estimated that he could not expect a reply under a week or ten days, and that it would more likely be ten days or even a fortnight. There was no fever of im-patience in him as there had been before; now, he felt, he could work patiently through the days until the miracle was once more re-enacted. But when no letter came at the end of a fortnight he began to be restive. Perhaps she had left Paris for the South and there was a delay whilst his letter caught up. He thought of sending a telegram, but did not care to start up fresh gossip in Ballyrannon. Mike also began to be restive; he wanted his own plans settled. Why the divil didn't the woman write? Then suddenly an idea flashed to him, and one afternoon when Bridie was out on her bicycle, on an errand for Tante Emma, he went into her room and pulled open a drawer.

He found what he was looking for under a pile of handkerchiefs—a letter in Stephanie's handwriting addressed to Flynn, and bearing a Paris postmark of over a week ago. It had been opened.

He took it to Flynn in the kitchen garden.

"Here's the letter you were expecting. I found it in Bridie's drawer——"

Flynn took the letter, wonderingly, then looked from it to his father.

"In Bridie's drawer?"

"It suddenly came to me that she might have intercepted it—she is generally in the avenue to meet the postman."

Flynn went pale. "This is the end," he said; "I can't bear it. She's been so sweet and good since I came home from hospital, and so penitent about that bogus telegram, and I'd completely forgiven her, and now this! I can't see her again. I must go at once——"

Mike suggested, "You'd better see what the lady says before you decide anything."

Flynn pulled out the letter.

My darling Flynn,
October 1st is splendid if you can't come before—in which case wire me.
All my love and longing,

S.

He crushed envelope and letter into his pocket.

"She says if I come before October first to wire her. I must leave at once. I can wire from Dublin. I'll get Foyne to run me into Galway, and if I can't get a train through this evening I'll spend the night there."

He flung down his fork and picked up his jacket from where it hung over a blackcurrant bush.

"Aisy now, aisy," Mike said. "If you go now you'll meet Bridie on the way back from the town. You'd much best wait till the morning."

"And have a scene with Bridie all over again? No, thanks. I'm off tonight. I never want to set eyes on her again. There's a limit to how much forgiving one can do. You can tip Tante Emma the wink to keep Bridie with her in the kitchen when she gets back, then if you'll come up to my room and let me know I can slip out without being seen. I can take a suitcase on the carrier of the old bike and leave the bike at Foyne's."

"What thou hast to do, do quickly," Mike muttered, and added, "It's probably best. You're all right for money?"

"Unless Bridie's stolen it whilst I was in hospital," Flynn said bitterly.

They went back to the house together and Flynn went up to the turret and Mike into the kitchen to instruct Tante Emma. She declared at first, when he had explained to her, "I'll not be a party to such wickedness. Whatever Bridie's done, I'll not be a party to further wickedness."

"There's no wickedness," Mike insisted. "Since when was it wicked for a young man to go abroad?"

"He's going to That One—'tis no use to deny it."

"He's going to Paris, and Mrs. Paul is there, along with a few million other people, and several friends of mine whom he'll also meet. If he stays here there'll be another scene with Bridie and one of them rushing out of the house, and God knows what! We've had enough trouble——"

"It's scene enough we'll have when we break it to her he's gone."

"She can scream the roof down, it'll make no difference once he's safely away."

So, quite suddenly, with no time for leave-taking, throwing his fork down in the middle of his work, breaking off, as it seemed to him, in the middle of a sentence, Flynn left Ballyrannon.

And Bridie did not scream the roof down when they told her, at supper-time, when Flynn did not come in and she was for waiting for him.

She stared from one to the other of them, and the colour went out of her face; she swayed a little, and Mike caught her as she pitched forward, fainting for the first time in her life.

PART II

PARIS—FIN DE SIÈCLE

'Yet but for the wild bed,
But for the body's flame——'

I

FLYNN sat on a green-painted seat under a little hawthorn tree on the terrace of the Luxembourg gardens and leaned his arms on the balustrade and looked down into the square below, with its formal flower-beds planted out with dahlias, its pond and leaping plume of fountain, its children running in all directions with small shrill cries, flashes of scarlet and yellow and blue in the pale September sunshine, and he watched a toy sailing-boat rocking perilously across the pond, and tried to realise that a week ago he was in Connemara.

He had arrived in Paris the night before, after what had seemed to him an incredibly long and exhausting and difficult journey, spending a night in Dublin and a night in London. By showing a taxi-driver a piece of paper with Stephanie's address written on it he had succeeded in getting from the Gare du Nord to the Observatoire, where she had an apartment in a block of studio buildings. He had somehow cherished a crazy idea that she would have been at the station to meet him, and had eagerly searched amongst the crowd waiting at the barrier; everyone who came off the train seemed to be met, everyone except himself—who so badly needed someone. He had been completely lost and confused, and then a porter had seized his suitcase, demanded "Taxi?" of him, and he had followed him, helplessly. He had had no idea how much to tip the porter, and had held out a handful of coins, from which the man had extracted ten francs and had gone off marvelling at the ease with which '*les Anglais*' could be fleeced. He had been too dazed to take in the Paris street-scene he was seeing for the first time. He had had a confused impression of very crowded pavements, of people sitting at tables under café-awnings, of streets choked with traffic even worse than London—that terrifying, grey inferno—of shrill noises, of everything utterly strange and different. Then there had been streets a little less noisy and crowded, and presently avenues of chestnut trees, and the dome of the Observatoire, and the taxi stopped. He had offered the driver a twenty-franc note and been given the correct change, but this he had not known. He had only known that he stood at last outside the house in which Stephanie lived.

After that, endless stairs, and landings with painted signs, 2*eme étage*, 3*eme étage*, and his heart plunging so heavily that he had felt sick with it. Then at last the number that corresponded with the address on the piece of paper, and a bell that ringing seemed to pierce his body, and the door opened by a uniformed maid who stared at him with hard black eyes and said things he did not understand, until, exasperated by his stupidity, she said in slow,

132

laboured English, "Madame is not here.   Return morning, two hours, three hours——"

He pulled out the envelope of Stephanie's letter and scribbled on it:

Arrived this evening.   Will come back in the morning about ten.

Flynn,

and handed it to the maid.

Back in the street, on the wall of a green-shuttered house across the road, he had seen in peculiar lettering but plain English the words 'Private Hotel'. He had gone in through a wrought-iron gate, with the concierge's lodge at one side, and crossed a courtyard and entered a small dark overheated hall. A slender, youngish man with an almost bald head and a melancholy, sensitive face, spoke a little English and had said yes he had a single room— thirty francs a day *demi-pension.*   Flynn had had no idea what this meant, but had been relieved to have secured a room so easily and so near to Stephanie, and to find someone who spoke English.

He had been shown into a small, dark, high-ceilinged room with a dark wallpaper.   The deep window framed the upper branches of a chestnut tree which shut out both light and air but gave the room beauty.   There was a divan bed in a corner, with bookshelves above, and covered with a beige cover of some coarse material matching the curtains and the carpet.   It had seemed to Flynn a very luxurious room after the glazed linoleum, iron bedsteads, and dingy imitation lace curtains of his two previous bedrooms. When the proprietor had pushed the shutters further back and opened out the window wider a little air came in through the tree's dense foliage and lifted the must from the room.

"You stay—how long, monsieur?" he had inquired politely.

But Flynn had had no idea; he had explained that he had to see a friend, that it all depended, and the proprietor had smiled and murmured that it was of no importance, 'but if you stay one month we make special terms'.   The opening of the window had admitted the clacking of a typewriter in the room above, and he had added, "We have writers stay here—English and American. You also write, perhaps?"

Flynn had hardly known the answer to that, and had said, confusedly, "Not—not really—just a little poetry—nothing to speak of . . ."

"There is here the young American poet, Raymond Farrow—you know the name, perhaps?   He is here one year now."   He had smiled, happily, then touched a bell by the door.   "The maid will bring you towels.   Do you wish something to eat?"

Flynn had discovered that he was hungry and was glad to be shown to the dining salon.   It also was high-ceilinged, and dark from the combination of dark wallpaper and tree-filled window.   There was a long narrow oak table which reminded Flynn of the refectory at the monastery at Ballyrannon; it was laid with rush mats and in the middle a rush basket was full of bread.

Monsieur had explained that most people preferred to go out in the evenings, but if anyone wished not to do so there was always something. "Tonight there is *potage St. Germain* followed by an *entrecôte garni.*"

Flynn had dined alone in the dark room and looked at the tree at the window and felt intensely lonely. He had wired Stephanie from London that morning—surely she had had the telegram? But perhaps, he had told himself, she had had an engagement she had been unable to break. It had occurred to him that now he had an address he would go back and slip a note through the letterbox of her apartment—in case she got back earlier than the maid had anticipated and could see him that night.

He had done this, and then walked under the chestnut trees of l'Avenue de l'Observatoire to the Luxembourg gardens, and since, they were closed for the night, gone along by the railings to the Rue de Medicis. He had crossed over and followed an instinct which brought him down the Boul' Mich' to the river. A river was something he understood, and the river had given him sanctuary in the shape of a church. He had gone into Nôtre Dame with a sense of homecoming. That he was in a Catholic country—that was something. Paris could never be as alien and strange as London.

In London he had stayed in a shabby hotel near the terminus, and the Euston Road had seemed to him the most heartless thing he had ever known. In Dublin he had taken a room in a hotel along the quays, near the Fourt Courts; it had been strange being in Dublin without Bridie, and not seeing Cousin Kate, but he had no wish to see his cousin; she belonged to a world to which he had already said goodbye. He had stayed the night in Dublin only because he could not get his passport through before the next day.

Sitting alone in the gardens of the Luxembourg it seemed unreal that only yesterday morning he had been in London, and only the day before in Dublin; and stranger still that on his first morning in Paris he should be alone. But Stephanie had sent a message round by her maid that she could not see him till the early evening, as she had a luncheon engagement, and after that had to go to her tailor. She hoped he had had a good crossing and was glad he was in Paris at last; they would have dinner together that evening and he should tell her everything—'À bientôt, S.' There was a postscript instruction, 'Come here about six.'

He leaned his arm on the balustrade and looked at the dahlias and the children and the leaping fountain and the toy sailing-boat, and filled with a consuming sadness. There was bright sunlight, and the sky a pale clear blue, and the air had a fresh autumnal sparkle, and smelled of coffee and garlic and strong cigarettes, and beyond the green oasis of the gardens there was the exciting, teeming wilderness of Paris waiting to be explored, and this evening he would be with the woman he loved, yet he had never felt so alone, so completely estranged from everything he held dear.

It was more than homesickness; it was the realisation of the absence of any real home in Stephanie herself. Her casualness over his arrival, which had at first been a shock to him, had subsided into a half-suppressed pain, out of which he asked himself why, because he was in love with her, should he ever have assumed she was in love with him? She had, after all, never pretended to be in love with him; he had no recollection of her ever having said 'I love you' even at the peak of ecstasy. Why should anyone so experienced and worldly love anyone so utterly inexperienced and unworldly as Flynn

Harrigan from the back-of-beyond? That he had said goodbye to everything he loved for love of her could not be held to be her responsibility. She had urged him to come to Paris probably as much because she thought it would be good for him—a spiritual and intellectual, and perhaps even emotional, education—as anything else. She wanted to 'emancipate' him from the Catholic Church and the parish priest, and all that nationalist insularity that was all very well as a romantic ideal—Yeats and the Abbey Theatre and Celtic Revivalism—but in practice was very 'limiting' and 'narrow'—from the world's-eye view of Mrs. Stephanie Paul, of London, Paris and New York. He smiled a little bitter smile, remembering the night they had sat in the Railway Hotel and she had urged upon him the narrowness of his Catholic, nationalist world—she who professed to love Ireland and the Irish. It came to him suddenly that his father was right in his contempt for these people who 'adored' their own romantic conception of Ireland and had not the slightest understanding of the soul of the country. They had this sentimental notion of a charming, poetic people moving in a perpetual Celtic Twilight, and not the slightest notion of what '98 meant— or '21; Ireland for them was a land of yesterday, never of tomorrow.

Everything in him flowing back to Ireland, he thought of Jameel for the first time since his 'return to life' after leaving the hospital; but that the horse he had loved was dead had no meaning beside the fact that the woman he loved lived and invited him to join her.

In his dreams she had been there the moment he stepped off the train at the Gare du Nord, her eyes and lips smiling their welcome, her hands clasping his as she led him through the strangeness of this new world back into that enchanted kingdom they had once explored together, and which must be the same whether it be an island in the middle of an Irish lake, in the turret of a crumbling castle, or in a room in a foreign city. That there could have been this hiatus of loneliness and waiting and disappointment had been unthinkable.

He started from his reverie as a ball rolled under his chair, and in the next moment a child was at his knees, a girl of about seven or eight, hatless, and wearing a very short scarlet coat, a cheeky-looking little girl with a snub nose and a dirty face, and a fringe of straight fair hair coming down to meet lashes that curled back from blue-grey eyes.

She smiled at him without shyness and addressed him in pert French.

"*Attention, monsieur, je veux trouver ma balle sous votre chaise.*"

Then because he hesitated and looked confused she said, in English, "You don't speak French? You're English?"

He smiled at her. "I'm not English."

"American, then."

He shook his head. "Guess again!"

A fair-haired boy of about ten came up; he had the same blue-grey eyes and snub nose and alert look.

"I know—he's a Colonial——"

"I'm Irish," Flynn told them, and bent down and fished a coloured rubber ball out from under the seat. "Is this what you were wanting?"

He threw it and the boy bounded away after it. The girl lingered beside him, regarding him with interest.

"Have you got an Irish name?" she demanded.

"Yes—Flynn. What's yours?"

"My name's French, because my Pappa is French. You guess what it is!"

"I don't know French names, I'm afraid."

"It's Jeanne, but in England it's Jean. We go there sometimes because Maman is English and we've got relations there. We can only go when Johnny has any money. His father sends it from America."

"Who's Johnny?"

She told him, simply, "He's Maman's boy-friend. He's always around except when Pappa's there. Pappa doesn't live with us, but he comes to see us sometimes. He would like to come and live with us. I'd like it too. I don't like Johnny, but Henri likes him better than Pappa."

"Does Johnny live with you?"

"Oh, no. He lives upstairs, but he eats with us mostly."

She skipped away a few steps and hung over the balustrade, tipping herself forward so that her feet were off the ground, and exuding some spittle from her mouth allowed it to fall very slowly. Then she spun round, wiped her mouth with the back of her hand, and, her eyes eager, announced triumphantly, "I got it right in the middle of a flower—a dead shot! See if you can do it!"

Flynn got up and leaned over the balustrade.

"It seems a pity to spit in the eye of a dahlia," he suggested.

"What shall we do, then?" She slipped a hand into his and looked up at him, hopefully.

"Perhaps we should find your brother and play ball with him?"

"He has a lot of boys with him—it's boring. I know what—if you like I'll take you for a walk and you can buy me a gob-stopper at the kiosk, and one of those feather windmills."

"Come on, then."

Flynn allowed himself to be led away by the small, sturdy person in the scarlet coat. She conducted him down the steps and past the pond, and across the fountain square and up the other side to the grassless avenues of chestnut trees strewn with autumn leaves. Some men and boys played bowls in a clearing. A very thin and arid wood it seemed to Flynn, and the Luxembourg gardens, generally, not a patch on Stephen's Green. At a rustic kiosk, like a little summer-house, Jeanne selected a 'windmill' of yellow feathers, and a fig dipped in toffee and impaled on a stick, and supervised his payment for these purchases, turning the different coins over in his palm till she had found a two-franc piece.

After this they sat on a seat and Jeanne sucked her toffee-fig and whirled the feather windmill round, and then suddenly announced that she must 'faire pipi'. Flynn had no idea what she meant till she laid the windmill and the sweet aside and slid down from the seat and scampered off into the wood. Then he laughed, remembering the child who had been Bridie, and her abrupt disappearances behind hedges and walls when they were out together.

When Jeanne came back they strolled under the trees, the child chattering, sometimes slipping a hand into his, sometimes skipping a few yards ahead, holding the feather windmill high to catch the breeze, and for Flynn it was the child Bridie who came and went at his side, and at any moment it seemed they must come down to the lake. . . .

They came, instead, back to the pond, with the museum of the Luxembourg in the background, and beyond the tall railings at the gardens' edge the low green-and-white buses of Paris, and the dome of the Pantheon against the pale blue sky. They stood and watched the fountain, and a race between two toy sailing-boats, for a few minutes, and then Jeanne said that she must go and find Henri, because if they were late back for *déjeuner* Maman would be angry.

"If you like you can come and see us," she informed him. "There are always people in the evenings. It's very boring."

"I don't know where you live," Flynn reminded her.

"Just near here in the Rue Bonaparte—right by St. Sulpice."

Flynn laughed. "I've no idea where all that is."

She tossed her head. "Everyone knows where St. Sulpice is."

"Not if they don't live in Paris."

"You can see it from here—look !"

She took his hand and pointed out the towers of the church to him.

"We live over the *alimentation* on the corner," she told him, "at the very top. Now you know."

She skipped away, then came back. "I shall be here again tomorrow, I expect."

"Don't you have to go to school?"

"Johnny gives us lessons in the afternoons. Maman wants us to grow up English, that's why. We would live in England, only it's cheaper here, and Maman wouldn't get any money from Pappa, and Johnny couldn't earn any money giving English lessons."

She skipped away again, and this time did not return, but waved to him, looking back over her shoulder, as she skipped along.

Flynn left the gardens thinking about this extraordinarily worldly bi-lingual child, wondering what Maman was like, and feeling vaguely sorry for Pappa, and made his way down to the river again. He spent the rest of the morning looking at the prints and books along the quays, and, wandering, found the market under the catalpa trees in the little square off the Rue de la Cité. He stayed a while, strolling between the stalls and sun-umbrellas, looking at the massed flowers, pink and white and mauve asters, bronze and yellow chrysanthemums, spreading sprays of autumn-tinted beech leaves, slender wands of Cape-gooseberries like tiny orange Chinese lanterns, lingering, fascinated, at the gold-fish stall with its swinging glass globes, and by the stalls of caged birds, and the man with a basket of kittens. An old black-shawled woman reminded him of Ireland, but instead of fish she was selling tortoises.

He came to the Place Dauphine, a little further along the island, and had lunch on the terrace of a small café-restaurant with a red and white striped awning. He liked the intimate feeling of the little square, with its thick-clustered chestnut trees, and the ornate lamp-posts from which trios of lamps branched with a candelabra effect. In a curious way, in spite of the trees, it was like coming into a room. The leaves were yellowing and falling, and there was the smell of autumn, and of the river, and workmen in blue overalls drank red wine and laughed and were gay at the bar just inside the café, and at the tables out on the pavement English and American voices blended with the French, and Flynn thought that if Stephanie had been there all this initiation into a new life would have been exciting, and he would have enjoyed sitting there in the sun . . . but as it was he felt desperately lost and lonely, and the language and money difficulties exhausted him.

Leaving the Ile de la Cité and resuming his wandering, wearing down the day, he came by chance to the hill of Ste. Geneviève, but he knew nothing at that time of Irish links with Paris, and though it occurred to him to wonder why a street should be called 'Rue des Irlandais' he passed the Irish College without realizing it.

When he came to the Pantheon he recognised the Luxembourg gardens at the end of the street and made his way back through them to the Observatoire.

It was still only five o'clock when he reached his hotel. He went up to his room and removed his shoes from his aching feet and lay down on the divan-bed. It was a relief not to be walking the hard pavements and hearing the scream of brakes jammed on to buses roaring along streets so narrow that it seemed a miracle they did not sweep people off the kerbs. He lay on his back and looked at the deep dark green of the tree at the window and listened to the clack of the typewriter in the room above, and thought of afternoon lying golden on Ballyrannon lake, and of the Twelve Pins growing misty with the slow approach of evening—evening seemed always to begin in their distant blueness—and of the stillness holding everything as in a sleep. He thought of the plums and apples falling ungathered in the wild orchard of the castle, and the rats once again in possession of the stables. He heard the bittern booming over the marshland at the head of the lake, and the cry of the wild duck heading down over the darkening water. He forced his thoughts away from Ireland and thought of Stephanie and that within an hour he would be seeing her again, hearing her drawling sing-song voice, smelling her perfume, tasting her lips—was that possible? He no longer had faith—knowing the touch of her hands; but now he could not feel anything except this dull pain of homesickness, and the sense of nervous and physical exhaustion of the city.

II

MRS. PAUL had never quite been able to determine what she felt about Flynn Harrigan coming to Paris. It was true that she had suggested it herself in the first place, and at the time it had seemed an exciting and romantic idea —there had even been a certain urgency about it. But how could one guarantee the permanence of one's emotions? In Dublin it had not seemed particularly urgent, and even less so in London, and back in Paris the whole thing had become quite astonishingly unimportant. Flynn had been 'a terribly sweet boy', and 'quite unusual', and not for a moment was anything to be regretted—in any case had it not been a valuable, educative experience for him?—but it was surely a profound thought that Connemara was one thing and Paris another. It had been an effort to write even from Dublin anything like the sort of letter he would be expecting. Then had come the letter from Mike with news of the accident, and she had been a little shaken. That terrible little sister! And that poor wretched desperate boy. When she had written to him of the chestnuts in the Luxembourg gardens, and walking there together, she had been full of tenderness and longing. . . . Montparnasse had been rather stale, and a little unkind, at the time. Flynn would bring a breath of fresh air into its staleness, a quality of newness to its blasé sophistication. But already by the time she had received his brief note suggesting the first of October for his arrival that mood had evaporated, and the prospect of Flynn Harrigan from Connemara descending upon her in Montparnasse became suddenly rather worrying. When his telegram from London had arrived saying that he was already on the way she had been positively dismayed. Without upsetting the whole evening program it was impossible to meet him. Even if she cut the cocktail party she couldn't get out of the dinner engagement, and it was similarly impossible to get free the following day until the evening. But as Philippa pointed out, it should surely not be difficult for a young man to amuse himself in Paris on his own, especially when he was seeing it all for the first time.

"You can't have him tied to your apron-strings all the time he's here," Philippa said—a little inaptly, since Stephanie had never worn an apron in her life.

So Stephanie smothered the pang she had when she got in and found his note scribbled on the envelope of her letter to him, and in the morning sent round the message that she would see him in the evening.

He arrived punctually at seven and she opened the door to him herself.

He stood there in his rough Connemara tweeds, with his red-gold hair a little untidy, as always, and it was as though he had come straight in off the bog-road—there was even a piece of faded heather in his buttonhole, and the tweed carried, faintly, the smell of smoke and peat.

"Why, Flynn," she said in her soft sing-song, and smiled at him, and put out a hand.

He felt a little dazed. She wore the long black dress she had worn at the dance, and he was intensely aware of her perfume. He followed her across a little hall that seemed all pale green paint and gilt mirrors and massed flowers, and lighting that seemed to come from nowhere, and into a long light room with a highly polished wooden floor and numerous rugs, and a great many brightly coloured cushions. The walls were white and there were very deep windows and a skylight. Flynn was vaguely aware of orange material at the windows and covering a low divan, and original paintings on the walls, and one of Stephanie herself on an easel. There were again a great many flowers, and lighting that seemed to come from somewhere round the ceiling.

Stephanie bent over a table and poured out something from a cocktail-shaker and handed it to him. Confusedly he heard her asking him how he was and what he had been doing all day and saying that she could hardly believe it was true that he was really here. . . .

She waved him to the divan and he sat down and looked round for somewhere to put the glass and became aware of stepped bookshelves. He stood the glass on top of a shelf and then pressed his hands to his face for a moment. Then he looked up and smiled.

"I'm sorry," he said, "but everything has been so unreal ever since I arrived—such a whirl. Isn't it the most confusing place?"

"Paris? Is it? I suppose it is after Connemara. But vurry lovely, I hope you'll agree?"

"I liked it down by the river, the poplars turning golden, and all those little bookstalls. I liked the cathedral, too, and I found a flower-market, and a little square like a room where I had lunch sitting out on the pavement, the way they do here. I went into those gardens in the morning and made friends with a little girl who told me she had a French father and an English mother who had a boy-friend called Johnny."

She laughed. "That's little Jeanne D'Alvray. You'll meet Nina and Johnny—your father used to go there. You'll find Montparnasse horribly like Dublin in one respect, anyhow—everyone knows everyone else! Nina will be terribly thrilled to meet Michael Harrigan's son—so will a lot of people. You'll have a success, darling."

"If I do it'll be under my own colours, as Flynn Harrigan, not as Mike Harrigan's son. I'd hate that. But I don't want to be a success—whatever that means. I don't want anything except to be with you—it's all I came here for."

He reached forward suddenly and took her hands, and then his head was against her breast and her arms were round him, and he had the blessed illusion of homecoming. . . .

Gilt swans wreathed their long necks amongst gilt reeds and lotus flowers at the head of her bed. The walls of the room were grey, and there was a pale pink and mauve Marie Laurencin pastel facing the bed, and a quantity of tall pale pink roses in an alabaster vase. But it could have been an iron bedstead in a tenement room in any slum for all he saw of it, blinded by the spell she put upon him.

Later he was aware of the soft colours, the roses, a mist of fine soft net draped at deep windows, and in time he was to know every detail of the room, every pot of cream, every bottle of perfume and lotion, on the dressing-table, the title of every book on the shelf near the bed.

They dined out, late. Stephanie hailed a taxi in the boulevard and they drove down to the Pont St. Michel, and an unpretentious-looking restaurant which, Stephanie said, was one of the best on the Left Bank, a gourmet's place, she said—though this meant nothing to Flynn. Stephanie ordered the meal and the wine and in due course paid the bill. He noticed that she seemed to be known there, and that she handed over what seemed to him an astonishing wad of notes at the end of the meal—remembering that his lunch had cost only ten francs. The restaurant's famous cuisine was as wasted on him as the fine vintage wine. He longed for the moment when they would be alone again.

In the taxi, when they left the restaurant, she shattered his dream by announcing, "I'll drop you at your place first."

He said, startled, "Must I spend the first night away from you, then?"

She laughed, nervously. "Flynn darling, don't be difficult! We shall have plenty of opportunities for being together—if you're good."

"Whole nights?"

"We might manage a week-end together sometime, out at the forest."

"Why not here? You've your own place——"

"Darling, is it fair to pester me like this? Isn't it just a little—ungracious, in view of everything?"

He was silent, completely bewildered, and she added, "Aren't you being rather greedy?"

"I waited a long time for you. I killed Jameel for you. I gave up everything for you"—what was the good of saying it?

Instead, he said in a low voice, "I suppose we look at things differently. You told me that night at the Railway Hotel that I ought to have *affaires*, and I told you I didn't want them, and I still don't. This isn't an *affaire* for me. I love you. I should like us to be married."

She laughed, shakily. "Flynn darling, don't be absurd!"

"That's the trouble, you see. What seems absurd to you seems natural and right to me, and the way you want things unnatural and wrong in every way."

She was both distressed and irritated. She said, a little harshly, "I divorced my husband, but in the eyes of your Church I'm still married to him. We couldn't be married, anyway."

He answered her, sadly, "I wasn't saying what could be, but what I should like to be. It would make me happy to know that if it could be you would want it too, but I know you wouldn't."

"You'll think differently about it all when you've been here a little while."

He made no comment on that, feeling the futility of contradiction. After a silence which she found 'awkward', but which for him throbbed with pain, he said, heavily, "When shall I see you again?"

He was almost surprised when she said, "Would you like to come tomorrow afternoon? I'd like to show you the sun-roof of the studio. We could have coffee up there. You can see right across Paris to Montmartre."

"What time shall I come?"

"About three? I have to go out at seven. . . ."

That was how it was to be, then; she would see him at odd times, when she could fit him in, like a hairdresser's or a tailor's appointment, of no more importance than that, and of rather less importance than a cocktail date. . . . He recognised now that in not meeting him at the Gare du Nord she had set the key for their whole relationship.

The taxi stopped and she told him, "This is your hotel."

He got out, then leaned back into the taxi to kiss her hand.

He said with an effort, "Thank you—for everything. I'll come tomorrow at three."

Crossing the pavement, it occurred to him that perhaps he should have offered to pay for the taxi. In time, he supposed, he would learn the etiquette and obligations of this new world; for the time being he felt dazed and unhappy and utterly unadjusted.

When he had gone, Stephanie leaned back in a corner of the taxi with a sigh of relief. Poor boy, he was very sweet, but he had a lot to learn. He was terribly young and romantic; he would need a little 'managing'. He had been desperately disappointed, of course; but she had been right to be firm; it was so important to begin as you meant to go on. . . .

III

EXTERNALLY Flynn very quickly adapted himself to the life of Montparnasse and the Quarter; mentally and emotionally he remained as alien to it as to the restrictions Stephanie imposed upon their relationship, which he never ceased to resent, in spite of his outward acceptance.

Determined that he should not cling too closely to her for companionship in a foreign city, one of the first things Stephanie did was introduce him to 'Nina and Johnny'. She took him to one of their parties at the top of a tall dark old house in the Rue Bonaparte; he hated it, but it served the purpose she intended. He met a lot of people, English and American, a number of whom had met his father, and all of whom accepted him easily and readily and invited him to do this, that and the other with them. It was tacitly assumed that he was Stephanie Paul's lover, and as there had been a good deal of speculation as to her precise relationship with Michael Harrigan a certain piquancy was added to this latest piece of gossip. But of this Flynn was for a long while unaware. . . .

So far as he could make out nearly everyone he met subsisted on allowances from families in England and America. They all had 'no money', but apparently managed without going on the bread-line. Most of them wrote or painted, in an obscure, unproductive sort of fashion, but some of them, he observed, did not even do that. They lived, for the most part, in dark little hotels in narrow streets off the Rue Jacob, the Boulevard St. Germain, the Boulevard Montparnasse. They gravitated between the Café des Deux Magots and the Flore, and the Coupole, Dôme, and Select. Nobody nowadays, they assured him, went to the Rotonde; that was terribly nineteen-twentyish.

In time Flynn sorted out the various cafés and bars. The Flore, it seemed, was 'rather literary', and the Select 'very queer'—this was duly explained to him, and it was something he never understood—and the Magots was the 'hang-out' of the surrealists, whilst all the 'bums' and down-and-out painters in Paris hung round the Dôme 'zinc' in the hope of being stood a drink, perhaps cadging a few francs, or even a meal. On the terrace of the Dôme you could find almost anyone any evening at the aperitif hour, and if not there it was understood that you would find them in the American bar of the Coupole. It was an accepted thing that you spent more on your drinks before the meal than on the food itself; you ate very cheaply at little restaurants in side streets to enable you to do so. Montmartre, he learned, was no longer fashionable with the literary and artistic set, not even with Americans; it, too, was 'terribly nineteen-twentyish'. But once or twice he heard it counter-suggested that Montmartre was the 'only possible' place now that 'everyone' was living in Montparnasse and the Quarter; either that or out by the Porte d'Orleans. Others, again, declared that the Observatoire was the farthest out you could go on the Left Bank without affectation. Ideally, of course, one lived on the Île St. Louis—and when he had found it in his wanderings along the quays Flynn was inclined to agree; it would be pleasant and peaceful to live in one of those gracious old houses looking through trees on to the river, and the quays there were quieter than elsewhere, or, more accurately, less noisy—for it was impossible to escape noise in Paris, he discovered, and he never accustomed himself to that fact.

He made, quite quickly, a number of acquaintances, but no friends—he never came close enough to anyone for that. He had a general impression of everyone being free-and-easy and friendly, but little Jeanne D'Alvray was the only person for whom he developed any real affection. Her mother had warmth, and a kind of vulgar good-nature, but she never ceased to shock him by an outspokenness on sex and morals which he found quite incredible and completely unacceptable. She knew that she shocked him, and it amused her. It was good for him, she declared—and it was an attitude which Stephanie endorsed.

'Johnny' was American, tall, loose-limbed, good-looking in what Stephanie called a 'collegiate' fashion. He was old at twenty-four, and went about with a perpetually worried expression on his boyish face. Nina was ten years older, and the general feeling was that he was a fool to 'tie himself up' in so domestic a fashion with a married woman with two children and an extremely jealous and resentful French husband from whom, it was asserted, she was only semi-detached. At twenty-four Johnny already had a married-man, father-of-a-family air.

Flynn met Monsieur D'Alvray once, a short, dark, unhappy-looking little man, very obviously deeply devoted to his children, and especially to Jeanne. Flynn found an intolerable poignancy in the whole situation—the look of love and pain on the father's face when Jeanne climbed on to his knee, twining her arms round his neck, and chattering eagerly to him in French, with an animation he had never seen her exhibit in the presence of her mother and Johnny. Nina had been ironing at a table in a corner of the room, occasionally glancing up at the clock; when the husband had gone—for another week—the boy Henri would slip upstairs to let the lover know. . . .

To Flynn it was all very shocking, and inexpressibly sad. But Stephanie insisted that that was just sentimental, because, she said, Nina's husband was 'a fiend of jealousy', counted every *sou*, and was altogether 'quite impossible to live with'; Nina was very good to let him come there and visit the children as she did, and Johnny was a lamb, and they were very happy together, and Nina had done him 'a world of good', because before he had linked up with her he had been 'in a terrible mess, psychologically speaking'.

Flynn found it all completely unacceptable; for him it was all a terrible mess, morally speaking, and it depressed him. He gave up going to the house in the Rue Bonaparte except occasionally to see Jeanne, on days when he could not find her in the Luxembourg gardens. Nina's parties, at which people sat round drinking Pernod out of soup-bowls—because there were never enough glasses for everyone who crowded into the two squalid rooms, with their hideous wallpaper, their naked electric light bulbs, their bare boards—seemed to him quite horrible. On the few occasions when he had gone, taken by Stephanie, who always assured him he would meet some 'vurry in-er-esting people' there, he had ended up in a corner with Jeanne, or outside on the stairs with her, telling stories, playing cats' cradles with a piece of string, or some paper-and-pencil game. He found the gossip at these parties tedious, the endless references to people variously described as 'camp' or 'queer' or 'so'; the endless strings of names that meant nothing to him, the endless discussions of obscure literary publications as though they were of the utmost importance, the alternations of back-biting and back-scratching that went with it all. He could never accustom himself to the candid sexuality of the conversations, and the fact that life amongst the intelligentsia was apparently a series of *affaires*; the word 'love' hardly came into it, he observed.

Above all, he hated the excessive drinking, which caused people to become loud and quarrelsome and to show off—or, as they put it, 'exhibitionist'; in the face of it, all his innate puritanism would rise to the surface, as it had as a child in the presence of his father's alcoholism and his hard-riding and hard-drinking friends.

The parties at Stephanie's studio were a little different in atmosphere, partly due to the fact of her intellectual snobbism, and partly to the fact that she never served Pernod, which she regarded as pernicious. When Nina came to these parties she was always, after a few drinks, a little aggressive, conscious that socially and intellectually the 'tone' was superior to that of her own parties. Then she would begin to pick a quarrel with Stephanie, accusing her of despising her. 'For God's sake!' Johnny would protest, and take her home. Later he would come back, alone, and, over-full of drink himself, get Stephanie into a corner, or another room, and confide to her that he was sick and tired of the squalid life with Nina in the Rue Bonaparte, and that of course he wouldn't tell this to a soul, only Stephanie was so understanding. . . . If she had had enough drink herself Stephanie's eyes would brim with tears of sympathy, and she would press his hand and murmur, 'Poor darling Johnny', and it would all become very emotional, and perhaps a little more than that. . . . In the morning Johnny would come round in a distraught state to ask what he had said last night, and apologise, and beg her to forget any goddam nonsense he might have gone in for, and Stephanie would reassure him, and he would walk back in a glow of gratitude, thinking how wunnerful Stephanie was. . . .

If only they wouldn't all drink so much, Flynn would think, despairingly; they did, literally, drink themselves silly. Very often they would move on from a party to a *boîte*—'Bricktops' or *Le Bœuf sur Le Tôit*—where there was a Negro cabaret and everything was wildly expensive. More often they stayed on the Left Bank and went to a Biguine dancing place, at which Stephanie would dance with the utmost abandon with coloured partners, conscientiously demonstrating her freedom from colour prejudice.

The first time they went she accused Flynn of colour prejudice because he would not dance, and, when he had finally convinced her that he had no such prejudice, that it had not even occurred to him that such a thing existed, and that he did not want to dance even with her, of being 'priest-bound' and a prude. Well, she could call him that. He tried to explain to her that deep down in him he had always had that feeling that the priests were right in their denunciation of modern dancing—this business of clasping someone of the opposite sex to you in intimate embrace in public, bodies pressed to bodies. That he had had this feeling about dancing even in Ireland, even, when he had danced himself. And this Biguine dancing was frankly sensual. . . . Then Stephanie would accuse him of being a hypocrite. At first he merely shrugged; if she saw it like that there was nothing he could do about it. But she taunted him once too often. There was a night when he suddenly sprang up in a rage and seized her and danced like mad, with a crazy abandon, and after that he danced with a half-naked little Martinique who had just performed a 'stomach dance' as a cabaret number, her costume consisting of a raffia skirt and several strings of beads.

After that he drank as wildly as he danced, and finally had no recollection of leaving the place.

He wakened in the morning in a strange bed and feeling quite incredibly ill.

2

He realised, gradually, that he was in a small, darkish room with very violent wallpaper, and that a serious-looking girl with horn-rimmed glasses and oilily smooth black hair sat on the bed and regarded him, solemnly. He had a vague recollection of having seen her before.

"How do you feel?" she inquired, adding, "There's some coffee here if you'd like it."

He sat up and she pulled the pillow up behind him. He realised that he was wearing his shirt and trousers; his shoes were on the floor beside the bed, his coat over the back of a chair, and his tie hung across the coat. He was also aware of intense nausea, and his head felt like bursting. He sank back against the pillow.

"What am I doing here at all?" he demanded.

The girl told him, "Several of us came back here in a taxi when we left the Biguine place, and you passed out on us, so we thought you'd better stay here, as nobody knew where you were staying, and Mrs. Paul seemed to have got lost. I managed to get your shoes and coat and tie off, to make you a little more comfortable——"

"It was very good of you." Was this how his father felt most mornings of his life? He pressed his hands to his throbbing forehead, and the girl continued, in her matter-of-fact tone, "You'd feel better if you could bring yourself to take something. A hangover's always worst on an empty stomach."

He took the coffee from her and sipped. There was a *croissant* in the saucer beside the shallow bowl and he ate a piece and discovered that she was right; to eat did make one feel rather less ghastly, physically, though it could not lift the deep sense of humiliation.

When he had finished the coffee and the *croissant*, she took the bowl and saucer from him and went over to the wash-basin and wrung out a face-cloth in cold water, and brought it to him with a towel.

"It would help if you sponged your face and hands," she suggested.

When he had done so she brought him a comb, and suddenly, running it through his hair, he laughed.

"You should have been a nurse," he said, and then, handing her back the comb, "I don't know your name, but I met you at Nina's place, didn't I?"

"Yes. My name is Mary Trant. I'm on the stage—dancing—when I can get a job."

"I remember. You want to be a ballet-dancer."

She corrected him, sombrely, "I am a ballet-dancer, but I have to take what I can get."

She went over to the window and looked out. "It's a lovely day," she observed. "Don't think I want to get rid of you, but the air would probably do you good. I've nothing to do this morning, worst luck, and I thought we could go and sit in the gardens for a bit."

Flynn heaved himself up off the bed, throwing off the blankets, groping for his shoes. He groaned a little as he pulled them on, and sat down on the bed again, his head beating agonisingly. The girl came over to him, owlishly solemn with her large glasses, and kneeling down began to tie his shoe-laces. He pulled away from her quickly.

"I'm not all that ill," he protested.

When he had tied his shoes he got up and took his tie and went over to the wash-basin. In the mirror, as he tied his tie, he saw her stripping the bed, and it suddenly occurred to him to ask, "Where on earth did you sleep last night?"

She told him, tranquilly, "With you."

He was startled, but he merely turned round and picked up his coat from the back of the chair and observed, drily:

"That can't have been very comfortable."

"It was better than the floor. There was nowhere else."

How could she tell him that it was the most romantic and exciting thing that had ever happened to her in her twenty-four years—night-long to watch his sleeping face, brush the hair back from his forehead, rest her face against his. . . . This should be her secret for ever, that just once she had lain beside a man, a young and attractive and normal man, even she, Mary Trant, who never attracted men and pretended to no interest in them to conceal that humiliation. . . .

He said, with sudden bitterness, "You should have thrown me out into the gutter."

He excused himself from her for a minute, and when he came back they went down the steep dark stairs together and out into the Rue Jacob. They did not get as far as the gardens; when they came to the Café des Deux Magots Flynn decided that they had gone far enough; he wanted to sit down and drink gallons of iced water.

It was nearly mid-day and there were a number of people he knew by sight on the sunny café-terrace. Mary spoke to several as they passed between the tables, and waved to others in the distance. She was very happy to be seen with the good-looking Irish boy, because it was well known that he wasn't 'queer' like most of the beautiful young men in the Quarter, but having an affair with Stephanie Paul. Several people knew that he had passed out in her room and that she had proposed to allow him to remain there for the night, and she hoped that already the story would be running round Montparnasse and the Quarter, bringing a new lustre to a name she secretly acknowledged to be as dreary as that of Philippa Bryce—drearier, in fact, for Philippa at least moved in the aura of the glamorous Mrs. Paul, whereas she was notoriously solitary.

She sat there in the pale autumn sunshine, drinking the burnt red wine that was her favourite aperitif, at her side a good-looking and quite normal young man with whom she had passed the night, and life, which all her years in Paris had been so astonishingly drab, put forth blossoms like the bare branches of an almond tree suddenly awake to spring. She was animated and gay, as though she had given herself, gladly, to a lover. And something of herself she had given, she felt, with a kind of pride.

She gossiped, energetically, of Montparnasse personalities, and Flynn made no attempt to follow it all. It was the usual stuff he had heard so many times, and it was easy to detach his mind from it so that her voice became lost to him in the general clatter and chatter of the café. She had been kind to him, but she was a bore. All this Paris life was altogether a bore. Paris was a lovely enough city, and if you were Parisian, living a normal life, with a job, and a home, it would be possible to enjoy sitting at cafés and lounging in bars and bistrôts by way of relaxation and change, but the life of this English and American colony camped out on the Left Bank was little but that, and there was something rotten at the core of their lives, he felt. Sometimes they merely bored him—as Mary Trant was boring him then—but sometimes they filled him with anger and contempt. Then he would ask himself, impatiently, what did they all amount to, anyway, all these conceited, egotistical, self-important nonentities, these parasitical rentiers and hangers-on, these dilettantes and poseurs? There were a few writers and artists of some distinction to be seen about, and perhaps a few serious people amongst the undistinguished, but it was not they who cluttered up the bars and crowded the café-terraces, and drank themselves silly at parties. It was the bogus people who did that, deriding the achievements of everyone outside of their own precious little cliques, but within their own particular circle attaching importance to every kind of affectation and triviality.

Sitting now at the Deux Magots, Flynn gave his companion an absent smile occasionally and murmured 'Really?' and 'Indeed?', and he thought, 'I want to be alone; I want to sit under trees and look at water and be quiet, with no one talking, and no sound of traffic. If I have to talk to anyone I should like it to be little Jeanne, who is honest and has no affectations, and who a great deal of the time inhabits her own private world.' These people, it seemed to him, had no private worlds into which they withdrew; nothing was sacred to them; they had no reticences and no quietness.

It was a relief when a stout, florid, middle-aged man came to their table. He had a high-pitched voice and a nervous tittering manner, and all the time he was talking to Mary—asking her what she was doing now, if she had heard or seen anything lately of Tony, Olivia, Juno—he was glancing round the café-terrace fearful of missing anyone, anything. Mary introduced him and Flynn murmured "How d'ye do?" without hearing his name, and seized the first opportunity of declaring that he must be going, and looked round for a waiter to give him *l'addition*. Until then he had thought that in return for her kindness he would invite Mary to lunch with him; then suddenly he knew that he couldn't face it. She was so humourless and solemn, when she was not being drearily malicious, and he had had enough.

He left her with a sense of escape, and crossing the Boulevard St. Germain made his way up to Montparnasse and walked in the direction of the Observatoire, wondering what had happened to Stephanie last night, how they had come to get separated, so that he had been carried off in Mary Trant's party. He had a hazy recollection of dancing a rumba with Stephanie, and then with a half-naked little coloured girl. He remembered that the atmosphere had been suffocatingly hot and smoky, and there had been that insidious throb of the Biguine music, with its drums, its wailing saxophone, its rhythm of shaken seeds ta-ti-ta-ing above the drums. It was a rhythm that got into your blood, and once you had succumbed to it you were lost. It came back to him that Stephanie had accused him of colour prejudice and of being a prude because he had stood out against it, declining to dance. After that he had been determined to 'show her' . . . and the rest was all confusion.

He stopped at the Café des Lilas at the end of the boulevard for black coffee, debated with himself as to whether he would sit for a while in the gardens or go and lie down in his room, and decided to do the latter—after first calling on Stephanie to find out what had happened last night, and when he might expect to be seeing her again.

He took the lift up to her apartment—shutting himself in with the usual slight misgiving—and Philippa answered the door and regarded him unsmilingly. Mrs. Paul, she said, was not in. Whilst he was trying to find out from her when she was likely to be in Stephanie's voice called out, "It's all right, Phil darling, if that's Flynn I wanna see him."

Frowning, Philippa admitted him. He grinned at her and went into the studio, where he found Stephanie reclining on the divan, cushions behind her back, on a low table beside her a jug of water with cubes of ice floating in it, and a half-full glass. She wore the moonlight-coloured négligé he had seen on more than one occasion at Ballyrannon. She was smoking a Turkish cigarette. He thought that she looked tired.

She smiled at him and held out her hand, languidly, with deliberate affectation.

"What happened to *you* last night?" she demanded.

He kissed her hand and sat down on the divan, facing her.

"I can't remember," he told her, "but I still feel quite awful, and I woke up this morning in Mary Trant's room."

"That must have been a thrill for her! How on earth did you get there?"

"Apparently I went back with her and some others to her place and passed out there and she let me stay. It was decent of her. How are you, darling?"

"Not too good, but recovering. After we lost you we went on to the *Boîte des Matelots*. It was fairly dull."

She passed him the shagreen cigarette box with Turkish cigarettes one side and Egyptian the other. He shook his head. "No, thanks. Listen, Stephanie, all this sort of thing's no good——"

"What do you mean, 'all this sort of thing'?"

"All these parties, and drinking too much, and places like we went to last night, and feeling like death in the morning. It's all such a waste of time. And I'm so tired of *people*. . . . I wish—so much—we could go somewhere quiet together, just the two of us. You said there was a forest not far out from Paris——"

"So there is, my pet. We might go this weekend as it happens—two young friends of mine are coming into Paris for a week and have offered me their villa, and if we like it there we can stay the whole week. We might go. Little Paulo's very tired of Montparnasse too."

She put up a hand and brushed back the lock of hair that always fell over his forehead. "I can't think why you don't put something on your hair," she murmured. She had said that so often since he had been in Paris —in Connemara it apparently hadn't mattered—that he had come almost not to hear it; he took her fingers and kissed them. He disliked, intensely, her reference to herself as 'Paulo', because it was Philippa's name for her, and for some other reason he could not define, except that it made him 'curl up' inside; but he let it pass because her promise made him hopeful and happy.

"It would be lovely to get out into the country for a week," he said, and added, after a moment's contemplation of the happiness ahead, "I've very little money left. If I'm to stay on in Paris I must get a job of some kind, when we get back. I was wondering if I could give English lessons, like Johnny——"

She laughed. "With a Connemara accent?" She mocked him, "Indade, what sort of English would it be at all?"

"Johnny has an American accent," he pointed out. "But if you think I'd be no good at that sort of thing I could get a job washing-up in a restaurant or something—I wouldn't mind what I did——"

"Darling, don't be romantic. You shall give Gaelic lessons to rich Americans. When we get back I'll give a special party for you and you'll be fixed up in no time—you only need five people taking an hour a week each at a hundred francs an hour."

He smiled. "I daresay, but isn't it yourself is being romantic now? Why should there be five rich Americans wishing to learn Gaelic? Outside of Ireland no one's interested in Gaelic—why should they be?"

"Because, darling, Americans are just naturally in-er-ested in anything *cultural*. Particularly American women. Why else do you suppose those women's clubs exist all over the United States, and English celebrities come over to lecture to them and make thousands of dollars?"

"Isn't that very odd, now?" He helped himself to some iced water. "Very well, then, I will try to teach Gaelic to rich female Americans at a hundred francs an hour." He swallowed a tumblerful of water, and then demanded, "When are you coming to see my room? All this time and you've never been—soon all the leaves will be off the tree, and then it won't look so nice."

"I'll come this evening, and then we'll walk down through the gardens and eat at the Medici Grill and have a quiet evening—if you'd like that."

"I'd like it fine, though I don't really care where we eat, or whether we eat at all."

"You really are an incorrigible romantic!" He was aware of the note of impatience in her voice, although she laughed. She had complained more than once that the places she took him to were wasted on him. She had demanded, once, why hadn't he his father's interest in food, and he had replied that perhaps the fact that he wasn't his father had something to do with it. . . .

He answered her now, himself a little impatient, "I meant only that where we go or what we do is immaterial so long as we're together. . . ."

"All right, honey, it's all settled. You must go now, because Julian Richards is arriving for tea any minute now, and he'd hate to find you here."

"Julian Richards—who is he?" This maddening habit they all had of assuming that one knew everybody.

"He's the editor of a fearfully highbrow monthly, and he's rich and an intellectual snob and in love with me." Her tone was a little defiant.

Flynn said, "He sounds a horror. Why do you have him here?"

"He's terribly sweet to me, and quite amusing—that's why. Also perhaps because he's middle-aged and charming."

Flynn was aware of the challenge but did not pick it up. What was the point of quarrelling? He got up, frowning a little. He said, "One of these days, you know, I'll not be dismissed like this."

She smiled. "Won't you, darling? That'll be just too bad. . . ."

She helped herself to another cigarette, and snapped the lid to with a little irritated gesture.

"I either mean something to you or I don't," he pointed out, "and if I don't I don't know what I'm doing here——"

Now it was she who frowned, and when she frowned her agelessness deserted her and she was middle-aged. It was something which always pained him—it was 'the wrong of uncomely things' that was the wrong too great to be told, something that wronged his heart's image of her.

She said, "Darling, don't *bicker*! Go home and sleep that hangover off, and I'll come round this evening between six-thirty and seven."

She smiled and was young again, and he said humbly, "I'm sorry." He bent and kissed her forehead and went out.

He met Julian Richards coming out of the lift and realised that he had seen him several times before without knowing who he was. He was smartly dressed, as always, with an elegant, careful negligence—the artist, but the artist who has made good and has a substantial banking account with which to back up his Bohemianism. He carried a bunch of long-stemmed yellow roses, and it occurred to Flynn to wonder whether he had chosen yellow because he happened to be wearing a yellow tie, and had a yellow silk handkerchief in his breast-pocket. He wore a topaz signet ring on the little finger of his left hand, and carried a malacca cane with a large silver knob. He was handsome, in a heavy, middle-aged, successful business-man, self-satisfied fashion, and smelled delicately of eau-de-Cologne. He smiled faintly and held the lift-gates with a murmured, "*Pardon*", but black hatred surged up in Flynn and he brushed past him and slammed the gates after him.

"Who was that extraordinarily boorish young man who has just left you, my Sweet?" was Mr. Richards' first inquiry of his hostess, whilst the maid relieved him of his stick, and his artistic wide-brimmed black hat, and

Philippa took charge of the roses—the usual two dozen, she noticed, with approval.

Stephanie told him, as he followed her into the studio, "A young Irish poet, the son of Michael Harrigan, the novelist. He's not long over from the wild West of Ireland and is still a little uncouth, but really a *vurry* charming young man, and I think when you see them you'll agree that his translations from the Gaelic are quite brilliant. You must ask him to let you have two or three for *Poésie*. He needs some money badly, the poppet . . ."

"And some manners," Mr. Richards observed, "but tell me, Angel, what has been happening whilst I've been in darkest London? I want to hear *all* the dirt !"

IV

STEPHANIE met Raymond Farrow, 'the young American poet', on the stairs the evening she came to see Flynn's room, and she brought him along with her.

"You two boys are neighbours and ought to know each other," she said.

Flynn had never felt that he wanted to meet his poet neighbour ; he had seen him a good many times, coming and going, and had thought he looked conceited—which he was, inordinately. He had also tried to read some of his poems in *Transition*, *Échange*, and *Poésie*, and not only had they not made sense to him but had not seemed poetry to him—as he understood it. He had also found it a little trying that Mr. Farrow's genius appeared to function chiefly at midnight and in the early hours of the morning, and only on the typewriter. When Flynn had mentioned Farrow to Stephanie she had assured him that he was 'a very charming young man,' adding, 'He's queer, of course.' Flynn had murmured, wearily, 'Of course.' . . .

When he opened the door and saw Farrow standing behind Stephanie his heart sank. Farrow had a handshake like a wet fish, and though he was still in his early twenties his thin fair hair had receded, and it was obvious that in a few years he would be bald. He had a puffy, rather petulant, look, with conceited eyes and a small moist mouth. He carried, Flynn noticed, as he came into the room, the current issue of *Poésie*.

For a few minutes, after the introductions, Stephanie walked about the room exclaiming—the bookshelves above the divan-bed were 'cute', and having the tree almost thrusting its branches in at the window was 'swell'. . . .

Flynn said, deliberately, "What isn't so cute, though, is Mr. Farrow's typewriter thumping overhead at two in the morning !"

He looked at Raymond, who, startled, exclaimed in his rushing, nervous manner, "Oh, my dear, I'm so terribly sorry. But what is one to do? The ideas come to one at all sorts of odd times——"

"Need you type them ?" Flynn inquired.

Stephanie put in, "Raymond types everything, even his love-letters, don't you, honey?"

Raymond simpered, "I'm afraid I do !"

Stephanie picked up *Poésie* from the table. She said, determined to cover up the offence Flynn's bluntness had given, knowing how touchy Raymond was, and how susceptible to flattery, "I liked your poem in this issue, Raymond."

He all but writhed with gratification. To Flynn he seemed to writhe away from his words as he uttered them.

"Oh, how sweet of you, darling! I'm terribly glad. I put a quite *frantic* amount of work into it!"

Stephanie passed the magazine to Flynn, open at Farrow's contribution.

"I think you'll like this, darling. I should think it's up your street—realism lit by poetic imagery."

"I think perhaps it has a teeny, weeny little bit of importance," the poet murmured.

Flynn read the poem. It was entitled, 'Balustrade'.

> Staircase murmurings
> In the elbowing darkness
> In coal-holes prisoned,
> And the soul's caverns
> Frenzied with spiritual
> Baksheesh.
>
> The concierge's daughter
> Is *enceinte*
> By the student
> In the attic.
> The floor is black
> With sobbing apples
> And weeping wishes.
>
> The silence screams
> Its head off
> And the stairs
> Are drunk with stars
> Crazily copulating.

Flynn looked up, smiling.

"I don't really understand it, I'm afraid. I find I never do understand modern poetry. I'm sorry."

" 'The silence screams its head off' is terribly good," Stephanie suggested.

"But it's false imagery," Flynn suggested. "Silence doesn't scream. It can breathe or brood or any other quiet thing, but it certainly can't scream, even metaphorically, any more than an apple can sob."

"Don't be so literal, darling!" She turned reassuringly to Farrow, smiling. "Flynn belongs to the Irish Romantic School, you know. Yeats, and all that."

Flynn said, violently, "I don't belong to any school! It's just that what passes for poetry nowadays isn't poetry as I understand it—and as Yeats understands it, and all those that went before him understood it. If what Mr. Farrow and all the others write is poetry, then what Shakespeare and Shelley wrote is something else. But what they wrote used to be called poetry, and it's what I call poetry. If you write 'the concierge's daughter is *enceinte* by the student in the attic' you don't make it poetry by writing it in four lines instead of one. It still remains what it is—a prose sentence."

Raymond Farrow had gone quite white. His voice shook a little, as he said, with what was intended as a sarcastic, superior smile, but emerged only as a curious twitching grimace, "Thank you very much, but fortunately we don't all have to have our ears titillated with little jingling rhymes."

Flynn replied, "Rhyme isn't essential, but metre is. There must be rhythm—and music. And the great poets were all intelligible. They had something to say and they said it poetically."

"Really! How very interesting! I suppose, then, you wouldn't call, 'I am aware of the damp souls of housemaids sprouting despondently at area gates' poetry?"

Flynn laughed. "Of course not. Is it meant to be?"

Stephanie was genuinely shocked. "Darling, it's by one of the vurry greatest of the modern poets—T. S. Eliot."

"I don't care who it's by, I wouldn't be calling it poetry! I don't think it's very good even as prose. Why should a housemaid's soul be any damper than Mr. Eliot's? What is a damp soul, anyhow?"

Farrow licked lips that had gone dry. It was an effort for him not to tremble, and his heart was beating so fast that the words came with difficulty.

"Perhaps," he said, "our one and only playboy of the Western world would give us a sample of what *he* is good enough to consider poetry?"

Flynn did not hesitate. There was an English poem that stood out for him head and shoulders above anything he had ever read; a poem he had known as a boy, and dreamed of as he lay upon the lake island on a summer's morning dreaming of a girl; a poem that thrilled him like Connolly's words on leaving the Post Office in Easter Week. Those words were poetry, too, a poetry that men lived, and never more richly than in those moments when they faced the firing-squad. . . .

"Yes," he said, "this. The poet is addressing night, and he says:

" 'Blind with thine hair the eyes of Day,
    Kiss her, until she be wearied out.' "

He gave the words their full music, and smiled confidently at the pale angry young man opposite him.

Raymond exclaimed, contemptuously, "Good God, at this stage of human history—Swinburne!"

"Shelley," Flynn corrected him, gently malicious.

"Shelley! Have you read Aldous Huxley on Shelley?"

Stephanie intervened at this point. "Darlings, this is all *terribly* in-er-esting, but why don't we go over to the Café des Lilas and thrash it all out over some nice cold champagne *natur*?"

Raymond Farrow picked up the copy of *Poésie*.

He said, the words tumbling over each other, torrentially, "It's terribly sweet of you, Stephanie darling, but I'll ask you to excuse me—I really feel rather ill. One isn't used to being insulted—it's all rather upsetting——"

"Raymond darling——" Stephanie protested, but he rushed out.

When the door had slammed on him Flynn flung himself down on the divan, roaring with laughter.

"Can you beat it?" he cried. " 'The damp souls of housemaids'! 'The silence screams its head off'! 'Sobbing apples'! And he doesn't even recognise two lines from one of Shelley's most famous short poems! He's probably never read Shelley, or Shakespeare, or any real poetry!"

Stephanie stood by the window, frowning.

"You were frightfully rude to him, you know, darling."

"Rude? I was perfectly polite. I simply asked him if he need bang away over my head at two in the morning, and told him I didn't understand his poem."

"And that you didn't consider it poetry, anyway! Now you've made an enemy of him for life, and he's a great friend of Julian Richards."

"Who cares?"

"If you had any sense, you would! You could sell Julian any number of your poems if you passed them off on him as translations from the Gaelic—and didn't quarrel with his pet protégés!"

Flynn stared at her. "You're not seriously suggesting I should pass my poems off on Richards as translations?"

"Why not? I suppose you've heard of the young English poet Thomas Chatterton?"

"I have, but because he was a literary impostor is no reason for anyone going and doing likewise!"

She eyed him, thoughtfully. "Your father was right, you know, Flynn—you are a prig."

He shrugged. "As well as a prude and a hypocrite?"

"There's no point in raking all that up. What is to the point is that I'm not suggesting you should take translations and pass them off as your own work—that would be dishonest, I admit. All I'm suggesting is that you make translation a cloak of anonymity which would enable you to get things published—and paid for. You were saying this morning you wanted money."

"But if Richards likes anything of mine, why can't he publish it and pay for it as what it is—the work of a young Irish poet? I thought one of the objects of *Poésie* was to encourage the younger poets——"

"So it is, darling innocent, but if Julian Richards knew that what you sent him was the work of the boorish young man he met at the lift he wouldn't look twice at them. Besides, dear Julian is *vurry* highbrow, bless his heart. Mr. Flynn Harrigan does not represent a highbrow cult—Celtic Revivalism does."

"Perhaps he won't fancy Celtic Revivalism presented to him by the boorish Mr. Harrigan—especially after dear little Raymond has been and wept on his shoulder about Mr. Harrigan's rudeness. It's something I'll have to think about before deciding."

She told him, "By the time you've done thinking Raymond will have queered your pitch for you. You'd better go and see Julian tomorrow morning and take him some things and interest him in them, and be very nice to him, and tell him how much you enjoy *Poésie*——"

"I must be a liar as well as an impostor, is that it?"

"I suppose you've told as many lies as the rest of us in your time——"

"It's the humbug I object to—pretending to admire all that affected rubbish."

"You can't just sweep it all aside like that! The revolt against formality is symptomatic of our age. You get the same revolt expressed in modern music and painting."

He sat up, brushing the hair back from his forehead.

"What you call the revolt against formality is revolt against technique —nowadays anyone can write what they call poetry because there's no technique involved. You just chop prose up into lines and the less meaning it has the better. I wonder if Master Farrow can write a sonnet—does he even know the technique of a sonnet, the difference between a Petrarchan and a Shakespearean and a pure English sonnet? Does he know the difference between a ballad and a ballade? Could he compose a villanelle—does he even know off-hand what it is? Wouldn't you think it would be time enough to dispense with technique when you'd demonstrated that you'd mastered it?"

He sprang up. "We'd better go and have that drink—I'm getting angry."

She had not known that he had such a capacity for vehemence. It might have been Mike Harrigan himself speaking! Paris was educating Flynn all right—if not quite along the lines she had anticipated.

She said, as they went down the stairs, "A Russian artist friend of mine has an exhibition of his work in a gallery in the Boulevard Raspail tomorrow. The private view is tomorrow afternoon. You'd better come with me and have a look at anti-formalism in modern painting. . . . Besides, you'd probably like Boronski. He's quite a person. . . ."

.2

She was right about that, at least. He did like Boronski, and came nearer to friendship with him than with anyone he met during that Paris phase. He disliked his work; he disliked it quite as much as he disliked Raymond Farrow's poetry; he saw no reason why a ladder should emerge from the stomach of a naked woman, but when he said this to Boronski he roared with laughter, and demanded why not?

"Because it's unnatural," Flynn said.

Boronski laughed. "So is the whole goddam business of painting." He spoke fluent English with an American accent, having learned it during what he called 'the American invasion of Paris' in the 'twenties.

Flynn never learned to like his work, but he learned to appreciate its drive, the dynamics of it, to recognise that his vision derived direct from those basic realities of which he had heard his father speak. What he painted came straight out of his zest for living—the things he understood, struggle, hunger, sex, self-preservation, the laugh that was always on the universe, not some high-falutin' intellectual conception of reality. The wild crazy imaginativeness of his work was the illumination of his belief; his clear brilliant colours were the pigmentation of a passion for survival that was a kind of genius. . . .

"It was André Breton who said that beauty had to be convulsive," said

Boronski, "but Gregori Boronski knew it from the time he knew anything at all."

Boronski had a great admiration for Michael Harrigan. "There's a man who loves life!" he said. "There's a man who creates straight out of his loins and belly—where a man ought to create from!

"You keep clear of Stephanie Paul's crowd," said Boronski. "They're punk—emasculated and brain-spun, so goddam intellectual their sex has withered up on them. Or else they're nothing but sex, like Nina and her boy-friend, like Stephanie herself—playing everything out on a stage with a permanent bedroom-scene backcloth."

"Not Stephanie," Flynn protested.

Boronski grinned at him. His thin grey hair was like a crazy halo round the wrinkled moon of his ugly-intelligent face.

"You're in love with her. Your father had more sense. She angled good and hard for him, but he saw through her. It takes more than a Stephanie Paul to fool a Michael Harrigan. She'll give you hell before you're through with her—but you'll be a better poet because of it. . . ."

Flynn could not accept all that Boronski so vehemently insisted on as truth, but he got a great deal from him without realizing it. Only when Boronski spoke about Stephanie as bogus and a man-eater and a parasite, as he frequently did, he would close his mind to it all, telling himself that Boronski was cynical, prejudiced, did not know Stephanie as he knew her. . . .

He enjoyed walking about Paris with Boronski. Boronski took him up to the 'flea-market' in Montmartre, and to Les Halles—where he fell in love with a sheep's head and bought it and took it home to paint. He spent a whole day painting it, and when he had finished the atmosphere of the *abattoir* was in his room; the painting positively dripped with blood. Flynn said this, and Boronski was delighted. He could not wish for higher praise, he said. That nobody would be likely to buy so repulsive a piece of work did not trouble him at all; only the bourgeoisie could afford to buy pictures, and why should one trouble with them, the dullest strata of society? Not, anyhow, when you had eaten for the day. Occasionally it might be necessary to paint a portrait, flatteringly, to make sketches with a photographic likeness, nothing to do with composition or interpretations of inner truth, nothing to do with creativeness. He had always despised the artists who hung round the Dôme and the Rotonde and 'scavenged' a living in this way, he told Flynn, on one of their walks, until he was driven to it himself. Once he had had an exhibition of his paintings at the Rotonde; it was the thing to do in the 'twenties, he said; they were all on wood, because he could not afford canvases, and people did not like paintings on wood. Well, but it hadn't mattered; somehow he had managed to stay alive without having to make a scarecrow of himself in a waiter's greasy dress-coat, or revert to the dish-washing he had done in the days before he had learned how to live on the bread-line. If he couldn't make a living at the one thing he knew, painting—well, then life could do what it liked with him. The only way to force the world to acknowledge him as a painter was to keep on painting. The rest was so much degradation—loss of personal integrity.

Through Boronski Flynn gained a new orientation, both on his father's recklessness with money when he had any, and on his bouts of drinking. Sometimes, listening to Boronski, he could have closed his eyes and have believed that it was his father speaking, and his mind would go back to the summer's morning scene in the library at Ballyrannon Castle when his father had been violent about art in relation to life, demanding of him had he never heard of a drunkard called Kit Marlowe, and a fornicating play-actor called Bill Shakespeare. . . . He had hated his father then, and known no love for him since, but he began to grow to an appreciation of his vigorous, full-blooded living, and the integrity that over-rode all his faults. Boronski also drank wildly when he had any money. He would suddenly stop propping up the Dôme bar and leaning against the radiators, on the look-out for a gullible American or an English Madam of whom to make an outrageously flattering sketch, for anything from twenty to two hundred francs, according to his model's susceptibility to flattery, and instead of cadging drinks would stand them. As often as not he would get drunk and go careering down the boulevard holding his coat high above his head, like a crazy bat, jumping out at people as they passed, or leaping on them as he came up behind them, making them jump, and occasionally getting himself hauled up by a gen-darme. Crazy, but all the world was so sane, he would point out to Flynn next day, in reply to his protests about crazy conduct; the world as a whole was so sombrely sane, so sanely-solemnly preoccupied with its buying and selling, its lying and cheating, its bourgeois formulas. You wanted to laugh, you wanted to yell, to run like a crazy bat all down the boulevard when you thought of it all, making them all jump out of their skins with fright, the sane funny little people with their sane funny little ideas about money and sex and art—and sanity. "Your father understands all this very well," he added, "and it has nothing whatever to do with the dreary self-conscious drinking of your Stephanie Paul crowd, who drink because it's something they call 'la vie Bohème', and releases their sex-inhibitions—which is what they all came to Paris for if the truth could be told—which it seldom is. . . ."

Boronski had a room at the top of a tall old house in a narrow street off the Boulevard Montparnasse, just behind the Dôme, which was convenient, he said—but it was the room's only convenience, as the water did not go up so far, and there was no heating. In summer the room was over-hot; in winter savagely and uninhabitably cold. But it only cost five hundred francs a year, and was complete with an iron bedstead and the remains of a mattress, a couple of faded, thin blankets, a deal table, and a kitchen chair. It was, as Boronski gaily referred to it, an 'appartement meuble'. He had first moved in six years ago, borrowing the money from an American woman who fancied herself as a patron of the arts—but not, said Boronski, to the extent of not allowing him to repay her—'and five hundred francs was nothing to her; she would spend it on a single dinner and a few drinks'—which he did by dish-washing in a workmen's café-restaurant out beyond the Lion de Belfort. It was always a struggle to find the five hundred francs at the end of the twelve months, but one way or another he found means to raise it in time.

"If you're going to live in Paris you want such an apartment yourself," Boronski told Flynn. "You don't want to hang out in any goddam bourgeois private hotel thirty francs a day demi-pension. For thirty francs you can eat once a day for a week if you go to the right places."

Boronski showed him the right places. The best place, he said, when you weren't actually on the bread-line, was a tiny dark narrow little restaurant in the quarter known to its patrons as 'the Ritz', because you could get a *plât* there for three francs, or even two-fifty, and if you were in the money you could have a slap-up meal with a carafe of wine for five francs. There was sawdust on the floor, and wine-stained paper that had once been white on the long trestle tables, and the plates were always greasy and thumb-marked. There was a fat, dirty, slovenly waitress, as bad-tempered as she was unattractive, but the food was not bad, '*pas vilain*', as Boronski called it. True you could never be quite sure the *lapin* wasn't one of the numerous cats always swarming about the place, but you could never doubt the *blanquette de veau* or, when you had the money, the *coq au vin*, and when you could afford nothing else there was always a marvellous onion soup. . . .

Boronski introduced Flynn to a Paris quite unknown to Stephanie, although she believed that she knew the Left Bank intimately.

"She only knows the recognised Anglo-American beat," said Boronski. "All that arty-party crowd think they know Paris if they go to the Bal Tabarin once a week and know a few cheap *prix-fixe* places and live somewhere off the Rue Jacob. But Paris is all things to all men—like love, and other things."

Boronski also introduced Flynn to the Russians. He produced for his interest battered English translations of the plays of Chekhov, the stories of Turgenev, Dostoievski's *Idiot* and Tolstoy's *War and Peace*. Flynn read Turgenev and Chekhov easily and with pleasure, but Dostoievski and Tolstoy he found too heavy and gloomy, though Boronski seemed never to weary of insisting on what a great work *War and Peace* was. But Turgenev wrote of first love and the torrents of spring, and that was something he understood. He could envisage Cousin Kate both as Gemma and as Zinaida —Gemma sitting in the garden sorting cherries, Zinaida lying under the raspberry bush listening to her young lover reading poetry. It was romantic and sad and beautiful . . . like the memory of Cousin Kate and Ballyrannon. With Turgenev's Gemma and Zinaida, and Chekhov's Anna in *The Cherry Orchard*, Stephanie had nothing to do. She did not belong to those delicate, tenuous worlds; she was a world in herself . . . and in moments of illumination he knew that he did not belong to that world; he came and went in it, but never as anything but an alien. As alien as Stephanie herself had been amongst the stones of Connacht.

V

THE forest of Fontainebleau, in its autumn colours, enchanted Flynn. He had never known a forest before. He wanted to walk deeper and deeper into it, insatiably. He could not understand why anyone, completely free as Stephanie was, should ever want to leave such a place—to live in a city, when she could live on the edge of a forest.

The villa Stephanie had been lent was an ugly pretentious affair of red brick, with ornate woodwork round the gables, and ramshackle balconies, but there was an untidy, unkept garden with old fruit trees and long grass and a few ragged autumn flowers—sunflowers, and mauve and purple and bronze and yellow daisies, plumes of golden rod, and a few straggling late roses that reminded Flynn, painfully, of Ballyrannon. The house looked one way across the wild garden to the forest, and the other across a white road flanked by poplars to the river. Inside, the house was smothered in hideous wallpaper, but there was a bedroom with a French window opening on to a verandah above the garden, and downstairs there were red brick floors, and in the kitchen a charcoal-burning Provençale fireplace, and for these things, and its position between river and forest, Flynn thought, you could forgive the pretentiousness without and the mural ugliness within. He looked longingly at the river and thought about a boat; it must be wonderful to live between forest and river in the summer months. . . .

"Why don't we try to find a house out here and stay on anyhow till the end of the autumn?" he suggested, eagerly.

"Because, darling, it would be *vurry* boring after a time, and how could you make any money?"

"I could probably get some kind of a job in the town——"

Stephanie smiled, tolerantly, as at an over-eager child, and he knew that whether he could earn a living out there or not was immaterial; the simple fact was that she wanted to live in Paris. Yet it seemed strange, lying listening to the deep silence of the forest, that anyone could wish to go back and sleep in the midst of the sleepless drone of the city.

Out at Fontainebleau he faced the fact, resolutely, that he and this woman Stephanie Paul had nothing in common once they had left the kingdom of the flesh. They went wild dark journeys together in that kingdom and scaled together shining heights of ecstasy, and afterwards he knew a great flow of tenderness for the woman lying in his arms, and this fusion of passion and tenderness, surely this was love? It was something he could not answer; he only knew that there was this underlying questioning and sadness. He tried to recall what it was he had felt for Cousin Kate, the lyric joy of running to meet her under ilex trees, of grasping her hands and knowing that it was true, that she was real, of laughing together, and running down through the warm summer night to the lake, the feeling of being one with her, of their shared love of Ireland and Irish poetry and all that Ireland stood for that was fine and beautiful, something to live for and if need be to die for. The eager response to beauty that had been bound up with his love for Katherine O'Donal, the sense of the wild and strange and impassioned —which was something different from sexual passion. He remembered it all, but detachedly, as though it had all happened to someone else. Was that love, all that wild, undefined longing, bound up in dreams and poetic imaginings, that white fire of devotion to something afar?

There were times when his whole mood could be summed up in a single stanza:

> 'When passion's trance is overpast,
> If tenderness and truth could last
> Or live, whilst all wild feelings keep
> Some mortal slumber, dark and deep,
> I should not weep, I should not weep!'

As it was, there was a recurrent inner weeping before the bitter realisation that for Stephanie the question of tenderness and truth did not come into the picture; for her he was merely a romantic boy, 'rather sweet', but in need of careful 'managing' if he was not to make 'impossible' demands upon her. To tell him that he was 'rather sweet' was her nearest approach to tenderness, and it was an expression he found intolerable. You gave a woman the strings of your heart to lace her shoes with, if she cared to, and she called you 'rather sweet'. . . . And you, poor fool, could do nothing about it, because, God help you, you loved her—or if it was not love, by any other name it held you as helplessly in bondage.

He discovered, during that week of living together, how little real intimacy there was between them. The physical intimacy of the shared bed carried no mental and emotional intimacy with it—because she would not permit it. He had dreamed of holding her night-long in his arms, of sleeping with his head upon her breast, of waking in the morning to the miracle of her presence at his side, of gathering her to him in the half-light and sleeping again, full of tenderness and sweet content. This, it seemed to him, was the real intimacy, the closeness of this after-flow of tenderness. But Stephanie declared all that to be so much romanticism. Intelligent people, she insisted, did not meet in the morning until they had made their toilets; the man had to shave, the woman 'see to' her hair and face. Nobody looked at their best first thing in the morning.

"But people can't be all the time thinking about how they look," Flynn protested, "and I wouldn't stop loving you because your hair was untidy and you had no make-up. I would love you like that. I don't really like make-up, though I suppose women have to do it if they live in cities. It's not done much in Dublin, though."

"Darling, this isn't Ireland!" She nearly added, 'Thank God!' There were times when Flynn's 'puritanism' was really very irritating.

She remained adamant on the question of their finishing the night apart. It was almost an article of faith with her that all 'cultivated' people had separate rooms. Personal vanity had a good deal to do with it, but it was not the whole of it. Her sensuality, as Flynn was beginning to learn, was a surface thing, a matter of sensation, with no roots in the emotions. It was fashionable to have a lover, it was 'amusing', it was exciting, it was 'fun'. And, when the lover was as young as Flynn, flattering. It was almost anything except an expression of fundamental urge. It came to him with a sense of shock that she was sensual but not passionate. Her response was to the excitement of having a lover, of being made love to, rather than to the man himself flowing out to her, blood and spirit, through his body. It was all surface excitement with her, a titillation of nerves and senses, and afterwards she had no use for the maleness of the man, his body was nothing to her; she wanted to be alone, pretending, as Flynn sometimes thought, in moments of bitter illumination, that nothing had happened.

He would lie alone listening to the deep silence of the forest, and he would feel cheated; deep down in himself he knew that he had been cheated, that she had given nothing, neither of flesh nor spirit, and he would feel degraded, as though he had been used, and then the sense of mortal sin, which he could evade in moments of happiness, would lay hold on him and his spirit writhe in torment. He would know at such times a terrible longing for Ballyrannon, a fierce hunger for its wildness and its simplicities, the regular rhythm of religious devotions giving pattern to life. With a kind of agony he would long to know again the limitations of that life—those limitations which in retrospect had a way of seeming so much wider in the things of the spirit than the freedom of the sophisticated world. The occasional lost, hunting cry of an owl would remind him of a water-bird moving over the lake at night with a long low whistle like a signal. He would watch the moon riding up over the black trees and picture it flecking the lake, indescribably—for there would never be words to describe moonlight on water—turning the monastery into a Spanish villa, pouring its soft milky light over the bogs and along the narrow boreens and over the hills, dim and massive like the hulks of ships, silvering the ragged stone walls and the smooth grey boulders. The castle would be standing there, staring at the moon, trailing a blown spray of ancient ivy across its face. There would be long wide blades of light on the bare boards of the floors, and all the apples laid out on old newspapers would be moon-ripened to silver. Everything would be there in the moonlight as he had always known it. At that moment it was all there, and to the moon, looking down impartially on both, Fontainebleau and Ballyrannon were not so far apart. . . .

'I must go back,' he would tell himself in the night, but in the morning the forest would put its own spell upon him; his inner unhappiness and dissatisfaction would recede, and with this the sense of guilt. He liked to get up early and go out into the forest whilst the dew still lay heavy on the bronzed bracken and the rough wiry grass. He found a curious satisfaction in the forest's big boulders; he liked to touch them and speculate upon the centuries they had lain there, like the stones of Connacht. He liked to think of the forest growing up round them, and of the ice or fire which accounted for their existence. He tried to interest Stephanie in these forest boulders and their possible formation, but she was more interested in a bistrôt in the town which she had been told was 'quite amusing', and in the possibilities of an American bar in the hotel. . . .

However bright and beautiful the morning she never got up before mid-day, and even the thought of anyone getting up and walking about in the dew before breakfast made her shudder.

"Your father is really much more civilised, darling," she told him. "He always boasts that he never gets up before the streets are aired! But being a puritan I suppose you wouldn't call it civilised, but merely decadent."

Flynn said, simply, "It's just a matter of whether you like the early morning or not. I do. You and my father don't." He refused, as always, to rise to the puritan jibe.

When she learned that he had been to early Mass at the church in the town on the Sunday she made another attempt to provoke him.

"You Catholics certainly do believe in keeping in with both worlds!" she drawled. "It beats me how you square it all with your conscience, but that's what the priests are for, I guess!"

But he was not to be drawn on that subject. She had made various attempts to invade the citadel of his religious faith, bringing all that materialism and worldliness she called her 'rationalism' to bear. She was

F

incapable of realising that the citadel was inviolable, being founded on faith. She would accuse him, alternately, of superstition and hypocrisy; and always he refused to discuss it with her. There was a world in which they moved together; outside of it they were strangers, and strangers who did not speak the same tongue. You could not prove a miracle; you could not give a person faith. It puzzled him that she could not accept this.

Walking alone in the forest in the early mornings he would turn and look back at the villa, at the open French window of the room in which Stephanie still lay sleeping, and he would ask himself what it was beyond the physical which bound him to her. Why had she this power over him even when his blood was stilled and his mind knew that they were worlds apart? She did not meet his conception of beauty, yet he never tired of looking at her; they had nothing in common, yet they could be happy together. It came to him that it was because she was perpetually strange to him, a creature from another world; and for her, too, he supposed, there was this fascination of strangeness—but Paris would lose interest in the strangeness of Ballyrannon naïveté he supposed she would call it—he thought, sadly, long before Bally- rannon got used to the glamour of Paris sophistication. He recoiled from the perversions and promiscuities and affectations of her world, but there was another aspect of that world which he found endlessly fascinating. It was a world of cultured elegance, elegant culture. A world of hothouse flowers, Louis-Quinze furniture, pleated lampshades, central heating, exotic books, fashionable and amusing people; a cellophane-wrapped world, bound in vellum. A world of books, music, painting, but all very chic and sophisti- cated. A great many of the books were privately printed and not for export; the concerts were all very fashionable, patronised by the literary and artistic smart-set, the paintings were shown only in the best galleries—though occasionally it was amusing and chic to patronise an exhibition in one of the smaller galleries. It was culture de luxe, in limited edition, for subscribers only. . . .

In Stephanie's world elegance was an essential part of culture. Occasion- ally, from force of circumstance, or for experience, you occasionally lived the barbarous life, as at Ballyrannon, but even in that uncultured desert you still made an oasis for yourself as best you could; you still used expensive per- fume, crêpe-de-Chine handkerchiefs, toilet lotions; still smoked Turkish cigarettes and kept your manicure immaculate. In short, you insisted on remaining civilised.

Flynn could never accustom himself either to the elegance of the studio- apartment in the Avenue de l'Observatoire or to Stephanie's personal elegance. She wore gardenias a good deal on her black suits, and it came to him that these exotically perfumed, waxenly exquisite flowers were exactly expressive of her. The scent of a gardenia, he discovered, was almost too much; it went to the head, made you, almost, a little drunk; yet the flower itself was utterly cool, utterly without flamboyance, almost severe, with its stiff white waxen petals, its smooth dark shiny leaves—Stephanie in a dark tailored suit, with an immaculately white silk shirt, a little masculine; and with her aura of expensive, exotic perfume utterly feminine. It was that quality of the exquisite, that gardenia quality, which characterised both her and her background, which enchanted him. It was all a kind of Grecian urn at which the longer he gazed the more exquisite it seemed. She was the quintessence of everything that was 'different' from anything he had ever known, and that quality of difference was endlessly interesting, endlessly exciting, so that every time he held her in his arms it was for him a miracle of wonder and delight. It wanted only that she should come as close to him in the spirit as in the flesh for all to be perfection; but it was here she cheated him, and defeated his dreams, and he never realised this more acutely than at Fontainebleau, walking alone in the golden days, lying alone in the silver nights.

By the end of the week, despite his love for the forest and the river, he was glad to return to Paris. In the crowded, artificial life of the city the separateness she imposed upon them seemed less unnatural. In Paris he had the companionship of Boronski and the friendship of a child, and in both there was more warmth than in Stephanie's amorousness.

Stephanie, also, in her own language, 'faced up to things' out at Fontainebleau, and she too was glad to get back to the city. Flynn was, of course, 'a terribly sweet boy', but charm, after all, was not everything, even if Voltaire—wasn't it ?—did say it was a form of genius. If you were going to stay around with people any length of time you began to find that charm in itself was not enough ; you got used to it, and then you began to feel the need to be a little more amused. It was more amusing, too, if people had a little money. Youth could be *vurry* overrated, you discovered, once you'd got used to the initial charm. . . .

Philippa, to whom she made these admissions on her return, almost wept with joy. "It's taken you all this time to get around to discovering that ! Of *course* youth is overrated—particularly when it hasn't a cent to bless itself with ! If you've had enough of the Celtic Twilight at last why don't we get away to the South and make a clean break ?"

"I don't want to hurt him, poor pet."

"You were bound to, sooner or later. You always knew that."

"I suppose so. It's all been *experience* for him, of course."

"I'll say it has ! When shall we go South ?"

"What engagements have I got ? Bring me my little book. . . ."

Philippa's heart swelled with love and gratitude. Darling Paulo ! She took a little time to get around to things sometimes, but she always got around to them in the end. That was what was so wunnerful about her. The South with neither of the Harrigans, neither father nor son, was almost too good to be true. There would be someone else before the season was out, of course, but with any luck the next one would be someone you could respect, someone with a little money, and who could therefore be relied upon to treat dear Paulo as she was entitled to be treated, someone who knew how to say it with flowers, and orchids at that. . . .

Stephanie smiled when Philippa said this to her and murmured that maybe she was right. There was no doubt that the Irish had all the charm in the world, but sooner or later you reached that point at which you had to ask yourself if charm was enough, and you had to face up to the fact that for practical, everyday purposes it just simply was not. After all, the Irish had never produced any great love-poetry or any great lovers—or any millionaires. It was significant, she said, thoughtfully.

Philippa beamed love and admiration and happiness at her through her thick glasses. Darling Paulo, so sensible, so profound. . . .

VI

A LETTER from his father awaited Flynn on his return. Mike wrote that he had postponed his Hollywood plans because Bridie had not been at all well; he had had Dr. Murphy to her and he had said that she was run-down and needed a change, so he had taken her to Dublin. She had made a great fuss about going, but there was no doubt that she had benefited by the change. Of late she had been quite tractable, in fact, and he was glad to say that she seemed to be losing her hostility to Katie and the two now seemed to get on fairly well together. They proposed to remain on 'chez O'Donal' till after Christmas; he expected to sail for New York early in the New Year, and he hoped that Bridie would stay on in Dublin. He had shut the castle up and Tante Emma had gone to Letterfrack. '*Your cousin,* he wrote, *is reported to be engaged to a young actor called Rory Mahon, but truth to tell Bridie seems more interested in him. I had a little windfall the other day, having sold a prodigiously bad story for a respectable sum to an English domestic journal, and I enclose five pounds for you to turn into francs and spend in riotous living—you can regard it as a belated birthday present. I have had no news of you since your postcard—with view of Eiffel Tower—announcing your safe arrival, and whilst I should not dream of urging any filial duty upon you, a companion postcard of the Étoile to acknowledge receipt of this and advise me as to your plans, if any, would be appreciated.*' The letter was signed simply, '*Michael Harrigan*'.

Flynn sat down immediately and wrote a long letter setting forth his reactions to Montparnasse, its alleged art, its morals, its affectations, its futilities, its personalities.

'*The only really likable people I've met so far*' [he wrote] '*are little Jeanne D'Alvray, whom you'll no doubt remember, and that crazy Boronski, who is such an admirer of yours. Both of them chatter incessantly, but Jeanne is the least exhausting of the two on the whole. A few days ago I took her out to St. Cloud and we had a lovely day in the woods and by the river. We meet a good deal in the Luxembourg gardens—which reminds me that I discovered the Parc de Montsouris the other day and it reminded me of Stephen's Green . . . which was very hard to bear.*

'*Boronski is having an* affaire *with an American girl to whom he is giving drawing-lessons—though he says she will never learn to draw in a hundred years—and this keeps him off the bread-line at present. When she first saw his work she told him that it was an expression of the unconscious; he had never thought of it like that before, and it turned him surrealist over-night, it seems, and now he paints ladders coming out of naked women's bellies and tea-kettles balanced on the top. The other day he did a painting of me which makes me look completely mad, but Stephanie says its an aspect of my psyche, and gave him a thousand francs for it. She has it framed in her studio, and it's much admired by the intelligentsia when they come to drink her drinks and talk high art and low morals, which they do in clumps and clots several times a week, turning the place into a mad-house.*

'*You will be amused to know that I have sold a few of my poems to that ridiculous publication, "Poésie", passing them off, at Stephanie's suggestion, as translations from the Gaelic. . . . But I have, it seems, earned the undying hatred of Master Raymond Farrow because I called his so-called poetry prose-chopped-up, and as he is very thick with Julian Richards I doubt if I shall pull this trick off again, because, as no doubt you know, it all works like that here.*

'*I have been thinking a good deal about poetry and form lately. . . .*'

Then followed a long and vehement exposition of the ideas he had outlined to Stephanie on the occasion of his meeting with Raymond Farrow. He thanked his father for the money, which, he said, represented '*another few weeks of assured living in this lovely city which would be so much healthier if the English and Americans cleared out—or at least the arty-party sections*'. He added, bitterly, '*I have added two new words to my language since I came here—"rentier" and "homo". The fashionable thing seems to be to be both.*'

He debated with himself as to whether he would tell his father about the week at Fontainebleau, and decided against it. He sent no messages to Bridie or to Katherine or Aunt Chris. He felt that he had none to send. He could still not think of Bridie without anger, Aunt Chris had quarrelled with him, and Cousin Kate disappeared long ago.

This letter delighted Mike, hugely. There was good stuff in the boy. Paris was doing him good; he was wide awake now, in the real world.

He replied briefly on a postcard. '*Thanks for yours. Suggest you write a few articles for Dublin periodicals on modern poetry—technique versus formalism. Katie now playing in "The Hairy Ape". Much improved. Remember me to Boronski, the rascal. Sorry about the ladders, but if it pleases Miss America no doubt it pays!*'

A few weeks later, near the end of October, he wrote another letter and sent another five pounds. He was leaving for New York next month, he said, and gave the sailing date. He had had a cable from Hollywood that his presence was desirable without delay, and since Bridie had settled down with the O'Donals there seemed no point in delaying. She had agreed to remain on in Dublin and was learning shorthand and typing and proposed to get herself a job in an office in due course. He could not, personally, see her settling down to office life, but it kept her occupied and out of mischief. She rode with Katie from Miss Moran's stables on Sundays after Mass. They had some quite good hacks. Rory Mahon usually went with them. *If he and Bridie should make a match of it it would solve the problem of her future. He will certainly never get the virgin of the Gate—of that both your aunt and I are convinced. Bridie never mentions you, and I have an idea that she and Katie are drawn together in their common unforgiveness where you are concerned.*

'*If you go to London look up my publisher, Augustus Hawes; he knows nothing whatsoever about books and boasts that he has never read one, but he could almost certainly give you a job for the asking, and he has a bored and highly decorative wife.*'

Flynn wondered what it was Katherine had not forgiven him—whether it was the old foolish quarrel, or his flight to Paris and Stephanie, of whom Bridie would almost certainly have told her. But that, surely, did not call for any forgiveness from her, however much she might disapprove. He had been unfaithful to his dreams, but not to her, since she had not wanted his love—and the girl to whom he had offered it had gone for good, it seemed, like the wild and lovely lost world to which she belonged. As always, the thought of Cousin Kate filled him with sadness. But when he thought of Bridie his heart hardened. She and her unforgiveness! What had she to forgive? If there was any forgiving to be done it was for him to forgive her. . . .

After getting that letter he was hardly equipped for the news Stephanie had for him when he called on her a few hours later.

She had decided, in discussion with Philippa as to the best way of breaking the news, that her health must be the excuse for her leaving Paris, and she accordingly retired to bed shortly before Flynn was expected. Philippa opened the door to him when he rang and told him that Mrs. Paul was in bed with a bad cold. "Paris is too damp for her in the fall," she added and showed him into the bedroom.

Stephanie sat up under her gilt swans, brocade cushions behind her back and did her best to look as though she were, as she described herself to Flynn, 'far from well'. She was very pale, as always when not rouged, and she wore white satin instead of the usual peach in order to emphasise her pallor. There was a decanter of cognac and the usual box of Turkish cigarettes on a table beside the bed, and a smother of hothouse white lilac and lilies in an alabaster bowl.

Flynn was alarmed by her pallor, and a mere cold would surely never keep her in bed at her favourite hour of the day, the aperitif hour.

"It's nothing to worry about, darling," she told him, "I am subject to these chills if I don't get away South as soon as summer's over. I would have gone, back in September, but for you. I've stood it as long as I could but I'll have to go, honey."

He said, desperately, "Perhaps I could find a way to come too. Boronsky was telling me only yesterday how he gets down to the South every year jumping trains."

Stephanie had not bargained for this. She said, quickly, "You mustn't think of any such thing, darling. If you were caught you would be deported."

"Perhaps I could borrow the money from my father and pay him back in time."

"Don't be foolish, darling. How could you make any money in the South?"

"In the same way that people like me manage to in Paris, I suppose—and those cultural Americans in the Riviera are just as interested in Gaelic presumably, as the Paris ones——"

"Of course they're not. They go to the Midi to play, not to be serious. No, darling, it's out of the question—you'll have to learn to do without me for a little while."

He was silent. For her, clearly, there was no question of him joining her; she was not even prepared to consider possible ways and means. She seemed positively anxious, on the contrary, that he should not come. He sat looking at her with a sense of creeping coldness and greyness within him, in his heart, in his mind.

She reached out and took his hand. "Don't look so shattered, honey. You'll survive. Maybe it's a good thing for you to get away from me for a while."

"Why do you say that?" He spoke sharply.

"I don't seem to make you vurry ha-a-ppy," she drawled.

He drew his hand away. "What you mean is that you're tired of me." He had gone very pale.

"Darling, aren't you being *vurry* unkind to poor little Paulo when she's not well?"

"I'm sorry you're not well. I don't want to try and stop you going to the South if the Paris winter's too much for you, but even if I couldn't go with you it would have been something to have known that you wished I could."

She was silent, trapped. If she said that she did wish it he would promptly devise a means of doing so.

He got up and stood by the white fan of flowers, then, finding their scent overpowering, moved away. He said, "I suppose Julian gave you these? I suppose that's what you really need—someone who can buy you flowers and take you to expensive restaurants. But you always knew I couldn't do that sort of thing—that I was merely what your little pansy poet was good enough to call the one and only playboy of the Western world!"

"Darling, don't be bitter, it doesn't suit you. Pass me the cigarettes."

He passed her the white shagreen box. "I didn't know people smoked when they weren't feeling well."

"Didn't you, honey? But one lives and learns, doesn't one?"

"By God, one does!"

He suddenly whipped the bedclothes off her and flung them in a heap behind him, white fur cover, white silk sheets.

"Come on, get up! We're going out! You're coming out with me. I've got some money and we'll spend it down to the last *sou*! Will you get some clothes on, or will you have me bundle you into a taxi like that?" He pressed the bell beside the bed.

"Are you crazy?" Stephanie demanded.

"I expect so. Isn't my name Harrigan?"

The maid answered the bell.

"Taxi," Flynn commanded, and then to Stephanie, "You'd better tell her to come back when she's ordered it and help you get dressed."

Half an hour later they were in the taxi together.

"Where are we going?" she asked.

"To a students' place I discovered along the Quai Voltaire. After that to the Bal Nègre."

"Not the Bal Nègre, darling—there are plenty of chic coloured places."

"But we're not being chic tonight. Tonight you're seeing my Paris, for a change."

"I thought you didn't care for these coloured dancing places."

"I don't care for any dancing places, but the Bal Nègre is the most coloured of the coloured places, and you said I was a puritan and had colour prejudices, so tonight I shall hope to correct that fallacy."

He suddenly leaned forward and tapped on the glass screen, and when the driver turned round motioned to him to stop.

"This is only the Boul' Mich'," Stephanie protested.

"I've just thought of something. I won't be a minute."

He climbed out and ran across the pavement, and she saw him dive into a florist's. In a few minutes he was back with a spray of small yellow brown-speckled orchids.

"Flynn, but how lovely! Only I thought you considered orchids vulgar?"

"I do. But you like them."

She fastened them to her dress, and then said, "If you're so anxious to please me tonight why are you insisting on the Bal Négre after dinner?"

"Because I think it'll be good for you. If you want the real Negro stuff not put on for tourists, you'll get it there." He grinned at her, and it suddenly came to her how like his father he was, physically and at heart. "Can it be that it's really Paulo who has the colour prejudices?" he mocked her.

She thought the 'student place' on the Quai Voltaire charming, in spite of the stained check tablecloths and the smoky atmosphere, and the food and wine were undeniably good. Flynn ordered aperitifs before the meal, and cognac after it, and when they finally left for the Bal Négre they were both a little drunk. It seemed to Flynn that though he was drunk there was a separate compartment of his mind functioning very clearly; it was like a dark building with one lighted window, one small square of light within which everything was clear-cut.

At the Bal Négre Stephanie demanded champagne. Flynn told her, "You don't have champagne at the Bal Négre. You have beer, or, if you want to be grand, cognac."

They had black coffee and cognac, and they danced all night, with each other, and Stephanie with anyone else, white or black, who asked her, and Flynn with the first female, white or black, he saw available.

At midnight Stephanie declared that she would die if she didn't have champagne, so they came out into the cool starry darkness and found a taxi and drove back to Montparnasse and the Jockey Club. Flynn bought Stephanie her champagne, and between the champagne and the deoxygenated atmosphere felt the one bright window of his mind filming over.

He had no recollection of paying the bill or of leaving the place, but he wakened in his own bed in the morning, fully dressed, with a blinding headache, and without a *sou*. It was mid-day, and pale sunshine was forcing its way in between the slats of the shutters.

He lay staring at the shuttered windows for a few minutes, the memory of the night returning to him, slowly, and presently he got up and opened the shutters and let the day into the room, and a black bitter despair into his soul.

VII

WHEN he had bathed, shaved, changed his clothes, he went out into the sunshine and walked slowly down through the avenues of chestnut-trees of the Luxembourg, their bare branches clipped with a toothbrush evenness, and sat down on a seat facing the pond.

He had no money, and no immediate prospects of acquiring any. He had sent an article on poetry to a highbrow English magazine, and an article on Paris to a Dublin literary magazine; if they were accepted it would be some time before he could expect payment. He thought it highly unlikely that Julian Richards would take any more of his 'translations', and Stephanie had not given the party which was to bring him rich cultural Americans eager to learn Gaelic at a hundred francs an hour. He had lived frugally for the last few weeks on the first five pounds his father had sent, and spent the second as his father would have wished, in riotous living—by God he had! He had no regrets about that. Even with a violent hangover he experienced a sense of triumph in the memory of the night. He had done what no other of Stephanie's lovers or admirers had ever done—spent every penny he had on her, and in one night. And now she could go to the South and be damned to her. . . .

Apart from the question of eating—and at the moment he felt as though he would never eat again—the money problem was not pressing for a few days, as he did not have to meet his hotel bill till the end of the week. As to the eating problem, he had no doubt that Boronski could show him how that could be achieved without money. One way was to lean against the radiators in the Dôme zinc, and sooner or later someone would ask you to have a drink, when you could always ask them to make it a café-crème. With luck you could touch someone for a few francs. It occurred to him that he could probably borrow from Nina and Johnny, but he shrank from the idea. You had to like people before you could tolerate being indebted to them. Boronski would probably have a much better idea, and if he went along now he might find him at home in his attic.

He made his way back across the gardens and up the Boulevard Montparnasse. He searched the Dôme terrace and looked in at the zinc bar to make sure Boronski was not there, and then turned up behind. His heart sank at the thought of all the stairs he must climb to the attic, but luck was on his side, for Boronski came out of the house as he approached it, a large painting under his arm.

He greeted Flynn boisterously, calling him 'mon vieux' and 'mon petit', and digging him in the ribs, and demanding what was this story about him being thrown out of the Jockey Club last night. Then without waiting for an answer, "Come and lunch with me and my girl," he commanded. "She has no brains and no looks and legs like a piano, but oh boy, has she the dough? She's bringing along a young American Jew who fancies himself as an art collector. She's sold Gregori Boronski to him as the coming painter, guaranteed to put Picasso in the shade in a few years. Come and have her buy you a lunch—what are the rich for?"

Flynn smiled, faintly. "I've got what my father would describe as the world's worst hangover and I couldn't eat a thing. But I need to know how to make some money, for I gave Stephanie a farewell dinner last night and I'm cleaned out."

"Is she leaving for Antibes today? I knew she was going but I didn't know it was at once."

"How did you know she was going? She didn't make up her mind till last night."

"She's been talking about it for weeks—ever since you got back from the Fontainebleau trip."

"She only told me last night."

Boronski shrugged. "Whatthehell! Come and meet my girl and the American Jew, and we'll find a way for you to make some dough."

He waved to a passing taxi. "My girl will pay when we arrive," he explained. "I shall save all our faces by saying I have no change—which is true."

In the taxi Boronski propped his picture up on the seat opposite and grinned at it, affectionately.

It was a hideous affair, Flynn thought, though he liked the bright clear reds and blues of it. It was a barnyard scene, full of stiff geese and sheep and cows, and stiff ugly Breughelesque people sitting about on kitchen chairs, and in one corner a small naked boy micturating into a bowler hat.

"It's called *Le Printemps*," Boronski informed him, with satisfaction. "It's really only a preliminary study for a much bigger work, a real *chef d'œuvre*."

But Flynn was not listening. He was busy leaning out of the taxi window. He felt so ill that if Stephanie had been on the opposite kerb he would not have cared.

2

Boronski sold his picture to the American Jew for a thousand francs, and persuaded his girl that every cultured American must know Gaelic. It was agreed that she should have her first lesson with Flynn at his hotel the following afternoon, one hour, one hundred francs, payable per lesson. . . . The American Jew said that he knew a man who could probably give Flynn a job on a weekly tourist guide he ran ; he would get in touch with him right away, and if Flynn would 'phone him in the morning . . .

"You see," Boronski said, as they walked away together afterwards, "that is how it's done. Now we will go and find you a cheap room so that you move in at the end of the week and live sensibly. After that we will find you a nice sensible girl ! 'A nice girl, a decent girl, one of the rakish kind'."

Flynn smiled. "I think not. I'm not even sure that I shall stay on in Paris."

"What, then ?"

"I don't know."

"When a man doesn't know he does well to remain in Paris. If one goes to London in the winter one cannot see because of the fog. If one goes to Wien the snow is three feet high, if one goes to the Midi there is the mistral, and one cannot make a living. *Alors*, one remains in Paris ! Paris in the winter is *pas vilain*. Then comes the spring, and one cannot leave because all the chestnut trees are coming out and one is in love—in love with Paris, in love with life, in love with love, in love with a woman ! Then it is summer, and one remains because everyone else has gone South, and Paris empty of everyone but oneself and a few million French is very agreeable. Then it is autumn, and Paris in the fall is almost as exciting as the spring. When it is winter one stays for the reasons that one stayed before, and so one stays for years and all one's life. *C'est comme ça.*"

"Is it so?"

"You will see," Boronski assured him; "and now let us take the Metro back to Montparnasse and search in the side-streets for a *chambre louer*."

They found one almost identical with Boronski's and in the same street. There was no heating and no water, and it looked out over roofs and chimneys, with yards and garbage-bins down below. It contained a table, a chair, and a bed. "It is all one needs," said Boronski. It was available for sixty francs a month, or five hundred francs for the year. Boronski got the concierge down to fifty francs a month. Flynn paid a month's rent in advance, borrowing from Boronski on the strength of the job he was to have on the weekly guide, which, said Boronski, was a sure thing. . . .

In this way Flynn began the second phase of his Paris life. He did not see Stephanie again. She left for the South that night—but this he did not know till some days later when he chanced to meet Nina in the Luxembourg gardens with the two children.

She said, "You must be missing Stephanie terribly. We had a postcard from her from Antibes this morning."

She produced it from her handbag and invited him to read it. It was written the day after her arrival. She wrote that it was lovely to be back in the South, and she was thinking of buying a villa. . . .

"I suppose you've had a letter by now," said Nina.

Flynn replied that yes he had had a letter. It seemed easiest. To have said no, he had not heard, would have been to have started a fresh spate of Montparnasse gossip, and if he was to go on living there he felt that his pride could not stand it.

Stephanie did not write to him, and he had not expected her to. She had made it quite clear to him before she left that she was tired of him, that he had never been more than an episode in her life, and that now that episode was finished. It had been finished, really, he thought, when they got back from Fontainebleau. She had been bored out at the forest; she did not really want to be with him except occasionally. She liked it to be known that Michael Harrigan's twenty-year-old son was her lover; it was flattering, a feather in that cap she insisted on wearing so rakishly . . . but it was tiresome that the dear boy had no money, and insisted on being so serious about it all, even to the point of wishing they could be married! Thinking of her, of it all, some lines from *The Torrents of Spring* came back to him, 'a biting, burning bitterness, like the bitter of wormwood, filled his whole soul. A sort of clinging repugnance, a weight of loathing closed in upon him on all sides like a dark night of autumn, and he did not know how to get free of this darkness, this bitterness.'

He felt old, and disillusioned, and empty—terribly empty. One day you held someone in your arms, mingled your breath with hers, were one flesh, and the next day she was pretending to be ill to cover her eagerness to get away from you. There was no scene, you did not quarrel; to the end she called you 'darling'. You dined and danced together, and the wine was a kind of slow-working anaesthetic; in the end you knew no more, and when you 'came to' she was gone. She was still in the same city, the same street, the house opposite, but she did not send for you, and you did not go to her because you knew the hopelessness of it. Nothing would stop her going. She had never pretended to love you, that you were ever any more than an episode, an *affaire*, but you had always kept that knowledge in the background, telling yourself you had love enough for two, deceiving yourself, even, that in time you might become important to her, that she might have some use for you other than as a feather in her cap. The end was inevitable; it came slowly, without drama, but relentlessly, like the end of summer. . . . She had said come before the last leaves fall from the chestnuts of the Luxembourg; she had said they would walk there hand in hand, but they had never done so. For her it was just a thing to say, a romantic idea; in actual fact if you wanted to get from the Observatoire to the Rue des Medicis a taxi was quicker than walking down through the gardens, or if you had made up your mind to walk in the gardens you had a drink or two at the Lilas first, and after that it was too late and you took a taxi to wherever you were going to lunch or dine. A small thing to be cheated of, that promise of the Luxembourg gardens, but it was symbolic. She had cheated him all along the line.

All the loathing in him was directed against himself, not against her. She had been honest, in her own fashion. Even her departure for the South, and her refusal to consider the possibility of his joining her there, had been part of that honesty. But he despised himself for having allowed himself to be used, for his helpless submission to her, for permitting her to violate his self-respect; and for the terrible emptiness in himself now that she was gone.

He talked about it all to Boronski; he had to talk to someone, and there was no one else.

He told him, "It was terrible the way she had me. In Ireland, at the castle, she would come out to me in the garden when I was working. When the sun was hot I would work stripped to the waist, and she would come up to me and pretend to be interested in the St. Christopher medallion I wore round my neck. I would feel her fingers below my throat, and then in all the world there would be nothing but that. She had such power over me! She would come into the stables when I was grooming my little mare and lean against her flanks, and when she had gone her perfume would remain. I could ride the mare all day and the perfume would still be on her coat—like a spell there was no escaping."

He told Boronski about the afternoon on the island, and the moonlight nights in the turret . . . and the disenchantment at Fontainebleau.

"It was so beautiful out at the forest. I didn't know it would be like that—that you could walk miles in it. I used to think we could take food and spend whole days there, or tramp to the next forest village. But she would never get up till mid-day and then she would want that we should go to some bar or bistrôt in the town, and then lunch at some expensive place. We used to lunch very late because of all the drinks beforehand, and half the afternoon would have gone by the time we got back to the villa. As often as not people would come in in the evening for drinks—we might just as well have been in Paris. They would be painters and writers living round about—there seemed to be a sort of colony of them. In Paris I could at least see her alone sometimes—by appointment. But that week out at Fontainebleau we seemed never to be alone except at nights, and she would never let me stay with her till morning, though there was no servant and no Philippa to have to think about. She used to offer that as an excuse in Paris. At Fontainebleau she just said that sophisticated people never did, that I was young and romantic, that no one looked their best in the mornings—all that sort of thing. The word 'affaire' wasn't in my vocabulary till I met her. She taught it me in Ireland and I hated it and said I didn't want that sort of thing. When I first came to Paris I began to understand exactly what the word meant, and it was all as squalid and cheap and tawdry as I had always felt it would be. Out at Fontainebleau I had the feeling that she was reducing what was between us to an *affaire*. I would lie awake at nights thinking about it and wishing to God I'd never met her. . . . But I went on loving her. I suppose I still love her. I don't know. What is love, at all? Once I thought I knew. Now everything seems confused. . . .

"Then we got back to Paris and she told me she was going to the South because she couldn't stand the Paris winter, and pretended to be ill, and made it quite clear there was no question of my joining her there. Something happened to me, then, something like the heart turning to stone inside the body. I couldn't stand the lies and pretence; I couldn't stand being treated like a servant who could be dismissed at a moment's notice. The Harrigan temper came up in me and I whipped the bedclothes off her and made her come out with me. We went dining and dancing, and I bought her orchids and we went from place to place by taxi, and at the end of the night I was cleaned out, but I'd been for the first and last time the sort of person she wanted—except that I didn't end the night by going to bed with her! Even when I held her in my arms dancing I didn't want even to kiss her. I hate that kind of dancing; I hate everything we did that night, and I think I hated her, too, then. I got drunk, and I don't regret that, either. Towards the end everything blacked out. In the morning my clothes reeked of her scent, and I hated it. I bathed, and changed everything I wore and went out into the gardens, and it seems strange now, looking back, that I didn't want to see her even to say goodbye. I felt there was no point in seeing her. She was determined to leave Paris and she'd made it clear she didn't want me. I could have made a scene, I suppose, pleaded with her, reproached her, but what would have been the use? She'd put a spell on me, and when it suited her she'd taken it off. It was the end of the story. There was a very simple young man from the back of beyond, who fell in love with a very worldly woman, and she allowed him to love her until it became a bore, and then she said goodbye, and he didn't die of a broken heart but merely died inside himself. It's not even a very interesting story. . . ."

"It's a very old story," Boronski pointed out, "a very ordinary story. Turgenev told it in *The Torrents of Spring*. Writers have been writing it, and men and women living it, for thousands of years. It's as old and ordinary and hackneyed as the story of being born and living and dying. It's a very ordinary love-story, but by no means the only one. Why are you so damned bitter? An artist has no right to be bitter. Experience is his raw material —and what richer experience than an unhappy love-affair?"

"A happy one," Flynn suggested.

"Happiness is uncreative," Boronski said. "The best school for an artist is privation and pain. 'All experiences are good, and the bitter ones the best of all.' There's no getting past old Voltaire. He was a wise guy. He knew. Let's go down to the Quai Voltaire and have a drink on the strength of it!"

He told him, drinking Pernod on the Quai Voltaire, "There are plenty of women like Stephanie Paul. They have to have lovers the way they have to have new hats—for the look of the thing, but each one means no more than that, a new hat. They like the idea of a lover, of a man, of being made love to. It makes them feel good. To have a man wanting them like hell—that excites them, flatters them. They don't have to do any wanting back, and in that way they save their self-respect. They give themselves because it's expected of them, because it's part of the game, and they even get a kick out of it—the way they get a kick out of a new hat. But the man in himself is nothing but a means to an end. Stephanie Paul, for all her lovers, has never really wanted a man in her life, because she's never had any real use for a man except as a bit of millinery to show off till she's tired of it. Emotionally she's married to Philippa Bryce. It's a kind of emotional Lesbianism. You don't get it amongst Latin women or Slavs—they're more natural, not over-civilised like English and American women. Stephanie Paul and her crowd have got sex on the brain, instead of where it ought to be, in the blood. It produces a kind of nymphomania—they're never satisfied. And there's always the woman friend, so sympathetic, so understanding, so comforting to turn back to after each fresh bit of male millinery has been tried on, worn for a while, and then discarded. Next time you go get yourself a real woman, *mon vieux*, a woman who really wants a man for himself, because she's a woman and he's a man, and never mind what's flattering or amusing or fashionable!"

"I'm thinking I left the country where such women are to be found."

"They wash up in these parts sometimes," Boronski assured him, "but they don't move about in an aura of Numero Cinq, wear pearls, sleep under ermine, or get themselves sent roses by elderly dilettantes. . . ."

VIII

FLYNN got the job on the weekly tourist guide, and spent most of his time running round Paris after the required information regarding new films, theatrical productions, concerts, cabarets, restaurants, art exhibitions. It gave him, very quickly, a working knowledge of French, taught him to know the Right Bank as intimately as the Left, and brought him five hundred francs a week. He thought of moving from his attic to somewhere more comfortable, but Boronski advised against it, urging that he had no idea how long the job would last, he might be 'fired' at a moment's notice; these weekly guides had a way of suddenly dropping out of circulation; it would be more sensible not to 'quit' the room but to pay the rent of it for a year. Then whatever happened he would at least be sure of a roof over his head. Flynn saw the wisdom of this and acted on Boronski's advice. He was, after all, very seldom in the room except to sleep, and an oil-stove solved the heating problem, though in this Boronski considered that he was 'fadding' himself. "It would be more profitable to get someone to sleep with on cold nights," he suggested. Upon which Flynn made no comment other than a slight frown of disapproval. The hunger—physical, mental, and emotional—for a given person was one thing, but sex as a recurrent appetite was something he did not understand. He did not even want that Stephanie should come back to Paris and claim him as her lover again—not on the old basis in which he was a charming boy whom it was a feather in her cap to have collected —and he could not imagine her experiencing such a change of heart that he could ever be anything else to her. The physical hunger for her died down in time, he discovered, but even when it was at its height, during the first few weeks, it was too much centred in her for the idea of anyone else to be possible. Then the body learned to readjust itself to the changed circumstances, and he felt the greyness of his spirit closing in on him in the physical sense, too ; there had been spring and the sap of life rising ; there had been a brief summer of boughs blossoming with an unimagined beauty, then the slow running back of the sap, and deadness of winter settling in, and under its weight of dead leaves the spirit could not reach to the thought of spring. It was all very well for Shelley to demand, 'If winter come, can spring be far behind !' Shelley wrote that in Italy, and in love. . . .

On the paper he worked as the assistant of a middle-aged Englishwoman, a Miss Barnaby, whom he had already met in Montparnasse at various parties and in various bars. She was so masculine that it was always a slight shock to notice that she was wearing a skirt. She was extremely efficient at her job, spoke perfect French, and gave the impression she wanted to give, which was that of being completely hard-boiled. In actual fact she was, as Flynn very soon discovered, to his dismay, very sentimental ; she was always forming romantic passions for pretty office and shop-girls— particularly lift-girls—whom she took to lunch and dine in expensive restaurants, lavished flowers and presents upon, and made mild love to, and who were always disappointing her. Flynn liked her well enough to work with ; she had a friendly, easy-going manner, and was good-natured ; but when she had had a few drinks, or a little too much wine, she would insist on what she called 'letting down her hair' to him—an expression which struck him as singularly inappropriate, her hair being cropped like a man's—which meant recounting endless stories of her infatuations and disappointments, and then she bored and, a little, disgusted him, and his one desire would be to get away from her.

All the time he was in Paris Flynn was never able to overcome his repugnance to the homosexuality he was always coming up against amongst the Left Bank resident English and Americans of both sexes. He was prepared to accept that it was the result of some psychological kink, or in some instances pathological, as he was assured by various people, but in that case it seemed to him to call for sympathy and condolence, instead of which it was apparently considered amusing, interesting, and the relationships involved were flaunted with an exhibitionism and egotism he found quite intolerable. Nor could he escape the feeling that a great deal of it was the sheerest affectation, because abnormality was considered more interesting than normality, and even an aspect of genius. In time, he would think, ironically, you would have to be heterosexual in order to be different; the wheel would go full-circle and normality become fashionable for intellectuals. But he suspected that a good deal of the little-lilac-sailor-boy stuff amongst the males, and the well-of-loneliness stuff amongst the females, was nothing more than a cover for an unwilling celibacy, a failure to attract the opposite sex disguised as lack of interest in it. If it was true, as he was constantly assured, that the most interesting work in painting, poetry, writing, music, was being done by homosexuals, then it was surely an indictment of the age, and probably accounted for the decadence of a great deal of the stuff being turned out; stuff like Raymond Farrow's alleged poetry, for instance. . . .

But Boronski, to whom he said this, with a good deal of vehemence, in one of his recurrent fits of impatience with 'Peter' Barnaby, reminded him that Shakespeare and Michelangelo both wrote some of their finest love-sonnets to their own sex, and what about Leonardo da Vinci, he demanded, was he going to dismiss him as decadent? Then there was that gal Sappho, poetess of Lesbos, not to mention a guy called Plato, and a whole bunch of Greeks. . . .

Flynn remembered, suddenly, that Stephanie had mentioned Da Vinci in this connection the first time she had been in his turret room and seen the picture of Saint Anne. He hadn't known then what she meant and wished to God he didn't know now.

He said, desperately, "All the same, Shakespeare wrote *Romeo and Juliet*, and *Antony and Cleopatra*, and *Venus and Adonis*, and *The Passionate Pilgrim*. He may have had his deviations after he left Shottery and Ann Hathaway and got mixed up with the court in London, but these people one meets here are nothing but deviation, and proud of it—they don't even want to be normal, and they don't produce any great art to justify it——"

"All the affectation and exhibitionism apart," Boronski replied, "a certain amount of serious work is being done—by the male homos, anyhow." He mentioned a few distinguished and promising writers and painters.

Flynn dismissed the names impatiently; they were hardly potential Shakespeares or Da Vincis. . . .

Boronski felt that it was little use discussing the matter with Flynn. The boy had this innate puritanism, and was himself too completely normal to understand these things. He was, too, both right and wrong. There was no denying that things had reached such a pass that just as you could not expect to make a success in the ballet without a Russian name, so you could hardly expect to make a success in the artistic world—particularly the literary world—without at least the affectation of homosexuality. It had become a sort of entrée to the various coteries and cliques. To be just ordinarily normal was unamusing, unsmart, terribly old-fashioned—like wanting poetry to rhyme and scan and be intelligible. In that sense Flynn was right. But he felt constrained to point out that the decadence of which he complained in contemporary art—with special reference to poetry and painting—was not to be attributed to homosexuality, but to a basic insincerity and sterility that led to the affectation of it as a mask for the inner emptiness.

"When you have no natural creative urge, what can you do but flaunt your abnormality—or pretend to it? When you have nothing much to say you'll do best to be obscure or perverse, and then with luck you'll be mistaken for profound. Pederasty doesn't necessarily produce good poetry—you're right there; but neither does it necessarily produce punk. You can't generalise. It's what a man is, fundamentally, that's important. Not who and where and in what way he loves, but how much. It's the zest for life that counts, the feeling for life, the creative urge—never mind how expressed. The artist can be anything except sterile. Doesn't your Catholic Church insist that it's the sins of the spirit, rather than the sins of the flesh, that are the most important, the really grievous ones? I seem to remember. . . . When you get around to figuring it out it applies as much to art as to ethics. *Par exemple*—Stephanie's little friend, Raymond Farrow, doesn't produce bad poetry because he's a ponce, but because he's closed up in himself in all the ways in which he ought to be wide open. Not because he loves his own sex, but because he doesn't love anyone except himself. Mike Angelo also loved his own sex, but he was wide open to life—he loved. . . . That's the difference. Your little Raymond Farrows only love themselves. It all gets back to that," Boronski concluded, grinning; "love, never mind how it expresses itself, so long as it's the genuine article. Never mind labelling it normal or abnormal. Genius is abnormal, anyhow !"

Flynn could only feel that there was a flaw in the argument somewhere, that in all this intellectual reasoning there was a basic fallacy, but that he did not know what it was, and that only a very simple and wise person like Brother Francis would know. People like Boronski were too complicated in their worldliness. Only very simple people, it seemed to him, had real wisdom. When he and Bridie were children running about the bogs in the wind and rain, their heads brimming with songs they never committed to paper or spoke aloud, it seemed to him they had a wisdom they lost with the knowledge of later years. Right and wrong were much simpler for the child because no questioning shadowed faith. Safe in the sanctuary of Mother Church you became a child again, with all the comfort and security of unquestioning faith, knowing it to be too beautiful to be untrue. He longed, passionately, to know this security once more, but though there was comfort in being reminded of the wisdom of St. Thomas Aquinas in the matter of the sins of the flesh, he was not yet ready for confession and abso- lution and the blessed privilege of Holy Communion. He could not have said why this was so; it was as though he had to reach a certain point along a given road.

He rushed round Paris day after day, week after week, month after month, earning a living, yet felt himself to be full of inner inertia. He wanted to get away from that sad autumnal Paris of falling leaves and wet, driving winds that reminded him intolerably of the previous autumn, and the foolish romantic unfulfilled dream of the Luxembourg. The wooded avenues of the Champs Elysées and the thin woods of the Bois in their autumn colourings reminded him of Fontainebleau, its happiness and its torment. The plane- trees and poplars along the quays, weeping their yellowing leaves to the river, were too painful a reminder of the eager hopes with which he had first walked those quays. Now when he ate at the little café-restaurant on the Place Dauphine, where, by October, the chestnuts were already stripped of their leaves, it seemed impossible to realise that it was only a year ago that he had sat there feeling so completely alien, incredible that he should now be only a year older ; already all that early Paris life seemed as remote as Ballyrannon—he had grown so much in a year. How young one had been, how vulnerable !

He hardly recognised himself now as the shy, callow youth who had been at first fascinated, bewildered, excited, exhausted, by Paris. He had acquired now that *savoire faire*, the lack of which Stephanie had at first found charming and then tiresome. You did not 'go around' with 'Peter' Barnaby for months, all over Paris, without becoming 'hard-boiled'. You learned how to do, all right. It wasn't, after all, so very difficult, especially with a few drinks under your belt—'Peter' taught him that, and he learned quickly enough, his name being Harrigan. . . . He soon lost that dreaming, off-the-earth look which had so fascinated Stephanie Paul at first. He still wore the Connemara tweed suit, but it had long ago lost the smell of peat and bog. His face developed a slightly dissipated look from the late hours and too many drinks. . . .

But on Christmas Day he went to early Mass in Notre Dame and could have wept his heart out with nostalgia for the whitewashed simplicity of the monastery chapel by the lake at home—or any church in Ireland where Mass was said that morning. There was nothing to stop him going back ; that is to say no material thing ; but in the reality beyond material things there was everything to stop him. His spirit was still chained to Paris—which meant still chained to Stephanie Paul. She did not write to him and he had no desire to write to her, but he could not get free of her. Her voice perpetually sing-songed in his brain by day, and he dreamed of her by night, helplessly. People asked him about her, gave him news of her ; there was always someone who had just heard of her ; she seemed to come up in every conversation.

The child, Jeanne, was the only escape from her, but it was not now so easy to see Jeanne ; he was kept running about all the time ; there was little time for the Luxembourg gardens, and the weather was against his finding her there, as often as not, in what free time he had. She was still the only person in Paris for whom he had real affection, the only person who could make his heart feel less like a stone. Before her simplicities and candours he would fill with tenderness, as once for the child Bridie. She would climb on to his knee and run her hands through his hair and laugh and call him '*poil-de-carrote*', and rub her head against his rough tweed coat, like a little cat, and murmur, "You are nice. I love you. I love you almost as much as I love Papa." She was all the child Bridie for him then, and he would laugh with a sudden sense of a rush of tears behind his eyes.

'O child ! I love, for I love and know.'

He found time to take her and Henri round the children's bazaars in the big stores during the week before Christmas. He did not feel drawn to the boy as to Jeanne ; he was much more French than his sister ; he preferred to talk French, and wanted to be a Frenchman like Pappa when he grew up ; the more his mother tried to make him English the more stubbornly French he became. He refused to have lessons from Johnny, and in the end Nina had had to give in and send him to school. Flynn could never get close to him as to Jeanne, but it had seemed unfair to him to take Jeanne to the Christmas shops and not take the boy as well. They plunged into fairy caves made of cardboard and hung with tinsel icicles, fished up mysterious packages from 'lucky dips', rode on scenic railways, and came back laden with parcels. For a whole afternoon Flynn did not think of Stephanie, and Henri forgot himself and spoke English.

With the '*manifestations*' of '*l'affaire Stavisky*' in the New Year, Nina was nervous about letting the children go out, and Flynn saw less of them. The city seethed with every kind of wild rumour—the monarchy was to be restored; there was to be Fascist dictatorship, a Communist revolution. In February the rioting became serious, and squads of *gardes mobiles* appeared on the streets. There was violence and bloodshed and people killed. If there were, as was said, machine-guns out in the streets, Flynn never saw them. Everyone talked politics and of the '*bagarre*'. The '*bagarre*' became an almost nightly occurrence round the Chambre des Deputies, in the Place de la Concorde, and by the Hôtel de Ville. The crowds tore up the palings from the boulevard trees, and seized tables and chairs from the café-terraces for weapons. There was a twenty-four-hour general strike and a revolutionary mass-meeting in the Place de la Republique. The Luxembourg gardens were closed, and the Boul' Mich' was curiously empty. The English and American colony felt safer taking its drinks up in Montparnasse, at the Coupole, the Dôme, the Select, rather than down at the Deux Magots and the Flore, in the storm-centre of the Boulevard St. Germain. For weeks the streets were empty of taxis; it went on for so long that it seemed as though there would never be taxis again. . . .

1934, the year of destiny, with the stormclouds gathering over Europe, and the Paris Americans beginning to book their passages back home. In Germany the death of Hindenburg, and the Reich Chancellor, Adolf Hitler, coming to full power; the burning of the Reichstag, the June 'purges'; in Austria civil war, and the murder of Dollfuss, and Italian troops mustering at the frontier. Everyone talking of Hitler, Fascism, War, reminding each other that the 1914-18 Great War began with an assassination in Central Europe. Paris emptying; the beginning of the exodus; Europe is no place to be now; it is only a matter of time before there is war, the air is thick with it, Fascism has become a political swear-word. Riots in Catalonia, armed risings, the formation of a Red Army, a short-lived Commune in the Asturias, and the workers going down for the count, as in Austria, but the damped-down fires still smouldering. . . .

Europe in the melting-pot; Americans going home; English rentiers getting their passports—stamped at so many European frontiers—visaed for New York, for Mexico, away from it all. Life as they had once known it is finished; it is all over now bar the fighting, and there is already the sinister sound of armies on the march. They know it now—'*l'affaire Stavisky*' was the beginning of the end, the beginning of the European landslide. Now there is this destroying feeling of disintegration; it is all *fin de siècle*; it is the end of serious work and dilettantism alike; and an end of prancing and cavorting. Hitler has abolished the 'so' places in Berlin; *Eldorado* and

Dorian Gray are no more. All the rentier homosexuals, so literary, so amusing, move down to Vienna, where there are still a few 'queer' places left on the Berlin pattern. . . . But that is all finishing, too, and soon there will be nowhere to go except to the Americas. Paris is dead, Vienna is dead, Berlin is dead—and one wouldn't go there any more, anyhow. Europe is doomed. . . . There will be war, this year, next year, sometime, but certainly, and it might come any day now. . . .

In England there was the Battle of the Belisha Beacons, and posters about 'incidents' in Abyssinia, but the Beacons were more interesting ; the Beacons were near and Abyssinia far. There was the launching of the great transatlantic liner, and a royal wedding . . . and consternation over 'the trick by fire and the purge by blood' in Germany, but hang out the banners for the royal wedding, and next year we'll have a jubilee. . . . Europe may go up in flames, but not just yet. . . .

"Paris is goddam awful," Boronski complained to Flynn at the end of that summer. "I'm going South. There are little cheap places just outside Toulon. We could jump a train. You'd find a way to live there just as cheaply as in Paris. You needn't be afraid of running into Stephanie and her crowd—they're miles further up the coast and not likely to migrate to the sort of places we'd go to."

"I've decided to go to London," Flynn told him. "The guide is finishing after next week, and the year's rent of my room is up about the same time. I've written to my father's publisher telling him I'm coming and asking him if he can find me a job, in his office, or anywhere else. If he can't I shall go all the same."

"But why London, of all places ? Why London in preference to Marseilles or Toulon—or Dublin ?"

"I can't go back to Ireland, and I'm tired of France. I've more faith in being able to earn a living in London."

Boronski shrugged. "London is the loneliest city in Europe."

Flynn offered no comment on that. He could hardly imagine that he would be lonelier in London than he was in Paris. He knew people in Paris ; he would, in time, know people in London. It was not how many people you knew that saved you from loneliness ; loneliness was a purely internal affair. He had been probably loneliest of all out at Fontainebleau with Stephanie.

It was not the feeling of impending war which finally decided him to leave Paris but the fact that his job was finishing, and that his year's rent had expired. There was no point in renewing the lease of the room unless he intended looking for another job in Paris, and apart from the fact that it was hardly a propitious time for a foreigner to go job-hunting in Paris he felt that he could not stay on in that atmosphere of disintegration, of political tight-rope walking and nervous excitability. There seemed to be no escape from the interminable talk of politics, or the sense of impending doom. He had moments in which he had a sense of watching a world crumbling before his eyes. There was no reason to suppose that England would be immune from the slogans and the forebodings, but England might be counted on to be less excitable, and her stolidity would crumble more slowly, less noticeably. In any case there was this strong urge to get out of Paris, and England was the nearest point. Whatever England held, or did not hold, Paris was a finished chapter.

2

His twenty-first birthday fell on a Sunday, and he took Jeanne out to St. Cloud—not because it was his birthday, but because it happened to be a fine day and he was free. They went down by river, on a crowded paddle-steamer. The sun shone, and someone on board played a concertina, and lovers sat with their arms about each other, and everyone was good-natured and gay and full of holiday-spirit.

At St. Cloud they climbed up into the woods and looked back at Paris, pale and shimmering in the distance, and ate their sandwiches of garlic sausage wedged between long pointed rolls, and Flynn drank red wine from a bottle, with little sips for Jeanne, and they found a kiosk where you could buy toffee-figs, and they talked a good deal of nonsense, threaded with bright ribbons of laughter, and Flynn had no heart to tell the child that he would soon be leaving Paris. He had had wild ideas of asking Nina if he could take Jeanne with him to London, but had dismissed them as impracticable. Even if Nina consented, what would the child do all day whilst he was at work? Even if she went to school there would be hours when she would be alone; had she been even a few years older it might have been practicable, but eight was such a very little age. . . .

They came back in the dusk by the last steamer. After a while Jeanne grew tired of watching the dim landscape slide by and huddled close to Flynn, drowsily full of the long day in the open air, and was soon asleep. He was aware of the child smell of her hair and small body, sweetish, indescribable; he remembered it with Bridie; and something ached in him. He brushed the fine soft fair hair back from her face and pulled his coat round her; she stirred, half wakened, then with a contented sigh slipped into sleep again. His heart swelled with tenderness. 'O child! I love . . .'

He sat holding her close to him on the crowded steamer and thinking of the day's happiness, and of all the birthdays since the unforgettable seven-teenth. His eighteenth birthday with the Doyles on Bream Island, dancing jigs and reels on the earth floor of their cabin; the light in Patrick's face when it was his turn to clasp hands with Bridie. His nineteenth birthday in Dublin; the Horse Show, the buying of Jameel, the lunch with Aunt Chris and Cousin Kate, and Bridie and his father. His twentieth birthday passing over him unnoticed in Galway Hospital. And now Paris . . . and 'the world's wonder of a horse' that had been his twenty-first birthday present 'well in advance' was dead, and Patrick had betrayed him, and Cousin Kate had vanished long ago, and his heart was hard towards Bridie, and the woman who had invaded him in the ivory tower of his dream-bound life was as remote from him as Bridie and Cousin Kate, as dead to him as Jameel. Now there was only this strangely sophisticated little Anglo-Parisian child to say in her heedless child's way, 'I love you', and to evoke tenderness, and she would forget him as soon as he was gone, whatever grief she might display at his departure.

It was dark when they reached the landing-stage and he picked her up and carried her ashore and was astonished at her lightness. She wakened and came to lively struggling life, kissing him, violently, half strangling him with her arms round his neck, as Bridie used to in her moments of demonstrativeness, and demanded that he carry her pick-a-back the rest of the way. People smiled at them as they passed along the quays and up the Boul' Mich', the tall thin young man with the untidy reddish hair, and the small fair child with a bunch of wilting wild flowers in the hands clasped so tightly round his neck, the two of them laughing and talking nonsense in their own private world.

It was the first really happy day Flynn had known in Paris, and it was the last.

A week later he left for England.

When he told Jeanne that he was going she clung to him, fiercely, crying, "I won't let you go! I don't want you to go!"

He told her, "You will come to England with Maman, and then we will do all sorts of things together. We will ride on the tops of the big red London 'buses, and walk round the top of St. Paul's Cathedral, and eat ice-creams at all hours of the day."

He drew her a London 'bus, marking with a cross their seats on top, up at the front. She wanted to know if they would be able to lean out of the windows and spit on the people down below. Flynn replied that he didn't see why not. He promised to send her picture-postcards of all the places they would go to together, and that there should always be kisses and hugs in the shape of crosses and o's on the back of each. They reached a point of enthusiasm at which Jeanne was positively anxious that he should get away so that the flow of postcards could begin.

Boronski came to see him off at the Gare du Nord. They dined together first on the Boulevard St. Germain, drank a good deal of 'onion' wine, went across to the Flore for cognac and coffee, and had further cognacs when they reached the station. You should always start out on a journey the better for drink, Boronski declared.

They swayed along the platform together, Boronski singing the Marseillaise. When the guard blew his little tin trumpet and called out 'En voiture', Boronski clasped Flynn in his arms, kissed him on both cheeks, called him 'Mon vieux', commanded him to give his love to 'the prettiest poule in Piccadilly', and Flynn finally extricated himself from the bear-like embrace, scrambled up the steep steps and bundled into the already moving train just in time. . . .

Then he leaned from the window and waved at the wildly gesticulating figure of Boronski, until a sudden puff of smoke cut him off from view, cut off everything like a curtain abruptly dropped down on a lighted scene, leaving only the surrounding darkness, and nothing but darkness ahead.

PART III

LONDON—ON THE EVE

'He will not hear the bittern cry
In the wild sky, where he is lain.'

I

MR. AUGUSTUS HAWES had been a little embarrassed by Flynn's letter; as he said to his partner, Mr. Sylvanus Merry, and to his wife Lesley, he already had various young men 'draped about' the office with nothing in particular to do, though of course it was true each one represented a premium of several hundred pounds a head. Mrs. Hawes suggested that it would be 'quite distinguished' to have Michael Harrigan's son in the office, and Sylvanus had the bright idea of putting him in charge of the poetry department.

"Poetry department?" said Augustus, patting his large stomach a little irritably. He fancied himself as a gourmet, and he suffered from indigestion. His wife always insisted that gourmand was the word he wanted. . . .

Sylvanus, who was tall and thin and fancied himself as literary, made vague gestures in the air.

"Why not? We could bring out an anthology. Best poetry of the year——"

"Costs a fortune in copyright fees," Augustus snapped. "If we're going to do poetry it must be the kind that pays—the John Oxenham, Wilhelmina Stitch stuff."

"I was thinking of *cachet*," Sylvanus said, dreamily.

"We've got Michael Harrigan—what more do you want?"

"He's our only author of any distinction. It takes a lot to live down a book like *Outposts of Passion*."

"Who wants to live it down? A hundred thousand copies and still selling at seven and six. We could do with more like it."

"It spoils our imprint. We can't compete with people like Cape, and Faber——"

"Who wants to? But for you we'd have published *Away with the Breeze*—that book must have sold half a million by now! And you said it was sheer novelette!"

"So it is. Look here, Augustus, we've had all this out before. I can't think why you don't go in for the sausage business—you could turn 'em out by the million then, to your heart's content."

Mrs. Hawes, who was present during the discussion, smiled.

"Don't be bitter, Sylvie darling!"

Sylvanus bored her as a person; she regarded him as 'a drear', but she was on his side in every publishing argument between him and her husband, who bored her both as a person and as a publisher. She never ceased to wonder how she had ever come to marry him ten years ago. Had she ever really thought there was any glamour in being married to a successful publisher? He hadn't been fat and bald then, of course, and she had admired his energy and drive; even he had talked of 'imprint' in those days, and they had kicked off with quite a good list and good production. Now it was said of them, 'in the trade', that they only kept their authors by paying bigger advances than anyone else. Augustus would add to that, drily, "We also sell more of their books than anyone else would!"

Sylvanus was bitter. He had put his money into the business with a dream of a distinguished list and fine production; they had started off quite well, and then Augustus had found out what paid. The works of Michael Harrigan were Sylvanus's one scoop. Harrigan owed the good production he always got entirely to him—yet whenever he came to London it was always Augustus he asked for. Sylvanus was determined to have this poetry department, and he would deal with young Flynn Harrigan himself.

He said stubbornly, "We'll have a poetry department and we'll make it pay. At least we won't lose money on it," and refrained from adding that even if they did, *Outposts of Passion* would cover it.

When Flynn Harrigan arrived he took him out to lunch and explained his idea and warned Flynn that he would find that Mr. Hawes was "nothing but a salesman. Your father told you, probably," he added.

Flynn smiled. "My father always says that Barabbas was a publisher."

Sylvanus frowned. "Augustus is perfectly straight," he felt constrained to say. "It's just that he's interested in profits, not art. He told one of our lady authors that if only he could write himself he would write a best-seller that really was a best-seller—'something spicy' was how he described it. Then he got hold of *Outposts of Passion*, and it was the book he'd been looking for all his life. But the trouble is that on the sliding scale we've contracted to pay the author, if it sells many more it'll no longer pay us to publish it!"

They lunched in Fleet Street, at the Cheshire Cheese, and Sylvanus pointed out Dr. Johnson's seat, and various Fleet Street celebrities—an editor, a journalist, a 'well-known advertising man'. It all meant nothing to Flynn; he had never heard of any of them, and disliked Dr. Johnson intensely.

They walked back along the Strand, and he thought the Law Courts beautiful, and then they turned down towards the river. It was a relief to get away from the traffic, and Sylvanus showed him a courtyard with plane-trees, and a fountain, and people sitting about on seats eating lunches out of paper bags and throwing crumbs to pigeons waddling about on the flag-stones. He resolved to go there every day it was fine whilst he worked at Hawes and Merry's. He was glad the office was in a street leading down to the river.

When they got back he was introduced to Mr. Hawes, who said he must come to dinner and 'meet the missis', and how did he like London, and this was Miss Featherstone who would look after him and show him the ropes, and he must meet the boys in the production department. It was all rather bewildering, and a little exhausting. The young men in the production department had Oxford accents and an indolent manner; one wore suede shoes, and another a yellow tie, but there was a young man who wore a cheap-looking blue suit, and who worked in his shirt-sleeves, in a very ordinary-looking striped shirt, and he spoke with a Cockney accent and seemed to be the only one doing any work. When Yellow Tie asked Flynn what he thought of T. S. Eliot and Stephen Spender, Striped Shirt winked. Suede Shoes said that what was wanted was a poetry department with 'a Leftist slant', and he did hope the Harrigan influence wouldn't result in a rash of Celtic Twilight —'Cathleen ni Houlihan and the Dear Dark Head and Dark Rosaleen and all that'. He had a sarcastic, superior smile, and Flynn disliked him quite violently.

He said, for devilment, "We might do some translations from the Gaelic."

"In 1934, with Europe on the brink of war?"

"Because of that."

"Escapism! How frightful!"

Miss Featherstone, who had been doing the introducing, said frigidly, in her refined voice defined in the production department as 'south-west-seven', "I don't think the policy of the proposed poetry section has been decided upon yet!"

"Lummy!" said Striped Shirt, and grinned. He had a friendly, rather monkey-like face.

Miss Featherstone took Flynn back to Sylvanus's office. "Those two are horrors," she said, vehemently. "We call them Lenin and Trotsky, because one's a Communist—the one who was talking to you—and the other a Trotskyist—d'you have that sort of thing in Ireland?"

"I wouldn't know," Flynn told her. "I lived out at the back of beyond, and the important thing to be there was a Republican."

"Ireland must be fascinating," Miss Featherstone said, irrelevantly. "All those bogs. 'The mountains of Mourne go down to the sea'. Killarney and all that."

Flynn smiled and did not answer. He had known for a long time now that English people knew nothing about Ireland. It was 1934 and they still referred to the 'Irish Free State' and believed that De Valera was president.

He asked her about the boy in the striped shirt.

She told him, "That's Freddie Fisher—he used to be the office-boy. He does most of the work in the production department. The other two are premiums, of course. We have a succession of them. It's rather a blight." She pronounced it 'blate', and Flynn had no idea what she was talking about, but he smiled his charming smile and murmured, "Is it now?" and afterwards she confided to Mr. Hawes that 'the Irish boy' had 'the loveliest Dublin brogue', adding that he would be 'really rather attractive' if only he were 'tidied up a bit'.

Under Sylvanus's guidance Flynn took a room in Bloomsbury, at the top of a tall dingy house looking into a square with trees and gardens. Bloomsbury, Mr. Merry explained, was the home of the intelligentsia. The intelligentsia, Flynn soon discovered, played gramophones and radios late into the night, and were apt to be sick on the stairs. He met them occasionally, and felt that he had met them all before in Montparnasse. The only difference seemed to be that they drank gin and beer instead of Pernod and wine. He got drawn into one of their parties once, by a crowd of gate-crashers who insisted that he was one of themselves, and were all too drunk to be argued with. It was rather like a Saturday night at Nina D'Alvray's, and after a girl in trousers had been sick into an umbrella-stand he managed to escape. It was after that that he decided that Bloomsbury and the intelligentsia were not for him.

It was Freddie Fisher who came to the rescue. He had already introduced Flynn to ABC's and Express Dairies, where he could eat cheaply—as alternatives to the art-and-crafty basement tea-rooms at which Miss Featherstone and the two 'premiums' lunched; such places were run by 'decayed gentlewomen' Freddie explained, and were 'no cop', and having been taken by Miss Featherstone to one of these places, Flynn agreed. He did not care for Freddie's choice, either ; he disliked the clatter, and the smell of steam and buns and fried fish, and thought with regret of the brasseries and café-restaurants of Montparnasse and the Quarter, to which Boronski had introduced him. But this was England, the home of tea and buns, decayed gentlewomen, gas-fires with rings, and a perpetual cheerful cheerlessness. When the days were fine he preferred to buy food and take it into Fountain Court, or down to the Embankment. The river fascinated him ; it drew him as the Seine had drawn him in Paris ; a river was something he understood ; it was the link with the sea and had commerce with gulls. One day he walked out to Tower Bridge, and felt that he could have gone on and on in the wake of gulls and barges and the smell of the sea, but the lunch hour was more than up.

The next day he lunched with Freddie and told him about his previous day's walk. "One day I'd like to get right out to the docks," he said.

Freddie was all enthusiasm immediately.

"Rotherhithe," he said. "The Surrey docks. That's what you want. If I had to live in London that's where I'd hang out—not amongst all them parlour-Communists in Bloomsbury ! We get enough of them in the office ! You could get a room in Rotherhithe where you could spit into the river, and half the rent you pay in Bloomsbury. I know a bloke that's got a place there. He's a merchant-seaman and not there half the time. He might let you share it with him—you'd have it to yourself best part of the time. What about it ? His ship's in now ; we could go out there on Sat'rd'y afternoon and, if you liked the place, fix up with him."

The idea stirred Flynn's imagination, and it was arranged that they should go out to Rotherhithe together on the following Saturday afternoon.

II

THEY went out by tram from Waterloo, sitting on the top deck and rocking along through a greyness that reminded Flynn of Dublin ; there was even the familiar smell of breweries. When they reached the Elephant and Castle he suddenly gave a cry, and pointed to a corner building that housed a fifty-shilling tailor's.

"What about it ?" Freddie demanded.

"Only that one of the addresses above the door is Dame Street, Dublin," Flynn said, suddenly a little ashamed of his excitement.

"Give you a turn, I s'pose," Freddie said, sympathetically.

Freddie was altogether a sympathetic person, Flynn found. He had a natural warmth and friendliness, and was refreshingly unconcerned with being either clever or amusing. He was very proud of having got into a publisher's office. Anyone could do it if they'd had a public-school education and got their dad to put down a couple of hundred quid, he said, but he was a board-school boy and had left school at fourteen and taken the first job that had come along—messenger in an advertising agency.

"That was how I broke into Fleet Street," he said, proudly, and after that, it seemed, it was an easy step to publishing.

"You got to make up your mind to a thing—that's half the battle," he insisted. "You got to know from the word go what you want. I always liked books. I was brought up to 'em. You oughter see my dad's collection, all in cheaps and second-hands, o'course, but the real stuff—Dickens and Tolstoy and Jack London and W. W. Jacobs. And William Morris. My dad was a William Morris socialist. You want to get him talking of the old days. He met 'em all—Morris, Annie Besant, John Burns. It was real socialism then. Look at the Labour Party today—don't know the meaning of the word socialism! You must meet my dad."

Flynn had no idea what it meant to have been a William Morris socialist, and knew nothing of the British Labour Party, but he was quite sure that Freddie Fisher's dad was a great deal more worth meeting than most of the people he was likely to meet in London. You could probably take root in friendship with a family like the Fishers, as you could with the Doyles. . . . Ah, but Patrick had betrayed him; the coldness closed round his heart again with that thought.

The tram rocked along the grey wastes of the Jamaica Road, with its tall tenement houses with their iron stairways spiralling up between white-tiled walls, and their landings and asphalted courtyards swarming with children, and again Flynn thought of Dublin. In a queer sort of way Rotherhithe was a kind of homecoming.

When they left the tram Freddie conducted him through streets of small houses whose front doors opened immediately on to the pavement, and across a waste-ground at whose edge stood a row of cottages with scrawny acacia trees reaching up to the upstairs windows. Then there were back-streets, with flour warehouses, and tall shabby houses with eighteenth-century porches and crinoline balconies and deep windows, and altogether so much of Dublin in it that Flynn knew quite certainly that so long as he lived in London he would live there and nowhere else.

"You wait," said Freddie, when Flynn exclaimed upon the old houses, and they plunged into an alleyway.

"Seven Steps Alley," he announced, triumphantly.

A woman wearing a sacking apron and a man's cap shook a mat at a front door. Bay-willow herb waved purple plumes on a roof beside decrepit-looking chimneys. A lilac tree reared up from a confusion of rickety sheds and lumber and zinc baths and rabbit-hutches in a back yard. There was the sour-sweet smell of unaired rooms; a smell of mattresses, and cats, and children, of a fried-fish shop, of a brewery, of the river.

Flynn leaned against a high fence covered with naïvely obscene chalk-drawings done by children and laughed.

"This is where I belong!" he said.

Freddie grinned, happily. "Knew you'd take to it," he said. "It's real down here, that's what. Better'n all that Bloomsbury intelligentsia stuff. Intelligentsia my foot! Let's go and see 'f my pal's at home."

They ascended the steps and came out into Rotherhithe Street. Next door to a fried-fish shop Freddie led the way in through a doorway and up some very dark narrow stairs. At the top he rang a bell. He rang several times, and when there was no answer said, "Charlie's not in, by the looks of it, but we can get in, all the same—the old girl in the shop down below has a key. I'll just pop down."

He disappeared into the darkness, and returned in a few minutes with a large key with a faded blue label attached.

The room into which he let himself and Flynn was small and darkish and crowded; there was no window, but light was admitted from the glass panes in a door which admitted to a small kitchenette which appeared to have been built on; it had a ramshackle air and a zinc roof. At the end of the kitchen-ette another door with glass panes at the top opened out on to the flat top of the roof of the fried-fish shop. Freddie opened this door and they stepped out on to the roof, which had a trellised fence at the end, and nasturtiums climbing up it from a flower-box at its base.

They leaned on the fence and looked down into the Pool of London, with the Tower Bridge away to the left, and behind, in the near distance, the dome of St. Paul's, delicate and misted in the sunlight.

"See what I mean," said Freddie, "you can spit right into the river!" and spat in demonstration . . . and took Flynn back to just such a bright autumn day in the gardens of the Luxembourg, and a child who leaned over a low balustrade and announced that you could spit right into the eye of a dahlia. . . .

The wind whipped up the river, frothing it like a sea; there was the wide wake of barges, chugging along, and gulls wheeling and swooping, the under-sides of their wings like green ice; the blue and gold air was full of their cries, and of the ring of hammers from across the water, and the excitement of movement of wind and water and gulls and ships.

"This is wonderful!" Flynn cried, exultantly, into the wind.

"Knew you'd like it," Freddie said.

Flynn turned and looked back at the jumble of roofs behind him; they were at different levels, and here and there a building had been built on to in the most astonishing fashion; the general result was an extraordinary onglomeration of eaves and attics, chimneys and roof-gardens.

"It's crazy, entirely!" Flynn said, and laughed.

"You've got an author living next door but one."

"That's not so good."

"Oh, he's all right—a quiet sort of bloke. Lives alone. That's something in the lit'ry world, these days. Graham Hayes—you may have heard of him? A bit life-and-letters-ish. No fiction. We did a book of essays of his some time back, but after *Outposts of Passion* he left us—said he wanted a better imprint. Nearly broke poor old Merry's heart—put years on to him. If your dad ever leaves the firm I think Merry will sell out."

They went indoors and Freddie said, "There's another room in this ormolu suite—just off the stairs. Not much bigger than a cupboard, but it holds a bed. There's a lav adjoining, all handy, you see. No bath, o'course, but you can always go out and get a bath, or invite yourself somewhere for the weekend. You could come and have your Sunday dinner with us and have your bath then."

Whilst they were examining the room off the stairs there came the slam of the front door, and Freddie exclaimed, "That'll be Charlie back, most likely!"

He ran out, excitedly.

"That you, Charlie? I got a lodger for you—chap from the office. I got the key from old Ma down below—knew you wouldn't mind. We was just having a squint round, and my pal thinks it's the goods all right."

He came back into the bedroom followed by a shortish, dark, thickset young man wearing a seaman's overcoat and a knitted white silk scarf knotted round his throat. He had bright blue eyes and a pleasant smile.

"Charlie Cray," said Freddie, "Flynn Harrigan."

"Pleased to meet you," Charlie said, and they shook hands.

"Freddie had the idea we could share this place," Flynn said.

"Look at the saving on the rent," Freddie pointed out, and added, with a wink, "I'll want my commission, of course."

"Sure," Charlie said. "Will you take it with you or shall we send it?" He turned to Flynn.

"It's not much of a joint," he said, "draughty as hell in the winter, and terrible damp—you get all the mists from the river."

"He's used to damp," Freddie put in. "He's Irish."

Flynn said simply, "I'd put up with a lot to live here."

"O.K. then. You'll have the place to yourself most of the time. Only thing is, when I'm home I'd have to ask you to doss down on the sofa in the other room—it's not that I give a dam' where I doss, meself, but I've generally got a skirt in tow when I'm on leave. If you wouldn't mind that——"

Flynn smiled. "Why should I mind?"

"Might make it awkward like if you was to bring home a tart yourself at the same time——"

"One of 'em have to finish the night out on the floor," Freddie said, cheerfully.

Flynn assured him, "I don't think that particular problem will worry us."

They went back to the living-room and Freddie began asking Charlie about his last voyage, what ship he was sailing in next, or was he signing on again in the ship he was last in. Charlie said no fear; that last was 'a hungry bastard', and Freddie translated for Flynn's benefit, "He means a ship where they don't give you enough to eat." Charlie then began a long involved story about how they were held up at Liverpool and the skipper wouldn't let them pay off, and what he had had a good mind to say to the Old Man, and what he had in fact said, and what the second mate had said. Flynn tried to take an intelligent interest, but the idiom was beyond him, and presently he slipped out through the kitchenette and went back to watch the river.

"He's fair taken with that view," Freddie observed to his friend. "But to get back to what you was saying——"

"Well, I says to the Old Man, do you take me for a ——, I says. Well, no, not exactly, he says——"

Flynn looked at the Pool, and from the window of the house that stood with its feet in the water, Graham Hayes looked at Flynn and wondered, and wished, as he frequently did, that he could paint.

He gazed so intently that after a few moments Flynn became aware of him and turned in his direction. The face he saw reminded him, startlingly, of Brother Francis. He went back into the house with a confused feeling of some sort of pattern in it all—that atmosphere of Dublin the moment he had boarded the tram at Waterloo, 'Dame Street, Dublin', above the tailor's at the Elephant and Castle, the reminder of Dublin in the tenements of the Jamaica Road, and in the 18th century façades of Rotherhithe; and now, in the house standing in the water, the reflection of Brother Francis. . . .

He saw the man again a little later, when he was in a public-house with Freddie and Charlie, having a drink on the arrangement by which he was to share the flat with Charlie. Freddie gave him a nudge. "See that grey-haired bloke over there? That's Graham Hayes. I'll introduce you if you like——"

At that moment, whilst Flynn was still looking in his direction, Hayes glanced up, and there was the flash of recognition between them.

Flynn said quickly, "No—not now. We'll meet sometime when I've moved in. Don't let's be literary this evening."

But it was not the desire not to be literary which made him decline the introduction, but the feeling—which Graham Hayes also shared—that they had met already.

III

CHARLIE did not sign on in another ship for three weeks, during which time Flynn remained in Bloomsbury, and it was October before he moved to Rotherhithe; he could have gone before, but Charlie had 'a skirt in tow', and he preferred to wait.

During those three weeks he went out to Freddie's home at Peckham at the weekends and felt as at home with the Fisher family as he had with the Doyles. 'Dad' Fisher showed him his collection of books with great pride, and was easily launched upon 'the good old days' of William Morris and the Kelmscott Press. 'Mum's' great concern was that he should have enough to eat, make himself at home, and take them as he found them; all of which he did, and, taking them as he found them, found them charming, and his heart warmed to them. They lived in an ugly red-brick and stucco house-in-a-row where they kept the coal in a cupboard under the stairs, washed in the scullery, and only used the 'front room' on Sundays. The rooms were small and overcrowded and, because Mrs. Fisher had a horror of draughts, stuffy. The house smelt of roast joints, boiled cabbage, polished linoleum, carbolic soap, and unaired rooms, and for Flynn this combination of smells was a smell of home, and he loved it.

Mrs. Fisher was house-proud, and perpetually bustling about. She had not much time for reading herself; she was, in her own words, 'no scholar',

but she had a great admiration and respect for 'Dad's' addiction to books;
it was one of the highest compliments she could pay to anyone to say that
he or she was 'a great reader', which was synonymous with being a 'scholar'.
She shared her husband's socialist ideas by instinct rather than from any
political knowledge or social consciousness. You did not have to read
books or pamphlets to realise that there was 'a lot of unfairness' in the world;
nor did you have to be 'up in' William Morris and Karl Marx and such to
know that everyone ought to have equal chances in life and an equal share
of the good things of life; it all 'stood to reason'. She had 'no patience with'
royalty, but equally no patience with the working-classes, who were so
'gormless', she declared, that they couldn't stand up for themselves and
demand their rights. Dad was interested in Irish Nationalism, and Mitchell
and Connolly were on his bookshelves. He prided himself on being what he
called 'a free-thinker', but was tolerant of Catholicism. If you was goin' to
be orthodox, he said, Catholic was the only thing to be. He had, he said, a
great respect for the Catholic Church in some aspects—"in some aspects,
mark you," he insisted, fixing Flynn with his bright intelligent eyes. "You
gotter be tolerant of everything except intolerance," was one of his favourite
axioms.

There were five children in the Fisher family, but there was a married son
and daughter living away from home, and only Freddie, Hazel, the youngest
of the family, and the eldest daughter, May, living at home. Hazel was a
typist; she was pretty, in a synthetic, film-star fashion; she was engaged to
a bank clerk, and was a great deal more interested in love, clothes, and 'the
pictures' than in social reform. May was 'the serious one' of the family.
She was twenty-eight, and a member of the Independent Labour Party; she
attended meetings of the local branch regularly every Monday night; she
also sold the Party paper in the High Street on Saturday afternoons, to the
embarrassment of her young sister, who, passing with her fiancé on the way
to 'the pictures', would pretend not to notice her.

May had no sweetheart, but occasionally at weekends she brought home
earnest-looking young men whom she addressed as comrades. Mum made
the comrades' tea and they all sat round and talked social revolution to Dad.
Mum usually got on with the ironing or mending or making a pie. May's
young men were shabby and had uncultured accents and their red ties were
not silk, like those of the cultured 'Left's' in Flynn's office. Whenever the
Communists were mentioned May and her comrades got very angry. They
referred a good deal to 'Stalin's henchmen' and 'the betrayal of the revolution'.
There was a good deal of Popular Front talk at that time, but May and the
comrades would have none of it, and had as little use for Blum as Mum had
for royalty or the gormlessness of the working-classes.

For Flynn it was all very confusing.

"Trouble with you, comrade," May once told him, caustically—she
was apt to address everyone as comrade—"is that you're wrapped up in your
Irish isolationism; you only understand nationalism, but the revolution is
international. World revolution must be the true socialist's objective!"

"Heil Trotsky and the Fourth International!" Freddie mocked her.

May frowned. "I'm no Trotskyist," she said bitterly. "I don't forget
Krondstadt!"

It was confusing, but Flynn found it enormously interesting. New worlds opened up for him. These people were at least serious and sincere. He had heard all the slogans in Paris, but there they had rolled off the tongue so glibly ; you could not feel that the decorative and amusing people who said them really cared about the revolution ; you suspected that if they saw it coming they would run for their lives.

May was musical as well as revolutionary, and she took Flynn to some Queen's Hall concerts, at which they stood for hours listening to 'good music'. Flynn found all the standing about a little tiring and would gladly have paid the difference so that they might have seats, but May declared that that was bourgeois, and with whatsoever was bourgeois May had no patience. In spite of the discomfort Flynn enjoyed these 'proms', as May called them, far more than the elegant concerts, with their gilt chairs and fashionable audiences, to which he had gone in Paris with Stephanie, hearing, for the most part, only very modern music which was for him a cacophony which was the musical equivalent of the formlessness of modern poetry ; with May he did at least begin to learn a little about real music.

He recognised that May was, as Freddie said of her, 'a good sort', but he found her a little exhausting ; she was inclined to be 'bossy', seeking a perpetual intellectual domination ; she wanted to break down his Irish nationalism—as Stephanie had wanted to break down his Catholicism—and turn him into an active international revolutionary ; world revolution would automatically free Ireland, she insisted ; it would free India, Africa, the Palestine Arabs ; it would free everyone. What were the Six Counties in comparison with the whole vast anti-imperialist struggle ? Flynn thought that they were a good deal, because whereas you mightn't get world-revolution—or even like it if you got it—you stood a good chance of getting the Six Counties back from the British eventually if you kept up the agitation. But he was never much interested in arguing with May ; it was too exhausting, and like every English person he had ever met, he felt that she did not really understand Ireland— Irish problems or Irish politics.

When he finally moved to Charlie Cray's place he invited the Fishers on his first Sunday there for a house-warming. 'Dad' admired the view—he was an enthusiastic Londoner—but took 'a very poor view' of Charlie's library, which consisted entirely of tattered magazines, 'Saucy Stories', 'Smart Set', 'Blue Stories', and paper-backed novels with covers depicting girls in very short skirts, long black silk stockings, and very high-heeled shoes, posed in attitudes which Mrs. Fisher defined as 'vulgar'—an expression she applied equally to the conduct of the monkeys at the Zoo and to the undraped statues at the Crystal Palace. May murmured something about 'the bourgeoisified proletariat' ; Dad insisted that it was 'edjercation' that was at fault ; 'you gotter edjercate the masses, see ?' Freddie said, Hell's bells, when a chap was at sea for weeks on end, with water, water everywhere, and never a skirt in sight, you could hardly expect him to read Shakespeare. . . . He adored Charlie ; Charlie was everything that was heroic and romantic —all those ships and foreign ports and women—and he could not bear that even a faint breath of criticism should touch him. Charlie was all right, and if they got the revolution they were all so keen on they'd find Charlie come out on the right side, as reliable a comrade as any of 'em. . . .

"That's right," Mum said, "I like to hear friends stick up for each other. We can't all be scholars."

Hazel and her young man were not included in the party. They had gone to see the film version of *Outposts of Passion*, Hazel for the second time—but it was such a *lovely* film you could really see it once a week. . . .

Mum bustled about the place dusting and tidying. The place really wanted a good clean-up, she declared. She had brought a bunch of chrysanthemums from the back garden and set them about the place, and Flynn was astonished at the difference a few flowers made, though they didn't constitute floral decoration as Stephanie would have understood the term. . . . But Stephanie, he reflected, would have been 'amused' by Rotherhithe, provided she hadn't to live there too long. . . . Stephanie, Stephanie, in everything he did—would he never escape her?

"The place is damp, of course," Mum said, critically.

"So's Ireland," Freddie observed.

Flynn smiled. He was getting a little tired of that one. . . .

"It makes it seem more like home," he said—since Dad or Freddie would almost certainly say it if he didn't.

"You ought to get a place of your own," Mum said, thoughtfully. "There's nothing like a place of your own."

"He's all right as he is," May said, firmly; "the fewer possessions one has the better in this life."

Flynn was inclined to agree. He had a sense of the importance of mobility. The world itself was in such a state of flux.

Yet it was the last year of peace, that year of destiny, 1934. The curtain had gone up on a stormy Prologue, but Abyssinia and Spain still waited in the wings to enact their tragedies.

IV

NEW worlds of a quite different kind opened up for Flynn with his friendship with Graham Hayes, whom he met when he had been living in Rotherhithe a week. He had gone down to the river one evening and was leaning on the low parapet when Hayes spoke to him.

"I'm your neighbour, next door but one," he said quietly. "We met one sunny Saturday afternoon a few weeks ago, at a window."

Flynn smiled. "And we didn't meet in the pub."

"Young Fisher 'phoned me after that and said you were coming to live here. He recommended that I should call, but I knew we'd meet somehow, sooner or later, without any conventional calling. Will you come and have some sherry at my place?"

"I'd like to, very much," Flynn told him, with sincerity.

The ground floor of the house in which Hayes lived was a boys' club. It was a little noisy some evenings, he admitted, but then he made no attempt to work or to read but went down and did what he could to help. He'd got an English literature class going, and the kids were interested. The people who ran the club, he said, were quite the better kind of social worker, admirably

G

free of that ghastly patronage of the poor which characterised so many of them. . . .

At the top of the dark stairs opening almost off the street they came into a panelled room which seemed mainly occupied by a huge oak table littered with books and papers. There was a massive Queen Anne silver inkstand, and a carved ivory paper-knife.

"I can't work looking on to the river," Hayes said, "I find it too distracting. This room looks out on to nothing more exciting than a brick wall, as you can see."

They went up more stairs and came into a room with a curved window recess built out over the river, and a window-seat encircling it. Both seat and window-ledge were littered with papers and books. There were books everywhere, on shelves along each wall, a row along the mantelpiece, piles on tables. There was a mask of Beethoven above the fireplace, and on the opposite wall an engraving of Shelley. In one corner of the room there was a gramophone with an enormous horn, and beside it a cabinet of records; records were also stacked on the floor.

Hayes brought glasses and a Georgian decanter of sherry.

"Help yourself to cigarettes." He indicated a box.

"I don't smoke," Flynn told him.

"But you drink, I hope?"

Flynn laughed. "Did you ever meet the Irishman who didn't?"

Hayes poured out sherry, then asked, abruptly, "Why did you leave Ireland?" He added, quickly, "I know it's a leading question. It's why I asked it. I have all of the writer's curiosity about people. We all spend far too much time being polite and getting nowhere, anyhow."

Flynn swallowed the sherry at a gulp; whilst Hayes was refilling his glass he said simply, "I left Ireland because an American woman I was in love with asked me to join her in Paris. I left Paris after a year there because I got tired of it."

"Not of her?"

"She got tired of me." Flynn sipped his second sherry and looked out of the window.

"Isn't that a very fine sunset?" he demanded, deliberately changing the subject.

Hayes gave him a quick glance. "We have very fine sunsets in Rotherhithe," he said, and then, "What are you doing at Hawes and Merry's? Is Hawes still talking about giving the public something spicy, and Merry still hoping to start a poetry department?"

"I am the poetry department," Flynn told him.

"Indeed! Who have you got?"

They talked 'shop' for a little while, and from there it was an easy transition to literature in general. Hayes was more at home with the ancients than with the moderns, and as most of Flynn's reading had been done in the Franciscan monastery library, and he had grown up in the tradition in which scholarship and literature are inseparable, Hayes' erudition came to him with a happy sense of familiarity. Hayes did not merely resemble Brother Francis physically, but intellectually, it seemed to him. And Hayes, also, it seemed, in his book-littered rooms above the river, lived the monastic life. He had been married at one time, he told Flynn, later in the evening, 'But it didn't work, and after five years that were hell for both of us she went off with someone more present in his body. She accused me of living in the dust of the past. I suppose it's true, but for me it's a living dust, whereas the present is just dust and ashes. The industrial revolution was the end of all real culture. History since then is mechanisation, imperialist ambition, wars, mass-thinking and mass-production. The cultural *fin de siècle* was the 18th century—there's been nothing since, nor likely to be."

Beneath the sweeping generalisations Flynn was aware of basic truths, and felt in himself an instinctive response. It might not be literally true that 'there has been no writer of real importance since Voltaire', and no composer since Bach, but it was, he felt, true in essence. He urged that in poetry there was Shelley in the 19th century. Hayes conceded that there was Shelley; he had a great admiration for Shelley 'in his moments of genius'; he was not a genius, Hayes insisted, he had genius in flashes; he was not to be compared with Milton, or Marlowe, or Donne. The cultural peak was represented by the Elizabethans; he was writing a book on them 'in order to escape from this revolting century and its Gadarene descent to destruction'.

The dusk settled in and star-points of lights came out along the river.

"If you've nothing better to do you might stay and eat here," Hayes said. "There's food in the house, and some claret. I hope you can drink wine? I'm not a beer-drinker myself. . . ."

They ate cheese and brown bread and tomatoes and drank claret, and Hayes discussed the Elizabethans and presently introduced Flynn to a Purcell sonata which seemed to him quite the most beautiful music he had ever heard—until Hayes put on the record of the slow movement of Bach's Concerto for Two Violins.

It was midnight when Flynn returned to his own place, and he took with him a sense of elation he had not known for a very long time—not since the first ecstatic days with Stephanie at Ballyrannon. Now, it seemed to him, he had a friend in the full rich sense of that fine word. In Paris he had liked Boronski and been amused by him, and grateful for his friendliness, but they had been too essentially of different worlds and outlook for real mental intimacy. Here in London he felt great warmth and affection for the Fisher family, but at no point, with any of them, was there anything approaching that complete communion of spirit, beyond need of words, which is the essence of friendship. He had come near to it with Brother Francis, but the saintliness of the Franciscan friar, for all his humour and humanity, was always present as a thin wall between them, a delicate, fine-spun veil of a wall, impalpable, but inescapable . . . whereas in Graham Hayes he was aware of a spirit that had known the vibrations of love and pain, of sensibilities heightened by experience, and of passion tempered by an innate austerity, a quality to which something within himself gave immediate response, and that Hayes should turn back to the past, away from the disillusion and dissatisfaction of the present, matched his own mood. Despite the fifteen years between them he had a sense of equality, of parallel experience and temperament. He was no more conscious of the disparity in their ages than he had been with Stephanie; he was in entire agreement with Hayes that it was the personality that was of interest, not the number of years a person had lived; nor was it the volume of experience that counted, but the intensity of it. You could live to be a hundred and know very little; you could die at twenty knowing a great deal. In this friendship he felt himself moving easily and naturally into that world of spiritual adventure for which he had been groping in Ireland, in the library of the Franciscan monastery, and in his researches into ancient Irish poetry—as surely as he had lost that sense of spiritual adventuring in Stephanie's self-consciously cultural world.

After that first occasion he and Hayes spent several evenings together every week, and within a month it was as though they had known each other all their lives. Gradually they filled in their backgrounds, each for the other. Graham knew all about Ballyrannon, Bridie, Cousin Kate, Jameel, and what Flynn was beginning to think of as 'the Paris interlude'. Flynn learned all about Graham's English county background, Oxford, his 'patriot's progress' to disillusionment in the Great War, his marriage with 'Eva', poet, painter, musician, brilliant, beautiful, impatient of the inward-turning flame, the final dissolution of the marriage in Paris, and the ever-recurring echo left in the heart, down through the solitary, ascetic years.

> ' "Eva!" the toast goes round;
> "Eva!" again.'

"Once you have loved a woman with your whole soul," said Graham, "there is no escape this side eternity—no escape in the spirit, though you never set eyes on her again in the flesh as long as you live."

Of the War, he said, "We really did believe, then, that it was the war to end war. We didn't believe it after Versailles, but we believed it at the time, God help us. Now there's nothing left to believe in. We have known *la grande illusion*—gone right through it and out the other side. We know that a second world war is blowing up as hard as it can blow—the same old struggle for the balance of power in imperialist politics."

"If the storm overtakes you," Flynn said, "you'll not be over military age if it happens within the next two or three years——"

Hayes shrugged. "I served *la grande illusion* last time—this time they can count me out. I'm not a pacifist. I don't hold human life inviolate. There are things for which I'd fight. I'd have taken up arms during Easter Week if I'd been Irish, and afterwards. I'd have been proud to have had a part in the October Revolution in Russia, though I'm no Communist. What I'm not prepared to kill my fellow-man for is high finance and power politics."

"They'll jail you——"

"At least one will have preserved one's personal integrity."

Concerning Stephanie he said, "She was a physical experience only, and it's with experiences as with sins, the spiritual ones are the more important. What is important to you is what you feel for your cousin. Your whole nature is involved in that."

"It can't come to anything."

" 'Yet will I love her till I die'."

"For what good that is," Flynn said, bitterly.

"Very good for the non-physical part of you we call the soul."

"Hardly a philosophy of happiness!"

"What has happiness to do with it? The important thing is to live! To feel! Outside of that you've got all that turgid D. H. Lawrence stuff, with the flesh triumphant and swallowing the spirit whole; if we're to accept that we might as well go on all-fours again. All that 'body's rapture' stuff— horrifying! As though whatever agreeable sensations the body feels the rapture isn't a purely cerebral affair! I'm not trying to disembody love. I agree with Wells that without one's body it would be bleak. What I am getting at is that it's what happens to one mentally and emotionally that is important in the end—not the calamities and brief ecstasies of the flesh. Heavens, it's not romantic love that needs debunking today, but romanticised sex! You're romanticising sex when you deceive yourself you were in love with your Mrs. Paul. Take my word for it, Stephanie Paul had no such illusions, either about what she felt for you or you for her!"

It was a difficult idea for Flynn to accept. Had he really quarrelled with Bridie, ridden Jameel to her death, left Ireland and everything he loved, for nothing more than a fever in the blood—'the wild bed', and 'the body's flame'?

"When people get into your blood they get into your imagination as well," he urged.

And Graham told him, "When the blood is fevered the mind is apt to run a temperature!" He added, "It can leave one sick for a long time——"

That at least Flynn knew to be true. But the sickness was subsiding—he knew that, too.

During Christmas week he went to confession.

V

As Christmas drew near he was seized with restlessness, and had wild ideas of going to Dublin, but told himself that the fact that Stephanie was no longer in the picture would not alter Bridie's and Cousin Kate's feelings about that episode; Holy Church might give absolution, but for them his sin remained, because he had sinned against them. Any gesture of reconciliation must come from them, since he had first to be forgiven by them; and the thought of meeting them with their hearts still hardened against him was intolerable. Then he played for a little with the idea of going to Paris; the Christmas shops brought little Jeanne d'Alvray vividly back to him; it would be sweet to see the child again . . . but that would mean Nina and Johnny, and the rest of the Montparnasse crowd, and he shrank from the thought of them, and Boronski, according to a recent postcard, was still in the South, and likely to remain there. Paris, he decided, was probably not a very good idea; he felt the old bitterness rising in him when he began to think of Montparnasse.

The Fishers invited him to spend Christmas with them, and he would have accepted, gratefully, but that suddenly Graham produced a better idea.

"Why don't we go to the Lakes?" he suggested.

They made an incredibly crowded night journey to Keswick on Christmas Eve, since Flynn was unable to leave town before then, and arrived in Keswick in time for him to attend the early Mass.

"Unless you're going up Skiddaw the great thing to do in Keswick is get out of it as quickly as possible," Graham said, when they left the church. They took the 'bus out to Borrowdale and made their way over to Stye Head Pass, for Wasdale Head. It was extremely wet going until they reached Stye Head, and miniature waterfalls cascaded down over every track and boulder of the ascent to it, but they were both completely happy, Graham because he was always happy amongst the high hills, in all weathers, Flynn because the bogs, and the wildness of the hills, reminded him of Connemara, and because of the blessedness of restoration to Holy Communion, of being again in a state of grace. He had a sense of inner purification, of having shaken off chains at long last. He was integrated after months of disintegration, and was filled with an extraordinary feeling of spiritual lightness and joy.

There was snow up in the Pass, and a bitter wind, but nothing could quench his exhilaration. He was back in Ballyrannon, running in the wind and rain with Bridie to a rhythm of endlessly unwritten poems, the two of them living out their lives in winter under the eternally blossoming boughs of fantasy. Were there not great bare hills behind that might be the Twelve Pins, and below, far down in the valley, a lake that might be Ballyrannon Lough itself? Any moment Bridie might come running with wild hair flying, or Cousin Kate with the dark hair blown across her eyes and her head thrown back as she called to him, 'Fly-nn! Flynn darlin' . . .' her voice echoing down into the valley, with a kind of sadness to it, like the cry of a curlew.

At the head of the Pass, Graham paused and looked along the valley to the distant white line of the sea.

"Ireland's over there," he said, "only that narrow strip of water between."

Flynn laughed, excitedly, leaning against the wind that caught them as though it would hurl them off their narrow track and roll them down over the loose flints of the scree and into the deep valley.

"Ireland's here," he said softly, " 'tis a piece God left on this side of the water to show he forgave the English their sins against the Irish."

They had rooms in a guest-house at the foot of Great Gable, and for three days lived in an atmosphere of ropes and nailed boots and ice-axes, and nobody mentioned Abyssinia, Mussolini, Hitler, or 'the international situation'; the talk was all of screes and traverses and rock-faces and 'chimneys'. They climbed Scafell Pikes and came down over the Lord's Rake in spite of the ice on the rocks; they made the traverse of Great Gable, and hacked steps up the steep snow slopes of Bew Fell . . . and promised themselves to come again at Easter.

Those few days together brought them very close; there was the unspoken thought in them both, 'Now we shall be friends forever.'

During those days Flynn found himself thinking again of his mother, which he had not done since he had left Ireland; he spoke to Graham about her for the first time, and of the fantasy he had had when he was sixteen, and trying to remake the gardens at Ballyrannon Castle, that she would one day return and find everything as she had left it.

"It seems strange," he said, "to think of her living out her life somewhere, perhaps in this country, perhaps in Paris, and the two of us never meeting."

"She may not be living," Graham pointed out, "and if she is alive and you eventually met it would be as strangers. Because you sprang from her womb it doesn't necessarily follow that you have anything in common. This assumption of a natural affinity between parents and children is the sheerest sentimental romanticism, you know. Having got out of the womb, with some difficulty, why this psychological groping down labyrinthine ways back to it?"

"Well, why?" Flynn challenged him.

"Pure neurosis," Graham said, shortly. "Inability to adapt to life in the outer world, and the desire to return to the womb. Perfectly understandable, the world being what it is, but a pity."

Flynn smiled. "I seem to remember Stephanie talking like that once——"

"People like Stephanie Paul are born parrots. Sometimes a parrot picks up and trots out something that happens to be true. Forget your mother. She walked out on you—which was probably a very good thing. A pity more parents don't walk out on their children early on instead of staying to warp their lives."

But you couldn't, Flynn discovered, eliminate by intellectual processes something rooted in the emotions. It was something beyond all reason, and something he could not tell Graham—whom he loved—but he needed that woman from whose womb he had sprung, needed her with a fierce and terrible nostalgic longing, because there was no one else in intimate relation to him to whom he could come close, and she, whether she liked it or not, was part of him as he of her, and the fact that they might pass in the street and not recognise each other did not destroy their relationship. The mother, it seemed to him—whether modern psychology recognised the fact or not—might have no emotional need of the child, but the child could never quite escape the emotional need of the mother. The Catholic Church, in its compassionate wisdom, recognised this need and became the universal mother, symbolising all maternal tenderness and love in the Mother of Jesus. It was something which at times Flynn felt intensely, and a grace for which he was devoutly grateful, but Wasdale's likeness to Ireland raised the ghost of that Irish 'pretty, witty Kitty', and bound up with that nostalgic longing was the nostalgia for Ireland itself, the mother who was Cathleen ni Houlihan, whose son he was. . . .

2

News of his father came to him through the office. Mike Harrigan wrote to his publishers from Beverly Hills asking for copies of his new novel to be sent over immediately to secure ad interim copyright in the States; also he wanted copies sent out to Hollywood for film purposes. He was, apparently, completely immersed in the film world, making money, and indicating no desire to return to Ireland or anywhere else in Europe. He wrote that he was glad to know that Flynn was in the office, sent him his love, and urged him to 'quit England' if the imminent Abyssinian-Italian war broke, as it would most certainly be the beginning of the European conflagration. . . . *'Tell him to go native on his native shores and leave the rest of Europe to smash itself to bits, as it will.'* Mr. Hawes frowned over this letter. The terrible insularity of the Irish. . . . He showed the letter to Flynn, and invited him to dinner.

Flynn found these periodic invitations to dinner at the Hawes's a little embarrassing. They had a beautiful house at Hampstead, overlooking the Heath; they had a good cook, and they collected interesting and amusing guests round their table; but Mrs. Hawes was, as Mike had observed some time ago, very bored as well as very decorative, and she was very anxious to know young Flynn Harrigan better. . . . Flynn thought her attractive, in her slim, dark, rather exotic, long-ear-ringed fashion. He was well aware of her interest in him, and it seemed to him a very good reason for keeping away from her. When possible he refused invitations to dinner; the fact that Lesley Hawes had a power to attract him disturbed him; he had believed—and quite desperately wanted it to be true—that the Stephanie business could never happen again.

But he felt that he could not refuse this latest invitation, having recently refused several, and on the appointed evening went out to Hampstead with Mr. Hawes. There were several other guests, and it was not difficult for the hostess, in the confusion of farewells at the end of the evening, to get Flynn a little aside from the others and ask him in a low voice when he was going to ask her to tea at Rotherhithe.

"I was so jealous that you had Sylvanus there. I hear it's enchanting—and I'm sure I should be a more entertaining guest than old Sylvanus!"

The Irish instinctive desire to please, in combination with the wine he had had at dinner—and the sherry before, and the whiskies after—made Flynn say Why yes, of course, and positively urge that she should come to tea the following Saturday afternoon. . . .

It would suit her perfectly, she declared, adding, playfully, "You won't forget between now and then, will you?"

He spent the rest of the week regretting having asked her, and then had the inspiration of inviting Graham as well.

Graham said frankly, "I'd much rather not. Lesley Hawes and I have a pretty good hate on each other."

"Might one ask why?"

"I'd sooner she told you herself. She will—her version, anyhow. But why do you have her to see you? She's your Mrs. Paul all over again. Ten years or so younger, perhaps, but the same thing, English version——"

"She rather forced herself on me," Flynn admitted.

"Of course she did."

"She's very charming and nice," Flynn said, "and anyhow," defensively, "I couldn't very well refuse."

"All right, all right. Let her come, and get it over, only don't drag me into it."

It was an ideal afternoon for seeing the river at its best when Mrs. Hawes arrived, just such a blue and gold day as that on which Flynn had first come to Rotherhithe. Mrs. Hawes, wrapped in mink, looked down on the Pool of London, admired the misty dome of St. Paul's behind Tower Bridge, smiled at Flynn and told him it was an enchanting place to live. It came to him that it was all rather like showing Stephanie Paul the view from the tower at Ballyrannon Castle that first time. . . .

She wandered about the living-room whilst Flynn was making tea, looked at the few books he had collected, and then alighted upon a small framed photograph of Graham Hayes. When Flynn came back into the room she turned away from the photograph and said, "I suppose you know it's frightfully indiscreet to have that man's photograph blatantly exposed for all to see like that?"

Flynn set down the laden tray he had been holding and stared at her in amazement.

"What on earth do you mean? He's my greatest friend—my only real friend."

"I daresay. But there's no point in getting oneself labelled, is there?"

"I really don't know what you mean."

"You're not going to tell me you haven't been in London long enough to discover that he's one of the most notorious queens in the literary world?"

Flynn had the feeling of the blood draining out of his heart. He said, violently, "That's a lie!"

Mrs. Hawes shrugged. "If you think you know the English literary world better than I do after twelve years in it. . . ."

"I don't know anything about the English literary world, but I do know that what you say about Graham Hayes is completely untrue."

"You're very naïve," she said, and reached for a sandwich.

After that he found it difficult to talk to her, and she was aware of his roused hostility. She had ruined the afternoon so far as making any headway with Flynn was concerned, but she liked to think that she had sown the seeds of doubt in the young man's mind regarding his great friend, and was a little avenged on the odious Graham Hayes in the process. Flynn Harrigan, she was convinced, was a very normal young man, and being Catholic into the bargain would no doubt be very shocked at the idea of scandal circulating about himself and his cherished friend.

She went within an hour, leaving behind a seething anger in Flynn's heart, and in his rooms a scent of violets which he found so intolerable that he flung windows and doors wide open to get rid of it. Then he went round to see Graham. He let himself in and ran up the stairs and found Graham in the river-room.

"No wonder you hate that woman!" he cried, "but why in God's name should she be so vicious? What has she got against you?"

"What she will now have against you," Graham told him—"the fact that I didn't respond to her advances. She started a story about me and a young German refugee lad I was interested in helping, having known his father in pre-Hitler Frankfort. I was so sick that I called at the Hawes's house and made a first-class row. . . . When I didn't renew my contract with the firm it was thought that I had gone after a better imprint; I expect you heard that story? I couldn't have gone on with them; old Hawes naturally defended his wife—it all became impossible. Now she'll start a story about us. Do you mind?"

"It seems that wherever you go the literary world is so full of scandals that one more can't make any difference. At least I won't be asked to dinner there any more—that's something!"

It had, however, wider repercussions than that. When Augustus Hawes heard that Flynn Harrigan was 'having an affair' with his great enemy, Graham Hayes, he was so indignant that he informed his partner that he intended giving Michael Harrigan's son a month's notice, and told Sylvanus why. Sylvanus disliked Mrs. Hawes and had never believed the story about Graham Hayes being a 'queen'—alternatively, he didn't mind if he was, he said, he had been a very distinguished author on a very shoddy list—and saw no reason for sacking Flynn because of his friendship with him. Mr. Hawes was adamant, and the upshot of it all was that Sylvanus declared himself fed-up and that he was clearing out.

He cleared out with Freddie Fisher and Miss Featherstone and Flynn, and they became the Merryweather Press—with Graham Hayes as their literary adviser. For Flynn it was all a little bewildering, so great an upheaval over so small a thing.

"The next thing is to get Michael Harrigan and Graham Hayes on to our list," Sylvanus declared, "as soon as their present contracts have expired. And what about a slim volume of poems by the young Irish poet Flynn Harrigan?"

But he recoiled away from that. His poems were few, and were intensely personal; he never wanted to show them, and only very occasionally to talk about them. They were as private as an intimate journal. There was something a little vulgar, surely, about rushing into print with one's thoughts and feelings when they were so very personal?

"Shakespeare and Shelley and a few others weren't so reticent, fortunately," Sylvanus said, drily.

Flynn felt that it was too difficult to explain. He never thought of himself as a poet. Most of the things he wrote he left unfinished; a lot of the visions that came into his head and assumed rhythmical form he never committed to paper. When he wrote it was not to be heard, but merely because things shaped in his mind in a certain way and they clarified on paper. What did get put down had, he felt, no real meaning for English people in any case. Cousin Kate was probably the only person he could freely have shown his poems to. He had shown a few to Graham at different times, and Graham had urged that he should collect and publish them, but had said no more about it when he had realised how genuinely and deeply repugnant the idea was to their author.

London, Flynn discovered, was much easier to 'settle down' in than Paris. It was like marriage with a very sensible woman; it was not exciting, it was not beautiful, it was not amusing; but it was workable. You had an 'affair' with Paris; it was gay, amusing, adventurous, exciting, beautiful; Paris was the perennial mistress as surely as London was the serious good wife. In Paris you lived; in London you settled down into regular existence. It suited Flynn very well; to live happily in Paris you had to be in love; it was essentially a lovers' city. London had its compensations. He found the Pool of London endlessly romantic and interesting, in spite of the winter mists that made the Rotherhithe rooms every bit as damp as Mrs. Fisher had prophesied. He liked the Park and Kensington Gardens, and the deep cool twilight of Westminster Cathedral. He liked the river at Chelsea, to which Graham introduced him—Turner's Reach, and Whistler's chimneys, and gulls flying low over the moored barges; he liked the old houses with their deep windows and crinoline balconies and tall narrow doors under stately porches; he liked the vines and the mulberries and the wrought-iron gates and general old-world charm. He liked the Chelsea of the King's Road that reminded him a little of Paris. He liked the bookshops of the Charing Cross Road that reminded him not so much of the Paris *quais* as the shabby quays along the Liffey in Dublin. He liked the heathery commons of the Surrey countryside where he walked at weekends, sometimes with Freddie Fisher, sometimes with Graham, sometimes the three of them together. Occasionally, as the good weather advanced, he went on the river at Richmond with May Fisher, and walked with her afterwards amongst the bracken in the Park, and had tea on the terrace. She was falling in love with him, but he was quite unaware of it, and she kept her quite unMarxist grief to herself. He went to the Russian Ballet with her, and with Graham, but much preferred going with Graham, because May Fisher was forever making a Marxist analysis of any story a ballet might possess, giving it a sociological significance, or deploring the lack of it. Her great ambition was to go to Moscow and see *Swan Lake* done in its full length, whereas Flynn agreed with Graham that there was quite enough of it as it was. May took him to Kew at Whitsun; they wandered in avenues of blossom and sat under a cherry-tree and had their tea from a thermos flask, and out of various paper bags which May produced. There were bluebells in the long grass and lovers in every blossoming avenue, and May Fisher talked energetically and interminably of the international situation. . . . He went again the following day alone, and was exquisitely happy and exquisitely sad. He was once again the boy who had lain face downwards on the lake island on a summer's morning and dreamed of a girl, of kissing her until she be wearied out, of love wild and bright as a seagull's wing in sunlight, sweet as the song of a blackbird on a blossoming bough, and a line from the Gaelic came into his head:

> 'It is the fragrant branch I would soonest pluck,
> And it is my own love I would soonest follow.'

He lay in a little orchard of Japanese cherry-trees, and looking up at the deep white and soft rose of the thick-massed blossom, he thought of Ballyrannon and the wild cherry-tree down by the broken wall that divided the castle gardens from the reedy beach of the lake. He thought of Bridie climbing into the boat with her hands full of cherries, and cherries dangling from her lips and her ears. He thought of Cousin Kate swimming naked with him in the moonlight of a summer's night, white breast lifted on the silver water like the breast of a gull. He thought of old Tante Emma wrapped in her shawl, and the rosary said in the whitewashed kitchen; he thought of Bream Island, and the seals with their great soft liquid eyes, and the curaghs upturned on the beaches like sleeping seals, and the Doyles gathered round the fire in the smoky cabin singing Gaelic songs and telling stories. Of Stephanie and Paris he did not think at all. He knew now that they had nothing to do with the blossoming bough invisibly stretched above the dreaming heart.

3

When Charlie Cray's ship returned to port and Charlie to his rooms above the river, Flynn went to stay with Graham for a few weeks. He liked

Charlie, but after a few nights under the same roof with him and his current 'skirt' he found it impossible. Charlie and the girl would come in late at night, very noisily, turn on gramophone or radio, and dance; very often Charlie would be accompanied by various other seafaring friends and their 'skirts'. The men produced bottles from their pockets, and there was generally a concertina, or at least a mouth-organ, in the party. It was 'fun' on the first few occasions, Flynn discovered, but when it happened night after night it became exhausting. Charlie could lie abed till mid-day the following day—and usually did, his girl in his arms—whereas Flynn had to be up by seven-thirty. He found, also, that it got on his nerves, badly, hearing the sounds of soft intimate talk and laughter from Charlie's room when he had a girl in there, which he almost always had. After a fortnight of it he acknowledged to himself that he could not stand it, and accepted Graham's invitation to stay with him till Charlie went to sea again, which would not be for some weeks, since he did not intend to sign on in another ship until he had spent all the money from his last voyage.

The dream of revisiting the Lakes that spring had to be abandoned because Graham was writing a new book and could not spare the time, but they went walking at weekends, and when the Jubilee came upon them escaped out of the beflagged and garlanded and vulgarised city into Sussex, and stayed for the entire week at an inn beside a wood full of wild rhododendrons and ancient stones. Graham went on with his book and Flynn wandered in the woods and thought that in the autumn it must be like a corner of the forest of Fontainebleau . . . and that was the first time he had thought of 'the Paris interlude' for a long time. He filled again with the restlessness he had experienced under the blossoming trees of Kew Gardens, and one soft May morning he sat on a boulder with a writing-pad on his knee and resolutely wrote to Katherine O'Donal:

Dear Cousin Kate: I am writing this in a wood in Sussex, and I am thinking of Connemara because of the great boulders that are strewn about, and of Ballyrannon Castle because of the wild rhododendrons, and of you because you are bound up with these things. I left Paris last autumn and am working in a publishing house in London. There's no reason at all why you should be interested in what I am doing, but I long, terribly, to have news of you and Bridie and Ireland. If I thought for a single moment you or Bridie would be glad to see me I would arrive at Dun Laoghaire by the next boat. The only thing that keeps me away is the thought that your hearts are still hard against me. If it helps at all for you to know it—I mean if it helps me to secure absolution at your hands for past sins—I was alone in Paris for the last year, and in that sense I am alone here. I wonder, endlessly, what you are playing in, what Bridie is doing, and if Aunt Chris is as beautiful as ever. At this moment I am so homesick I could die of it, but it's more than a homesickness for Ireland, though perhaps you'll not understand that.

He signed the letter simply, '*Flynn*', and gave the Rotherhithe address. With any luck, he told himself, feverishly, there should be an answer awaiting him when he got back to London.

There was no letter when he got back, and after a fortnight he gave up hope. Then, when he was no longer looking for it, there came a letter with an Irish stamp. His heart turned over, but the writing was neither Cousin Kate's nor Bridie's, but Aunt Chris's. She wrote:

My dear Flynn: Since neither Katherine nor Bridie feel they can write to you, I am doing so to let you have news for which you ask. Bridie has been working for a year and a half now as secretary to Mr. Seamus Moyne at his bookshop in Dawson Street. She was engaged to young Mr. Rory Mahon of the Arts Theatre at Christmas but it was broken off. We think her heart was never really in it at all. She is as high-spirited as ever—still the wild one. Katherine had a success as Pegeen in the 'Playboy'. Your father keeps urging me to go to Hollywood and make films, but it would be the world's wonder if I should ever leave Ireland. We are rehearsing for the 'Moon in the Yellow River'. I had hoped Bridie at least would write to you herself, but people get ideas into their heads and there is no unfixing them, and she cannot get over this idea that you deserted your family, your home, and Ireland itself for 'that woman', and even though all that may be finished now she remains unforgiving. She says that it is not a matter of forgiving, but that the world you once knew together does not exist any more because, she says, you smashed it up, and it cannot be put together again. What Katherine thinks or feels I have no idea; I never have known what goes on inside her. She showed me your letter, and when I asked her would she be answering it, replied that she didn't feel she could— whatever that may mean. I hope you are happy, Flynn, and that that unfortunate Paris episode is truly finished. Your affectionate aunt, Christabel O'Donal.

When he had read that letter Flynn sat for a long time with his head in his hands. The unforgiveness it conveyed lay like a physical pain at his heart—as a letter of Cousin Kate's had once lain. He wrote briefly and thanked his aunt for her letter; he was glad to have news of them all, he said, dully, and still hoped that one day they would all meet again and laugh and be happy. . . .

Katherine did, in fact, write to him, within a few hours of receiving his letter. She wrote:

Flynn darling, it was wonderful to get your letter. I have thought of you, too, endlessly. If you were to come home I would meet the boat at Dun Laoghaire, in the early morning, and we would travel out together to Westland Row in the little train, sitting very close and holding hands. Perhaps I shouldn't write that to you, but I love you, Flynn; I have never ceased to love you . . . why haven't you known? Come home, my darling, come home. . . . Kate.

She wrote it with the tears streaming down her face, and when she had written it she tore it up, and knew, then, that she would never write at all.

VI

His twenty-second birthday Flynn spent with the Fishers. Mrs. Fisher made a cake and decorated it with twenty-two candles. Various 'comrades' came in, including, what was unusual in the Fisher household, some girl comrades.

Freddie brought in bottles of beer, and May some cheap sherry. "It's nice to have a bit of a do on an occasion like this," Mrs. Fisher said, approvingly. "You want to forget politics once in a way." She took up the rugs in the 'front room', and pushed the furniture back against the walls, so that there was room for three couples to dance at a time, but Flynn smiled ruefully and said he was sorry, but he didn't dance; he had known that wild night in Paris when he had taken Stephanie out for the first and last time that he had danced for the last time—unless it was the old Irish dances which did not involve the intimate embrace of modern dancing. That he didn't dance was a great disappointment to the girl comrades, and not least to May, who had hoped, wildly, that the combination of sherry and dancing would induce Flynn to be a little more 'coming on'. . . . She offered to teach him, and was so persistent about it that he was forced to tell her that he didn't dance 'on principle'. It sounded, he knew, abominably priggish, but there was no other escape from her persistence.

She asserted, severely, "It's time you emancipated yourself from all that priest-ridden puritanism, you know."

He smiled. "I've been told that before."

Freddie came to his aid. "Principles aside," he said, "he's quite right, all this jigging round clamped together. It's not dancing at all, properly speaking."

Freddie himself didn't dance—not on principle, but from shyness, and a complete lack of any sense of rhythm.

"You can't beat the old-fashioned polkas and waltzes," Mrs. Fisher said, and later she and 'Dad' gave a demonstration.

It was all full of warmth and good-nature and fun, but Flynn was glad when it was over. He was not in the mood. He would far rather have sat with Graham in the river-room listening to a Purcell sonata, or the slow movement from Bach's Concerto for Two Violins, whilst the twilight crept along the river. He could not shake off the sense of heaviness and hopelessness which Aunt Chris's letter had left in him. There was a destroying sense of pointlessness in everything. His personal life was utterly disintegrated, and the world itself was in a state of slow disintegration, or at least moving towards it. He had the feeling of going on from day to day with no meaning to any of it. He clung to his friendship with Graham Hayes as the only thing left of any value, a city of refuge. He became aware, as time went on, that scandal attached to their friendship, thanks to Lesley Hawes; he was aware of nudges and murmurs sometimes when he was at the ballet with Graham, or in restaurants favoured by the 'intelligentsia'; but he was completely indifferent to it—since Graham himself was. Graham was fond of quoting, 'People say—what say they? Let them say!' The slander was symptomatic, Flynn felt, of all that *fin de siècle* decadence and disintegration he had felt in Paris. He felt no bitterness towards Mrs. Hawes; nearly two years in Paris had taught him not to be surprised at anything in human nature.

In October Mussolini's troops invaded Abyssinia, and the war clouds darkened over Europe more heavily than in 1934. It looked like another world war, with 'poor little Abyssinia' replacing the 'poor little Belgium' of 1914. Everyone was talking 'sanctions' and was passionately for or against. Everyone, forgetting their own imperialist past, was highly indignant over this act of Italian aggression. Graham observed, "It's interesting to speculate on how long it takes for an act of imperialist aggression to become merely part of the historic past, and respectable. . . ."

At Christmas they went to Dieppe together; neither was in the mood for Paris, but both felt a strong need to get not merely out of London, but out of England. They had a leisurely few days, sitting on café-terraces, eating in unpretentious little restaurants renowned for their cuisine, loitering along the quays and looking at the fishing-boats, and strolling out into the country and drinking the local cider. There was a pale cold clear sunshine and a smell of France. It was a 'break' they both needed, but Graham was worried about Flynn; he knew very well that what he needed was to fall in love again, not with an impossible Irish cousin who refused to write, or with any worldly Stephanie Paul; something, he felt, had to happen soon if Flynn was not to have a breakdown; he was very obviously in a very bad nervous state since the letter from Ireland. He talked wildly, from time to time, of trying to get sent to Abyssinia with Quaker or Red Cross organised hospital units. Or as a newspaper correspondent. Graham dissuaded him from these ideas, and tried to interest him in new publishing projects he was planning, with Sylvanus, for the Merryweather Press. But it was no good. The sense of impending world disaster made the production of *de luxe* editions of poetry, *belles lettres*, and the more literary type of short story seem to Flynn hopelessly unrealist, a form of ivory-towerism. The word 'escapism' came into the language; the success of a book called *Away From It All* seemed significant. Flynn's need was not so much to get away, as for action, the need to move, if only with the landslide; what was intolerable was sitting still and waiting for it to overtake you. You could not just go on bringing out good books, listening to Bach and Purcell, going to an office every day, and leading a normal, orderly, uneventful existence, when you had this sense of your whole being in a state of disintegration, and the world itself moving towards chaos. Something had to happen in one's personal world, Flynn insisted, something which removed one from the deadly artificiality of the static in a doomed civilisation.

When Charlie Cray came back at the end of January he discussed with him the idea of going to sea. Charlie thought it could be 'wangled'; he knew a chap in the Shipping Federation who would always 'fix it for a pal'.

"I can't stand this backwater existence any longer," Flynn said, "I need the open sea," and Graham knew that it was true, and this time made no attempt to dissuade him.

In mid-March he signed on as ordinary seaman in a tramp steamer bound for South America.

2

The days, then, resolved into a series of impressions, curiously unreal. The ship rolling heavily with a cargo of sheet-tin; the smell of the fo'c'sle; the greasy smell of the galley. Stumbling out of a bunk in the middle of the night, in the small hours of the morning, for the turn at the wheel; the long watch poised between black sea and thick-starred sky; the sense of ploughing on into eternity. The blasphemy of men's tongues, the endless fornicatory talk of leisure moments. The struggle against odds for physical cleanliness; the slow demoralisation. Growing used to being called Paddy; growing used to cockroaches in the food; growing used to the obscenity of men's minds.

Then at last Montevideo, and a strange spicy smell blown off the land, and the curiously tidy wharves. The plane-trees of the Plaza de la Constitución, and a sudden pervading sense of loneliness in the neat town. Exploring the old town and thinking of Graham and Rotherhithe and the twisted acacias and the shabbiness.

Buenos Aires, and the flat, wide skyline, and the curious irrelevancy of small skyscrapers. The fine, spacious docks, with the unexpectedness of trees and grass. The broad streets with their imposing buildings, their smart cars, and little scampering 'buses of different colours. The magnificence of the Plaza del Congreso with its trees and fountains; the tree-lined Avenida de Mayo; the palatial beauty of the Opera House; squat palms with trunks like pineapples. At night the double row of lights strung like a necklace along the Avenida de Mayo, and, with the lights and trees and noble sweep, an echo of the Champs Elysées. The flashing sky-signs and the changing colours of the fountains—and an echo of the Rond-Point. The endless din of cicadas. The bursts of music and rowdy laughter from the bars and cafés of 'The Arches', that sailors' synthetic Paradise of drink and women and garish lights. The Liverpool Bar; the Welcome Bar; the Moulin Rouge—is this the South American Montmartre? Prostitutes in lighted doorways. 'You know gay Paree, Paddy; what price this?' Lights everywhere, till the head spins, and a beer that tastes of chemicals, and a *vino tinto* harsh as truth.

Then Rosario and the impatient days of waiting out in the roads for a berth. The brown-skinned natives of the shanty town outside the city coming out in boats to exchange bottles of beer for pieces of wood. Berthing at last under the precipitous 'cliffs', loading grain; the endless racket of the grain in the long pipes; dust everywhere; the dockers arriving in city clothes and changing on board into striped pyjama-like jackets and trousers, and aprons. The Greek bars in the dock area, the endless games of dice. The magnificence of sunset over the wide, swift river.

Then back to Buenos Aires in the cold bright sunshine of the Argentine winter, and only by an effort realising that in England it is June. But England is a world away, and Ireland remote as heaven. In the Argentine newspapers, in English and Spanish, Spain is in the news; there are strikes all over Spain, and people no longer appear on the streets of Barcelona wearing hats or collars and ties—symbols of the bourgeoisie. But you are a sailor ashore and you do not read the newspapers, and you do not speak Spanish, and so do not know what people are saying in the cafés and bars. The only talk you hear is of drink and women; you are a merchant-seaman, adrift in one foreign city after another, out of touch with the world as a whole.

VII

FLYNN was back in London when the Fascist military revolt started in Morocco, and an English major flew General Franco from the Canaries to lead the insurgent troops in Spain. Visiting the Fishers, Flynn found them in a state of great excitement. They had always known, they declared, that the Spanish workers would rise again; now they were pouring out into the streets of Barcelona to face the machine-guns of the Fascists armed with no more than sticks and stones, and a great number of the troops had refused to obey their officers' orders to fire and gone over to the workers. In one barracks a sergeant and his men had arrested the officers, and the sergeant had then placed himself at the service of the P.O.U.M.—the Spanish equivalent of the I.L.P., May Fisher explained. The P.O.U.M., together with the anarchists, organised in the great Catalan trade union organisation, the C.N.T., and the F.A.I.—the Federation of Iberian Anarchists—stood for more than the war against Fascism, but for the workers' revolution. The workers were coming out on to the streets crying *'Viva la Republica!'*, and *'Viva la Fai!'* The crews of warships were rising against their officers and shelling Moroccan ports to prevent the transport of Moorish troops to Spain. The civil guards and shock police had come out on the side of the government. Workers were forming themselves into militia, and when the government refused them arms were seizing them from the ships in harbour.

"It's the Revolution!" May Fisher declared, triumphantly, and was immediately busy working with comrades organising truth-about-Spain, the revolution-behind-the-Spanish-war, meetings.

The entire Fisher household, even Hazel, was startled when Flynn hung fire in his enthusiasm not merely for the Spanish revolution but even for the Republican cause. He was troubled. It might be true, as the Fishers so vehemently insisted, that General Franco stood for the ruling classes, vested interests, private profit, but he also stood for the Catholic Church, whereas the 'Reds', as the Republicans were called, were frankly anti-clerical and were accused of sacking and destroying the churches. The Fishers, horrified, read him long and impassioned lectures on the tyranny of the Catholic Church in Spain. May Fisher was particularly passionate about the grip of the Church on Spanish women, frustrating their emancipation. May Fisher, it seemed to Flynn, was as anxious to free the Spanish women from the influence of the convents as Stephanie Paul had been to free him from the parish priest; it was a line of attack before which his resistance always hardened. Irish nationalism was bound up with the Catholic Church, and had been for six hundred years, yet the Fishers, and people liked them, gave their support to Irish nationalism in spite of the tie with the Church; why, then, should they fight Spanish nationalism, which was also tied up with it?

"Because it's not a liberating nationalism," May Fisher said, impatiently, "any more than Hitler's or Mussolini's brand. You've got to distinguish between imperialist nationalisms and liberating nationalisms—such as the Irish, the Indian, the Arab. Franco's so-called nationalism isn't nationalism at all; it's straight Fascism. As to the Church—haven't you seen about the Basque priests being on the side of the Republic?"

Flynn hadn't, and the news shook him a little. As did the fact that Graham came out so strongly on the Republican side. Graham was sympathetic to the Catholic Church, but the Church, he insisted, must be above the strife. In Ireland the nationalist struggle was bound up with the Church because the struggle had its origins in a people's right to the Church of its choice; it was part of the struggle for Catholic Emancipation. The Azana government was no more anti-Catholic than it was communist; it was put into power by a Catholic people. Franco might set himself up as a gallant Christian gentleman, the champion of the Church, but it did not alter the fact that the Moroccan rising was nothing more or less than a military *coup*, and it was not a case of Franco and the Catholic Spanish people against the 'Reds', but a case of Franco and an army of mercenaries against a Popular Front government elected by the people. He personally had no use for the Popular Front government, but it was elected by the people, and was no more communist than the British Labour Party was socialist. . . . To call it 'Red' was ridiculous, when it was hardly pale pink. But better a pale pink republic, since it at least had some relation to democracy, that tattered, frayed-at-the-edges word, than Franco's black-shirtism, backed by German and Italian Fascism. You might not think very much of the Spanish Republic, but at least it was a step forward, whereas Fascism was a step back, a clamping down on all personal liberty and social progress.

"You may not have a very high opinion of De Valera's government," Graham urged, "but that would be no reason for wanting to see it replaced by a dictatorship, or a swing-back to British rule."

"I keep wondering what line my father is taking on all this," Flynn said.

"Michael Harrigan is far too good a Republican not to be on the Government side in the Spanish issue," Graham declared, emphatically.

A little later Graham was proved to be right; a symposium of replies from established authors as to which side they were on was published, and Michael Harrigan declared himself uncompromisingly on the side of the Republic, for the same reason, he declared, that he had been on the Republican side during the Irish civil war—'for the principle of the thing'!

The Republican principle. . . . Flynn turned it over in his mind endlessly those July days. He went to a number of meetings in Spain organised by the I.L.P., and it began to seem to him that much more important than 'the Republican principle' was the revolution being waged by the workers, organised in the P.O.U.M, the C.N.T. and the F.A.I., behind the anti-Fascist struggle. The communist slogan, 'the war first, the revolution afterwards', seemed to him a good way to lose the revolution. You had, as May Fisher and her comrades were always insisting, to take advantage of the revolutionary situation created by the war. Better the Republic than the Fascist dictatorship a Franco victory would mean, but better than any capitalist democracy would be workers' control and an end of the exploitation of the many by the few. And the more you thought along those lines the more you inclined to the anarcho-syndicalist idea, with its absence of any centralised government and the risk of any privileged class of commissars and intellectuals springing up to form a new bureaucracy. The case, it seemed to him, was not for the dictatorship of the proletariat as laid down by the Marxists, but for the abolition of all dictatorship, under any label.

He had intended going to sea again after a few weeks in London, but now it seemed to him that there was something more important to do; in Spain there was a cause to be fought that was worth the fighting, a cause for which there was little support or even knowledge outside Spain itself, a revolutionary struggle for a juster and more rational order of society. He had no desire to join the communist organised International Brigade and fight for the preservation of the *status quo*, but a growing desire to join in the revolutionary struggle being waged by the anarchists and the P.O.U.M. This was something which, once the civil war in himself was settled, fired his imagination. He read Ramon Sender's *Seven Red Sundays*, describing the strikes which preceded the civil war, and everything concerning the revolutionary struggle which he could get hold of. The more he read the more he realised that the popular press on Spain was completely misleading, and that the British masses were not being allowed to know the tremendous social upheaval being the straight Republican versus Nationalist issue. When the majority of people said 'revolutionary' they meant 'communist', whereas the communists, in alliance with the Republican government, were in fact doing their best to smash the revolution—in the interests of Soviet foreign policy, which looked for a protective alliance with democratic governments.

Instead of hanging round the Shipping Federation after a ship, Flynn was constantly in and out of the I.L.P. office finding out how he could get himself to Spain. Graham declared that it was the innate Irish inability to keep out of a scrap; Flynn retorted that it was 'the Irish passion for liberty'. He added, "I don't see how anyone can be neutral—any more than anyone could have been neutral in the Irish civil war. It's one of those things in which every man knows where he stands—where you can't help but take sides!"

His voice was eager, his eyes alight. He had already forgotten his early uncertainties as to which side he belonged. These Irish, Graham thought, this fanaticism and its passionate espousal of lost causes. Because, of course, the revolution was a lost cause, whatever might be the outcome of the war. But for that reason it was worth fighting—magnificently worth fighting. It did not take a lot of thought to decide him to go to Spain with Flynn. What was there to remain for? He had been extraordinarily lonely whilst Flynn had been away at sea; it had not been easy, he had discovered, to revert to greyness and solitude after the warmth and light which friendship with Flynn Harrigan had come to mean. Flynn was right; you could not sit in an ivory tower isolated from human struggle, producing *de luxe* books for the bourgeoisie and the intelligentsia; you could not remain detached from such issues as Abyssinia and Spain and their potential world repercussions.

Flynn's twenty-third birthday passed almost unnoticed in the busyness of meetings and in the Spanish preoccupation generally. There was a meeting on the actual day, and the Fishers could think of nothing else for weeks beforehand. Flynn remembered on and off during the day, and mentioned the fact to Graham in a pub after the meeting. Graham stood him another drink and said, "I wonder where you'll spend your twenty-fourth?"

Flynn laughed. "If we get to Spain I may not have a twenty-fourth!"

At that point, Freddie Fisher, who was with them, looked up from the evening paper whose columns he had been skimming, and exclaimed, "Here's a bit of news! An Irish company is coming to London at the beginning of September. That'll mean your cousin'll be coming over, Flynn, doesn't it? How does that affect the Spanish proposition?"

VIII

GRAHAM said, "You realise your cousin's show opens in London the day before we're due to leave it?"

Flynn nodded. He said, bitterly, "She'll probably refuse to see me in any case. I shall ask her to have supper with me after the show—I'll send a note in to her dressing-room."

"You'll see the play, I suppose?"

"I thought we might go together."

"I'd like to. But why don't you try and see her the day before? I daresay we could find out from the theatre where she's staying."

"I'd sooner not. I wouldn't want to disturb her before the night—it's her first time in London, and she'll probably be nervous."

They secured a box—Graham said it called for that, and the weeks that stretched ahead between acquiring the ticket and the opening night seemed to Flynn to stretch away into infinity. He moved restlessly between the Merryweather Press office and the I.L.P. office. He addressed envelopes for appeals for funds for Spanish causes, to send an ambulance, to send dried milk to Valencia, to finance meetings; he stuck on stamps, he licked envelopes, he folded handbills; at the publishing office he checked proofs, helped in the packing department—anything to wear down the hours, the days. He was eaten out and in with restlessness. When at last the great day came he went out early and made his way by 'bus and tram into the West End, where he bought an armful of cream roses from a street flower-seller, then went into a stores and bought a cooked chicken and a bottle of champagne. He completed his shopping in Rotherhithe, with fruit and salad and white candles.

He put the cream roses about the living-room and stuck the candles into bottles, then went along to Graham to borrow a tablecloth, glasses and some cutlery. Charlie had all these things, but they were not good enough for the occasion; there had to be silver, and cut-glass, and a good cloth. Graham offered to lend him silver candlesticks, but Flynn said the candles had to be stuck in bottles—"It's how we did it at Ballyrannon on that great occasion." It all had to be as much like that as possible.

Graham was worried. Flynn was making all these preparations, but supposing Katherine O'Donal refused to come back with him after the play?

"Aren't you rather taking too much for granted?" he suggested.

Flynn said, "Some things have to happen. This has got to happen."

"Are you going to tell her you're leaving for Spain in the morning?"

"No. That would be too much like emotional blackmail. I'm just telling her it's very important we should meet tonight. If she refuses, which is unthinkable, I shall throw the roses into the river, present you with the chicken and the other things, and drink myself insensible with the champagne."

He wrote to her:

Dear Cousin Kate. In spite of the fact that you didn't answer the letter I wrote you from Sussex last summer, I write now to ask you if you will come back with me to Rotherhithe, where I am living, and have supper after the show tonight. It is very important it should be tonight. No other night will do. I will wait for you at the stage door; I would sooner not come to your dressing-

room, as after all this time I would like to see you for the first time alone.
                                                                        Flynn.

He sent this letter in to her at the theatre with a sheaf of red roses, then went with Graham to a pub and drank several whiskies. He had not been in so nervous a state since the evening on which he had gone to Stephanie's apartment after the day spent wandering in the streets of Paris. When they went back to the theatre and were mounting the red-carpeted stairs he suddenly gripped Graham's arm.

"I can't face it," he said. "Let's go into the bar and have another drink."

In the bar several people spoke to Graham, and Flynn overheard a girl remark to her companion, "There's Graham Hayes and his boy-friend."

He felt completely indifferent. What did it matter what anyone said about anything? In a few minutes he would see Cousin Kate in the living flesh, after four years.

In spite of the whiskies he was shivering when he and Graham finally went into their box; he sat with his hands locked round his crossed knees in order to control the tendency to tremble. Graham made conversation, pointing out people in the stalls—dramatic critics, celebrities and near-celebrities. The orchestra played Irish airs. "If they play *The Londonderry Air* I shall burst into tears," Flynn warned him. They played it, and he was hardly aware of it, staring at the curtain, waiting for it to go up.

Then at last the lights were lowered, the music trailed away, the hum of voices dwindled into silence, and the curtains swung back, and at a table in the centre of the stage a dark-haired girl sat writing. At one side of the stage was an open fireplace, the fire on the hearth, and at the other side a small bar, with shelves and bottles above it. Through a window there was an indication of grass and boulders. The girl's voice, slow and deep and rich, came upon the stillness out of the pool of light that was the stage.

"Six yards of stuff to make a yellow gown. A pair of laced boots with lengthy heels on them and brassy eyes. A hat is suited for a wedding."

Flynn rested an elbow on his knees and covered his eyes with a hand.

"Flynn darlin'! Darlin', darlin' Flynn! . . . Don't frown, Flynn darlin'. Look, the moon's coming up. Let's do a crazy thing and take the boat out. . . . Isn't it strange to think of people lying asleep in their beds, with all this shut out from them? Let's not go to bed all night! The night's too beautiful to sleep it away. . . . Jameel! It's a curious name. Is she very beautiful?"

Bursts of laughter broke like waves in the darkness of the auditorium. There were other people on the stage now. Flynn got up, whispered to Graham that he would be back, and went out. At the end of the act Graham found him drinking in the bar. He looked at him anxiously.

"Aren't you rather over-doing the whisky?" he suggested.

"I couldn't get drunk tonight if I wanted to," Flynn assured him. "Everything in me's wide awake—everything I am and ever have been."

"You are drunk," Graham said. "Come and have some black coffee."

Flynn laughed. "Sure, I'm not drunk at all!" and then, with the full Connacht accent, " 'It's little I'm understanding myself, saving only that my heart's scalded this day'." He laughed again, excitedly, and gripped Graham's arm. "I'm not drunk, and I'll not be getting drunk, but you must let me drink—it's the only way I can keep a grip on myself. Otherwise I'll be shouting down to herself on the stage, answering her all the things she isn't saying except in my mind!''

Graham could not persuade him to return to the box with him, but he came back halfway through the second act; at a slight sound at the back of the box Graham turned and saw him standing at the door, looking at the stage, waiting for the speech he had begun to quote in the bar, 'and I going off stretching out the earth between us, the way I'll not be waking near you another dawn of the year till the two of us do arise to hope or judgment with the saints of God. . . .' 'Pegeen' went off the stage soon after that and he came and sat down beside Graham and stayed till the end of the act.

He did not drink during the next interval, but paced the foyer with Graham.

"Isn't she very beautiful," he demanded, "with her high cheekbones and her great burning eyes? Did you ever see the like of her?''

Graham thought that he had seen many women both more beautiful and more striking, but he smiled and said, quoting from the play, "She's 'a lovely, handsome woman' all right—and a remarkably good actress. The part suits her perfectly, of course—I don't think Maire O'Neill herself did it better.''

"She must be very proud and happy this night," Flynn said, softly. "It's the part she always wanted, and to be playing it in London must be a great thing for her.''

He was flushed, his eyes almost feverishly bright. He too was proud and happy, Graham thought, and his heart breathed a crooked pagan prayer that the heart of Katherine O'Donal be soft towards him when the curtain had fallen for the last time.

He came back to the box for the third act, and during the love-scene between 'Pegeen' and 'Christy Mahon' he never took his eyes from the stage. Everything that Christy Mahon said to Pegeen the heart of Flynn Harrigan was saying to Katherine O'Donal, but it never for a moment occurred to him that everything Pegeen said to Christy Mahon in that scene Katherine O'Donal was saying to Flynn Harrigan, and she with his red roses lying like a great fire of love at her heart. When Christy said, 'Me there toiling a long while, and walking a long while, not knowing at all I was drawing at all times nearer this holy day', she could answer him in an anguish and ecstasy of passionate love, 'and I not knowing at all there was the like of you drawing nearer, like the stars of God', because she spoke to Flynn, convinced that he was in the house.

The players received a tremendous ovation at the end, and 'Pegeen' and 'Christy Mahon' took curtain after curtain, but when he left the box with Graham Flynn was unaware of the buzz of praise for 'the new young Irish actress' and her interpretation of 'Pegeen'. He could only hear her voice in his ears saying the wild extravagant lovely words which held everything he felt for her but had for a while forgotten.

When they came out of the theatre Graham said, "I won't wait—you'll want to meet her alone. But if she fails you you'll come round to my place, won't you? Promise me that!''

"I promise," Flynn said, "but she won't fail me.''

"You can't possibly be sure, you know.''

Flynn laughed, excitedly. "She couldn't have said those lines like that if her heart were hardened against me.   There was a kind of radiance on her.''

Graham felt constrained to say, "For all you know she might be in love with the actor who played Christy Mahon !''

"Ah, sure she might be. . Sure, the heart's a, wonder—didn't you hear herself say it this night ?   She'll come with me tonight for the same reason that she came across all Ireland on my sixteenth birthday, because in the end there's nothing so powerful as a dream in the human heart !''

Graham laughed.   "You're a little tight, aren't you ?''

Flynn said, softly, rapturously, "Sure I'm a little tight, but not on whisky !''

He pressed his friend's hand and they parted, Graham to lose himself in the chattering crowd pouring out of the theatre, Flynn to make his way round to the dimly lit stage door where a few people loitered hopefully in the murk.

2

It seemed a very long time to Flynn, and a great number of people emerged and disappeared into the darkness before Katherine came.   To his great relief she was alone, but there was still a small group of autograph-collectors.

"Could I trouble you, Miss O'Donal ?''

"You were fine, Miss O'Donal.   If I could have your autograph——''

They closed round her and she was lost to him for a few moments, then they melted away from her and they were alone in the dim light, and he heard her low, warm voice saying, "I'm sorry I was so long, Flynn, but I wanted to shake off the others——''

She came close to him, took his hands, and looked at him, smiling.

"I was good, wasn't I ?''

"You were wonderful, alannah.''

"It was because I knew you were in the house !''

He put an arm round her waist and she leaned her head against his shoulder and they walked away down the dark passage at the side of the theatre and out into the crowded street.

She said, "I loved your roses.   A lot of people sent flowers, but only you sent red roses.''

"Why didn't you answer my Sussex letter ?''

"I did—but I tore it up !''

"Was that the kind thing or the cruel thing to do ?''

"It was the proud thing.   I was wanting not to give in to you.''

"How is it you can give in to me now, then ?   I'm the same person.''

"Perhaps I'm not, though !   I had so strong a feeling of your presence in the house tonight, and something seemed to break down in me, so that I said all the lines of the love-scene to you.''   She laughed, nervously.   "Isn't that a terrible confession, now ?''

He pressed her close to him.   "It's a very beautiful confession.''

He guided her into a side-street and in a patch of shadow they turned to each other instinctively, and clung together for a moment, lost in a world

of their own, whilst people passed them on the pavement—a strolling prostitute, a man whom she accosted, and who hurried past, a couple arm in arm.

When they walked on Katherine said, shakily, "All these years and we've
never kissed in that way, and now we do it in a city street!"

"I was thinking that, too, and that I never expected to find beauty in a
London street. Ah, but sure it isn't a street any more, but a private world,
and only we two inhabiting it."

A taxi turned into the street, and he secured it for them.

The long drive out to Rotherhithe melted into nothing under the eager
flow of their talk. She was astonished to learn that he had been to sea, and
asked him quickly, "Are you going away tomorrow—that it had to be tonight I should come to you?"

He told her, "I am going away, but not to sea."

"Where, then? Not to Spain?"

He was startled. "Why should I be going to Spain?"

"So many of them are going over now. O'Duffy got up a brigade—
you're not thinking of joining them?"

He had wanted not to tell her till the end of the evening, but there seemed
no help for it now.

"I am going to Spain, but not on the nationalist side."

"Not on the nationalist side? As a Catholic, how can you go on the
other? Or have you turned your back on the Church along with Ireland?"

There was a note of bitterness in her voice. He took her hand.

"I haven't turned my back on the Church, but there are Catholic priests
in Spain who are on the Republican side. You must believe me, Katie, I've
been into it all, and I haven't any doubts any more. My father has come out
on the Republican side, too. Only I don't want to talk about it all now.
Now I want to hear all about everything—about Bridie, and all the Dublin
gossip, and what you and Aunt Chris have been playing in, and how Bridie
ever came to be engaged to that actor person who was supposed to be in
love with you, and whether the view from the O'Connell Bridge is as beautiful as ever, and the latest books to be banned. . . . Tell me first about Bridie
and why she won't write to me all this time. 'His sins they were forgiven
him'—why must she keep on with the hard heart year after year?"

"It was a terrible shock to her, you know, when, in spite of everything,
in spite of your accident, and Jameel getting killed, and the reconciliation
there was between you when you came out of hospital, you went off to Paris
in the end. She just hasn't got over it, that's all. You were everything to
her, and you abandoned her. It's something she can't forgive. She never
forgave your mother for abandoning you both, though she was too young
ever to have known her. Her trouble is that she can't forgive you and she
can't replace you. The Rory business never came to anything for that
reason. Sometimes she talks about going back to Ballyrannon and marrying Patrick Doyle. She's had two summer holidays there with Tante Emma,
and warned us she would probably marry and not come back, but she came
back each time."

"Has she changed at all—in appearance, I mean? And does she still
steal things?"

Katherine laughed. "The last person she stole from was Mrs. Paul, so far as we can make out—she has a heap of her handkerchiefs to this day! We've not noticed anything in the last few years. She's rather beautiful now—rather like those portraits of Mummy when she was young—a lovely proud look—like a thoroughbred horse."

"I know. Like Jameel." He sighed. "She was the world's wonder of a horse, and when Bridie rode her the two of them made a piece of music, or a poem. In this country the riding's terrible. You should see them in the Park on a Sunday morning—and the broken-down hacks they bring out. You would be wanting to laugh, if it wasn't after making you cry! I discovered a lovely book the other day; it was called *The English—Are they Human?* Would you believe it, over here they still refer to the Irish Free State, and believe that De Valera's the president? And the other day I was talking to a woman who said she had a nephew in that part of Ireland where the religion was Orangemen. . . ."

They both laughed. "She wasn't so far out," Katherine said.

They had slipped back not merely into the Connemara idiom and accent, but into the old easy cousinly comradeship of four years ago—she was Cousin Kate and he was the boy who loved her beyond telling.

When the taxi stopped in Rotherhithe Street, and he had let her into the dark narrow little hall, he had her wait whilst he ran up and lighted the candles stuck into their bottles, then came back to her and took her hand up the steep stairs.

At the sight of the candles and the cream roses, the champagne, and the spread feast, she gave a little cry and said what was for him the perfect thing.

"Oh, Flynn—Flynn darlin'! We're back at Ballyrannon entirely!" She stood gazing, rapturously, then added, a little sadly, "Tante Emma should be here, and Bridie."

"Ah, no." He spoke softly. "Sure, everything is perfect as it is."

He opened the champagne and they stood together above the roses and candles, looking at each other.

"The toast," said Flynn, "is Cathleen ni Houlihan."

She smiled, and when they had drunk that toast she said, "'There's another toast, though, and that is for you, my darling—may God bring you safely back from Spain."

"Amen to that. When I come back we shall be married, isn't that so? Then we will serve Ireland together."

Her eyes filled with tears. "Yes," she said. "Yes," and put down her glass, and buried her face against his heart.

He said, stroking her hair, "Do you remember saying once, when there was champagne, and candles and roses, and a feast, 'Let's not go to bed all night. The night's too beautiful to sleep it away.'? Do you remember that, alannah? There's no moon tonight, and no lake, but there's stars and the river. Come and see."

He put her coat round her shoulders and led her outside.

There were dim lights along the river, the sudden scurry of a police launch and the white fan of its wake spreading on the black water, a golden glow of light that was the City, the bright oblongs of attic windows, the steely blue of an arc-light flooding a wharf, and below them, looking towards the City, soft light between the curtains of Graham's river-room.

Flynn told her, pointing out that light reflected in the black water, "There lives the great friend with whom I am going to Spain." He told her about him, briefly, and concluded, "If you had not come we should have drunk the champagne together and thrown the roses into the river, but I knew you would come. I have never been so sure of anything."

She leaned her head against his shoulder. "You were so sure, and we are actually here together, yet it all seems like a dream."

He said, "It is a dream. It began a long time ago when we were both children running wild in the bogs of Ballyrannon and watching the king-fishers along the lake. It never had to come true because we were living it all the time. There are some dreams from which we never wake."

He laughed, pressing her close to him, and kissed her hair.

"You'll say I am talking in riddles, and Graham would say I was drunk, and drunk I am, but on water itself I would be drunk this night! As to riddles, who would look for the meaning in a holy mystery?"

She smiled up at him, and this was Cousin Kate, laughing and gay and tender, as on that night when they had drunk champagne at midnight at Ballyrannon Castle. He kissed her lips, and the night-wind, and the smell of the river, strong and brackish as the Ballyrannon lake, was part of the consciousness of that moment, and ever to be remembered.

They went back into the room where the candles held their small blue and yellow spear-heads of flame motionless above the flowers and the spread feast, and they laughed and ate and drank and talked nonsense as on that other night seven years ago, and presently sat together, as then, she in the room's one shabby armchair, he on the threadbare rug at her feet, his head against her knee, but now her hands strayed without shyness through his hair, softly caressive and infinitely tender.

In the end she asked the question he had been dreading she might ask. "Must you go to Spain—now? Why don't we go back to Dublin together?"

He told her, "I must go, alannah." How explain to her that sense of being committed beyond any last-minute withdrawal, committed in the name both of revolutionary idealism and of friendship? How explain to her that sense of spiritual necessity, of expiation? He added, "I don't know if you will understand at all, but the more I have thought about this thing the more it has seemed a way of wiping out the past——"

"You have already received absolution for that."

"There are things one feels one must do. Once, if you remember, I felt I had to restore the gardens at the Castle, dedicating the work to the memory of my mother; it satisfied me for a little while, but only for a little while, because then I was reaching back into the past, whereas now I am reaching forward into the future. You know *The Cherry Orchard*, and you'll remember what the Eternal Student tells the young girl——"

"You mean the piece about 'The moon is rising—happiness is coming nearer'?"

"I mean the piece that comes before that, about expiating the past——"

"I remember—'in order to start to live in the present we must first of all redeem our past—have done with it——' I forget how it goes on——"

"—'and its redemption can only be achieved through suffering, only through tremendous, incessant labour'." He laughed, eagerly, excitedly. "Like the Eternal Student, my soul is full of 'inexplicable anticipations'."

She stroked his hair and turned on him a look of tenderness and sadness. She said, smiling, "And do you 'anticipate happiness', and do you 'experience it already', my Trofimov?"

He caught her hand to his lips. "I do! I do! Truly I tell you, the moon is rising, and you can hear the footsteps of happiness drawing nearer. . . ."

IX

MAY and Freddie Fisher took time off from work to come and see 'the Spanish contingent' off at Victoria, May full of comradely enthusiasm, Freddie insisting to the last that it was not men that the Spanish anti-Fascists wanted, but arms; what was wanting was an end of non-intervention and a lifting of the arms embargo. As the train steamed out they gave the clenched-fist salute with gallant disregard for the communist implication to the uninitiated in Left politics.

Graham settled himself with a book he had bought on the station bookstall at the last minute, *Brush Up Your Spanish*, and Flynn, who had no Spanish to brush up, and had intended studying a book May Fisher had given him as a farewell gift, *Spanish in Twelve Easy Lessons*, sat gazing out of the window lost in the dream of the night before. It seemed incredible that only a few hours ago he and Cousin Kate had watched the dawn breaking over the Pool of London, had made tea and buttered bread together, and finally gone out together into the cool freshness of the September morning and parted in the street. He had found a taxi for her, given the driver a ten-shilling note, and watched the taxi till it was out of sight, Katherine waving from the little window at the back over an armful of cream roses. . . . Then he had gone to call for Graham. Katherine had preferred not to come to Victoria, but she would be on the platform to meet him when he came back, she promised, recklessly.

Not until they reached Calais did he realise that he was going to Paris, that there would be a few hours to spend there, before getting the night-train to Perpignan. He found himself wondering, suddenly, whether Boronski was in Paris, still propping up the Dôme bar; he had written to him a few times when he had first come to London, but it had been impossible to maintain contact with so erratic a correspondent. It would be fun to see 'the ould divil' again, and perhaps Nina and Johnny were still in partnership and living at the same address, and little Jeanne would remember him, though he had long ago given up sending her picture-postcards of the Tower of London, the Tower Bridge, St. Paul's Cathedral, Trafalgar Square, the Thames Embankment with Cleopatra's Needle . . . but more likely, he thought, she would have forgotten him, or anyhow that she had ever loved him. . . 'O frankly fickle, and fickly true!'

Something stirred in him with the first smell of Paris at the Gare du Nord. He gripped Graham's arm.

"Let's go up to Montparnasse!"

Graham smiled. "Of course. Where else? But let's take our ruck-sacks over to the Gare d'Austerlitz first——"

That accomplished, they took a taxi to the Dôme. The terrace was as full as ever, but there was no one that either of them knew in the zinc bar, and no one hailed them on either the terrace of the Dôme or of the Coupole.

"It is, after all, 1936," Graham said. "They probably all got out whilst the going was good in 1934. Abyssinia no doubt settled it for any that remained behind, and the 'palmy days' with the franc at 160 to the £ and more have gone for good."

They turned into the American Bar of the Coupole, and there, leaning against the bar, was Boronski making a sketch of a smart young woman perched up on a stool, with a smart and amused-looking young man seated next to her. Preoccupied with his drawing, Boronski did not see Flynn enter, followed by Graham. Flynn gave a start, then went up to him and laid a hand on his shoulder.

"You ould divil!" he said.

Boronski took one look, then flung his sketch-book on the floor and his arms round Flynn's neck and kissed him violently first on one cheek and then on the other, with loud joyous exclamations in English and French in between.

"Where did you spring from, for goodness' sake?" he demanded, grinning all over his great moon of a face, and still gripping Flynn's shoulders.

"I arrived with a friend this evening," Flynn told him. "We're off to Spain by the night-train. Let me introduce Graham Hayes, or do you know each other?"

Graham laughed. "Of course we know each other. Is there anyone who has lived in Montparnasse during the last ten years who doesn't know Gregori Boronski? What are you drinking?"

Boronski grinned. "When you came in I was attempting to earn a *pour-boire*." He retrieved his sketching-block from the floor, tore off the half-finished sketch, and handed it to the young woman.

"*Voilà, Madame!* I guess this is where I get off!"

Flynn said, eagerly, "I suggest we drink Pernod here, then go down to the Boulevard St. Germain and drink another at the Deux Magots for old times' sake and then go and eat at the Café des Sports and drink *vin à l'oignon*, after which we should be in a fit state to fight *la guerre* in any country!"

They sat on the red plush *banc* opposite the bar, and Bronski kept gazing raptly from one to the other and exclaiming that gee it was good to see them both.

"Tell me about everyone," Flynn said. "Are Nina and Johnny still here?"

"They went to England last year," Boronski said. "Didn't they write to you?"

"They did not—but no reason why they should. Nina knew I hated her parties and only went there to see the child. Did they go to London?"

"They were going to a place called Cornwall," Boronski said vaguely.

"What about my ex-colleague?"

"Peter Barnaby? She's in New York—fell in with a blonde heiress. Mary Trant is there, too—got fixed up with a Russian ballet company at last. Raymond Farrow has published a volume of poems entitled *Venus*

its 'baffle' walls the stern examination, the smiling acknowledgment of comradeship, and the word 'Salud!'   At Figueras the first glimmer of light in the sky, a halt at a roadside *taberna*, long and low, whitewashed, stone-floored, with a trellised arbour over which a vine sprawled with bunches of grapes like Chinese lanterns.   Glasses of wine, thin and pale, and black coffee, and rolls, and a cheese made from goat's milk.   Trestle tables, and benches along the walls, and dark eyes alight with an inner fire.   In the eager babble of speech the words '*Compañero*', and '*Viva la Fai*', emerging, and the language barrier overcome by a kind of Esperanto of comradeship.   Full daybreak in Gerona, and the snow-crested line of the Pyrenees now clearly visible in the distance, and on either side the road the vineyards crimson and gold with autumn.   At Gerona another halt and more black coffee and rolls, and more comradely enthusiasm, and then the long final run into Barcelona in bright sunshine.

The trees of the broad boulevard of the Ramblas, the red flags hanging from the windows of the buildings, and the red and black flags of the anarchists; everywhere P.O.U.M. and C.N.T./U.G.T. posters and revolutionary slogans, and the hammer-and-sickle chalked on walls, and the initials of the workers' political parties.   Lorries rattling past with these initials painted on them, and occasionally a chorus of '*Fai! Fai! Viva la Fai!*' breaking out like a burst of song.   Then the shabby Hotel Falcon at the bottom of the Ramblas, the headquarters of the P.O.U.M.

The feeling of the body aching all over, the eyes burning from lack of sleep, the sense of mental and physical exhaustion.   The sense of confusion and everyone talking at once.   The sense of irrepressible enthusiasm, as though to say, This is the revolution, comrade; here no one rests and no one sleeps; here there is neither night nor day, but only the triumphant red dawn. . . .   Outside in the Ramblas the perpetual flow of the crowds under the trees, a shabby crowd in workers' dungarees and improvised militia uniforms, and loudspeakers blaring revolutionary slogans and songs.   This is the revolution, comrade; you can hear it, you can feel it; you can hear the beat of its heart, feel its throbbing pulse.   Even the bootblacks have been collectivised, and the prostitutes have taken over the brothels and claim comradely equality with their clients . . .

Henceforth you will not sleep, comrade; the revolution hath murdered sleep.

(Ah, but the excitement of it, the feeling of being at the very heart of the revolution; the big hotels controlled now by workers' syndicates, fashionable restaurants turned into communal kitchens, shops and cafés 'collectivised'; no more the fat greasy prosperous business-men and their fashionable women and sleek shiny cars; they have fled, the bourgeoisie, and the workers promenade the streets triumphant in overalls and the uniform of their own militia.   Have they, with their hammers-and-sickles, smashed the starry diadem of the Mother of God?   We are fighting the Church as well as the State, comrade.   *Viva la revolución!*

"I don't see why they have to do this to the churches—even if you don't want to worship in it, a Catholic church is a beautiful thing!"

"The Church in Spain has always stood for everything that's reactionary —you can't blame them.   This is the revolution. . . ."

"But I do blame them. I do, I do! They can revolt against the reactionary regime and still keep their faith."

"They never had any. Their faith was always in the revolution. There's no analogy with Ireland. Ireland is another world. This is Spain—and the revolution.")

After the shabby Hotel Falcon the imposing building of the Lenin Barracks.

"Can you handle a rifle, comrade? Very good. You will go to the front tomorrow.'

But there are no rifles to be handled, and it is always *mañana, mañana*.

Sleeping in the cavalry stables, empty of horses; drilling, in haphazard fashion, on the cobbled parade-ground, and in the public gardens; everyone calling the officers *Compañero*. Drinking harsh red wine, realising the hopelessness of trying to learn Spanish when everyone speaks Catalan, yet feeling all the time behind the barrier of language the warmth of comradeliness. 'We understand each other, comrade; we are comrades; it is enough.'

Then at last the great day when the order comes to entrain for the front, and the half-trained, undisciplined, ill-equipped rabble of a unit in makeshift uniforms, zip jackets, corduroy breeches, red, or red and black, neckerchiefs, party badges, marches off to the station, along roads lined by waving, cheering crowds.

The fantastically crowded train, sheep and hens and humans, peasants and militia, all crowded in together, but everyone good-natured, gay, singing revolutionary songs, eating garlic sausage, drinking wine from longspouted bottles; women waving from platforms, a few going to the front.

Goodbye to Catalonia in an interminable crawl, and at long last the high Aragon plateau.

2

Is this war—this weariness of cold and inaction and spasmodic, ineffective sniping from filthy trenches, this defending of positions that none attack? The occasional bursting of a shell, the rattle of a machine-gun, a volley of rifle-fire, both sides wasting their ammunition. The savage red mountain dawns, the bitter cold mountain nights, the endless patrols and fatigues, the sense of futility. The nearer to the war, the further off from the revolution. Rifles that jam; bombs that fail to go off—or go off before they have been thrown. An army of enthusiastic amateurs, most of them in their teens. . . .

'They may ransack and burn and demolish their churches, but they have their own kind of faith.'

Mud and excrement at their feet, but the wild white boughs of idealism blossoming above their heads—Mother of God, forgive them their blasphemy and have pity on their crazy courage!

One day very like another, but the shadows lengthen on the mountains. On the lower slopes and in the valleys behind the front the grapes are gathered in and the peasants are clipping back the vines. Most of the time the cold seems a greater enemy than the Fascists, for the cold is there always, actively present, and intensifying at nights, whereas the Fascists only seem to be there in bursts, when a mortar comes flying over, or a machine-gun opens up, as a reminder.

The mind growing numb, with the cold, with inaction, with the sense of unreality that began at Perpignan and which not even the spattering of a machine-gun or the drone of a Fascist bomber overhead can disperse. No sense of time; the day of the week, the month, nothing. Christmas is something that happens in another life—a life in which you undress at nights, sleep in beds, go to Mass; in this no-man's land there are no days of the week, no months of the year, no seasons, neither feasts nor fasts. Here the food comes out of tins and the water comes by mule or donkey from God knows where and tastes like God knows what; here are parapets of sand-bags and a human rabbit-warren of dugouts, and antiquated machine-guns defending 'fortified' posts. Here are bare mountains, and men of the same nationality firing at each other across a valley under different flags.

'*Viva Franco !*'
'*Viva la revolución !*'
'*Arriba España !*'
'*Viva la Fai !*'

Both sides shouting their slogans into loudspeakers for the benefit of the enemy, and at nights saying it all with flashes of fire under the still, indifferent neutrality of the stars.

February, and the fall of Malaga, and the sense of dismay, and the bitter sense of betrayal; the sudden end of inactivity and the move off to Huesca. The lorry jolting across the plain, and men's spirits rising in the bitter cold despite the thunder of artillery. 'We have served our apprenticeship in guerilla warfare; now we go to make the war in earnest. Huesca in the hands of the *Fascistas*; here comes the army of deliverance !' . . . raggle-taggle and inadequately armed in the pale wintry sunshine.

'Both sides saving Spain from the Spaniards ?'

'We stand for something beyond both Republicanism and Nationalism—we stand for the Revolution. . . .'

Within sound of the guns—they were Russian guns, someone said—but another period of inaction. You could be hit by a stray bullet, or a stray shell come too close, and there were a few casualties, but it was accident rather than warfare.

The spring like a rising tide, and an end of the period of inaction on the eastern Huesca front. The raggle-taggle unit is sent up the line to the central front of the general army besieging Huesca.

And to the very last it never seems quite like warfare, all the wire-cutting in the darkness, all the belly-crawling over the mud of ploughed fields and through the icy water of marshes, under a raking machine-gun fire before which you die so many deaths that the whole thing ceases to have reality. Even when a fragment of a shell embeds somewhere in your living flesh and you crumple up and become part of the darkness and confusion. . . .

3

After that, the dressing-station, the hurried bandaging, the shot of mor-phia; the ambulance to the collection of wooden huts that was the base hospital. Somewhere in time, the next day or another day, a hospital train and another hospital, a brick and stone building standing in a garden. A long ward full of men ; a half-world, of strange and horrible sights and sounds, of pain a long way off but sometimes coming closer, stinging the flesh like a thousand whips, and presently out of all the phantasmagoria of reality and unreality, a familiar face, a familiar voice, a familiar smile. Graham, with his right arm in a sling.

"Mother of God, how did you get here?"

"I came down with you. Most of our crowd that survived that night were casualties. They're sending us off to Barcelona today—they've got a fresh lot coming in here."

The sanatorium in the suburbs, the great hills going up behind, the gardens where it was pleasant to sit in the warm April sunshine with the feeling of slowly returning strength. Graham discharged first ; going every day to the General Hospital for electric massage for his arm, and coming every afternoon to see Flynn. Thinking, 'I must write to Kate, and the Fishers, and send a postcard to Boronski, the old devil,' but it is all too much effort. But the mind writing endless letters to Katherine, detailing every smallest thing, a nurse with an 'Irish' face, a wall covered with papery purple bougainvillea, an image of Our Lady poised triumphantly above the rubble of a ruined shrine, children running, laughing and playing, in and out of an arcade, moving between sunlight and shadow, the feel of spring on the air, the thought of the daffodils at Ballyrannon Castle, flowing down over the broken terraces in golden waves to the lake's edge, and the new shoots of the wild fuchsia thrusting up from the moist earth beneath broken stone walls. All day and every day this endless communion with Cousin Kate, this endless reverie of Ireland, and all round the sights and sounds and smells of Spain.

Then leaving the hospital, walking away with Graham, boarding a tram, coming into the city, walking again under the trees of the Ramblas, sitting on café terraces. . . .

Is there a subtle difference of atmosphere since those exciting early days when everyone was comrade and the workers held the field ? The red and red-and-black flags still flutter from roofs and windows, the revolutionary posters still exhort from walls and hoardings, but there are, now, also posters boosting the Popular Army, a conscript army, well-equipped by the Government, and surely there are more cars on the roads ? What has happened behind the scenes that the *milicianos* are no longer seen off or welcomed back with cheers and waving flags ? Has something evaporated from the revolutionary spirit, in spite of the persistent bravery of the flags ? There are stories of attempts by the Government to disarm the anarchists, and of arrests everywhere. Stories of skirmishes between anarchists and communists. The red-and-black flags rise and fall upon the spring air, but there is this uneasy feeling of all not being well behind the scenes.

But whatever insidious draining of workers' power is going on there is no recognition of it at the Hotel Falcon, or at the P.O.U.M. executive offices across the road from it ; here revolutionary enthusiasm runs as high as ever. Drafts of militia are still being sent up to the front ; the achievements of the revolution still stand ; the anarchists still control the Telephone Building; the workers' syndicates still function, and despite the Government the mass of revolutionary workers are still in possession of arms . . . *Viva la revolución!*

Then the afternoon of May 3rd, and lorry-loads of armed police, and communists suddenly appearing on the Plaza de Cataluna at the top of the Ramblas. There is the sound of rifle-shots, the sudden spatter of a machine-gun that seems to rip the afternoon wide open. Suddenly every window looking on to the great square appears to hold a sniper. On the Ramblas groups of men hug the walls at street-corners with rifles lifted. There is a slamming down of shop and café shutters, a panic-stricken scattering of people in all directions; unless you want to be mixed up with the shooting, the important thing is to get off the street. The afternoon is ripped wide open all right. Lorry-loads of armed men, Assault Guards, anarchists, race past. Everyone seems to be shooting at everyone else.

Graham bitterly cursing the fact that his right arm is out of action. Flynn, caught up in the excitement, feeling fit for the first time since he has left hospital, and handling his rifle as though he loved it. . . .

The usual shortage of arms. Helping to erect barricades on the Ramblas from the torn-up cobblestones. The hotel seething with a confused and confusing restless mob—journalists, militia, lorry-drivers, members of the P.O.U.M.; no one knowing what is happening or who is who, a perpetual coming and going, and the din and confusion of street-fighting continuing daylong through the bright sunny May days, the long boulevards with their new-leafed trees empty of everything except bullets and bombs, and the occasional armed car or lorry racing madly past. . . . The police are hourly expected to attack the P.O.U.M. headquarters, and there is a feverish working at the erection of barricades at doors and windows, whilst snipers take up positions behind sandbags on the roof.

On the third day the firing ceases, and the boulevards, at first cautiously, and then with gathering confidence, come to life again . . . then suddenly it all begins again, scattering the crowds, snapping down the shutters of shops and cafés. At the Hotel Falcon the food is giving out, and no one sleeps except for an hour or two at a time, on the floor, on couches, everywhere and anywhere. . . .

Next day the rumour that the Valencia Government is sending troops, and in the evening their arrival. It is the beginning of the end. The following day the Assault Guards are in control of the streets; the 'rising' is crushed. The police and communist plot against the anarchists has succeeded. The red and black flags have disappeared completely; the flag of the Republic is everywhere. Popular Army officers swagger past; no one says 'comrade' any more. The militia is to be reorganised along Popular Army lines. The bourgeoisie, as though they have been in hiding all this time, begin to reappear on the streets.

A communist-inspired campaign of slander is let loose on the P.O.U.M., which is accused of engineering the rising, of being 'Trotsky-Fascist', and the agents of Hitler.

In the hotel lounge a couple of Spanish communists and a young Englishman from the International Brigade, a little drunk, on victory as much as wine, make sneering remarks about O'Duffy's Irish Brigade sending its agents to the P.O.U.M. They have come there for the express purpose of making trouble. They speak in English, deliberately loudly enough to be heard, and look at Flynn and Graham, and immediately Flynn's temper is up and he is on his feet and advancing towards them, blue eyes blazing, "It's a lie ! A damned dirty lie !"

It flashes to Graham instantly, "My God, now we are done for !" and with it the counter-thought that it doesn't matter, because everything is finished now anyhow—everything that was idealistic and crazily courageous, everything that stood for comradeship and selfless purpose, everything that was heroic in the larger sense, beyond the beating of drums and the waving of flags, beyond physical courage. Two lines of poetry read in another world long ago stir somewhere at the back of his mind : '*There was a thing to do, and it is done now ; There was a thing to say, and it is said now*' . . .

The three communists are on their feet, the two Spaniards intent and menacing, the English youth flushed, smiling insolently, swaggering. Rising, he has knocked over a glass of red wine ; it is running down over the table-cloth and to the ground, like blood.

"A lie, is it, Paddy ? You didn't come over with the Irish Brigade, I suppose, and O'Duffy isn't in the pay of Berlin ?"

Graham cutting in quickly, "To hell with O'Duffy ! We came over together from London to join the P.O.U.M. militia, and for your information we were both wounded on the Aragon front a few weeks ago——"

One of the Spaniards begins to say something, but the boy makes a gesture of waving him aside and over-rides him.

"We know all about you, Mr. Graham Hayes, you *and* your boy-friend——"

The same old lie following them even to Spain. . . . Graham's answer was to swing up a clenched fist and lunge at the sneering face, but it is not easy to strike a man effectively with your left hand when your right is in a sling and there is a table between you. The boy ducked, his Spanish companions seized Graham by the shoulders, and two Assault Guards closed in from behind, just as Flynn whipped out the revolver he had secured from the P.O.U.M. armoury after his rifle had been taken away by a young Spanish anarchist who claimed that he could use it more effectively.

One of the guards swooped down on Flynn and grabbed the revolver, triumphantly ; the other Flynn caught a blow with the butt of his rifle which re-opened his wound and sent him crumpling to the floor, his shirt crimsoning with blood.

"You filthy swine !" Graham tore himself out of the grip of the two Spaniards and tried to force a way over to Flynn, but instantly the Guards were upon him ; three of them held him whilst one of the Guards fastened the handcuffs round his wrists. A number of people in the hotel lounge had gathered round, and there were some protests when Flynn was dragged to his feet, only half-conscious, but they fell back as the party advanced to the door. These arrests were taking place every day now ; it did not do to get mixed up in them. . . .

The prisoners were taken by car to the Cuartea Carlos Marx, the barracks whose cellars already housed several hundreds of alleged 'Trotskyists' and 'agents of Franco'.

XI

THE arrest was illegal, like so many at that time, and there was no question of any trial. Every day there were floggings, and 'confessions' extorted by every form of third-degree method, and every night there was the sound of a car in the barrack square. At first Flynn and Graham did not realise the significance of that car leaving and returning; but the three young Spanish anarchists with whom they shared the cell were under no illusions. They did not speak English, and Flynn's and Graham's Spanish was a mere handful of words, but the Spaniards offered them a single, terse word in explanation.

"*Paseo!*" they said, simply.

Flynn and Graham looked at each other, and Graham said, "Do you get it?"

Flynn shrugged. " 'Taken for a ride' is how it would be translated in good gangster American, I imagine. It makes no odds. I thought they'd shoot us here, that's all."

Every day the young English communist who had started the row in the Falcon came to see them. He was always flushed and excited, sweating a little from his sadistic pleasure. He told them early on, "You think that because one of you is English and the other a citizen of Eire that we shall never dare to shoot you, but that is where you are so wrong; it will never be known that you are shot. You will simply disappear. Your sorrowing relatives will think you were killed in action. Or that you died of appendicitis after your arrest and pending trial. Or simply that you died of your wounds. The truth will never be known."

"The usual Cheka methods, in fact," Graham observed, drily.

"Precisely," the other agreed, and smiled.

Flynn said, wearily, "What are you waiting for, then? One night is as good as the next. Why not take us all out in lorry-loads and turn a machine-gun on to us and have done with it?"

"Have you never heard of the pleasures of anticipation?"

The next time he visited them they refused to answer him. He motioned to the guards, who stepped forward and manacled Graham and took him out of the cell. He was brought back twenty minutes later unconscious, and thrown face downwards into his bunk. The back of his shirt was soaked in blood.

That night the three young Spaniards were taken out. They were glad to go. They believed implicitly that it was 'better to die on your feet than live on your knees'. They were weak from floggings and lack of food, but they walked out proudly, their heads high. At the door one of them turned, and smiled faintly at Graham and Flynn.

"*Salud!*" he said.

Listening to the commands outside in the square and the car starting up, Graham said, "I hope they take us tomorrow."

As a result of the manhandling he had received from the Assault Guards who had arrested them, and the flogging, he was in great agony from his injured arm. He had asked for medical attention on arrival at the barracks and been refused. Flynn had tried to rebandage the arm for him to give him relief, but had been unable to ease the pain in any way. He was in great pain himself; in the filthy conditions of their confinement the reopened wound had turned septic, and he also was refused medical attention.

He said, in reply to Graham, "If they don't hurry up, one of us will be slipping off without the benefit of the firing-party." He knew that it was useless to ask for a priest; he had seen too many desecrated churches, and this, anyhow, was the citadel of Karl Marx himself. His chief sin, it seemed to him then, was so great a preoccupation with physical pain that it was an effort at times quite beyond him to contemplate the state of his soul as befitted one about to die. He prayed a good deal in the intervals in which the pain receded a little; they had taken his rosary from him, and his St. Christopher medallion, and he had a sense of being naked before God. Graham would lie on his plank watching him kneeling on the stone floor of the stinking cell, his eyes closed, his face, gaunt from suffering, lack of sleep, starvation, rapt in religious ecstasy, and in the midst of his own pain envied him, passionately. For him, he knew, death was not extinction but merely transition. For him, Graham Hayes, there was nothing beyond; death was final, and life completely purposeless, without meaning; when possible you enjoyed it; when that was not possible you bore with it; you endeavoured to express yourself, creatively, and to contribute to the society from which you took; you could do no more. At the end, whether you died in bed of one of the diseases of old age, or faced a firing-squad at an age most people thought too young for shuffling off the mortal coil—what was the odds? You might think that nearing forty you had had enough; that to go on could only mean tedious repetition. Nor was it so tragic to die young in the early twenties; it meant that you kept your illusions intact; you were spared the humiliation of physical deterioration, and of having lived too long. Flynn Harrigan would die in ecstasy, in the tradition of Easter Week; in ecstasy and illusion. He would believe that he was dying because he had chosen to serve the Spanish revolutionary cause; that was true enough, but where the illusion came in was that he had not served the revolutionary cause, and having survived the wound he had received in fighting the war against the Fascists he was now to be bumped off by a bunch of political gangsters. In the Irish civil war, whether you were bumped-off by the Black and Tans, or your political opponents, you could truthfully say you had died for Ireland; here in Spain you got bumped-off by the very people on whose side you had fought, with the Assault Guards, as the opposite number of the Black and Tans, co-operating on that side, and in your decease. It had a kind of ghastly humour. Flynn Harrigan would be, like Lycidas, dead ere his prime, 'yet who would not sing for Lycidas, since he knew himself to sing?' He saw clearly, that old blind Milton. . . .

Flynn became less and less conscious of the filthy cell, and, towards the end, even of his pain. He was back in Ballyrannon, with songs that would never be written down running in his head; Cousin Kate was standing in the bows of the boat, dark hair blown across her eyes, and Jameel the Beautiful whinnied to him at sundown across the stable yard. Tante Emma was saying the rosary in the castle kitchen, the light was dying over the lake, and the wild geese flying home. He and Bridie were at the Galway races together and lying in the sandy grass out at Salthill, content and close. He was paddling about amongst the rocks on Bream Island with the Doyle children; there was the boom of the great Atlantic breakers, and the sudden sobbing cry of a donkey. The curaghs lay upturned on the strand like sleeping seals; and a seal sometimes appeared for a moment between the rocks of a cove, gazed for a moment with sad soft eyes, then disappeared in a swirl of waters. He was sitting round the turf fire in the Doyles' smoky cabin, listening to the romantic stories and wild sad songs of Connacht. He was browsing over ancient books written in the Gaelic in the monastery library, kneeling in the monastery chapel and feeling its peace flow over him, pacing the grounds in talk of ancient or saintly things with Brother Francis, the lake blue and sparkling beyond its ragged edge of twisted thorn-trees that in May were white and sweet with blossom; he was bringing branches of yew to the monastery chapel at Easter and Christmas, his heart crying with Father Burke, 'O fair and lovely Church!' It was fair-day in Ballyrannon and the two broad streets were choked with sheep and cattle, and the air quivering with their bewildered, frightened cries. It was spring, and the gorse fires burning on the low near hills, and in the distance the Twelve Pins were mistily blue. On the island lake the daffodils thrust up between the dead bracken and dry heather—in memory of Herself, she who was beautiful, pretty witty Kitty Shann. It was summer, and the grey and brown wilderness of stones and bog broke into a crimson splendour of flowering fuchsia. It was winter, and an endless fine soft rain, and endlessly he moved through the familiar scene. Paris and London did not come into his mind at all; he had left them finally and for ever and gone home. He had never in any sense belonged there; he had never belonged anywhere but to Ireland.

There was a night when he was delirious, and the cell was full of voices.
'*We are going out to be slaughtered, but has it not been a full life, and is not this a good end?*'
'*We stood for something beyond the Republic; we stood for the Revolution.*'
'*They shall be remembered for ever; they shall be alive for ever . . .*'
'*In order to start to live in the present, we must first of all redeem our past.*'
'*Redemption can only be achieved through suffering.*'
And a voice calling across a lake, 'Fly-nn! Fly-nn', and the echo dying away into the soft still sunshine.

The dream that began a long time ago when we were children running wild in the bogs of Ballyrannon, and ending here in Republican Spain; the dream in which we lived out our lives under eternally blossoming boughs; the dream that never had to come true, because we lived it all our lives. . . .

2

After a feverish night he was so weak by morning that he could barely stand. He observed to Graham, "This damned wound! If they keep us here much longer they'll have to shoot me sitting down—the way the English shot Connolly!" It troubled him; it was somehow important to die on your feet. He prayed that God would send him strength to die in the spirit of Easter Week, and on his feet.

There was something else which troubled him and which had kept recurring to him ever since their arrest.

He said to Graham in the early hours of that morning, "If I hadn't lost my temper in the Hotel Falcon they wouldn't have arrested us. I ran us both into this by flaring up like that—the Harrigan temper!"

Graham answered, "Actually it was probably my attempt to sock that young swine on the jaw that made them arrest us—it might have passed off but for that. But does it matter? The round-up of the P.O.U.M. and the anarchists was in full swing before we got back to Barcelona, don't forget, and it'll go on. They'd have taken us in the end—within the next few days in all probability."

"They mightn't have shot us."

"After a certain point is it important whether one lives or dies? It ceased to be important to me years ago. I wish you could have lived—to have married your cousin and seen Ireland again, though you'd probably never have been as happy as on that last night in Rotherhithe after the play. It's never how long one lives, but how intensely, that's important."

Flynn lay on the plank bed smiling a little, his eyes closed. He repeated like a prayer, '*Me there toiling a long while, and walking a long while, not knowing at all I was drawing at all times nearer this holy day.*'

His grey, hollowed face had the rapt ecstatic look of a martyred saint.

Graham did not know whether he meant the day on which he brought Katherine O'Donal to Rotherhithe, or the day of their execution. Actually the two were fused in Flynn's mind. You reached the point of perfection, the apex of beauty, and beyond that in terms of living you could not go. You were ready, then, to die, if need be. In the end it all made an intelligible pattern. As it said in the ancient Gaelic, it was the fragrant bough you would soonest pluck, and your own love you would soonest follow, but for a time the bough was out of your reach, and your own love withdrawn from you; you lost sight of the dream and were false to it, and fell into sin, and suffered like Lucifer fallen from heaven; the Paris interlude led to London, and London led to the rediscovery of the dream, and to Spain. You might have stayed in Ireland all your life, the fragrant bough growing further out of reach with the years, and the ivy growing in your soul. You might have stayed in Ireland and been spared much spiritual tribulation, but felt your spirit slowly crumble; whereas now it was a flame that stood up bright and strong as a sword before God, seeing death as release, as the completion of the picture, the final thread in the intricately woven tapestry, and the thread which gave meaning to a pattern obscure till then. You had this sense of the necessity for expiation; a way was indicated, and you followed it—to the end. In the end it was as simple as all that; it was acceptance; it was faith.

The day dragged on, timelessly, like all the other days. They lay on their planks, dozing in snatches, and when exhaustion overcame pain, talking fitfully, and lying for long stretches in a kind of coma, their minds blank, waiting. They had no idea what hour it was when the cell was unlocked and two guards entered, manacles in their hands, but they had heard the car on the barracks square a few minutes earlier and knew that it must be night. The guards muttered something in Spanish which neither Flynn nor Graham understood, but there was no need of explanation. Their waiting was at an end. They exchanged glances and half smiled.

Graham's hands were manacled together in front, because of his left arm still in the sling; Flynn's behind his back. Graham winced at the tug on his bad arm, and in the same moment the thought crossed his mind that it was odd that a man about to die should be aware of a minor pain.

He said quickly to Flynn whilst they were being handcuffed, "As this will probably be the last chance we'll have of speaking to each other, I want to say how glad I've been of our friendship. It's meant more to me than I can tell you even now——"

"But for me you'd never have come to Spain!"

There was a glimpse of the old ironical smile. "I've no regrets. The ripe old age idea never attracted me, as you know."

As they left the cell he looked over his shoulder at Flynn behind him. "Goodbye," his lips said.

Flynn smiled, faintly. He was desperately weak and all his will-power was involved in the effort not to collapse.

"God bless," he murmured, swayed, then rallied, and concentrated his whole being in a prayer for the forgiveness of sins and the strength to die upon his feet.

He had no consciousness of the stone steps up from the cells, or of the corridor out into the yard; he stumbled along with his eyes closed, offering up the contrite heart, and beseeching strength.

Behind locked doors men listened to the jangle of keys and the shuffle of feet, and the atmosphere was tense as always at that hour with the realisation that smote each man's heart. Each man listened in his blood for the tramp of boots, the curt commands, the starting-up of the car.

There were those watching from upper windows who saw them go, the two foreigners, the Englishman and the Irishman, bareheaded, coatless, wearing the shabby corduroy breeches and broken boots of the militia. Their shadows lay black and long and thin across the moonlight that filled the yard. Their light shirts gleamed whitely. They held themselves erect, their heads high.

Flynn opened his eyes at the impact of the clean, cold night air. Both men drew in deep breaths of it, gratefully, after the foetid air of the cells. The barracks buildings cast deep shadows across the square, and the moonlight glinted on roofs and windows like water. From behind closed shutters a concertina jerked out a catchy tune, and there were men's voices rough with laughter. A dog barked, querulously, from somewhere beyond the walls, and there was the distant clatter of a tram.

It seemed to Flynn that there was a smell of flowers on the air; a spicy smell, almost like incense. Then he was crowded into the back of a closed car with Graham and two armed guards; in front, at the wheel, sat the young English communist, and beside him a surly-looking Spaniard who nursed a rifle across his knees. The Englishman turned and looked over his shoulder for a moment, his hand on the clutch.

He smiled his sarcastic smile. "It's a nice night for a drive out into the country," he observed.

Neither Flynn nor Graham answered him. Flynn had closed his eyes

again and was lost in prayer; there was so little time left for that essential
final confession. Graham stared through the windscreen at the moon-
silvered square and had no thoughts at all; it was as though he had already
finished with living and awaited only the physical act of annihilation. Everything that happened now happened in a dream from which there was no
waking. The car jolted along over white roads full of pot-holes; the long
low whitewashed walls of farm-houses and vine-trellised taverns flashed past;
and the ancient, twisted trunks of olive and cork trees, and the nakedness of
boulders thrusting up on wild mountainy land, and everywhere sharp black
shadows imposed on the tremendous silver flood of the moonlight.

The young Englishman at the wheel hummed snatches of song. He was
immensely happy. It was such a lovely night, and he had the satisfaction
of being personally responsible for getting this pair of Trotsky-Fascists
bumped-off. They would stop at the *taberna* on the way back and drink to
the rounding-up of all agents of Franco and their successful and speedy
liquidation. . . . Soon, now, they should come to the farm-house, and see
Roderiguez's party digging the grave that would hold the lot of them. A pity
these two bastards were too dam' weak to lend a hand. Ah yes, there they
were. . . . He drew the car in to the side of the road and switched off the
engine. Another car was drawn in a few yards further on. Across a
stretch of rough ground there was the shell of a burnt-out farm. Three men
were digging a trench in front of the whitewashed wall of an outhouse; a
couple of armed guards paced up and down, and a small group of men wearing raincoats stood leaning on their rifles, waiting.

As they all bundled out of the car Flynn looked up at the moon, high in
the clear sky, and for the last time saw moonlight on the lake at Ballyrannon.
He was no longer aware of physical weakness; he walked firmly over the
rough, boulder-strewn grass. Now the scent of flowers seemed as tremendous as the moonlight itself. Then suddenly he saw. Above the wall before
which in a few moments he would stand a tree reached out branches thick
with blossoms that glistened like snow in the moonlight.

A step or two behind Graham, he whispered, "Will ye look at that blossom
now? Did ye ever see the like of it? Isn't it the tree of heaven itself?"

Graham looked, and he saw the white wall, pockmarked from bullets,
and the broken red roofs of the outhouses, and he saw the glint of moonlight
on the barrels of the rifles of the firing-party as they moved up into position,
and a radiance that was more than moonlight on Flynn's ecstatic face, and
for the last time smiled the old ironic smile.

"Can an unbeliever see the tree of heaven?"

But Flynn was by then beyond hearing human voices or seeing earthly
sights. Skirting the open grave, and walking towards the wall in front of
which the three Spaniards of Roderiguez's party now stood blindfolded, he
approached closer and closer to the blossoming boughs that reached out to
him like the arms of an eternal mother, and his soul filled with joy.

Even when they bandaged his eyes he could still see those outheld arms,
and he knew then that everything he had ever known had led up to this
supreme ecstasy of release.

EPILOGUE

THERE was a little stir of consternation in the Left press over the disappearance of the English writer, Graham Hayes, and 'the young Irish poet', Flynn Harrigan—the son of the well-known novelist, Michael Harrigan—who had gone to Spain to join the militia, been wounded at Huesca, caught in the Barcelona rising, arrested and taken to the Karl Marx barracks, and not heard of since. Some inquiries were set afoot; a 'comrade' was going out to Barcelona on a political mission and undertook to visit the barracks and ascertain whether the two men were still held there. He experienced a good deal of obstruction, but finally elicited the information that Flynn Harrigan had died of his wound, septicaemia having set in, and that Graham Hayes had been released and had returned to the front. It seemed possible to accept the story concerning Flynn Harrigan, since it was known in Barcelona that he had received a body wound, but considerable suspicion and dissatisfaction was felt over Hayes. Attempts were made to trace him, and various trails were followed, unsuccessfully; there were quite a few English writers on the Aragon front, and in any case the comrade making the inquiries had to return to London, and the investigation fizzled out. As a writer Graham Hayes was little known outside of a comparatively small literary and intellectual circle, and there appeared to be no relatives interested in his disappearance.

The Fisher family were very dissatisfied, and May and Freddie talked wildly of going out to Spain to find out for themselves. Other people, May declared, violently, had disappeared before now into the secret prisons of the O.G.P.U.; pamphlets had already been written—and sold by her on the streets—concerning the terror inaugurated by the communists in Spain. The entire family was very upset—and May was heartbroken. But it is one thing to talk of getting to a country in the grip of civil war, and another to get there, particularly when faced with the necessity for raising the necessary money and sacrificing your job. . . . In time it came to seem not to be of importance whether Flynn had died of his wound or been shot; he was dead, and it could be fairly safely assumed that Graham Hayes had been shot with him, since they had been jointly arrested.

Sylvanus Merry cabled the news to Michael Harrigan in Los Angeles, but he had already received a cable from Bridie, who had read the news in the Irish papers; 'Michael Harrigan's son, Flynn, fighting on the Government side, and wounded on the Aragon front, is reported to have been arrested in Barcelona after the 'May rising' and to have died of his wound in the Karl Marx barracks', and 'Novelist's Son Dies in Spain'.

The ice that had encased Bridie's heart ever since the bitter quarrel in which Flynn had rushed out of the house and ridden Jameel to her death cracked. She was filled with the wild grief that had seized her after his accident, and the same terrible consuming remorse. Had her father been there she would have clung to him as she had then, but he was beyond reach, and there was no one . . . but back at Ballyrannon there was Tante Emma

. . . and Patrick Doyle. She had to get back; she had to go home. Her aunt made no attempt to dissuade her; what was the use? She would go, anyhow; nothing could stop her. The Harrigans always did what they wanted to do, whatever the obstacles and opposition.

Bridie, wild-eyed, told Katherine, "This time I'll not be returning."

"You'll be marrying Patrick Doyle, I suppose, and—" she smiled, wanly remembering what Bridie had told her on previous occasions of flight back to the West, " 'raising up sons to the glory of Ireland'—is that it?"

Bridie nodded, then added, in a low voice choked with suppressed tears, "You have to have someone to love."

Her cousin answered, a little bitterly, "You seem to have managed with no one these last years."

A flame spurted up in Bridie's eyes. "I never stopped loving Flynn! Never for a single minute! Any more than you did! Why not admit it?"

Katherine shaded her eyes with her hand. "I do admit it. It's true, God help me, but why didn't we let him know, the two of us? Why did we harden our hearts against him, God forgive us?" She rocked herself to and fro in her agony of remorse. "That woman was nothing—nothing. His real love-affair was with Ireland, anyhow! It was Cathleen ni Houlihan he loved, not Katherine O'Donal. O God, what am I saying? He loved me. He held me against his heart and asked me would I marry him, and yes, I said, yes. . . ."

She buried her face in her hands. "It's true, all the same. Ireland was his real love-affair. He wanted that we should serve her together——" Her voice had sunk to a whisper—" 'servants of the Queen'." She began to weep softly into her hands.

Bridie said, stonily, "It isn't any use crying. There isn't anything we can do now except ask God to forgive us our sins against Flynn, and pray for his soul. . . ." Her voice cracked and broke; she rallied herself and went on, "And go on living, the way he would have us. You will give Ireland your art, and I shall give her sons, please God." She lifted her head with the old proud, challenging gesture. "Perhaps one will be a poet and fight for freedom—in the service of the Queen. . . ."

Christabel, looking at her daughter's suffering face, thought, 'Poor child, poor child. But at last she has served her apprenticeship; now she will begin to act, because now love and pain are real to her, not something merely poetically imagined. . . . Now the springs of real feeling are released.'

They both went back with Bridie to Ballyrannon for the Requiem Mass.

Michael Harrigan cabled from Hollywood to Bridie, *'Shall I return? Gladly do so if any help.'* It seemed to him possible that she might be needing him, remembering her wild grief when Flynn had met with the accident, and again later when he had made his get-away to Paris; she had, it seemed to him, no one to turn to. It was a relief, nevertheless, to get Bridie's reply, *'Leaving immediately for Ballyrannon for Requiem Mass and to marry Patrick Doyle.'*

She might have done better for herself, he thought, but it was followed immediately by the thought that she might have done worse—made a dashing, brilliant marriage, and eventually run out on it like pretty witty Kitty, whose daughter she was. She was doing what she wanted to do; what it was natural, instinctive, for her to do; what she would have done long ago but for the emotional tie-up with Flynn; she had gone home, in every sense of the word. He cabled her his congratulations and to sell up at the castle everything that was of no use to her for her new home. He followed this with a letter enclosing a cheque for a thousand dollars as a wedding present, with the injunction not to spend it sensibly, for the love of God; let the two of them be off to the Galway races in August, and on to Limerick and Dublin, and coming back with the world's wonder of a horse, the like of which there had not been seen in the West since Jameel went daisy-clipping over the turf, stepping out as though she owned the earth, and let her not be grieving for Flynn, God rest him, for it was better to die at twenty-three on the right side of the barricades than live on fighting freedom's battles on paper till the ivy twisted in your soul. . . .

And let her make copies of every scrap of poetry she would find in Flynn's drawer in his room, and he would edit it and write a Foreword and arrange for its publication in England and America, and let her write to Mr. Sylvanus Merry in London—he sent the address—and inquire if he had any of Flynn's poems, however fragmentary, to add to the collection, and to inquire also of any friends Flynn might have had in London if they had any. . . .

Bridie and Katherine went through Flynn's manuscripts together, sitting on his bed in the turret room. Most of the poems were fragmentary—delicate, tenuous things, full of the tentative approach to experience, unaware of the implications. Katherine had been a little nervous of the task; if there should be love-poems written to Mrs. Stephanie Paul it was not going to be easy. There were love-poems, but they were not immediately recognisable as such, and they were not written to Stephanie Paul. His ecstasies, when it came to poetry, were of the spirit, and when Katherine O'Donal came into them she did so as the personification of Cathleen ni Houlihan, not as Cousin Kate whom he loved, she of the warm laughing voice and the dark wind-blown hair; with Cousin Kate you walked in enchanted moonlit worlds, but in the love of Cathleen ni Houlihan—tall and dark as Katherine herself—you were swept up to the starry heavens on wings of light. To that love you dedicated your life, and for it you were prepared to die, if need be; with the lips and breasts of mortal love, however beautiful, however tender, however full of sweet longing, it had nothing to do. Poetry as he saw it was no corporal tune but a music through which to convey the adorations and ecstasies, the aspirations and dreams, of all that was incorporeal.

So Katherine found no love-poem that could wound her, and the task was all wonder, and a strange sad beauty. There was a longish poem called *The Blossoming Bough*, and it seemed to her that this should be the title for the collection, since it set the motif—the unspoken dream in the heart of man, the dream of love and beauty and truth, the heart's eternal spring, eternally renewed.

Patrick attended the Mass with his family, and outside the church afterwards, came up to Bridie, twisting the cloth cap, which he always wore on solemn occasions, in his fingers.

"If I could help ye in any way at this time, Bridie——"

She pressed his hand. "I am going to sell up at the castle, and after that I shall be needing some place to live, but I'll not be leaving Connemara."

She lifted her head and looked him full in the eyes.

"Are you of the same mind about marrying, Patrick?"

The blood rushed up into his face. He said, eagerly, "There's never been anyone but yourself I would be marrying, Bridie."

She smiled. "It's settled then. After the sale we'll go to Father Faherty together."

His hand tightened on hers a moment, and the look of sheer radiant happiness he turned on her was more than anything he could have said.

Bridie rejoined her aunt and cousin, and she told them, "That was Patrick Doyle. I was telling him I would be wedding him soon now. Isn't he a fine tall handsome lad?"

Christabel was aware of the challenge in Bridie's voice, but she could concede quite sincerely that he was all that. She had, in fact, no more opposition to the marriage than Mike had. Patrick Doyle had established himself in a small-holding on the mainland two years ago, and a sister was keeping house for him until such time as she herself married, or Bridie married Patrick; this Christabel knew, and also that the Doyles were Bream Island folk, peasants. But if anyone was going to say that the 'Whisky Harrigans' were superior to the natural aristocracy of the Gaeltacht it was not going to be Christabel O'Donal, who was herself a Harrigan. Bridie's young man had personal beauty and charm; he had proved his devotion over a course of years; that he was hard-working was self-evident—and anyone who thought that Bridie Harrigan would have done better to have married a Dublin playboy, or one of the hard-riding, hard-drinking landed gentry, would be a fool, and Christabel O'Donal was certainly not that. . .

She and Katherine returned to Dublin after the Requiem service, and Bridie and Tante Emma stayed on at the castle.

The sale was a purely local affair; there was so little to dispose of that it was not worth advertising—a few tables and chairs and cupboards, odds and ends of cracked and chipped crockery, some worn cutlery, gardening implements, stable accessories. There were no fine ornaments, clocks, pictures. Everything of value had gone in the great sale seventeen years ago. Michael's library, and Flynn's few books and his picture of Saint Anne, were not for sale. The star features of the sale were the threadbare red carpet which had been bought for the guest-room, when 'the American ladies' had been expected, the settee purchased at the same time to 'furnish' the drawing-room, and the saddle-horse—but this Bridie withdrew from the sale at the last minute, to the great disgust of Charlie O'Brien, who had been planning to buy it for a few shillings and sell it for a few pounds. There was some haggling between two old women over a pair of broken steps, and some keen bidding for some strips of wire netting from Flynn's chicken-runs.

Bridie watched it all go without a pang.   It all belonged to a life that was
over; all that was important of that life she carried in her heart, imperishably.
All the work that Flynn had put into the place had disappeared long ago.
Even the *Kingfisher* was rotting down at the edge of the lake; sometime she
and Patrick might bale it out and repaint it, sometime . . . Maybe it was
better left buried in its watery grave, since he had painted it blue in honour of
Her, That One, she who never should have been honoured. . . .

(Back in Paris Mrs. Paul read in the papers of Flynn Harrigan's death in
Spain, and immediately wired her condolences to his father.   Poor boy; she
had really been very fond of him; it was terribly young to die.   Later, when
she saw the announcement of his poems, she said to Philippa that they must
be sure to get them.   He had been, really, turribly sweet. . . .)

When the sale was over and the last bargain-hunter had gathered up the
last spoils and straggled away into the May evening, Bridie and Tante Emma
stood on the crumbling steps of the castle and looked across the overgrown
terraces to the lake, touched with apricot from the sunset, and waited for
Mr. Foyne to arrive in his ramshackle car and run them in to Letterfrack,
where Bridie would stay until her wedding.   From within the house a door
banged suddenly in a gust of wind and kept up a dull continuous knocking
as it swung loose from a broken hinge.   Most of the windows had been
broken for some time past, but the emptying of the rooms had somehow
robbed the place of its last vestige of life, and it stared now at the sunset
with a completely derelict air.

The old woman rearranged her black shawl and sighed.

"Aye, aye.   'Tis lonesome th'ould place'll be with the last sticks gone
from it, and none of us comin' or goin' from this out."

Bridie lifted her head with the old defiance.   "It was all finished the day
Flynn went away.   We should have sold up long ago."

"Ah, sure, weren't we always thinkin' and hopin' and prayin' he'd be
comin' back one of these fine days?"

Bridie did not answer.   She had always believed that Flynn was convinced when he left that he would not come back; it was as though he had
known.

There was the sound of a car approaching along the boreen and she
stooped and gathered up the bundles at their feet, then took the old woman's
arm.

"Let's go now," she said.

They descended the steps and, crossing the terrace, turned into the weed-
grown drive and waited under the darkness of the ilex trees.   Mr. Foyne
passed them with a wave of his hand, turned the car at the top of the drive,
and came level with them again, and they climbed with their bundles into the
musty-smelling interior.

" 'Tis a fine evening, God be praised," Mr. Foyne observed.

"It is that, thanks be to God," Tante Emma answered.

The car rattled away down the drive, through the wrought-iron gates,
pushed permanently back into the tangle of shrubs and bramble on either
side, the paint Flynn had lavished on them long ago peeled off, their hinges
red with rust, and out of the shadow of the castle's belt of trees and on into
the luminous light that held the boreen.

At a bend of the road Mr. Foyne slowed down, and turned in his seat.

"Ye'll be wantin' to take a last look at th'ould place—" he suggested.

"Ach no, man dear, get on wid ye!"

Bridie said, "It's bad luck to look back," and gazed resolutely ahead.

"Flynn!" her heart cried. "Flynn! Goodbye! Goodbye!"

THE END

LONDON,
 May–December, 1942.

PRINTED IN GREAT BRITAIN, BY THE
ANCHOR PRESS, LTD., TIPTREE, ESSEX.